Praise for ...

CARNAL GIFT

"[Written with] verve . . . The prose is lush, and the author clearly has a talented way with plot and pacing."
—*The Romance Reader*

"Sizzling . . . steeped in sensual fantasy, strong characters, and intense emotions." —*Romantic Times*

"*Carnal Gift* speaks directly to a reader's heart. If you are seeking a romance with suspense, passion, and an astonishing love, don't miss this exceptional tale."
—*Romance Reviews Today*

"Wonderful . . . fans will enjoy Pamela Clare's fine tale."
—*Reader to Reader*

"Historical romance with richly drawn characters and a charismatic love story." —*Sensual Romance Reviews*

continued . . .

SWEET RELEASE

EXTREME exposure

PAMELA CLARE

BERKLEY SENSATION, NEW YORK

THE BERKLEY PUBLISHING GROUP
Published by the Penguin Group
Penguin Group (USA) Inc.
375 Hudson Street, New York, New York 10014, USA
Penguin Group (Canada), 90 Eglinton Avenue East, Suite 700, Toronto, Ontario M4P 2Y3, Canada
(a division of Pearson Penguin Canada Inc.)
Penguin Books Ltd., 80 Strand, London WC2R 0RL, England
Penguin Group Ireland, 25 St. Stephen's Green, Dublin 2, Ireland (a division of Penguin Books Ltd.)
Penguin Group (Australia), 250 Camberwell Road, Camberwell, Victoria 3124, Australia
(a division of Pearson Australia Group Pty. Ltd.)
Penguin Books India Pvt. Ltd., 11 Community Centre, Panchsheel Park, New Delhi—110 017, India
Penguin Group (NZ), Cnr. Airborne and Rosedale Roads, Albany, Auckland 1310, New Zealand
(a division of Pearson New Zealand Ltd.)
Penguin Books (South Africa) (Pty.) Ltd., 24 Sturdee Avenue, Rosebank, Johannesburg 2196, South
Africa

Penguin Books Ltd., Registered Offices: 80 Strand, London WC2R 0RL, England

This is a work of fiction. Names, characters, places, and incidents either are the product of the author's imagination or are used fictitiously, and any resemblance to actual persons, living or dead, business establishments, events, or locales is entirely coincidental.

EXTREME EXPOSURE

A Berkley Sensation Book / published by arrangement with the author

PRINTING HISTORY
Berkley Sensation edition / August 2005

Copyright © 2005 by Pamela White.
Excerpt from *Hard Evidence* copyright © 2005 by Pamela White.
Cover photo of couple in bedroom by Chad Ehlers/Indexstock.
Cover photo of office buildings by Steven Weinberg/Getty Images.
Cover design by Rita Frangie.
Interior text design by Stacy Irwin.

ISBN: 0-425-20633-5

BERKLEY® SENSATION
Berkley Sensation Books are published by The Berkley Publishing Group,
a division of Penguin Group (USA) Inc.,
375 Hudson Street, New York, New York 10014.
BERKLEY SENSATION and the "B" design are trademarks belonging to Penguin Group (USA) Inc.

PRINTED IN THE UNITED STATES OF AMERICA

10 9 8 7 6 5 4 3 2 1

This book is dedicated to the more than 1,400 American journalists who've died, mostly through assassination and murder, while trying to expose the truth. Their names are inscribed on the Freedom Forum Journalists Memorial in Arlington, Virginia, a landmark to democracy's often overlooked heroes.

ACKNOWLEDGMENTS

With special thanks and much love to R & K.

Special thanks to Mark Kertz, sommelier and general manager at Laudisio Ristorante Italiano, for his expert advice on sexy wine and food; and to Scott Weiser, for sharing his knowledge of forensics and firearms.

With deep gratitude to Cindy Hwang, my editor, and Natasha Kern, my agent and friend, for opening this door.

Personal thanks to Michelle White, Timalyn O'Neill, Norah Wilson, Kally Jo Surbeck, Vickie McCloud, Sara Megibow, Joyce Farrell, Kelly LaMar, and Amy Vandersall. Your support and encouragement keep me sane.

Additional thanks to Joel Warner, Vince Darcangelo, Stewart Sallo, and *Boulder Weekly*. I wouldn't be able to pursue my dreams without you.

And as always, thanks and much love to my family and to my sons, Alec and Benjamin. You mean everything to me.

CHAPTER 1

KARA MCMILLAN was going to kill her best friend. It was Holly's fault Kara stood alone, margarita in hand, in Denver's skankiest meat market, wishing she were invisible. Holly had brought her here—and then deserted her.

This time Holly had gone too far.

"Just go up to a guy who turns you on and start talking," Holly had said before she'd disappeared into the crowd. "Make it clear you want to get laid, and you'll find yourself on your back in no time."

On her back.

Kara hadn't been on her back for five long years—not since she'd learned she was pregnant with Connor—and the thought of ending the evening with her legs wrapped around some strong, sexy man while he drove himself into her, hot and hard, was almost enough to make her moan out loud.

But she was nothing if not a realist. She'd never hooked up with a man in a bar before, and there was no way she was going to meet anyone worthwhile tonight, no matter what Holly said. Why had she let Holly talk her into this? Was she truly that desperate?

Kara pressed herself farther back against the wall and took a sip of her drink just to have something to do. She stood next to an enormous potted fern not far from the entrance. The fern's lacy fronds made her feel somewhat sheltered but allowed her a view of both the bar to her right and the restaurant to her left.

The Rio del Sol, or The Rio as locals called it, was a spawning ground. The air was heavy with pheromones, the bar so crowded it was impossible to walk anywhere without brushing up against someone. Music pumped from overhead speakers but was drowned out by shouted conversation until the bass tones were nothing but a throb against the soles of her feet like a heartbeat, or the pulsing rhythm of sex.

Most everyone wore black—black leather, black Levis, black T-shirts, tiny black dresses that revealed black bra straps. It looked like a funeral, except everyone was smiling, flirting, touching. Kara's mind flashed on the prairie chickens she'd seen doing their mating dance at a nearby wildlife refuge—a sultry glance, the bulge of a bicep, a bit of exposed cleavage little more than the flash of mating plumage.

In the back corner, one couple had already paired off. They stood against the wall, all tongues and hands and writhing bodies. The woman had lifted her leg, had all but wrapped it around the man's waist, and he obligingly ground himself into her.

For a moment, Kara couldn't pull her eyes off them and found herself wondering what it would feel like to be that woman, to have a man maul her with the same kind of intensity. When the man reached up and cupped the woman's breast, Kara's pulse skipped.

She looked away, took another sip of her drink, and savored its salty tang. At least the margaritas were good. Signs on the wall said patrons were limited to three, so the drinks must be potent. She took another, bigger sip. If she had to be here, she might as well get a bit tipsy. Tomorrow was Saturday. Holly was driving, and Connor was staying with her mother tonight. She could afford to have a little fun for once—if drinking a margarita with an overgrown fern for company could be called fun.

Just go up to some guy who turns you on and start talking.

It ought to be easy. Kara talked to people all the time. In the ten years she'd been a journalist she'd talked to literally thousands of people—corporate CEOs, government officials, convicted drug smugglers, war survivors, rock stars, even a retired assassin. She'd gotten angry phone calls, hate mail, death threats. None of it fazed her. So why did the idea of approaching an attractive man in a bar seem so overwhelming?

Just go up to a guy who turns you on and start talking.

It was certainly easy for Holly, who was younger, platinum blond, and had the kind of body that rendered men stupid—big boobs, a slender waist, and plenty of booty. Kara had stretch marks on her belly from pregnancy and had never gotten out of a B-cup, except when she'd been nursing Connor. Her only striking asset was her hair, which attracted attention because it was long—that and maybe her eyes.

Even had she been a supermodel, casual sex just wasn't Kara's style. Not that she didn't *wish* it were her style. She'd give anything to have Holly's confidence and smorgasbord attitude toward men and sex. Kara was thirty-two and in her sexual prime, after all. She hadn't been with a man for so long she felt her sexual frustration could generate enough electricity to power the entire Denver metro area.

"You're pathetic, McMillan," she said to herself. "Pa-the-tic."

What was she doing here? She should be home snuggling her son and reading *Fox in Sox* for the millionth time, not standing in The Rio drinking by herself while Horny Holly went trolling for sperm.

Cold air rushed in as the front door opened again and more people strode inside. As they streamed toward the bar, one face caught her eye.

State Senator Reece Sheridan.

Though she'd never met him in person, she recognized him from the many photos that had run on the front page of the paper since he'd been elected two years ago. She'd interviewed him over the phone a few times when the bills he was carrying overlapped with one of her columns or investigative stories. She'd found him smart for a politician and unusually well spoken—which, in Colorado, set him apart.

She took another sip and studied him as he walked closer.

He was, she decided, even better-looking than his photographs. He was tall, easily over six feet. His dark blond hair was cut conservatively—short at the back and on the sides, a bit longer on top for style. His eyes were large with unusually long lashes, his lips firm and full. His square jaw bore a trace of five-o'clock shadow. He wore a gray wool trench coat over a white shirt and gray slacks, his gray silk tie visibly loosened.

He reminded her of a *GQ* model—handsome, well dressed, smooth. She imagined he'd been one of the popular kids in high school. He'd probably been president of his fraternity in college and had no doubt dated sorority girls and cheerleaders, who'd swooned for him—and the sports car he inevitably drove.

Kara could almost hear their annoying squeals. *"Oooh, Reeeece!"*

An overgrown frat boy—definitely not Kara's type.

Kara took another drink of her margarita and was surprised to find she had only ice left. No wonder she felt a bit buzzed. She lifted her gaze back to the senator, remembered what he'd said last time they'd spoken on the phone.

"You've got a pretty voice. It's very feminine."

She had dismissed the compliment as nothing more than a politician's attempt to suck up to the press. But she hadn't forgotten it.

He surveyed the bar area as if looking for someone, slipped the heavy coat from his broad shoulders, and kept moving. He was probably looking for a woman, Kara decided. A man like him wouldn't go long without one.

He hadn't seen Kara and had almost passed her by when she heard herself speak.

"Senator Sheridan?" Kara could have kicked herself. Why had she opened her mouth? She didn't want to talk to him!

It occurred to her to walk quickly away, but it was too late.

His gaze met hers, and she could tell he was trying to place her.

Then he smiled and walked over to her, hand extended. "Kara McMillan?"

Kara took his hand, shook it, and slipped behind the mask of her journalist persona. "Congrats on passing your alternative energy bill."

"Thanks." His hand was large and warm, and he held hers a bit longer than was necessary. "Your coverage was one of the reasons the bill made it out of committee."

Kara shrugged, irritated by the way his compliment warmed her. She wasn't supposed to care what he thought. "I felt I had to give it some ink. It's an important issue to our readers."

"It's good to meet you in person. I've been meaning to call to tell you how much I enjoyed the interview. Of all the journalists who called about that bill, you asked the best questions."

Her face grew warm, and she was horrified to realize she was smiling. "Well, that's my job."

What a stupid thing to say! Of course it's your job, McMillan!

"I was warned about you." He smiled. It was the kind of smile that made women melt.

But no way was an overgrown frat boy going to charm her. "Warned?"

"I was told you eat legislators for breakfast."

The statement was so outrageous it made Kara laugh. "Only when I can't get a hold of murderers, drug kingpins, or rapists."

His smile brightened, and he chuckled. "Ouch! I think I've been insulted. I need a drink to soothe my wounded pride. Can I get you something?"

Good journalists never let politicians buy them drinks. "Oh, no, I—"

"Another margarita?"

Blue. His eyes were blue. "On the rocks with salt."

He smiled, took her empty glass, and turned toward the bar. The crowd seemed to part for him, and in a matter of moments he was back, two drinks in hand. He gave her one and took a sip from the other—amber liquid in a small glass. "I don't know about their margaritas, but they have the best selection of single malt in town. Cheers."

"Cheers." Kara drank, tried to recover her sense of detachment. She had no business getting cozy with a senator. Particularly not a handsome one who oozed charm the way slugs oozed slime.

He gestured toward the fern and grinned. "Are you undercover or something?"

Kara felt her aloofness slip to the floor and shatter. She took a step away from the plant. "I'm waiting for someone."

"Your boyfriend?"

"No! No—a friend from work. She's somewhere out there." Kara gestured toward the undulating crowd. "We put our names in for a table and—"

"Reece! There you are!" A young woman who reminded Kara of Malibu Barbie emerged from the crowd and reached for the senator.

Kara watched as Senator Sheridan took Barbie's hand and bent down to kiss her cheek. He seemed happy to see her. Blond, curvy, tanned—she was just the sort of woman Kara had imagined he would find attractive. For some reason, being right disappointed her.

He put his arm around Barbie's shoulder and drew her nearer. "Melanie, I'd like you to meet Kara McMillan of the *Denver Independent*."

Melanie—Kara thought Barbie was a better name for her—reached out a delicate, well-manicured hand. "Oh, I've heard of you. You're the reporter who got that city official fired, right?"

Kara shook her hand and forced a smile. "Right."

Melanie turned to the senator. "I've saved us a little table in the back corner. You can talk some more if you want. I'll head back to the table. I'm afraid someone will steal it."

Blond hair swinging, Malibu Melanie disappeared back into the crowd.

Senator Sheridan shifted his gaze back to Kara, a look of regret on his face. "I hate to end this conversation, but I need to go. Are you going to be here for a while?"

Kara wanted to tell him to drop dead, but he hadn't done anything wrong. "We were planning on having dinner."

"I'll look for you in the restaurant." Then he flashed her another smile and disappeared into the crowded bar.

He'd been gone perhaps two seconds when Holly reappeared, eyes wide, a big smile on her face. "Who was that?"

"Nobody." Kara took another sip of her marg.

Holly's big brown eyes narrowed. "Nobody, my ass! You were talking to the hottest guy in the bar! I saw him buy you a drink!"

"You were watching?" For some reason Kara wasn't really surprised.

Holly crossed her arms. "Who was he—or didn't you bother to get his name?"

Kara gave up. "That was Senator Reece Sheridan."

Holly's eyes widened. "A senator? Oooh!"

"YOU'RE TOO damn picky. That's your problem." Holly dug a corn chip into the salsa, popped it into her mouth, and crunched. "You don't know anything about this senator guy, and you've already written him off."

They'd gotten a table, had placed their orders, and still Holly wouldn't quit harping at Kara.

"He's here with a woman." Kara drank the last of her second margarita. "Besides, he's not my type."

"Tall, sexy, and blatantly male isn't your type? Good God, Kara, what is?"

"I want someone real."

Holly considered her for a moment and sipped her Diet Coke. "This is all *his* fault."

"Oh, don't start—"

"If he'd been a man instead of a rat bastard, you might have a love life."

"You can't blame him for my decisions."

"The jerk should be neutered."

Kara opened her mouth to protest, shut it again. She had once been in love with Galen Prentice, had believed he loved her, too. But he had betrayed her and dumped her when she'd needed him most. She'd found herself in the exact same situation as her mother—raising a child by herself.

"You know what I think?" Holly took another sip of her Diet Coke.

"I feel certain you're going to tell me."

"I think you were so hurt by that S.O.B. you're afraid to spend time with any man who might actually turn you on. That's why you haven't been on a date in five years. You hide behind motherhood and your job and use your responsibilities as a way to hide from life." Holly nodded her stylish blond head decisively, and, apparently done preaching, bit into another chip.

Kara felt tears prick behind her eyes, fought them back. "I've been on dates. I went out with Todd Myers, remember?"

Holly gave Kara a withering look. "Todd Myers is gay as a daisy, and you knew it! You prove my point."

The waiter arrived at the table with two plates, a sizzling platter and all the fixings for fajitas for two. "Is there anything else I can get you ladies? More drinks?"

Kara started to say no, but Holly had already answered for her.

"More Diet Coke for me, and definitely another marg for her."

By the time the remains of the fajitas were cleared away, the conversation had moved from men to having sex with men, and Kara was feeling better than she'd felt in ages. She was floating, and everything in the world seemed warm, fuzzy, perfect.

She glanced at her empty glass and wondered what exactly

they put in their margaritas. Whatever it was, it was really, really, really strong.

"What I miss most is kissing." She closed her eyes for a moment and tried to conjure up the sensation. "I love it when you feel that first brush of his lips on yours. And when his tongue slips into your mouth—mmmm."

Holly smiled at her and poked at the ice in her glass with her straw.

"You know what else I love?"

"Hard cock?"

Kara heard Holly, of course, but she wasn't going to let Holly interrupt her train of thought. It was so like Holly to go straight for the crotch. "I love it when a man licks my nipples. It makes me crazy! I can't even think about it without feeling turned on."

Holly shrugged, still smiling. "That's nice, but I prefer his mouth a bit farther south."

"Galen refused to do that. But I knew this guy in college who said he really liked it."

"And?"

"And what?"

"Was he any good at it?"

Kara nodded and felt heat suffuse her cheeks at the memory. She leaned forward and looked straight into Holly's eyes. "I think it's soooo erotic when you kiss him afterwards—and taste yourself on his mouth!"

A man's voice interrupted the conversation. "What are you ladies talking about?"

Senator Sheridan. He stood beside the table, his coat draped over his arm.

Kara looked up, felt the heat of his smile, and answered without thinking. "I was just saying I think it's really erotic when you kiss a man and taste yourself on his mouth."

Some part of her wondered through a tequila haze whether she had just said something she shouldn't have. But before she had time to consider it, the senator pulled out a chair and sat.

"I'd have to agree." He gave her a lopsided grin. "That is erotic."

She could smell his aftershave—something warm and enticingly male. He had taken off his tie and unbuttoned the top button on his shirt, exposing a bit of chest. His shirtsleeves, too, had been unbuttoned and were rolled up to reveal the muscles of his forearms.

Kara couldn't remember noticing a man's forearms before.

Holly was right.

Senator Sheridan was hot.

Reece knew he should be going. He had to finish editing the last of his five bills for the session, as it was slated to be heard in committee next week. He also needed to read through the bills he would be expected to vote on next week. And there were always phone calls and e-mails from constituents to return. But he found he couldn't budge.

Kara McMillan was nothing like he'd expected. The black-and-white photograph that ran every week with her opinion column showed a rather stern woman, hair pulled back, staring gravely into the camera. But the real Kara McMillan was much softer, more colorful, and much more feminine than her photo revealed.

He could tell she was tipsy by the color in her cheeks, a pink glow against her otherwise creamy skin. Her features were delicate, almost elfin. Her eyes were an unusual shade of green, dark with flecks of gold. Her hair was almost black and fell, thick and shining, to her waist. She was almost a foot shorter than he and willowy, with delicate curves in the right places. She looked more like a ballet dancer than a tough reporter.

Kara had a reputation for being ruthless. When she called, people worried. Last year she had lost a city department head his job after discovering he was writing thousands of dollars in checks to a nonexistent contractor who turned out to be his mistress. Reece had been impressed.

Then she had called him.

He'd been taken aback by her voice—soft and sexy. He had

answered her questions—surprisingly insightful questions—
and found himself wondering if her reputation wasn't more
the result of her determination and her success. As he knew too
well, nothing pissed people off like success—and a refusal to
break the rules.

Kara turned to her friend. "Holly, I'd like to introduce
Senator Reece Sheridan."

"Please, just call me Reece." He reached out a hand to the
pretty blonde who sat across the table from Kara.

She shook his hand. "Holly Bradshaw."

"Don't let me interrupt your conversation. You were just
talking about—"

"Oral sex," Kara supplied, apparently unembarrassed.
"So tell me the truth, Senator, how do men really feel about
going down on women?"

"She's had three," Holly mouthed, pointing toward Kara
and holding up three fingers.

But Reece had figured that out for himself. "It's Reece,
and I can't speak for all men, but I—"

Kara shook her head. "How like a politician to dodge the
question!"

Reece tried not to laugh. "If you'd let me finish my answer . . ."

"Let the man talk." Holly shot Kara a stern look.

More pink crept into Kara's cheeks. "Oh. Sorry."

"I can't speak for all men, but I enjoy it just fine—
provided the woman gets into it. Not all women are comfortable enough with their bodies to enjoy it, you know."

Kara looked puzzled by this and stared at . . . his mouth.
"Do you like to kiss women?"

"Yes. But not as much as I like to go down on them."

Kara's gaze met his. He saw her pupils dilate and heard
her little intake of breath. Her reaction, unguarded and sensual, intrigued him, and he found himself wondering if she
was anywhere near as fiery in bed as she was in print.

A voice in his head reminded him he was treading on
dangerous ground. Kara McMillan was a journalist. There

was nothing to stop her from printing every word he said, nothing to stop her from taking her embarrassment out on him once her hangover had passed. He had a feeling she wasn't used to drinking and that, while she might be adept at asking tough questions, those questions probably never involved anyone's views on oral sex.

But in short order, she'd peppered him with an array of queries.

"Do women really taste like tuna?"

"No. Absolutely not."

"Is it fair that some men expect a woman to give them head but refuse to return the favor?"

"Hardly."

"Do men like regular sex or getting head more?"

"That depends on the moment—and the woman."

If she was trying to turn him on, she was doing a good job of it. He took a sip of whisky and nearly choked at her next question.

"What does it *feel* like to be inside a woman?" She leaned toward him, her gaze fixed on his, her chin resting on her hand.

"Um—"

"Good grief, Kara, are you interviewing him?" Holly laughed, stood. "If you'll excuse me for a moment, I need to use the ladies' room."

Kara giggled, then made a grave face and spoke with mock severity, as if quoting a newspaper headline. "Sen. Sheridan Says Not All Women Like Oral Sex."

Reece laughed. "It's Reece, and please tell me this isn't tomorrow's lead story."

"I'm afraid it is, Senator." She looked at him sternly. "It's a senatorial sexposé."

A moment later he caught sight of Holly as she waved good-bye to him and slipped out the front door.

In his mind, he heard the doors of the trap swing shut with a clang.

CHAPTER 2

REECE SHIFTED his gaze back to Kara, who was licking salt from the rim of her margarita glass with a distracting pink tongue. "How are you getting home?"

She glanced across the table at Holly's vacant spot. "Holly is driving me. Coming here was her idea."

From her tone of voice, Reece gathered Kara hadn't wanted to come along, an intriguing notion, since she'd obviously gotten very much into the spirit of the place. "I think Holly has deserted you. She just walked out the door."

The look of panicked surprise on Kara's face as Holly passed them outside the window and blew them a kiss convinced him Kara was as caught in Holly's snare as he. He felt oddly relieved. He didn't have much respect for women who tried to manipulate men into bed. Since he'd been elected, he'd met far too many women like that—grasping women who sized up men according to social status and potential future earnings and saw sex as the fastest means of securing their share.

That sort of woman hadn't been interested in him at all when he'd been nothing more than a high school social studies teacher and youth soccer coach. But once the title "Senator" had been placed before his name, they couldn't spread their legs fast enough. He had learned the hard way not to take a sexy, willing woman at face value.

But it was obvious Kara hadn't been privy to Holly's

scheming. She sat for a moment, eyes wide with astonishment. Then she grabbed her purse, threw her credit card on the table, stood—or tried to stand. But three margaritas had taken their toll.

Reece jumped to his feet and reached out with both arms to steady her before she fell into the aisle. "Careful."

"I have to catch up with her. I don't have cash for cab fare. I'll have to walk home." There was genuine worry in her eyes.

Reece couldn't blame her. The streets of Denver weren't the safest place for a woman at night—particularly one who'd had three. He reached for his coat. "It's allright, Kara. I'll drive you."

She looked at him, her green-gold eyes clouded by uncertainty. "Are you sure you don't mind?"

"Not at all." Reece was a bit surprised to realize he was telling the truth.

As soon as Kara had paid the bill—her friend had thoughtfully abandoned that, as well—Reece led her out into the cold January night and down the icy sidewalk.

The shock of Holly's trickery seemed at first to rob Kara of her tequila-induced chattiness, and they walked in silence. This wasn't entirely a bad thing, as Reece wasn't sure he could have endured more of her seductively blunt questions without embarrassing himself.

What does it feel like to be inside a woman? Holy hell!

"I can't believe she left me! Why would she—?" But Kara never finished the question. With a gasp, she slipped on ice and would have fallen had Reece not caught her.

"You'd better hook your arm through mine, or you're going to end up flat on your back."

"Oh!" Kara felt the strength of his arms as they encircled her and looked into his blue eyes. Her stomach did a flip.

Flat on her back.

The next moment, he deposited her squarely on her feet, wrapped a strong arm around her waist. This was a good thing, as the sidewalk was not only slippery, but seemed somehow slanted, as if gravity were stronger in some places than others.

She hadn't had that much to drink. Had she?

Reece led her to the door of a yellow Jeep Wrangler that was covered with mud up to its headlights and stuck a key in the lock.

"This is yours? It isn't a sports car." Kara took his hand and climbed up the step into the passenger seat.

He shut the door, walked around to the driver's side, and got in. "Sorry. I left my Jag at home in the garage next to my Porsche."

It took Kara a moment to realize he wasn't serious. "You're joking, Senator."

"It's Reece. And, yes, I am." With a grin, he turned the key in the ignition, turned on the heater, and slid into traffic. Then he reached across her and buckled her seat belt. "Where am I taking you?"

She had to think for a minute. "Corona four blocks south of Colfax."

"Close to the Capitol."

Kara nodded. "And close to my son's day care and the paper."

"You have kids?"

"One. He's four."

"What's his name?"

"Connor."

"So you're divorced?"

"Oh, no! No, no!" Kara couldn't get the words out fast enough. "I was never married."

As Reece drove through the city's slushy streets, Kara found her gaze traveling over his face, only vaguely aware of what he was saying—something about state law and aid for single parents. Watching him, she felt something she hadn't let herself feel for years—an overwhelming attraction to a real, live man.

Then she remembered Malibu Melanie.

Reece already had a girlfriend, a gorgeous girlfriend.

There was no way he would break up with her to spend time with a woman as unglamorous as Kara.

Then again he had left the bar with her, not Malibu Melanie. But a little voice inside her mind shot that hope to bits. He was giving her a ride home because Holly had run off, not because he was attracted to her. She felt her mood plummet.

"Corona, right?"

Kara realized they had reached her street. "Take a right. It's that one."

He turned into the driveway and left the Wrangler running. "I'll walk you to your door. It's slick out there."

By the time Kara had opened the passenger door—the handle was a bit confusing—he was standing beside her, offering her his hand. The ground seemed ten feet away.

"Easy." He helped her down, slipped his arm through hers, and walked with her up the flagstone path that led to her front door.

Even though she was wearing a thick winter coat, the contact was unsettling. She wanted to savor it. She wanted it to end. It had been a long time since she'd been physically close to a man.

"Watch the steps. That's it." He helped her up her front porch one stair at a time and then released her.

A feeling not unlike desperation welled up inside her. She didn't want him to leave. Not yet. "You're nothing like I thought you'd be."

"No? How so?" He stood so close she could feel his body heat.

"I had you figured for an overgrown frat boy."

He frowned. "Now I *am* insulted. I was never in a frat."

Kara giggled at the irritated tone in his voice. "Did you date cheerleaders?"

"No. They wanted nothing to do with me."

"And you don't drive a sports car."

"They're no good in three feet of snow, and I like to snowboard."

"Like I said—you're nothing like I thought."

His lips curved in a wry grin. "I'll take that as a compliment."

Then, ignoring the voice of warning in her mind, she asked the question she'd wanted to ask all the way home. "Who is Malibu Melanie? Your girlfriend?"

He looked puzzled, his brow furrowed. "Who?"

"You know—the blond bimbo you were with earlier." She watched recognition dawn on his face.

He smiled, chuckled. "Who is Melanie?"

"Yeah."

He cupped her shoulders in his palms, an amused smile on his face. "Melanie is my little sister."

KARA STARED unseeing at the stack of new press releases in her hand.

She wanted to die, to wither, to vanish from the face of the earth.

All weekend she had tried to forget, but she could not. She'd drunk enough to act like an idiot, but not enough to blot out her memory. Like a bad song, her own words played over and over in her mind, just as they had all weekend.

I was just saying I think it's really erotic when you kiss a man and taste yourself on his mouth.

Why hadn't Holly done her a favor and stuffed a napkin in her mouth?

Do women really taste like tuna?

Would it have been too much to ask to have been struck by a lightning bolt?

But that wasn't the worst of it.

You know—the blond bimbo you were with earlier.

If only she could spontaneously combust. She had called his little sister a bimbo!

Kara dropped the press releases on her desk, buried her face in her hands, and moaned, her dignity in tatters. She had made a complete fool of herself in front of a state senator, a man she would have to interview sooner or later, a man in a position of power who could easily malign her to any number of important people.

To his credit, Reece—Senator Sheridan, she corrected herself—had kept his sense of humor and behaved like a gentleman. He'd driven her home, walked her to her door, and declined her rather blatant invitation to come in for a cup of tea and whatever might follow.

"Not this time." He'd brushed a strand of hair from her face. "Ask me again when you haven't had three."

She had found herself staring up at him, wishing he would kiss her. "I'm glad I got to know you better."

He had smiled. "I sure learned a lot about you, sweet-heart."

Then he'd turned and walked down the stairs, calling back to her to take some aspirin and drink lots of water.

One thing was for certain. Kara would never speak to Holly again. And she would never, ever drink more than one margarita at The Rio.

She forced her mind back to the press releases.

A motivational speaker promising financial gain to those willing to pay $500 for his workshop. A company vowing to make the world's largest chocolate-chip cookie using organic dairy products. A health department notice about free vaccination clinics.

None of them touched on her current beat, which focused on the environment. She tossed them into her recycling bin and picked up her phone to check the five messages on her voicemail.

She had called his sister a bimbo!

Kara dialed her access code, determined to put her stupidity—and the devastatingly sexy man who had inspired it—out of her mind.

"Hi, Kara, it's Holly. I guess you're still not in. Buzz me as soon as you get this, OK?"

Delete.

"It's Holly. Are you in yet? I want to hear how it went."

Delete.

"Hi, Kara. It's Holly. I hope—"

Delete.

"Hi, Kara—"

Delete.

"Hi, Ms. McMillan. I really need to talk with you. I work at a factory outside the city, and some bad things are happening out here. Pollution and all—it's right up your alley. People need to know about this. But I can't be seen with you, and.I have to know I can trust you not to use my name or tell anyone you got this information from me. Meet me at noon in the parking lot behind the abandoned warehouse at Quebec and Smith Road. Come alone. Don't worry about knowing who I am. I'll recognize you."

Kara replayed the message several times, listening closely to the man's voice. It was no one she knew. He sounded gruff, nervous, but not threatening.

There was every chance he was just another weirdo, someone who thought his boss was a space alien or had an ax to grind with management. But something told her he was authentic—perhaps the current of very real fear in his voice, or perhaps the fact that he knew his story fit her beat.

She glanced at her planner and saw she had scheduled a lunch downtown with a member of the state water board for her story on water conservation. Colorado was prone to drought, and with the population explosion of the past decade, water resources were stretched to their limits in some areas. It was an important story, and she couldn't afford to cancel the interview.

She listened to the message again and saved it. Then she pulled up the number of the state water board and was about to dial when her phone beeped. The LCD display showed it was Holly calling on the inside line—again.

"I know you're there, Kara," Holly's voice said over her speaker. "If you don't pick up—"

Kara picked up the receiver and dropped it back into its cradle, disconnecting her ex-friend. Then she picked up the receiver again, pressed an outside line, and dialed. She had just managed to postpone her lunch meeting until one o'clock when she spied Holly making straight for her.

"Thanks for being so understanding. I'll see you there." Kara hung up and glared at Holly as Holly entered her cubicle. "I'm not talking to you ever again. Go away."

"I called four times this weekend, and you didn't call back!" Dressed in a mauve peasant blouse, a short tweed skirt in mauve and yellow, and knee-high black boots, Holly looked like she'd stepped out of the pages of *Vogue*. "Now tell me what happened!"

"If you hadn't deserted me, you'd know exactly what happened. Instead, you walked out and left me with him—and the bill!"

"I only did that to make sure you didn't have fare for a cab." Holly exposed a twenty she had crumpled in her palm and tossed it on the desk. "Here. That ought to cover my part of it."

"Don't you ever get tired of manipulating people?"

Holly frowned. "You didn't sleep with him, did you?"

"What makes you say that?"

"If you had, you'd be grateful this morning instead of surly."

Kara grabbed for her notebook and pencil, then stood. "He was too much of a gentleman. He took me home and walked me to the door, and that was it. Now if you'll excuse me, I have an I-team meeting. You arts and entertainment writers might have all day to gossip, watch DVDs, and listen to music, but we investigative reporters actually work for a living."

She ignored the insulted look on Holly's face and walked off toward the conference room.

"WE NEED a shooter in Boulder by five. Another protest about breast-feeding in public."

Kara fought to keep her thoughts off Reece Sheridan and on the meeting as Tom Trent, the editor in chief, doled out last-minute assignments. A big man whose linebacker body matched his bulldog personality, he was more than a little intimidating to most people. His green eyes had a way of seeing through people that made even other men squirm. Only his curly gray hair, which more often than not he let grow until it covered his eyes, softened his appearance in any way.

"I'm on it." Joaquin Ramirez, by far the best photographer at the paper, tapped the time into his pocket planner. Young and sexy, he reminded her of Antonio Banderas. If only he hadn't been twenty-five. "Will your mother be at this one, Kara?"

"Probably." Kara hid her irritation behind a smile.

Joaquin had covered the first such protest in Boulder a few weeks ago and come back with a photograph of Kara's fifty-two-year-old mother topless, her bare breasts barely concealed behind a sign that read "Nursing is nurturing." Only company policy, which restricted the paper's use of photographs of employees' family members, had kept that photo off the front page.

"Alton, what's on your plate?" Tom had the irritating male habit of calling everyone by his or her last name like a football coach.

Sophie looked up from the notes she'd been poring over and tossed her sleek auburn hair over her shoulder. With freckles, a bright smile, and baby-blue eyes, she had an all-American, outdoorsy look that immediately set people at ease, and Kara knew she used it to her advantage. "There was another murder at the state prison last night. Some young kid was put in a cell with two lifers. They eviscerated him."

"Good God!" Kara's expression of disgust joined the others.

"What is that? Three prison killings this month?" Tom was the only one without a look of shock on his face. But Kara knew he'd heard and seen it all during his thirty years at the copy desk.

"How much space do you want?" Syd Wilson, the managing editor, sat with a calculator, tried to figure out how to make all the news fit.

"Can I get twenty inches?"

Syd ran a hand through her short, spiked salt-and-pepper hair and shook her head. "Can you do it in fifteen?"

"If I have no choice." Sophie met Kara's gaze and gave her that "Why do I bother?" look. The two of them had been coworkers for the better part of three years and had grown to be good friends. "Want mug shots?"

"Get one of the victim if you can," Syd said, still calculating. "And the killers, too."

"Harker, what have you got for us?"

Matt, whose red hair and freckles left him looking like a kid even though he was almost forty, waved a packet of documents. "There's a special City Council meeting tonight. They'll be taking public comment on the proposed homeless shelter. I don't need more than six."

Syd nodded. "Perfect."

"Novak?"

Tessa, a transplant from Atlanta and the newest member of the team, fiddled with a sharpened pencil. With a sweet southern accent; long, wavy, honey-blond hair; and big, blue eyes, she'd immediately caught the attention of every straight man in the building, including a few who had wives, but had told the lot of them to get lost. She was at the paper to work, not to flirt, she'd said. Kara had instantly come to respect her. "The mayor has called for an internal investigation of the Gallegos shooting. Ten inches ought to do it."

Syd nodded, calculated.

Tom leaned back in his chair, apparently done with his notes. "Maybe the mayor can hire a consultant for hundreds of thousands of dollars to teach the boys in blue the difference between a gun and a cell phone. McMillan?"

Kara had just taken a sip of her rapidly cooling tea and swallowed quickly. "I've got that meeting with the water board at one and should be ready to wrap that story this week. Also, I got a tip from some anonymous caller who says he's got damning evidence against a factory outside the city. I'm meeting with him at Quebec and Smith at noon. He was very cloak-and-dagger about it. Could be a wingnut, but there's only one way to find out."

KARA SLOWLY pulled her silver Nissan Sentra into the empty parking lot, glanced around for any sign of the man who'd left her the strange message, but saw no one. Grass and weeds grew up through the cracked and crumbling asphalt that passed beneath her tires. To the west stretched an empty field. To the south ran a line of rusted railroad tracks and, beyond that, the always-crowded lanes of I-70. To the east stood an abandoned warehouse, its windows broken, its wooden beams stripped of paint and falling from the walls. There was no billboard or sign to show what kind of business had once been housed here, nothing but emptiness and decay.

Tap. Tap.

She gasped, startled to find a man standing just outside her window, where seconds ago there had been no one. He stood so close she could see only the faded denim of his jacket and jeans and a bit of white T-shirt. With a work-roughened hand, he motioned for her to roll down the window.

She hesitated. What if he wasn't the man she was supposed to meet and just some rapist on his lunch hour? Even if it was the right person, how did she know she could trust him?

There was nothing to do about it now.

With one hand on her cell phone, she rolled down the window.

He bent down, and she got just a glimpse of his face—reddish-blond moustache, blue eyes, shoulder-length blond hair under a baseball cap—before he shoved something roughly through the window.

Whatever it was struck her chin, made her gasp. It fell into her lap—a heavy bundle of documents with her name on it.

"What . . . ?"

But when she looked up, the man was gone.

CHAPTER 3

REECE STEPPED off the Sixteenth Street Mall and into Bravo Ristorante. He slipped off his sunglasses and looked about for the men he'd come to meet. They had contacted him prior to the legislative session in hopes he'd sponsor a bill for them in the Senate. He had agreed to have lunch with them to at least discuss the matter.

The tuxedo-clad host greeted him and led him to a table near the back where three men in business suits sat mulling over menus. They sat apart from the other lunch customers— the better to avoid being overheard, he supposed. Although the good citizens of Colorado probably imagined new laws were born in the marbled halls of the Capitol, most of the real work was done clandestinely in restaurants and on golf courses, with deals cut over prime rib, cigars, and holes-in-one.

Reece didn't much like it and had entered office determined never to be used or bought. There was only one way to hold public office, and that was honestly, openly, and in the spirit of service. He paid for his own meals and drinks, turned down gifts, and refused to discuss important issues in secret. But to accomplish anything he had to at least appear to play the game.

The men rose as he approached.

"Senator Sheridan." An older man with a head of thinning white hair extended his hand. "Carl Hillman. So good to finally meet with you."

Hillman was a lobbyist for a number of mining companies in the state and stood across the aisle from Reece on every environmental issue. Ordinarily, Reece wouldn't have given him the time of day, but the bill Hillman had proposed had intrigued him.

Reece shook each man's hand in turn, returned their greetings, and recalled what he knew about them.

"Mike Stanfield, Senator. Thanks for joining us."

Stanfield was the CEO of TexaMent, a Texas-based cement company with a processing plant somewhere in Adams County, north of Denver. With Stanfield at the helm, TexaMent had become the second-largest cement company in the world, with $10 billion in profits last year. His gold ring and diamond-studded platinum Rolex were evidence he took a fair amount of that $10 billion home with him.

"Galen Prentice of Prentice, Burns and Prentice. Pleased to meet you, Senator."

Prentice was the lawyer representing TexaMent. He appeared to be in his mid-forties, with a bit of gray at his temples and a hairline that was in full retreat. From the look of his Armani suit, he'd made a killing off his corporate clients. His firm represented high-profile companies—pharmaceutical firms, oil and gas companies, insurance companies—in their dealings with the state bureaucracy.

Reece sat and accepted a menu from the waiter. "Just water, please."

As the others placed their orders, he glanced over the menu and decided on the seared ahi tuna.

Do women really taste like tuna?

A pair of green-gold eyes flashed through his mind, and he fought back a grin.

Kara McMillan.

He'd spent far too many hours over the weekend thinking about her. He was certain she'd been mortified by her behavior once the tequila had worn off, and he was content to let her squirm for a while. She'd called his sister a bimbo, after all.

Not that her words had truly offended him. The whole thing was too damned funny to make him angry. The look on her face when he'd told her Melanie was his sister had been priceless. Besides, Kara's cattiness likely meant she hadn't liked seeing him with another woman. And that satisfied his male pride in a way he couldn't explain and didn't care to examine.

Truth be told, the hour or so he'd spent with Kara was the most fun he'd had with a woman in a long time. When she had asked him in for tea, her eyes smoky with female sensuality, he'd been hard pressed to refuse her. But he'd been certain they'd end up sharing more than tea, and he'd always made it a policy never to have sex with a woman who might wake up the next morning and claim she didn't know how he'd gotten into her bed.

There would be another time. He would make sure of it.

The men laughed at some joke and jerked Reece out of his own thoughts. They were looking at him, broad smiles on their faces. He smiled back and chuckled as if he'd been listening. He needed to pay attention, not let his mind drift off with thoughts of women—or one particular woman.

Stanfield's smile faded, and he glanced at his watch. "Shall we get down to business, gentlemen?"

"Certainly." Reece met his gaze and found the man's blue eyes as cold and hard as flint.

KARA PORED over the page, ignoring the chatter of the newsroom around her. Clearly these were chemical measurements of some kind. The looked like the kinds of readings the EPA took when monitoring air emissions, but they weren't official government documents. Perhaps they were the company's own measurements, part of a self-monitoring program.

Most of the elemental symbols she recognized: *As* for arsenic, *Si* for silicon, and *Hg* for mercury. All showed elevated levels, particularly mercury. But someone had altered the measurements, deleting some, rewriting others.

The chemical charts dated back over a period of two years. They were accompanied by a series of unsigned memos on plain paper reminding the company's environmental compliance officer to "correct false readings and eliminate unnecessary data." Someone had gone over those words in yellow highlighter to make sure she saw them.

Last was an EPA report documenting a plume of pollution running for almost a mile beneath the plant where it threatened to contaminate groundwater. The report was ten years old.

She was about to flip through the report when it opened on its own to a page near the center. Several photographs had been tucked inside. Each bore a date stamp indicating the photos were taken four days ago.

The photos were dark and had obviously been taken at dawn or dusk—she couldn't tell which. They appeared to have been shot in close sequence. The first showed several men in hardhats, their faces cloaked by darkness, in the midst of unloading metal drums from the back of a heavy truck. The license plate of the truck was not visible, and the name of the company on the door was obscured by mud. Kara could just make out the letters "r-u-p."

The second photo was much like the first, but more drums now sat on the ground. The third showed men carrying drums toward a ditch just off to the left of the truck—a ravine or perhaps an irrigation ditch. The fourth showed a man with a crowbar prying the lid from one of the drums. The fifth showed two men dumping the contents of the drum into the ditch as the others watched and the man with the crowbar pried open yet another drum.

Chills ran down Kara's spine.

She had a bona fide whistleblower on her hands.

The man who had given her these photos had taken a serious risk. The deliberate dumping of toxic waste—she was sure the drums didn't contain Kool-Aid—was a felony. If he had been discovered either shooting the photos or delivering them to her, he'd likely lose his job, maybe even face harassment from his coworkers and his employer.

But which company was this? She looked carefully at each photograph once more and again felt chills when she got to the last one. But all she could see were those last three letters—r-u-p.

She turned to her computer and was about to begin an Internet search when she saw the time—5:42. Outside her window the sun had already set.

"Damn!"

She quickly shut down her computer, stuffed the documents into her briefcase, grabbed her keys, and dashed down the hallway past the busy production department and out the side door. If she didn't hurry, she'd be late picking up Connor again. Worse than the money the YWCA would charge her would be the sad look in her son's eyes. He hated to be the last to go home.

She rushed to her car, opened the door, tossed in her purse and briefcase, and slid behind the steering wheel. It was only a few blocks to Connor's day care, but downtown Denver was a tangle of one-way streets that were inevitably choked with traffic during rush hour.

It was 5:58 when she pulled into the YWCA parking lot. Two other cars were parked there, and one of them belonged to Connor's teacher.

Kara scrambled out of the car and up the walkway just as a father stepped out with his little girl. As she reached for the door handle, she spotted Connor staring dejectedly out of the window at her—last again. She felt the familiar twist of regret in her stomach.

She stepped inside the foyer and unfastened the childproof wooden gate. "Hey, pumpkin!"

Connor gazed up at her from his perch by the window, a look of resignation in his brown eyes. He shuffled over to his cubby and pulled his blue down coat from its hook.

"He's had a good day." Janice, Connor's teacher, wiped down a shin-high table. "You ate all your lunch and helped me keep an eye on the little kids, didn't you?"

Connor nodded and stuck an arm in a sleeve.

"I'm happy to hear that. Thanks, Janice." Kara helped Connor the rest of the way into his coat, knelt down, and zipped it. She kissed him on his tiny nose. "I'm so happy to see you!"

He reached for his lunch box, while Kara took the papers and drawings from the top shelf of his cubby and looked through them. "What a nice butterfly! I love its pretty blue wings."

"There's a permission slip there I need you to sign. The Friday after next, we're taking the four- and five-year-olds on a field trip to the museum to see the dinosaurs."

"That sounds like fun, doesn't it, Connor? You love dinosaurs."

Connor looked up at her, his little mouth curving into a smile.

Janice lifted tiny chairs onto the newly cleaned tables. "We need parents to help chaperone, and as you work so close by, I was hoping you could be one of them."

"Well, I . . ." Kara glanced at the permission slip. She would love to come along, to spend a part of her day with her son and other children, but Tom would never give her time off for that. "I don't know. I save all my personal time to use when Connor is sick."

Janice gave Kara a look that said she heard excuses like this from all the parents and had little respect for them. "Well, see what you can work out. We can't take the trip without chaperones, and so far only one parent has signed on."

Kara took a breath and fought back a sense of overwhelm. "I'll let you know. Are you ready, pumpkin?"

The look on Connor's face said he'd been ready an hour ago.

KARA RINSED the shampoo from Connor's hair with a pitcher full of bathwater, then grabbed a towel and wiped water from his eyes. "There you go—no more sea slugs or slimy snails in your hair."

This was her favorite time of day. Dinner was over, the dishes were done, and she had uninterrupted time to spend with her son.

She'd made spaghetti—his favorite—then listened as he'd told her about the tower he'd built with blocks and how it had been the tallest tower ever. Her heart had ached to think she hadn't been there to see it.

The tallest tower *ever.*

"Draw me a picture!" Connor smiled up at her from beneath a tousle of wet, blond hair.

"Okey-dokey." Kara grabbed the can of generic shaving cream she kept just for this purpose and shook it. "What do you want this time?"

"A bunny rabbit."

"One bunny rabbit coming right up." She drew a circle on the tile wall with shaving cream and made a little triangle nose and two big eyes. Then she shook the can again and added long whiskers and two big, floppy ears. It wasn't Monet, but it would do.

Connor giggled and stood up, sloshing a wave of water over the edge of the tub and into Kara's lap. She never escaped bath time without getting soaked.

Connor was smearing the shaving cream across the tile when the phone rang. Kara didn't want to leave Connor alone in the tub, nor did she particularly want to talk to anyone, so she let the call ring through to the answering machine. Connor had completely smudged her rabbit and transferred most of the shaving cream onto his belly by the time the machine picked up.

Kara scooped up a bit of the cream with her finger and dotted it on her chin. "Do you like Mommy's beard?"

Connor reached out, brushed it from her chin, and placed it on his own, a mischievous smile on his face.

"You stole my beard!"

It was then she heard the voice. Her heart stopped. She had expected it to be a telemarketer.

"Hi, Kara, it's Reece—Reece Sheridan. I was just calling to see—"

Kara couldn't hear because Connor was laughing and chattering about her beard. She stood and listened. Was he asking her out? After everything she'd said to him?

"I thought you might enjoy it. If you're interested, give me a call."

She made a mad dash for the kitchen and grabbed the phone just as he finished leaving his number. "Hello?"

"Kara?"

Kara tried to act like her stomach hadn't just tied itself in knots. "Senator Sheridan?"

"Call me Reece, please. Did I catch you at a bad time?"

"I'm just giving Connor a bath."

"Should I call back later?"

Kara glanced down the hall toward the bathroom, where Connor was humming to himself. He was old enough to be left alone for a short time. "No, I can take a few minutes."

"How are you?"

"Oh, I'm . . ." What should she say? That she was mortified? That she couldn't believe he was calling? That she'd thought about him constantly since Friday? "I'm fine. And you?"

"I'm doing well, thanks. Still at the Capitol."

"Late night?"

"Yeah. I'm introducing my last bill for the session tomorrow." He paused. "I was wondering if you'd let me take you to dinner—perhaps a trip up to Boulder?"

"Uh . . ." A thousand emotions raced through Kara's head—disbelief, excitement, doubt, fear. "I don't know."

"Is the People's Republic of Boulder too granola for you?"

Kara laughed in spite of herself. "No, I like Boulder. It's just . . ."

"Just what?"

"Well, I'm a journalist, and you're a senator." *Way to state the obvious, McMillan.*

"I'll try not to hold it against either of us."

Fragmented thoughts chased one another through Kara's mind. There were lots of reasons she should say no, good reasons, reasons that made sense both personally and professionally. "Really, we . . . I shouldn't."

"Was it something I said?"

The self-deprecating tone of his voice and the ridiculousness of his words made her smile. He was letting her off the hook. "No, it was something I said. I can't imagine why you'd ever want to talk to me again. I called your sister a bimbo. I'm sorry."

"Make it up to me by having dinner with me."

"I think that's a bad idea."

"Why, Kara?" This time his voice was sincere.

Because I find you irresistibly sexy. Because you make me feel things I haven't felt for a very long time. Because I'm afraid what will happen if I start to care about a man like you.

Was Holly right about her?

I think you were so hurt by that S.O.B. you're afraid to spend time with any man who might actually turn you on.

Kara couldn't let Galen define her life forever. "We'd have to agree not to discuss our work."

"Darling, work is going to be the last thing on my mind. Would this Friday work?"

Momentarily speechless, she felt her heart literally skip a beat. "Friday would be fine."

"I'll pick you up at 6:30."

"Okay, 6:30."

She said good-bye, hung up the phone, and wondered if she'd just done something incredibly stupid. A date with Reece Sheridan? She hurried back to pull Connor from the tub.

She was so distracted as she got him ready for bed that she forgot to have him brush his teeth until he reminded her and her tongue got tangled a dozen times while reading *Fox in Sox.* Finally, she tucked the blanket under his chin. He was drowsy, his eyelids heavy.

"Mommy, will you be late tomorrow?"

Kara sat down beside him on the bed and stroked his downy hair. She savored the smell of baby shampoo. "I don't know. I'll try very hard not to be late. I love you, and I want to be with you as soon as I can every day."

"If I had a daddy, would he pick me up so I didn't have to be last?"

Kara felt a pricking behind her eyes and swallowed. How could she tell him that he did have a daddy, that his daddy lived in the same town but didn't want to have anything to do with him? "Maybe, but daddies have to work, too."

"Will you come with us to see the dinosaurs?"

"Yes, pumpkin." She vowed silently to work it out somehow. She bent down and kissed the baby-softness of his cheek. "Sweet dreams."

She quietly slipped out of Connor's room and into her own, where she took off her still-damp sweat pants and sweatshirt and slid into her nightgown and bathrobe. Then she stepped into the bathroom and began to brush her teeth.

She could lie. She could simply tell Tom she had an interview that morning. There's no way he'd know she was chaperoning a preschool field trip instead.

But she didn't want to do that. She was in the business of telling the truth—that's what being a journalist was all about. Lying to her editor didn't seem right. Yet if she told Tom the truth, he would surely begrudge her the time.

Though Tom knew she put in more than forty hours a week, he'd never really accepted the fact that she was a mother and needed to leave work to pick her son up from day care every evening by six. He'd never actually verbalized it, but Kara knew he felt motherhood had compromised her as a reporter. His idea of a good journalist was someone who routinely worked until 1 A.M. and had no personal life to interfere with the job.

Not that Tom was a complete jerk. He put as many demands on himself as he did his staff, and he knew the Denver metro area like no one else. A consummate journalist, he'd taught Kara the ropes and encouraged and berated her until she'd found her investigative legs and a coveted spot on the I-team, the paper's investigative team. The result was a slew of state and national journalism awards with her name on them.

She'd never been able to explain it to anyone—had never even tried to explain it to Tom—but she'd fallen in love with her baby from the moment she'd learned she was pregnant. And though she hadn't enjoyed the constant fatigue and nausea that went with pregnancy, she'd cherished the thought that someone new, some little person, was growing inside her.

For a time, her condition had been her special secret. She'd hidden it from everyone at the paper—everyone except Holly, who'd found her sick in the bathroom and had guessed immediately—until she was five months along and Tom had finally noticed the growing bulge of her belly.

He hadn't taken it well. Though he tried hard to act like a feminist, his idea of liberation was acknowledging every woman's inalienable right to work long hours and to have sex with him. He seemed to think pregnancy and motherhood were an extreme inconvenience, some primitive biological reaction women ought to have evolved beyond by now.

Kara had worked hard throughout her pregnancy, had pushed herself to prove to him she could still do her job. There was no reason she couldn't both raise a child and continue to be one of the top journalists in the state. Lots of men combined parenthood with successful careers. Why couldn't she do the same?

She'd gone into labor at her desk and had finished her story before driving herself to the hospital. She'd given birth alone, with a nurse whose name she didn't know holding her hand. When she'd finally pushed her baby out in a rush of fiery pain and held him in her arms, she'd discovered that she loved him far more than she could possibly have imagined.

Tom had always told her the true job of the journalist was to make the world safe for the future by shining a light into dark corners. Connor's birth had put a face on that future.

Kara rinsed her mouth and toothbrush, pulled her hair back into a ponytail, and felt the urge to talk with her mom. Besides, she needed to make certain her mother could babysit Connor on Friday.

A date with Reece Sheridan. What had she been thinking?

She walked down the hallway to the kitchen, picked up the phone, dialed, and got her mother's voicemail. She left a quick message and then went back into the bathroom to wash her face. She had just finished slathering on moisturizer when the phone rang.

She hurried back to the kitchen and picked up the receiver, sure her mother was calling her back. "Hello."

"I frightened you today, and I'm sorry."

The whistleblower.

Kara hit record. "I'm fine."

"You're a nice lady, and I know you're single and all with a kid, so I didn't mean to spook you."

How did he know so much about her? Kara held back the question. "I read through the documents this afternoon. I saw the photos. Thanks so much for trusting me with this."

"Do you understand now why no one can know where you got them?"

"Absolutely. What you've done is very brave, and I would never, ever reveal your identity to anyone."

"Not even your boss?"

"Not even my boss."

"That's good. That's real good."

Kara could tell he was nervous. "There are laws that protect whistleblowers, and there are things we can do to help keep you safe. But I do need you to trust me. I need to know who you are and how I can reach you. And I need to know the name of the company. I can't do anything unless I know who and what I'm dealing with."

"Fair enough. Can you meet me at the same place at the same time on Wednesday?"

"Yes, I—"

The phone went dead.

CHAPTER 4

"I'D LOVE to take Connor Friday night, but I'm going to an overnight retreat at the Dharma Center. It's a Tantric workshop for singles." Lily McMillan's voice sounded tinny coming across the bad cell phone connection.

Kara rolled her eyes and wondered why she couldn't have a normal mother like everyone else, someone who would bake cookies, wear an apron, and let her grandson call her Grandma instead of insisting he use her first name. "Tantra for singles? What is that—masturbation for Buddhists?"

"They prefer to use the term *self-pleasuring. Masturbation* is such a moralistic word."

"So you're going to go to a workshop on self-pleasuring? Isn't that something a person's supposed to practice on their own?" Kara didn't want to imagine what actually happened at the workshop.

"Tantra is about more than sex. It's about channeling sexual energy in a spiritual way. Really, Kara, you need it more than I do. Your second chakra is clogged to overflowing, and it's throwing your whole mind and body out of sync."

Kara had heard this more times than she could count. "Leave my second chakra out of this, Mom. Is there any way to reschedule to the next workshop?"

"No, honey. I've already paid my tuition, and I can't afford to lose it. I'm sorry."

"How expensive is this workshop?"

Her mother's voice took on an evasive tone. "It's being taught by a husband-and-wife team who trained in India."

A husband-and-wife team who trained in India. They were probably divorced and hated each other. "Mom, how much?"

"Well, with vegetarian meals and daily guided meditation it's twelve hundred."

Kara's jaw dropped. "Twelve hundred dollars to listen to a couple of self-styled gurus talk about masturbation?"

"I told you—Tantra is more than that."

Kara watched the rest of the I-team head off to the conference room and fought a growing sense of frustration. She needed to find someone she could trust to watch Connor, or she needed to cancel her date with Reece. "I've got to go, Mom. I-team meeting."

"I hope you find a sitter. Would you like me to ask around?"

"Yeah, that would be great. Thanks. Talk to you later." Kara hung up, grabbed her files, and hurried off to the conference room, wondering if perhaps she'd been adopted.

REECE LOOKED through the report Carl Hillman and TexaMent had prepared for him, intrigued. Every year, the company's Colorado plant burned one hundred thousand tons of coal in its kiln to turn rock into the clinker that, once ground, became cement. This resulted in the release of tons of mercury and other pollutants into the air that were picked up by moisture in the air and dropped into the state's soil and lakes whenever it rained or snowed.

But TexaMent's board wanted to burn old tires as a fuel source instead. Based on the data they had from their plants elsewhere around the country, changing to scrap tires as a fuel source would reduce air pollution while keeping almost a million tires out of the state's landfills each year and reducing the need for coal. All TexaMent needed was a change in state law that allowed them to burn tires in a cement kiln.

The company was being up front about the fact that burning tires would save them millions of dollars each year, as the state paid industry to dispose of waste tires. Instead of spending money to fuel their kiln, they'd be earning money, adding to their bottom line. On the surface it seemed like a mutually beneficial solution to a serious environmental problem.

So what was the catch? Or was there a catch? Had Reece already grown so jaded that he looked for ulterior motives where there were none? Perhaps. But something about Stanfield left a bad taste in his mouth.

Reece pored over the EPA data on tire-burning until the columns blurred. He glanced at his watch. It was almost midnight. He'd just finished packing his briefcase when the scent of a woman's perfume wafted into his office, followed by Alexis Ryan.

"Working late, I see." She leaned against the doorjamb to his office, arms crossed to emphasize her artificially enhanced cleavage. Dressed in a fitted gray suit, her bleached-blond hair pulled back in an elegant French braid, she somehow looked as fresh now as she had when he'd passed her in the hall early this morning.

"What do you want, Alexis?" He slammed his briefcase shut and grabbed his jacket, keys, and cell phone.

"Are you this rude to all lobbyists, or is it just me?" Her cherry-red lips turned down in a slight pout.

He strode toward her, reached for the wall beside her, and flicked out his office light. He looked into her blue eyes and smiled. "I'm not being rude, Alexis. I just know you well enough to know you don't come around unless you want something."

She leaned toward him, gave him a better view of her breasts. Her perfume surrounded him like a cloying fog. "I thought we should meet this week to talk about the budget bill."

"Let me guess. There are a few expenditures you want to make certain don't get cut from the prison budget."

She tilted her head coyly and looked up at him from beneath smoky lashes. "Something like that."

He reached for the doorknob and pulled his office door shut, forcing her into the hallway. "You can't win my vote this way, Alexis. You know that. You've already tried, remember?"

It was hard for Reece to fathom why he'd ever found her attractive. It was even harder to believe he'd had sex with her. He'd met her shortly after being elected, accepted her invitation to get acquainted over lunch, and found himself living every man's fantasy when for dessert she went down on him in the front seat of his Jeep. They'd had a heated affair that had ended a month later when he'd failed to vote in favor of a huge increase for the state's prisons. The experience had left him feeling sullied and more than a little used. But it had opened his eyes.

The flirtatious look on her face turned into a scowl. "You're so arrogant, Reece. You really believe you're better than the rest of us, but your self-righteous idealism won't get bills passed."

"You're wasting your breath, Alexis." Drew Devlin strode down the hallway on his way to the elevator. Devlin was the Senate president and on the opposite side of the aisle from Reese on every issue. Their loathing for one another was mutual—and very public. "Another two years, and he'll be back to teaching high school social studies."

Reese paid no regard to Devlin's attempt at an insult. Deliberately, he smiled and looked down at Alexis. "I don't suppose my methods are as effective as yours, but at least I don't work on my back."

He ignored her outraged gasp and walked casually down the rose marble stairs into the foyer and out into the chill of night.

KARA TURNED on the digital recorder and slipped it into her pocket as she rounded the corner onto Smith Road. Before her stood the abandoned warehouse and the parking lot where she'd met the whistleblower on Monday.

An old, blue battered Chevy truck was parked in the lot, the whistleblower inside.

"Colorado plates—MAI-2431." She spoke the license plate number aloud, knowing it would be picked up on her recorder and saved for later.

As she turned into the lot, the whistleblower got out·of the truck, walked to the passenger side of her car, and tried to open the door.

It was locked.

Despite her misgivings, Kara unlocked it, allowing a total stranger to climb inside.

Dressed in jeans and a heavy plaid work jacket, he looked at her through a cheap pair of mirrored sunglasses, then craned his neck to look around them as if he expected someone to be following him. "Drive."

"All right." Kara eased the car back into the empty street, headed back toward Quebec, and ignored the voice in her head that warned her to be wary of this man. "You know my name. You know how to reach me. I've given you my word that I won't give you away. It's time you told me who you are and why we're meeting in an abandoned parking lot on the edge of town."

He was still looking over his shoulder. "Henry Marsh."

She had worked whistleblower cases before and knew it made people jittery to break ranks and divulge wrongdoing that their bosses and coworkers were covering up. But fear was rolling off this guy in waves. She could see it in his jerky movements, hear it in his rapid breathing, and smell it in his sweat.

Either he was paranoid, or he was truly terrified.

Feigning a calm she did not feel, Kara spoke in slow, soothing tones. "I'll just keep driving, Mr. Marsh. No one is following us. Tell me what has a big man like you shaking in his work boots."

* * *

TWO HOURS later, Kara pushed her way into Tom's cluttered office.

He looked up from his computer. "Have a seat, McMillan. What's up?"

Kara sat, notepad in one hand, cup of tea in the other. "He's a foreman for Northrup Mining Corporation, a gravel-mining operation north of Denver. And if he's telling the truth—and I have strong reason to believe he is—dumping toxic waste is just one of a host of serious environmental crimes taking place out there."

Tom listened, asking the occasional question, as Kara told him how the whistleblower went to work for Northrup three years ago and had noticed immediately that strange things were happening. Emissions data he'd recorded during the day were altered between shifts. Oils and solvents recorded as having been disposed of at a toxic-waste facility were warehoused in leaking drums—and then magically disappeared. And the primary air-pollution-control system on their main building hadn't been operational since before he'd gone to work for the plant, despite data in the company's state reports that claimed the system was fully operational and sucking up millions of pounds of pollutants each year. As the plant paid the state by the pound for emissions, Northrup's lie could be saving the company hundreds of thousands of dollars each year.

Tom frowned thoughtfully from beneath his mane of hair and matching bushy eyebrows. "Does he have an ax to grind with management?"

Kara had already thought of this. The first rule of dealing with a whistleblower: find out if he or she has reason to get back at the company.

"He says his record is clean except for a workmen's comp claim last year, which he disputed and won with the union's help. Of course, he could be lying. We have no way to know for certain unless we ask Northrup, but then we'd be giving him away."

"Any record on Northrup?"

"I'm putting together an open-records request on them as soon as we finish. I'll have that out before I leave today. If the health department or the EPA has anything on file for them, I'll find it."

As soon as the state government received her request for public documents, the folks at the health department would legally have three days in which to respond. Not that the state government always complied. But that's what lawyers and courts were for.

"Request any health studies done in the area. Maybe there's a cancer or asthma cluster in the areas surrounding the plant."

"Already on it. Can you think of anyplace else I can look?"

Tom's hazel eyes bored into hers. "You could always go out to the plant, but, of course, you'd be trespassing."

Kara nodded. "I'll see what I can arrange."

"I CAN'T believe I agreed to this." Kara drove Holly's car down the highway toward the Northrup plant and glanced at her watch. She hadn't been able to drive her own car because of the Colorado Press Association license plate. "You shouldn't be here. This isn't a game."

"Hey, you can't have all the fun." Holly sat in the passenger seat dressed in a long black wrap skirt and a red silk blouse, looking as excited as a child on her way to the zoo.

"I wouldn't call committing felony trespass 'fun.' "

"You can't fool me, Kara. You live for this stuff."

Kara couldn't deny the rush of adrenaline was exhilarating, but she wouldn't give Holly the satisfaction. "You get to interview rock stars, movie stars, reality TV stars. You don't think cozying up to Bono after the U2 concert at Red Rocks qualifies as fun?"

"Oh, sure. But there's no risk in that. No risk, no glory. How is this supposed to work again?"

Kara spotted the Northrup gate down the highway ahead of them, pulled off the road, and braked to a stop. "In two minutes, I'm supposed to drive through that gate and follow the water truck that will be waiting there. I'm supposed to follow at a distance as the truck passes through the razor wire and the security checkpoint. Where the truck turns left, I'm supposed to turn right. If I keep following that road, he says I'll come to a little wooden shed. Off in the trees past the shed is where they're dumping the drums. I'll shoot some photos, get proof of my own, and then we'll head back out the way we came."

Holly clapped her hands together. "Good lord, it's just like in the movies!"

"If this were like the movies, I'd be Julia, you'd be Brad, they would be shooting at us, and somehow we'd manage to look gorgeous and have sex while the bullets were flying."

"Bullets?" Holly sounded abruptly subdued. "What exactly will they do if they catch us?"

"Call the cops. Have us arrested. Throw our butts in jail."

"That doesn't sound good."

"I warned you. But we're not going to get caught. He says lots of wives drive in to pick up their husbands at this time of day because there's a change of shifts, so no one will notice two more women in a car."

"We hope."

"Yes. We hope." Kara looked at her watch again and felt her pulse quicken. "Show time."

She pulled back out on to the highway, drove the remaining quarter-mile to the gate, and turned right onto Northrup property.

Large signs stood on either side of the road. "No Trespassing. Violators Will Be Prosecuted To The Fullest Extent Of The Law."

"Oh, great." Holly groaned.

"I told you not to come. It's too late to let you out now."

Ahead of them, a large green-and-white truck pulled into the road, water spraying onto the asphalt from nozzles at its rear.

Kara glanced at her watch. Three o'clock sharp. "Right on time."

"Well, now I know what a water truck is. Why do they do that?"

"They process mined gravel here. Spraying with water helps keep dust out of the air. Now, I'll just follow him at a casual distance and see where he takes us."

Nice and easy, Mr. Marsh. Kara knew he couldn't hear her, but she sent him calming thoughts anyway. The poor guy had been horrified when she'd first suggested he help her get into the plant.

"If they connect me with you, I have no idea what they'll do to me or my family," he'd said.

Kara had tried to reassure him. "They can arrest me, but they can't do anything to you. There are federal laws that protect whistleblowers from retaliation."

"Laws don't do no good if you're dead."

"No one is going to die, Mr. Marsh."

To his credit, he'd calmed down and had come up with this plan himself. And so far it was working perfectly.

The road curved to the west, and a concrete wall topped with razor wire appeared before them. A guardhouse separated the right lane from the left, but no one was on duty. The change of shifts.

Kara smiled as they drove through. "Smooth as silk."

They'd gone only a short distance when the water truck crossed a set of railroad tracks and turned left.

She spied a dirt road on the right and turned onto it. "Breathe, Holly."

Holly took a ragged breath, her hands clutched into fists in her lap.

Kara followed the road, one eye on her rearview mirror, as the car was swallowed by a stand of cottonwoods. Where there were cottonwoods in the West there was water. It couldn't be far now.

They'd driven perhaps a quarter mile when a small wooden shed appeared on her right. Her heart thrumming, she stopped the car, glanced around her, and saw no one.

It was now or never.

"Stay here. If anyone discovers us, tell them I was driving and got sick."

Holly looked like she might be feeling queasy herself. "Okay, but don't take forever! This place is freaking me out!"

Kara grabbed her digital camera, opened the door, and hurried behind the building. The faint smell of coal smoke, carried on the chilly wind, tickled her nose. The snow made crunching sounds beneath her feet and recorded her every step as she hurried into the trees. Muddy tire tracks and dozens of old footprints suggested this was the spot in the photographs, just as Mr. Marsh claimed it was.

And then she saw.

A few feet beyond her, a frozen irrigation ditch pooled in a small lake of ice. Rusted metal drums lay half-submerged, set like trashy gems in the ice among the dead husks of last summer's cattails. The ice had a sickly green tinge to it, and the water beneath seemed iridescent. In several places, dark liquid lay thick and congealed on top of the ice—the most recently dumped material, she guessed.

A burning anger grew in her belly. This was likely someone's bright idea of how to cut costs. But whatever this stuff was, she'd bet her reputation it wasn't good to drink. No doubt it was seeping into the groundwater and spreading onto other people's property. Folks out here drank, washed, irrigated, and watered their animals with well water. If, indeed, the toxins had made it into the groundwater, there was a good chance that people, livestock, and crops were being contaminated as well.

No wonder Mr. Marsh was so afraid. An environmental crime of this magnitude could easily land someone—or several someones—in prison, to say nothing of the fine the company itself would face. Whoever was behind it would likely go to some lengths to keep it secret.

A shiver that had nothing to do with the wind ran down her spine. She needed to get these shots and get out of here.

She held up her camera, and sparing a moment's thought for photographic composition, clicked as fast as her camera allowed.

Someone would pay for this. She would make certain of it.

Then, struck by an inspiration, she reached into her pocket for the empty sandwich bag that had held her lunch. She'd eaten her sandwich while driving and thankfully hadn't thrown the bag away. Treading carefully, she worked her way to the edge of the ice and, using a stick to break off a chunk, slipped it into the bag. A good chem lab ought to be able to tell her exactly what this stuff was and whether it was truly toxic. It certainly smelled terrible—like brake fluid, only stronger.

She zipped the bag shut, hurried back to the car, slipped into the driver's seat, and handed the plastic bag and the camera to Holly. "Let's get out of here."

In silence, Kara turned the car around and drove back the way they'd come. She made a left turn back onto the paved road and saw the checkpoint ahead of them.

A uniformed security guard sat at his post, checking the ID of someone trying to enter the facility.

"Don't look this way," Kara muttered under her breath. "You don't even see us."

Slowly, casually, she guided the car through the checkpoint and heard Holly's relieved sigh as they passed unchallenged.

"Smooth as silk."

When they reached the highway, Holly finally found her tongue. "What was that?"

"What was what?"

"You know. 'Don't look this way. You don't see us.'"

"Don't tell me you never saw *Star Wars*." Kara smiled, feeling the heady aftereffects of adrenaline. "That was a Jedi mind trick."

CHAPTER 5

REECE GLANCED at his watch as the Legislative Audit Committee hearing dragged on. He was supposed to leave to pick up Kara in twenty minutes, but testimony was running long. Although he'd be only too happy to excuse himself—there were more than enough members present for a quorum without him—he didn't want to tilt the majority in favor of Devlin, who, as Senate president, had appointed himself chairman of the committee. Devlin had the ethical standards of a snake-oil salesman. There was no rule the man wouldn't bend, nothing he wouldn't sell. His bottom line, as far as Reece could tell, was whatever increased the size of his ego.

Yet if Reece canceled his date with Kara, he knew in his gut he wouldn't get another chance. He was surprised she hadn't already called him to cancel. He knew she wasn't entirely enthusiastic about their date. Was it only the possible conflict of interests that held her back, or was she truly uninterested in him?

"The bottom line, Mr. Chairman, is that there are more than a handful of senators who seem to be charging expenses to the state inappropriately." Carol, director of Senate Services, was clearly growing short-tempered with Devlin's constant stonewalling.

"It seems to me this is a matter best taken up with those senators who are causing the problem. Why waste this committee's time?" Devlin's voice held a strong note of condescension.

His words drew nods of agreement from his fellow party members.

An expression akin to outrage hardened Carol's face. "Our efforts thus far have been ignored, sir. Clearly the system is not working. It is the task of this committee to hold lawmakers and government agencies within the state accountable. I suggest the committee do so with regard to this problem. Or are senators reluctant to scrutinize their peers?"

Reece felt the tension between them and realized that for Devlin this issue was personal. Perhaps he was abusing the system. Reece decided to test that theory. "Are you suggesting the committee audit every senator's spending, ma'am?"

Devlin's head jerked around, and Reece didn't miss the alarm in his eyes. "She hasn't said any such thing. Don't put words in her mouth, Sheridan."

In the front row, reporters who'd all but drifted into a coma seemed to wake up and scribble furiously. They were, Reece knew, hoping for another confrontation between the two of them.

But it was Carol who spoke next. "That is exactly what I'm suggesting, Senator Sheridan. All we need is this committee's authorization—and the cooperation of each and every senator."

Reece smiled. This meeting was about to end—and he was about to send Devlin from the room with a bad case of heartburn. "Then I make a motion that this committee conduct an audit of senators' spending to be completed within thirty days. Does this address your concerns, ma'am?"

Carol's face radiated triumph. "Yes, it does, Senator."

Two seats down from him, Senator Miguel de la Peña leaned toward his microphone. He and Reece had entered office the same year and had quickly become allies and then close friends. "I second the motion, Mr. Chairman."

Reece met Devlin's furious gaze. "Mr. Chairman, a motion has been made and seconded. I believe it falls to you to call for a vote."

*   *   *

KARA GAZED at her reflection and fought with the zipper of her skirt, her stomach filled with butterflies. She ought to have called Reece to cancel. Then she'd be free to enjoy a quiet evening with Connor instead of feeling anxious and wasting time trying to look pretty for a man who probably only wanted to go out with her because he thought she was an easy lay. And who could blame him? After the things she'd said to him last time, he'd be more than justified in making that assumption.

I sure learned a lot about you, sweetheart.

She would set him straight on that score. He didn't know anything about her.

Unable make the skirt's zipper lie flat, she stripped it off and tossed it on the floor beside the other outfits she'd tried on. Then she turned to face the catastrophe of her closet. It wasn't like her to fuss over clothes. But then she hadn't felt much like herself all day.

She'd barely been able to concentrate at work. The lab results on the ice she'd taken from Northrup wouldn't be available until the middle of next week, and the state had until Monday to respond to her open-records request. She'd tried to focus on deciphering the documents Mr. Marsh had given her, only to have her thoughts drift time and again to Reece.

The hard feel of his arms around her as he'd kept her from falling on the ice. The hot kiss of his fingers on her cheek as he brushed a strand of hair from her face. His devastating smile.

No man had the right to be that sexy.

No, she corrected herself, Reece Sheridan wasn't a man. He was a politician. As long as she remembered that, she'd be fine.

She glanced at her alarm clock and felt her stomach knot. He would be here in fifteen minutes, and she still wasn't dressed.

"Mommy, what's this?" Connor held up her mascara. He had long since grown bored with the *Sponge Bob* DVD she'd put on to entertain him and had taken to playing with the antique perfume bottles on her vanity.

"It's mascara. It makes women's eyelashes longer and darker." She searched through the hideous assortment of work clothes hanging in her closet and reached for the black velvet dress she'd worn to last year's Christmas party.

"Why do women want their eyelashes to be longer?"

"Because we're silly and think longer, darker eyelashes will make men fall in love with us." She slipped the dress over her head, pulled it down over her hips, and looked in the mirror. The soft material clung to her skin, while the plunging princess neckline made it seem like she had breasts. But would he think she was wearing it to impress him? She certainly didn't want him to think she'd put any special effort into getting ready for this date.

"Is a man going to fall in love with you?"

She turned sideways and gazed at her profile. "Apparently not in this lifetime."

The doorbell rang.

Her heart gave a violent leap, and she hurried to her bedroom window.

The baby-sitter.

"Come, Connor. Sierra's here."

Kara quickly filled Sierra in on the basics—how long to heat Connor's mac and cheese in the microwave, which DVDs he liked most these days, how to reach her in case of trouble—while trying to ignore the way the teenager constantly flicked the metal in her newly pierced tongue against her teeth. She had just slipped into a pair of black tights and Victorian-style boots when the doorbell rang again.

Pulse racing, she took one last look in the mirror and touched up her lipstick.

What in the world were you thinking, McMillan?

She turned away from her reflection, forced herself to take a deep breath, and walked down the hallway to answer the door, trying to pretend that she was like Holly and went on dates with gorgeous men every night.

Another man, another night.

She opened the door and forgot to be nervous, forgot to think, forgot to breathe.

He stood outside in his long gray overcoat, a smile on his firm, sensual lips. "Kara."

Despite the cold, his coat was unbuttoned, giving her a glimpse of the crisp, white shirt, burgundy silk tie, and charcoal tailored slacks he wore beneath it.

If he ever gets tired of politics, he can always model for Playgirl.

The thought flickered through her mind and then vanished as embarrassment set in.

"Reece. Come in out of the cold. I'll just get my coat." She opened the door for him and walked down the hallway to the coat closet. She had just pulled her dress coat from its hanger when Conner came bouncing out of her bedroom and down the hallway with something in his hand.

"Mommy, what's this jiggle stick?"

She looked up to see her son standing not two feet away from Reece with her purple jelly vibrator in his hand. And he was shaking it, making it waggle back and forth.

"Oh, my God! Connor!" Blood rushed to her face, and she grabbed it from her son's hands. "Give me that!"

If she could have vanished from the face of the earth in that instant she would have gladly done so. Unable to meet Reece's gaze and ignoring Sierra's amused giggles, she hurried down the hallway, feeling utterly and completely humiliated.

Beautiful, McMillan! Now Senator Reece Sheridan has seen your vibrator!

There was absolutely no chance that he had mistaken it for anything but a sex toy because the damned thing looked just like a penis.

A huge, purple penis.

A huge, purple, veined penis, for God's sake!

Her insides withered and shrank, and she wondered for a moment if she could barricade herself in her bedroom and stay there forever.

Then she saw that her sock drawer was open. It wasn't hard to figure out what had happened. Connor had been with her while she'd been putting on her tights. She must have left the drawer open. And he'd found her vibrator lying on top—right where she'd left it last night after fantasizing about a certain state senator.

She dropped the device back into her drawer, slammed it shut, and sat on the edge of her bed.

She was never going to be able to face Reece Sheridan again.

REECE BIT his tongue and vowed not to laugh. He'd seen the look of horror on Kara's face and knew she was embarrassed beyond words.

Jiggle stick.

"Mine's black," offered the teenage baby-sitter with a shrug before walking over to the television and shuffling through a pile of DVDs.

Reece kept a straight face and knelt down until he was eye to eye with Kara's son. "You must be Connor."

The kid was adorable, with his mother's elfin facial features and her dark hair, paired with big, brown eyes. He eyed Reece curiously and nodded. "Who are you?"

"My name is Reece, and I like the Broncos, too." He pointed to Connor's Denver Broncos T-shirt. "I bet you have your own football."

Connor smiled, nodded. "Do you want to see it?"

"You bet." Reece found himself wondering who the boy's father was and why Kara had never married the man.

Connor turned and scampered down the hallway just as his mother reappeared.

She was dressed in a black velvet dress that seemed to be airbrushed onto her slender body. It was cut low enough to reveal the soft curves of her breasts. Her long dark hair was pulled back from her face in a barrette. Simple pearls adorned her ears. The faint scent of perfume floated gently in the air around her.

Classy. Elegant. Sexy as hell.

Reece's gut instinct was to skip dinner and focus instead on satisfying a more basic hunger. He wanted to get her out of that dress as quickly as possible, to peel away the black velvet and let his hands savor the silk of her skin. But first he would use his mouth to smear that glistening red lipstick of hers all over the place.

Unfortunately, he could tell that was not what she had in mind.

"Reece, I've been thinking maybe this isn't a good idea." She didn't look him in the eye, and he could tell she was mortified.

"I think it's the best idea I've had in a long time. You look beautiful." He took her coat from her arm, and held it up for her, refusing even to consider leaving without her. "Come to dinner with me. We'll talk. Nothing more."

She looked into his eyes as if measuring the sincerity of his words, then turned her back to him, and slid her arms into her coat sleeves. "All right."

Just then Connor dashed into the room, an orange and blue Nerf football in hand, and threw a wobbly pass straight for Reece's groin. Reece caught it and tossed it gently back. "That's a nice football, buddy. You've got a strong arm. Next time I come over, we'll throw a few passes."

The boy smiled, then roared and ran across the room as if heading for a touchdown.

"Call my cell if you need anything, Sierra. Have fun, Connor. Can Mommy have a kiss?"

KARA WAITED until they were seated at the restaurant—an upscale Italian place called Laudisio Ristorante Italiano—

before bringing it up. "The way I acted the night we met—you should know I'm not really like that."

"Considering how much you'd had to drink, I think you handled yourself pretty well." His voice was serious, but Kara didn't miss the smile that tugged at his lips. "I doubt anyone could drink three margaritas at The Rio without saying something . . . colorful."

"I appreciate your tolerance, and I hope you'll understand when I say I didn't come here so we could have sex."

His eyebrows rose. "That's good, because I'd disappoint you otherwise. I came here to eat."

Kara felt herself blush. She never blushed. "I didn't mean . . . You know what I mean."

He took a sip from his water glass and nodded. "This is your way of telling me you're embarrassed about the things you said last time and making certain I know you're not going to sleep with me tonight."

Relieved to have it out in the open, Kara nodded. "Exactly."

He set his water down and met her gaze, his blue eyes boring bluntly into hers. "If all I wanted was a quick fuck, I would have taken you up on your offer for a cup of tea that night. You were more than willing then, but I turned you down. Remember?"

Not this time. Ask me again when you haven't had three.

For the second time in less than a minute, Kara felt her cheeks flame. She closed her eyes and took a deep breath. "I'm sorry, Reece. I always seem to be saying or doing something stupid around you. Can we start over?"

He grinned. "Sure."

Kara leaned forward and held out her hand. "Hi, I'm Kara McMillan."

He took her hand in his and stroked the back of her hand with his thumb—not the conventional handshake she'd been expecting. "Delighted to meet you, Kara. I'm Reece Sheridan."

By the time he released her hand, her heart was beating noticeably faster than normal.

The black-and-white-clad waiter arrived. "Are you ready to order, sir? Perhaps wine and an appetizer?"

The wine list was the size of a three-ring binder. Kara had glanced through it and had been astonished at how much a bottle of wine could cost. Did people really drink this stuff?

Reece flipped to a specific page and then looked up at her. "Do you trust me?"

"Yes." Taken aback by the question, she answered reflexively. Trust him? She barely knew him.

Reece looked up at the waiter. "We'll have a glass of the Lacryma Christi del Vesuvio 1999 Mastroberadino with the polenta con funghi as an appetizer." The Italian rolled off his tongue as if he spoke the language.

The waiter looked surprised and grinned. "You know your Italian wines, sir."

"Some of them, anyway. Do you eat meat, Kara?"

She nodded, quickly glancing through the menu.

"Then make it two orders of your Vitello Saltimbocca, please, with a bottle of the Barolo 2000 Ginestra Domenico Clerico."

Kara had never had a man order for her before, and she found herself torn between a feeling of feminist irritation and one of strange feminine delight. But then the food arrived—first the polenta and mushroom appetizer and then the tender veal—and all she could feel was gratitude. And although she knew nothing about wines, the varieties he had chosen were delectable. Taken together, it was the most delicious meal she'd had in years. By the time the waiter cleared their plates away, she was feeling surprisingly relaxed.

She watched as Reece poured the last of the Barolo into their glasses. "Why did you decide to go into politics?"

"I thought we agreed not to talk about work." He set the empty bottle down and leaned back in his chair, wineglass in his hand.

She couldn't help but notice how broad his shoulders

seemed compared to the high back of the chair, and she found herself undressing him with her eyes. Would his shoulders be hard and muscular? Would his chest have lots of hair or just a little? Were his nipples red like wine or tanned and brown? "I would really like to know."

"My students challenged me to run for office. I was teaching U.S. government to juniors and seniors that year and gave a passionate speech about the need for citizens to participate in their government if our democracy is to succeed. So they called my bluff, told me that if I cared so much I should run for office."

"So you did."

"Yes. I decided they were right. Besides, real-life experience is a better teacher than a textbook, and whatever I learn, I can pass on to my students."

"You plan to return to teaching?"

"I'm not a career politician, if that's what you're asking. As soon as I feel I'm no longer contributing effectively—or when the voters send me packing—I'll go back to what I love."

Kara was almost sorry she'd asked. Throughout dinner she'd reminded herself repeatedly that he was not a man but a politician, motivated by an oversized ego and unhealthy ambition. Now he'd gone and shattered that perception. He was making her see him as not only a man—and an unbelievably sexy man at that—but also an ostensibly decent man. She hadn't imagined anyone actually ran for office these days simply because they wanted to help people.

They sat for a moment in silence.

"You like children then?" She was certain she knew his answer, almost dreaded it.

Please let him say he hates kids.

"I adore kids. They have such a unique way of seeing things. If we stand any chance of making this world a better place, it's through them."

She ran her fingers over the damp stem of her wineglass, finding her mental checklist of reasons she shouldn't spend time with him growing perilously short.

"Is Melanie your only sister?"

He shook his head. "I'm the eldest of four—one brother, two sisters. My parents got divorced when I was nine. The younger kids went to live with my mother and her family in Texas, while I stayed with my father here in Denver. Melanie just moved here two months ago. We're just getting acquainted really."

"That sounds like a lonely way to grow up. It must have been hard being so far away from your mom and the other children."

He shrugged. "I suppose so. I think my mother thought of me as being my father's son, while my brother and sisters were her children."

Kara couldn't imagine a mother abandoning her own child that way. "Are you and your father close?"

A troubled look crossed his face, and his gaze dropped to the table.

"I'm sorry. Is that too personal?"

"No, Kara. You can ask me anything you like." He looked up, gave a sad smile. "My father died last May. A car accident on I-25."

And then she remembered seeing it in a headline. She hadn't even bothered to read the article. To her it had been nothing but another news story, ink on newsprint. To him it had represented overwhelming grief, the loss of someone he loved. "I'm so sorry."

He reached across the table, took her hand in his, and caressed the back of it with his thumb. The contact was white-hot, made her breath catch in her lungs.

"Thanks. And, yes, we were close."

The waiter approached with the dessert tray.

"Have you ever had Laudisio's tiramisu?"

Kara shook her head, almost unable to speak. She'd seen a program on the Discovery Channel once, something about how the human hand has more nerve endings than most other parts of the body. She decided it must be true, as every nerve from her fingertips to her wrist was alive and tingling.

"Then you really must try it. We'll split one order of tiramisu with two glasses of the Reciotto della Valpolicello 1997 Mazzi."

"Yes, sir." The waiter hurried away, a big smile on his face.

"Enough about me, Kara. You've been 'interviewing' me all evening. Now it's my turn." He leaned forward in his chair, his hand still holding hers. "Tell me about your family."

Distracted by his touch, by the heat of his gaze, she fought to find her voice. "There's nothing to tell really. It's just my mom and I. My father left when I was a baby. I've never even met him."

He interrupted his relentless caresses to give her hand a sympathetic squeeze. "That must have been hard on you both."

Unable to help herself, Kara stroked him back, running a finger slowly across his knuckles. She felt dizzy, almost drunk, but it wasn't the wine. "My mother would never admit that. According to her, it was the best thing he could have done for either of us. She's a bit of a . . . free spirit. She never remarried and swore she had no use for a man in her life."

"Regardless of how she felt, it must have been difficult for you to grow up without a father."

A strange pain Kara hadn't allowed herself to feel since she was a teenager crept into her stomach. She forced it down, irritated with herself. She hadn't thought about her father for years, and she couldn't imagine why Reece's question—no different from those she'd asked him—should have called up an emotional response. She was grateful when the waiter interrupted them with one dish of tiramisu, two small glasses of wine, and two spoons.

Reece watched Kara swallow her emotions and decided to let the subject drop. He'd been about to ask her whether she, like her mother, felt no need for a man in her life. After all, she, like her mother, was raising a child alone. But he knew instinctively that would be going too far.

He snatched up her spoon before she could reach it, scooped a small bite of their dessert, and deliberately lowered his voice. "I want your first taste of paradise to come from me."

She looked at him, her eyes wide, a sexy flush stealing into her cheeks. "You must be joking. You're going to feed me?"

He'd surprised her, caught her off guard. Good. She'd kept herself too tightly reined in all evening, asking him questions from behind the safety of her journalist's mask, seeming to him more like the serious, controlled woman whose photo ran in the newspaper than the passionate pleasure-seeker he suspected she was.

"That's right. Now taste." He slipped the spoon between her parted lips, felt the tug of her mouth against the spoon.

Her eyes closed, and she moaned.

Christ! Blood rushed to his cock and made him painfully hard.

Had he really promised her that all they would do tonight was talk? Well, yes, in not so many words. And she'd made it clear she wanted nothing more from him—yet.

You should know that I'm not like that.

Try as she might to deny her nature, he wasn't buying it. Tequila—and now the tiramisu—simply released a part of her she kept hidden. But no woman who owned a large purple jiggle stick could suppress her own sensuality forever. And despite his raging hard-on, he could be a patient man— when the reward promised to be sweet.

"It's delicious!"

He took another spoonful and held it to her lips.

This time she took it eagerly. Again she moaned. "I've never tasted anything like this."

He fed her another bite and imagined kissing that mouth, feeling those lips around his throbbing erection. "Their tiramisu is a full-blown culinary orgasm."

As soon as he said the word *orgasm*, her gaze locked with his, and he saw a response in her eyes that had nothing to do with her taste buds.

CHAPTER 6

REECE PULLED into her driveway and turned off the engine. She'd been silent since they left the highway and entered the city. She was pulling back, walling herself off from him. Did she think he was going to try to make her pay for the meal with sex? Had their conversation gotten too personal? What was she afraid of?

He hadn't imagined that a woman as sexy, smart, and successful as Kara McMillan would feel nervous around men. Then again, he hadn't known she'd been abandoned by her father. What did that do to a little girl, to a woman?

"Thanks, Reece. I had a good time." She said it as if she hadn't believed it was possible.

"Don't sound so surprised. Besides, the pleasure was entirely mine." He reached over and took her hand. Her fingers were cold. "In case you're wondering, I'm planning on walking you to your door and giving you a good-night kiss. I hope you don't object."

"That might not be a good idea."

"Just a kiss, Kara. Nothing more. Don't tell me the woman who brought city hall to its knees is afraid of a kiss."

Even in the dark he could see the flash of fire in her eyes. "Of course I'm not afraid of a kiss! But you're assuming I want to be kissed."

He leaned across the seat and brushed her lips with his. "Don't you?"

He heard her quick intake of breath, saw the heat in her eyes, and knew he had his answer.

He pulled her closer, tasted first her upper lip, then her lower, forcing himself to go slowly. He wanted to get past her reserved exterior, to awaken that part of her she tried to hide, to force her to admit, at least to herself, that she felt some attraction to him. He wasn't trying to seduce her. Not tonight.

But then her lips parted, and her tongue flicked his, one timid touch.

With a groan, he fisted his hand in the dark silk of her hair, crushed her against him, and kissed her the way he'd wanted to all evening—deep and hot and hard.

He's kissing you, McMillan.

It was the last coherent thought in Kara's mind as Reece's tongue penetrated deep into her mouth. But this wasn't just a kiss. It was a full-on assault on her senses—the velvet thrust of his tongue, the musk and spice of his aftershave, the press of his hard upper body.

If she'd been able to think it through, she might have pushed him away, told him to stop. But she couldn't think. Not with her brain. So it must have been some other part of her that decided she should slide her arms behind his neck, press herself against him, and kiss him back.

And that other part of her was already aching and wet.

Oh, lord, but the man knew how to kiss! He ravished her mouth with delicious attention to detail, stroking her sensitive inner cheek with his tongue, sucking and nipping her lips, and angling his head to take the kiss deeper, stealing her breath, breathing for her.

She was lost in him, lost in the scent and feel of him, as he consumed her, devoured her, seduced her with his mouth. Something that sounded suspiciously like a purr came from her throat, and her hips rose reflexively off the seat as she squirmed against him, wanting to get closer, needing to get closer. It had been so long since a man had touched her, so long since a man had kissed her.

Abruptly, he broke off the kiss and ran his thumb across the swollen wetness of her bottom lip. "I told you I was going to kiss you good-night and nothing more. If I'm going to hold to that, we'd better stop now." He sat back in his seat, and Kara heard a click as he unlatched her seat belt. "I'll get your door."

As he walked around the front of the Jeep to her side of the vehicle, Kara tried to still her trembling. She shook from head to toe, her body quaking with raw need. But no matter how she tried, she couldn't stop shivering.

Get a grip, McMillan!

He opened her door, helped her to the ground, and held her before him. "You're cold."

Unable to meet his gaze, Kara spoke without thinking. "N-no, it's not that."

His brow furrowed for a moment and then he seemed to understand. He grinned, a sexy know-it-all grin, and ran a finger down her cheek. "I'm glad I was able to provoke a reaction."

Her sexual frustration became irritation. She glowered at him. "How is it you remain so unaffected?"

His eyebrows rose, and he gave a snort. "Unaffected?"

Without warning, he cupped her bottom, pulled her hard against him, and she felt the unmistakable evidence of his arousal. He was rock-hard, huge.

Her inner muscles clenched—hard—and the air rushed out of her lungs. "Oh!"

He thrust against her, his eyes dark with obvious male hunger. His voice was deep and husky. "Nothing about you leaves me unaffected, Kara."

Then he released her, slipped his arm through hers, and walked with her to the doorstep, where they stood for a moment in silence.

"Thanks, Reece. I—"

He pressed a finger against her lips to silence her. "Next Friday night—dinner at my place? I'm a good cook."

He was standing so close to her, his nearness, his scent

playing havoc with her ability to think, to breathe. If only he would shut up and go away. If only he would kiss her again!

"Okay."

Then he ducked his head and brushed his lips lightly over hers. "Good night, Kara. Sleep tight."

And then he was gone.

"THE TROUBLE is that they're lumping all senators' expenses into one sum. We can't tell one senator's legitimate claim from another's dry-cleaning bill." The audit was in its first day and already Carol was facing resistance.

Reece switched the phone to his other ear and pulled on his other jacket sleeve. "Do you mean to say there are no individual records? Nothing at all?"

Stanfield stood in the doorway to Reece's office with Galen Prentice and glanced impatiently at his watch.

"That's right. Nothing."

"What about the payroll system? Surely the state has records of compensation paid to each senator. Could we get at it that way?"

Stanfield glared at him, tapped the face of his watch, and mouthed the word, "Now!"

Reece deliberately turned his back on the man. He didn't dance to TexaMent's tune. The tire-burning bill wasn't the only issue on his plate today, nor was it the most important bill he was carrying. He'd be damned before he'd let any corporate CEO treat him like he'd been bought and paid for.

"Probably, but you know most of the senators will put up a fight. Paychecks aren't public records."

"Of course not, but the Legislative Audit Committee isn't a public body. See what you can do, and get back to me. I've got to go. Press conference. And Carol—thanks."

Reece hung up the phone and reached for his notes with deliberate calmness.

"Couldn't you handle that later?" Prentice scolded. "The press is waiting!"

Reece pretended to glance through his note cards. "They'll wait. They won't want to leave without getting the story."

Would Kara be there?

His stomach tightened with anticipation at the thought. It had taken every ounce of willpower he possessed not to call her over the weekend. He didn't want to tip his hand, to scare her away. He had a feeling that if she knew how badly he wanted her she'd never go out with him again. So he'd resolved to call her mid-week and had tried to put her out of his mind.

He'd worked out hard at the gym on Saturday, lifting weights until his muscles felt like linguine and running ten miles on the treadmill. He'd come in to the Capitol and tried to read through a few dozen of the bills he was expected to vote on in the coming weeks. On Sunday, he'd driven up to his cabin in the mountains and split firewood. He'd even taken his snowboard to Eldora and carved some turns on the double-black-diamond runs.

But never once had she left his thoughts.

He wanted to see her again.

See her? Hell, he wanted to get her into bed. It was that simple.

Then again, forget the bed. The floor would work. A couch. The kitchen table. The bathtub. The bare ground.

He'd known she was fiery, but he hadn't realized what it would do to him when she finally let that fire loose. They'd shared only one kiss, and yet in those few minutes, her responsiveness had driven him to the brink. She'd actually begun to writhe in her seat.

One kiss had done that.

He couldn't fathom what she'd be like stripped naked with his head between her thighs. But he intended to find out.

Stanfield's angry voice jerked him back to the present. "We have a lot riding on this bill, Sheridan, and we're not going to tolerate a less than fully committed effort from you!"

This was the opening Reece needed. He looked up from his notes, met the older man's soulless gaze, and allowed an angry edge to creep into his voice. "Let's get one thing straight, Stanfield. I agreed to carry this bill for my own reasons. I don't work for you. I don't report to you. I report to the taxpayers. I decide what my priorities are, not you. Is that clear?"

Stanfield's face turned crimson. "Of course, Senator. I didn't mean to imply—"

"Good." Reece interrupted him and strode past him toward the pressroom, only one thing on his mind.

Would Kara be there?

NOTHING ABOUT you leaves me unaffected, Kara.

If she tried, Kara could still feel his lips against hers. She could feel the roughness of his five-o'clock shadow, the slick glide of his tongue, the surprising hardness of his chest and his—.

She pulled to the side of the highway, slammed on her brakes, and realized it was too late. She'd missed her turn.

She swore, scolded herself. "Quit thinking about *him,* McMillan!"

She'd been thinking about *him* all weekend. When she'd burned Saturday's dinner. When she'd put her line-dry-only rayon shirt in the dryer. When she'd gone to the grocery story and remembered to buy batteries but not milk or bread or eggs. When she'd lain awake last night, every nerve in her body alive and wanting.

Wanting him.

But life was not about what she wanted. She'd learned that lesson a long time ago.

She waited for traffic to pass, made what was probably an illegal U-turn, and headed back the other direction, passing the entrance to Northrup Mining on her left, resolved to think no more about Reece Sheridan.

Okay, so Reece was an incredible kisser. She'd give him

that. He kissed her the way she'd only ever dreamed of being kissed. My God, the man had what felt like prehensile lips—to say nothing of his tongue! But did that mean she had to go witless over him?

That question was drowned out by another: if that's how he kissed, what would it be like to have sex with him?

"Stop it, McMillan! Stop it now!" She spied the little dirt road on her right, flicked on her turn signal, and made the turn.

She forced her mind back to her work. The state health department had faxed a response to her open-records request, asking for another week to organize the requested documents, some of which were supposedly in storage. Legally, they could get away with it. Colorado law required only that they respond within three days. They didn't have to fork over the actual documents in three days. Now she had a week to wait.

She'd decided to do some footwork. She'd come out here to interview Northrup's neighbors, hoping to make good use of her day. If the plant truly had been polluting the air and water for the past few years, surely the neighbors would have noticed something by now. Perhaps some of them had witnessed strange activities at or around the plant.

She came to the first farmhouse, a little white house flanked by enormous cottonwood trees. She parked, gathered her notebook and a pen, and slipped her digital recorder into her pocket. Then she stepped out into the chilly morning air.

The house looked run down, its paint worn thin. A flower garden in full hibernation took up most of what would have been the front lawn, the dried remains of sunflowers jutting up from the still-frozen earth. A wooden plaque on a little wooden fence surrounding the flowerbed proclaimed "Grandma's Garden."

Kara made her way up the sidewalk, climbed the front steps, and knocked.

After what seemed a very long time, a thin, elderly woman

with short white hair—probably Grandma herself—opened
the door. "Yes?"

"Hi, I'm Kara McMillan from the *Denver Independent*.
I'm investigating Northrup Mining Corporation, and I wondered if you might have a few minutes to talk with me."

"You're a reporter?" Grandma opened the door a bit
wider.

"Yes, ma'am." Kara held up her press card. "I'm working
on an article about your neighbor, Northrup."

"I wish they weren't our neighbor." The woman opened
the door. "Come on in."

Kara stepped into a small entryway that opened into a little kitchen. There was the heavy scent of bacon and coffee
in the air. Immaculately clean, the kitchen held a small table
with four chairs, an old stove, and a refrigerator. The appli-
ances and countertops were the same shade of golden yellow
that had been so popular in the '70s. On the wall was a clock
shaped like a cat, its swinging tail and moving eyes ticking
off the passing seconds.

"Have a seat, dear. I'll fetch my husband." She shuffled
off in a pair of slippers and a floral housedress, the bare
white of her spindly calves laced with purplish varicose
veins.

In a moment, she returned and motioned Kara down the
hallway into the living room—a small, homey room with an
overstuffed sofa decorated with white, hand-crocheted doilies.
An elderly man, presumably Grandpa, sat in an armchair, an
oxygen tube running beneath his nostrils. His cheeks were
sunken, his mouth open, and a shock of thin gray hair fell
over his forehead. But his eyes were keen. He gave her a
toothless grin and pointed to the sofa.

"This is Kara McMillan, dear. She's a reporter come to
talk about Northrup."

"Hi, Mr.—"

"Farnsworth. I'm Moira. That's Ed."

Kara shook Mr. Farnsworth's thin hand and sat on the
sofa. "I'm investigating claims that Northrup is polluting the

air and water around its plant. I decided to come out and talk with those of you who live around the facility to find out what you've seen. How long have you lived here?"

It was Moira who answered the question. "We've lived here all our married life, nigh on fifty years. Raised five kids in this house. As for Northrup, they can go to hell."

Moira spent the next hour telling Kara exactly why Northrup could go to hell. Although the plant had been a decent neighbor for most of its thirty years in existence, the past decade had been rough with night blasting at its mine and a big increase in the clouds of dust that wafted across their yard and fields. It had gotten so bad that they'd quit opening their windows, Moira said.

"If we leave them open, everything in the house gets coated in the stuff. Isn't that so, Ed?"

Ed nodded and spoke in a raspy, wheezy voice. "It plum near stripped the paint off my Ford."

"Stripped the paint off your truck?" Kara took notes, knowing also that the entire conversation was being recorded digitally. State law allowed her to record any conversation she was a participant in without notifying those she was recording. She didn't do it to be sneaky, but rather to enable her to double-check her notes later. Sometimes even she couldn't read her handwriting.

"Stripped the finish off," Moira corrected her husband. "Took away the shine. It did the same thing to the paint on our house."

Kara remembered the dull, chipping paint job and wondered if the harsh Colorado sunshine and the extreme shifts in temperature weren't to blame rather than dust. "Do you mind if I ask why you're on oxygen, Mr. Farnsworth?"

He started to speak, was cut off by his wife. "Chronic Obstructive Pulmonary Disease, isn't that right, Ed?"

Ed nodded.

"My Ed was a two-pack-a-day man when he was younger. He quit about twenty years back, but it caught up with him anyway, I guess."

Kara met Ed's gaze. "I'm sorry. I don't suppose the dust helps much."

Ed grinned and shook his head. "No, I reckon it don't."

"If you want to know more about Northrup, you should talk to the Perkinses two houses down. They've been complaining to the county health department for years about the dust. Hasn't done them one bit of good, though."

Kara thanked Moira and Ed and gave them a copy of her business card. "Please call me if you think of anything else. And thanks for being so generous with your time."

She headed farther down the road to the Perkinses' home and knocked on the door.

A middle-aged man with long hair and a beard opened the door, a growling wolf-hybrid at his side. "Who are you, and what do you want?"

In his hands he held a rifle, and it was aimed at her stomach.

CHAPTER 7

KARA TRIED not to roll her eyes and held up her press card. "I'm Kara McMillan with the *Denver Independent*. I'm investigating Northrup and was told by some of your neighbors that you might have something to say."

Mr. Perkins lowered the rifle, pushed the wolf-dog back with his leg, opened the door a crack, and took the ID card from her hand. After reading it closely, he opened the door and handed it back. "Sorry about the gun. We get some weird people out here. You never can be too careful."

"No, I guess not." Kara slipped her card back into her pocket.

"Come on in. Don't worry about Yukon here. He's a big chicken. I'll get my wife."

In short order, Kara was seated in another living room, this time with a couple of aging hippies, a large marijuana plant, and a snoozing wolf-dog, listening to an almost identical story. Dust clouds that blew in through the windows, stripped the finish off cars and houses. Dust that coated peonies, tomatoes, and apples. Dust so thick it drifted across the landscape like a suffocating fog.

Two years after moving into their home, Dottie and Carl Perkins had both been diagnosed with asthma, which they blamed on the dust but which their doctor blamed in part on their penchant for smoking ganja. They disagreed with their doctor, of course.

"We've called the county health department at least a hundred times to complain about the dust, but they say they have to see it themselves in order to fine Northrup," Dottie Perkins said. "We've taken pictures and showed them, and they always say they're going to investigate, but somehow nothing ever happens."

"They think we're just a couple of kooks who like to complain."

"Really? May I see the photos, perhaps borrow them?"

Carl Perkins nodded. "Sure. They're not doing us any good."

"What about the water? Are you on well water?"

Dottie shook her head, her long, graying flower-child hair swaying around her waist. "Oh, no! We quit drinking our well water years ago. It tastes funny. We drink bottled water."

"Would you mind if I took samples?"

They both looked at her, surprise on their faces.

Yukon, who'd been a snoring ball of fur a moment ago, sat up and watched her through wary, dark eyes, apparently sensing the shift of mood in the room.

"You think there's something in there, don't you?" Carl looked almost excited at the prospect.

"I can't say for certain, but it's worth checking, isn't it? The paper will pay for it, of course, and I'll let you know what we find."

"Fine by me. Dottie?"

By late afternoon, Kara had spoken with three other families, faced down an overly protective pit bull, and enjoyed a cup of Southern sweet tea prepared by an insistent displaced South Carolina belle. All the people she'd spoken with complained of wafting clouds of chalky dust. Some had told her of funny-tasting well water. All said they'd contacted the health department at one time or another and had gotten nothing but reassurances and promises.

As she drove south on I-25 back to Denver, Kara ran down her growing list of questions. With evidence as clear as photographs, why had officials at the health department, whose job it was to protect people from polluters, done nothing about the dust problem? How could dust from a gravel mine strip the finish from a car or a house? Could the dust be responsible for Ed's lung disease or the Perkinses' asthma? Could the chemicals Northrup was dumping in the ditch water be the cause of the funny taste in people's well water?

Lab tests might give her the answer to that one. She'd taken samples from three separate wells and would get them sent off before heading home this evening. As for the rest of her questions, she would simply have to keep digging.

"COME ON, Reece. Out with it. Who is she?"

Reece glanced over at Miguel, who was running on the treadmill beside his. "What makes you think it's a woman?"

"Oh, please, *amigo*. When a man is as distracted as you have been all day, it can only be a woman. Some lovely *muñequita* has you tied up in knots."

"It's that obvious?" He didn't like that.

"It's not that lobbyist again, is it?"

"Give me a break! I wouldn't touch Alexis Ryan if I were wearing latex gloves."

"Well, that's good. Who is it, then?"

Reece hesitated for a moment and realized he actually wanted Miguel's opinion. "She's a reporter."

"A journalist? Who? Do I know her?"

"Everyone knows her."

"Who? You're killing me!"

"Kara McMillan."

"Kara McMillan?" Miguel's voice seemed to carry across the entire gym. "You're kidding!"

"Would you pipe down?"

Miguel's sweating face split in a big grin. "You're dating Kara McMillan?"

"No. We went out once. That's all. One date is not dating."

"But you wish you were dating."

"I guess you could say that. She thinks the two of us shouldn't see one another, says it's a conflict of interests. But I think there's more to it than that. I'm not sure she likes men."

"You think she's a lesbian?"

"That's not what I said! And, no, she's not a lesbian. She just seems . . . hesitant. Ambivalent." Hot and cold was a better description.

"About men or about you?"

This was the crux of what had been eating at Reece. "I don't know. Men. Me. Both."

Miguel shrugged. "We all have our ghosts."

That was certainly true. And at least two of Kara's ghosts were men—her absent father and her son's absent father. "I hoped she would come to the press conference today."

"Maybe it's a good sign that she didn't."

"What do you mean?"

"Well, perhaps by choosing not to cover your bills she's trying to put enough distance between the two of you on the job so she can get closer to you after hours."

Reece hadn't thought of it that way. He liked that idea.

Then something on the television caught his eye. His press conference. He hated watching footage of himself on TV and was about to look away when the image of him at the podium vanished and was replaced by Drew Devlin's smirking face.

It took a moment to sink in. For the first time since he'd entered office, he and Devlin were sponsoring the same piece of legislation. Behind Devlin stood Galen Prentice and a beaming Mike Stanfield.

"What the hell?" Reece was so surprised that for a moment he quit running and was almost thrown off the back of the treadmill.

Miguel laughed. "I guess there really is a first time for everything."

"I don't believe it."

What kind of game was Stanfield playing?

* * *

TUESDAY WAS as frustrating and unproductive as Monday had been productive. Kara paid a visit to the county health department and got a refresher course in mindless bureaucracy when she spoke with the air-quality director, a middle-aged woman who smelled like cigarette smoke.

Yes, regulations did, indeed, require them to see dust emissions themselves before they could charge Northrup with a violation. Yes, it was at least a forty-five-minute drive from the office to the Northrup site. No, they had never actually witnessed these clouds of dust the neighbors had reported. Yes, they took such reports very seriously, but sometimes people just liked to complain. Yes, cement kiln dust could cause lung disease, but, no, they'd never done a health study of the area downwind from the plant. They simply didn't have the money for that sort of thing.

Then Kara moved on to air-pollution emissions. But the county health department air-quality division didn't actually deal with emissions from smokestacks.

"That's EPA," the director told her. "But the EPA leaves it up to the state air-pollution control division to handle most in-state cases."

"So the state health department makes regular inspections?"

"They come out twice a year just like we do."

"Do you make unannounced inspections or schedule an appointment with Northrup?"

"We make an appointment. They know when we're coming. But you need to understand that a plant that size can't be cleaned up overnight. If there are problems out there, we'll find them whether they know we're coming or not."

"Do inspectors verify a company's self-reporting, do air testing, make sure the company is telling the truth?"

"No. They wouldn't do that sort of thing unless the company was up for a new permit or had reported problems.

Besides, no company would lie about their emissions. They'd be in big trouble if they got caught."

"But it sounds to me like it would be hard to get caught if no one's checking."

The director glared at her openly.

"What about water pollution? How often does the county check well water?"

"We only check residential wells when someone requests it or when there's evidence of contamination."

"Have you ever had reports that Northrup is dumping toxins in the irrigation ditch that runs through their property?"

"Not that I recall. We would have referred the caller to the state water-quality people anyway. Something like that is the state's jurisdiction, maybe even EPA."

The flow chart Kara had drawn in her notes ended up looking like a knotted ball of yarn, and at the end of two hours of questions, she was certain only that no one was keeping an eye on Northrup. EPA left it up to the state, which left most of it up to the county, which, in turn, left the important stuff up to the state and the EPA. Inspectors visited the plant twice a year, taking Northrup's records at face value and being escorted on what was surely a canned tour of the facility. Based on the documents Mr. Marsh had provided, it was pretty clear that Northrup was laughing all the way to the bank.

On her way out of the director's office, Kara asked one more question. "Why would dust from a gravel mine wear the finish off a car or ruin the paint job on a house?"

"Northrup crushes the gravel, heats it, and turns it into cement. Any dust coming off their property would probably be CKD."

"CKD?"

"Cement kiln dust. It's got a very base pH, so it's caustic. It can strip the paint off a car or burn the skin, particularly if the skin is damp."

Kara digested this bit of information and then met the director's gaze full on. "If you know this, why haven't you paid any attention to the ruined paint jobs on cars and houses downwind from Northrup? Wouldn't that, together with photographs and eyewitness accounts, be sufficient evidence for some more in-depth investigation?"

The woman's face turned bright red. "As I've already explained, we need to see the dust ourselves to write a citation. How do we know what ruined the finish on their cars?"

Kara didn't bother to hide her disgust.

It wasn't until she'd reached her car that she realized she'd actually gone most of the morning without thinking of Reece.

KARA LISTED some of the chemicals found in the chunk of ice she'd taken from Northrup. The lab results had been waiting for her—together with about a zillion e-mails, many of them offering to enlarge the size of her penis—when she'd arrived at eight-thirty. She'd just had time to read through the report before the I-team meeting.

Typical Wednesday morning.

"Borated polyisobutenyl succinic anhydride nitrogen, ethylene-propene copolymer, and methyl ethyl ketone—these are common components in engine oil, the kind one uses in heavy industrial machinery. They're in the water in high concentrations."

Tessa smiled and spoke with her lazy southern drawl. "Soak your teabag in that."

Tom twirled a badly gnawed pencil in his fingers, a thoughtful scowl on his face. "So they're dumping waste oil in the water instead of paying to have it removed or recycled."

"That's my guess. But there's more. The water has dangerously high levels of methylene chloride. Methylene chloride is an extremely toxic substance found in solvents used to degrease industrial machinery. It looks like Northrup is changing the oil on their machinery, cleaning up, then dumping everything—oil and solvents—into the water."

Sophie shook her head in disgust. "That's got to be criminal, even a felony."

Kara nodded. "If it could be proved that Northrup's management was willfully dumping these chemicals in the water, it would definitely be a criminal violation of pollution laws. Northrup could be looking at a fine of millions of dollars, and management might face prison time. It's proving intent that's tough. They can always plead ignorance."

"You've got the whistleblower," Matt offered. "Does he or she know where the order to dump came from?"

"No. The source was asked by a shift manager to help with the dumping a couple times but has no idea if the supervisor is the only person behind it or whether the orders come from higher up." No one but Kara knew the whistleblower's name, and she was careful not to reveal his gender. It was part of the game, and everyone understood, though speaking without using pronouns could be awkward.

Tessa took a sip of her designer latte. "It would be the source's word against that of Northrup's legal team and their management. And unless this individual witnessed a manager giving the order, this individual's testimony would be little more than hearsay. A judge might rule it inadmissible."

"The big question is whether Northrup's criminal activity has resulted in groundwater contamination. We should get the lab results on the well water by Monday." Kara shifted to the topic that had kept her awake most of last night. "I've put the whistleblower in touch with the folks at OSHA. Unfortunately, they can't really help our source unless or until our source is threatened or faces some kind of retaliation. But the whistleblower is afraid retaliation will come with a bullet or car bomb. If that happens, of course, OSHA will be too late."

Tom waved his hand in a gesture of impatient dismissal. "That's not going to happen. Every whistleblower gets nervous. Sounds like you just need to do some hand-holding."

Kara knew Tom was probably right, but something about Mr. Marsh's very real fear gave her pause. "What if the whistleblower is right? I've promised the paper will do everything it can to keep everyone safe. If there were any immediate threat—"

"The source would have to call the cops. We're not the goddamned cavalry." And just like that Tom changed the subject. "Speaking of cops, Novak, anything new on the Gallegos shooting?"

Sometimes he could be an insensitive ass.

Kara could only imagine what he'd say when she told him that she needed Friday morning off so she could help take a bunch of preschoolers to see dinosaurs.

"This is politics, Senator Sheridan. We'll take support wherever we find it." Stanfield sounded defensive, even through the telephone.

Reece nodded his thanks to Brooke, his intern, as she handed him a cup of coffee and then winced at the strong burned taste. "Of course. But one has to wonder at the timing of Senator Devlin's support for this bill. It's almost as if he was waiting in the wings for me to announce it so he could jump onboard. I wonder how much he knew before I even agreed to carry the bill. Was this some kind of stratagem for ensuring my support—keep him in the shadows until I've gone public with the bill?"

"You think I've got that kind of time, Senator?" Stanfield laughed, his reaction and his words a bit too rehearsed for Reece. "You're giving us way too much credit here."

"Perhaps I am. But I don't like being used, and if I find out you've played me or that this bill will accomplish something other than what I hope it will accomplish, I'll withdraw my sponsorship so fast, you'll hear the sonic boom up there in Adams County."

There was a thick, uncomfortable silence on the other end of the line. "I can assure you that's not the case, Senator. I'm stunned you could think such a thing. We're straight-talkers here at TexaMent."

Reece glanced at the mountain of work he had left to accomplish before he could leave tonight. "I'm glad to hear that. Then you'll appreciate that I have a very low tolerance for bullshit. Play straight with me, Stanfield, or the bill is dead."

With that, Reece hung up. There was someone else he wanted to call.

KARA TOOK a sip of her chamomile tea, determined not to lie awake all night tonight, and settled onto the couch with today's paper. Connor was finally asleep, giving her a few moments of peace and quiet before her own bedtime. They'd read dinosaur books tonight in preparation for the field trip on Friday, and he'd been full of questions. Would a T-rex eat a boy? What about a baby T-rex? What did dinosaur poop smell like?

Kara smoothed the paper and began to read the state government page. She'd missed Reece's press conference—somewhat deliberately—while she'd been out interviewing Northrup's neighbors. An intern had covered it for the *Independent* and had done a reasonably good job with the story, asking all the questions Kara had told her to ask.

Kara read through the lead—decent, straightforward. She considered the nut graph and decided it needed a little work. Then she sat up straight, astonished.

Senator Drew Devlin had immediately signed on to Reece's tire-burning bill.

"What the hell?"

Devlin had the worst environmental record in the State Senate, and he hated Reece. She read farther, then laughed out loud when she read Reece's response.

" 'I'm a bit startled myself,' Senator Reece told reporters Tuesday evening. 'Perhaps someone ought to check the weather report in Hell.' "

A few weeks ago, she might have thought his response to be the result of calculated PR, an attempt to garner press attention. Now she knew he was shooting from the hip, just saying what came into his mind.

She leaned back on the couch, touched her fingers to her lips, and allowed herself to relive every moment of his kiss. His lips had been so firm and full and warm, and he'd known just how to use them. He'd been aggressive, but not over-powering, his tongue possessing her mouth with supreme confidence. His body had felt stunningly hard beneath her hands—his chest, shoulders, and arms so different from hers. And that masculine growl he'd made just before he kissed her—.

The phone rang.

Kara's pulse raced. Despite the chorus of voices in her head that told her she should end their acquaintance before it became an actual relationship, she'd been hoping he would call. Every night since Friday she'd hoped, and every night she'd gone to bed disappointed.

She hesitated and wondered if perhaps she should let her machine pick it up. But the next ring had her off the couch and dashing toward the kitchen.

She yanked up the receiver and tried to sound casual, calm. "Hello?"

"Listen, little girl, you have no idea what you've gotten yourself into," a man whispered, his voice a malevolent hiss. "You can't handle this, and if you try you're going to end up dead. Back off now, or face the heat."

CHAPTER 8

BELATEDLY, KARA hit the record button on her machine, but the caller had already hung up.

"Damn!"

Immediately, she dialed star-six-nine to get the caller's phone number, but the number came back as a pay phone. She hung up the receiver, furious with herself. Why hadn't she hit record sooner? She was a journalist, for God's sake!

She turned away from the phone and realized with some astonishment that she was shaking. That bastard hadn't actually been able to frighten her, had he? She'd received death threats before. Lots of them. More than she could count. Why should this one shake her up?

And then it came to her.

No one had ever called her at home before. Whoever this was knew her home phone number, possibly even knew where she lived.

Listen, little girl, you have no idea what you've gotten yourself into.

Her gut told her the call was related to her investigation of Northrup. But how would anyone at Northrup know she was investigating the plant? She hadn't contacted them for an interview yet. The only people who knew were her coworkers, the people she'd interviewed, the staff handling her open-records request for the state, and the whistleblower.

It was possible that someone in the state or county health

department had passed a tip to Northrup officials. It was also possible, though less likely, that one of the neighbors had said something to someone who'd passed it along the line until it reached someone who worked for Northrup. As for the whistleblower, he couldn't give her away without also giving himself away.

The phone rang again.

She let the call go to her machine.

Hi. You've reached Kara and Connor. Leave a message, and we'll get back to you.

But after the beep, there was only silence, followed by the buzz of the dial tone.

Twice more the phone rang, and twice more the caller refused to leave a message. Whoever it was didn't want to be recorded. And Kara realized that if she wanted his voice on tape, she'd have to answer. She would have to talk him, let him spew his venom in her ear.

She waited. Five minutes passed without a call. She paced the hallway and watched the clock. When the phone finally rang, she gasped and jumped. She lifted the receiver, angry that anything should make her so skittish. "Listen, whoever you are, you don't scare me!"

There was a moment of silence. "Kara? It's Reece. Is everything all right?"

The relief she felt was coupled with embarrassment, and for a moment she found herself stumbling after words. "Reece! Oh, God . . . I, um . . . I'm sorry! I thought . . . I'm fine. How are you?"

Reece heard the awkwardness in her voice. But he'd heard something else just a moment ago: anger and, beneath it, a slick undercurrent of genuine fear. "Is someone bothering you, Kara?"

"No. Not really. Just, you know—a prank caller. He's called a couple times tonight."

Reece sensed she was trying to make light of it. "If he calls again, you should notify the police."

She laughed as if that were the stupidest suggestion she'd

ever heard. "If I had a dollar for every death threat I've gotten, I could buy you a bottle of that fancy Italian wine."

So it had been a death threat. He didn't like that one bit. In fact, it really pissed him off. "It's a crime to threaten someone, Kara. You really ought to contact the police."

"The last time I called the police, do you know what they said? They told me to call if the guy actually showed up and tried to kill me. That's how helpful the cops are." She sounded angry now.

"Okay, fine. Forget the cops. How about I stop by? I can stay for a couple hours, make sure you're safe. I can even sleep on the couch if it makes you feel better." Then, sensing she was about to refuse him, he added, "That's what I'd do for my sister."

"Oh! Well . . . I don't think that's necessary. It's kind of you to offer, Reece, truly, but I don't need you to rescue me." She sounded . . . surprised, flustered, uncertain.

Hadn't anyone tried to "rescue" her before? Even as the question occurred to him, he knew the answer. She'd never had a father or a husband. She was used to taking care of herself.

"I don't mean to steal your feminist mojo, sweetheart, but what if I *want* to rescue you? I'm on my way out of the Capitol right now, so I'm only ten minutes away. I'll just stop by, make sure everything is okay."

She didn't seem to know what to say to that. "Well, I . . . I look like a slob. I'm wearing sweatpants and—"

"I spilled salsa on my shirt at lunch, so we're even. See you in ten. Keep the doors locked."

He hung up before she could object, locked his office, and hurried out of the building to his Jeep, which was parked outside the west portico. He headed east on Colfax, and the weight of the day seemed to vanish from his shoulders, replaced by a strange mix of protectiveness and anticipation. In the short time it took to reach her house, his thoughts had ranged from loaning her his gun and teaching her to shoot to all the things he would do to her sweet body Friday night when he got her into his bed. As he pulled into her driveway, he found himself having to remind his hard-on that he had not come here to fuck her senseless but rather to make certain she was safe.

His hard-on didn't seem to care.

He was glad to see her porch light on. She was taking precautions. He knocked lightly, assuming Connor would be asleep by now. He saw her shadow darken the security peephole and heard the deadbolt tumble as she opened the door.

"Hi," she said, a bit shyly. She stepped aside to make room for him, a slight smile on her face. "Come in."

She wore dark navy sweatpants with a flannel shirt of hunter green and navy blue plaid that revealed the soft curve of her breasts—which were clearly not bound by a bra. Her hair was pulled back into a ponytail, a few dark wisps floating around her face. She wore no makeup, her skin dewy and clean, newly washed and ready for bed. In short, she looked sexy as hell.

But it was her scent that just about killed him. Clean skin. Woman. And something more—something that made him feel like dispensing with five thousand years of civilization, dragging her off to a cave somewhere, and filling her with babies.

He decided to mark his territory, ducked his head, gave her a quick kiss on the lips. "Has he called again?"

She looked up at him, clearly startled by the kiss, then hastily turned away, and shut and locked the door behind him. "No. I'm sorry if anything I said on the phone made you feel you had to come over. It's probably just some wingnut. He hasn't called again. I get a lot of crazy phone calls. It comes with being a journalist."

He slipped off his coat. "I know what you mean. I get e-mails and phone calls from people threatening to kill me for being a fascist. If only they would come to some kind of consensus with the people who want to kill me for being a communist."

That made her laugh. She took his coat and hung it on a peg by the door. "Can I get you a cup of tea?"

"That would be great."

Her gaze fixed on his shirt, and she smiled. "You did spill salsa on your shirt. I thought you'd just made that up. The tomato will stain it, you know. Would you like me to wash it? I can have it dry for you within an hour. It's what I'd do for a friend."

He was about to say that his cleaners would undoubtedly remove the stain with no trouble, but he stopped himself. If she wanted to get him out of his clothes, he wasn't stupid enough to stop her. "Thanks. I'd appreciate that."

He slid off his tie, pulled the shirt out of his slacks, and began to unbutton it.

Her cheeks flushed, and she turned abruptly away. "I'll just put some water on to boil for tea."

He followed her into the kitchen, where the dishwasher hummed in mid-cycle. Everything was clean and shiny from the granite countertops to the homey wooden table with its pewter salt-and-pepper shakers. Every inch of the white refrigerator was covered with alphabet magnets and drawings made by a child's hand. One showed a small, stick-like figure with slashes of short brown hair standing beside a taller sticklike figure with slashes of long brown hair. Beneath the shorter figure in shaky letters was written, "Me." Beneath the taller one in the same unsteady script was, "Mommy."

He slipped out of his shirt and watched Kara as she filled a silver teakettle and put it on to boil. Her movements were feminine, graceful, and her ass was positively scrumptious when outlined by the soft fabric of her well-worn sweat-pants. He could definitely see how she had ended up as someone's mommy. Clearly, he wasn't the only man who re-acted this way around her.

And what was that scent? God, it was driving him insane!

She stood on tiptoe, searching through the cupboard above the stove. "Would you like Earl Grey, Lemon Zinger, Hazelnut Vanilla, True Blueberry, Almond Sunset? My mother has a friend who works at the Celestial Seasonings factory and brings me tea every time I see her. I could also make coffee if you don't like tea."

"Earl Grey sounds perfect."

He saw her reach for it, and realized he'd chosen the tea farthest toward the back of the cupboard. Quickly, he moved up behind her, reached beyond her, and retrieved the sought-after box. "I've got it."

She spun about to face him before he'd had time to step back, her breasts grazing his ribs, her pupils dark, a look of surprise on her face. And he smelled it again—that scent. It rose off her skin like body heat, like pheromone, like lust. Faint but intoxicating, it grabbed him by the gonads.

Caves. Neanderthal sex. Babies. That's what he wanted.

Kara knew she was in trouble. He stood close, too close, wearing a T-shirt that revealed the very muscles her hands had discovered last Friday. Through the white cloth, she could see the dark circles of his nipples, the swell of his pecs, the distinct ridges that could only be a six-pack. His raised arm revealed a hint of dark blond hair and a well-developed triceps.

Oh, come on, McMillan! You are not *turned on by armpit hair!*

But she was—that and the whole delectable sexy male package that came with it.

She sucked breath into her oxygen-starved lungs and slid out from between him and the stove, box of Earl Grey in hand. "Thank you. I'll get your shirt in the wash while the water heats."

Trying not to run, she grabbed his shirt from where he'd draped it over a kitchen chair and sought shelter in the laundry room, which was just off the kitchen by the sliding glass door.

"Tell me about this caller." He walked over to the window above her sink and looked like he was about to open it.

Then she realized he was testing it, making sure it was securely locked. She stopped and watched him, taken aback. He *really was* trying to make sure she was safe. "There's nothing to tell. A pretty standard run-of-the-mill death threat."

"Has he called before tonight?"

She rubbed detergent into the stain, dropped the shirt in the washing machine, turned the dial, and set it to wash. "No."

He walked over to her sliding glass door and tested it. "Could it be connected to anything you're working on for the paper?"

She hesitated to answer. "Yes, but I can't talk about that."

"Can you tell me what he said?"

Kara repeated the caller's words. "Pretty vague."

A muscle tensed in Reece's jaw. "You can buy special locks for these doors, you know. They're more effective than this wooden dowel at keeping intruders out."

"Really?" She had never seen such a thing, but then again she didn't spend much time patrolling the aisles at hardware stores.

He smiled. "Really. I'll pick you up a couple next time I'm out."

She shook her head and walked over to the cupboard to fetch two stoneware mugs for their tea. The kettle was just starting to whistle. "You don't need to do that. I can ask about them next time I'm shopping. Do you take sugar or milk?"

In a few minutes, they sat in the living room on the couch, each with a steaming cup of tea. The next half hour passed in comfortable conversation, as Reece asked Kara questions about Connor. She felt herself begin to relax and told him of their upcoming trip to the museum and Connor's rash of funny questions. She had just put Reece's shirt in the dryer and returned with a second cup of tea for each of them, when she found him reading the article about his bill.

"That was a pretty hilarious quote you gave our intern."

He shrugged off the compliment. "So I merit only an intern, do I? I had hoped to see you there."

Her alarm bells ringing, Kara set their tea down, and sat.

This is what she'd feared—that he would feel their budding relationship earned him special consideration. "I felt it was best that someone else cover it. I can't compromise my job, Reece."

"It was just a joke, Kara. I'm not asking you to compromise anything."

"Oh. Well, then, you understand that if we're going to be friends—"

"Is that the direction we're heading, Kara? Are we becoming friends? I sure as hell hope not." He pinned her to the couch with his gaze and reached across to brush a strand of hair from her cheek, the touch of his fingers scorching her like fire. "Please tell me you've thought about me at least once since Friday."

A blush crept into her cheeks. How did he do this to her? He was just a man.

Not just a man, McMillan. A very, very sexy man.

"Okay, I'll admit I thought of you once. For a second or two."

"I guess it's time I made more of an impression on you." He scooted closer, his gaze never leaving hers, pulled her against him, and kissed her.

The phone rang.

Kara hopped to her feet, her pulse already racing. "It can't be him again. He hasn't called for an hour."

Reece was already walking toward the phone. "Can you record on your machine?"

"Of course. I'm a journalist, remember." She hurried into the kitchen, took a deep breath, clicked record, and picked up the receiver. "Hello?"

"Kara, it's Holly. I almost screwed the Orkin man! Can you believe it?" Holly's voice came over the speaker loud and clear.

Kara shot Reece an embarrassed glance and clicked off the record button so he could no longer hear Holly. "That's, um, very interesting. I can't talk just now. Can you tell me about it tomorrow?"

Kara hung up and looked up to find a smirk on Reece's face.

"The Orkin man?"

KARA LAY in the dark, sleep once again eluding her.

Things were moving too fast. One minute she'd been chatting with Reece like the Drunk Whore of Babylon in a bar. The next he was getting all protective, offering to buy locks for her sliding glass door and acting like he was really, truly interested in her.

Is that the direction we're heading, Kara? Are we becoming friends? I sure as hell hope not.

When had a man ever gone out of his way to make sure she felt safe? When had any man acted like she was something delectable that he just had to get his hands on? When had any man asked her about Connor or listened to her talk about the sweet and silly things her son said?

"Are we still on for Friday evening?" Reece had asked on his way out the door.

She'd nodded. "My mom is driving down from Boulder to watch Connor."

His voice had dropped to a masculine rumble. "Good." Then he'd leaned down and given her a lingering kiss on the mouth, before turning and heading down the front steps. "Lock the door, and think about contacting the police."

Kara figured there were more than a few police officers who wouldn't mind terribly much if she turned up dead, but she didn't tell Reece that. "Okay. And, Reece, thanks."

The grin on his face as he'd opened the door to his Jeep had nearly turned her knees to Jell-O. "My pleasure, as always."

But as she closed her eyes and drifted into a troubled sleep, it wasn't Reece's smile or his words that passed through her sleepy mind, but the rough voice of a stranger.

Listen, little girl, you have no idea what you've gotten yourself into.

* * *

Reece unlocked the door to his condo, tossed his keys on the counter, and set his briefcase on the floor. Then he reached for the phone. The dial tone told him he had messages, but he ignored them and dialed the number for Denver police dispatch.

He wasn't pulling rank. He wasn't using his status as a state senator to ask for any favors. He just had a few questions that needed answers. "This is Senator Reece Sheridan. Get me Police Chief Irving, please."

It was a crime to threaten someone. According to Kara, she'd spoken to the police in the past over previous death threats, and they hadn't taken her seriously.

Reece intended to find out why.

CHAPTER 9

KARA CALLED the whistleblower first thing Thursday morning and left a message on his cell phone. It bothered her that she hadn't reached him right away in person. If someone connected to Northrup knew she was investigating the plant, it was possible, however unlikely, that he knew about Mr. Marsh, as well.

She'd just gotten her notes about the latest lab results ready for the I-team meeting, when Holly bounded into her cubicle dressed in a very tight black dress and a wide smile. "Sorry I called so late, Kara, but I just had to tell you!"

"Talk fast. I've got an I-team meeting in five."

While Kara sharpened a day's supply of pencils—like any self-respecting reporter she held pens in disdain because they froze in cold weather, couldn't write on wet paper, and ran out of ink when you needed them most—Holly related how the Orkin man had come to kill her roaches and ended up almost shagging her on her living room carpet.

"He was a hottie, blond, and really enormous like a Viking or something. His hands were huge!"

Despite her best intentions, Kara couldn't focus on Holly's narration, her mind on the meeting and what was sure to become a confrontation with Tom. "Well, he'll probably be back, won't he? It's not like roaches ever die."

Holly looked at her, irritation on her face. "You haven't been listening. I said I kept thinking of all the chemicals that might be on his hands, and I couldn't go through with it."

"Oh, well, that's probably a good decision. Gotta go." Kara grabbed her notes and sharpened pencils and hurried off to the conference room, trying to ignore the butterflies in her stomach.

Today was the day. She was going to tell Tom she was taking time off tomorrow morning. And when he acted like a jerk, as he inevitably would, she was going to stand up for herself and not make excuses or apologize. The newspaper owed her more comp time than she'd ever be able to collect. She ought to be able to take three hours off on a Friday without taking flack for it.

She listened while Tessa gave an update on the police shooting du jour. It seemed cops from the drug task force had exercised a no-knock warrant at the wrong house and shot the wrong man. Several members of the force had been suspended pending the outcome of the internal investigation, but citizens were calling for an overhaul of the entire department.

"I think this is front page, above the fold—twenty inches at least," Tessa said.

Syd punched the numbers into her calculator and scribbled the results on her control sheet. "Get mug shots of the suspended officers if you can."

Joaquin grinned. "Already on it."

"McMillan." Tom turned his gaze to Kara.

"The three water samples I took from neighbors' wells show varying levels of petroleum products and of methylene chloride. It's the same soup that's in the drainage ditch."

Tessa shook her head in disgust. "Nail 'em, Kara."

Matt gave a low whistle of appreciation.

"Great work, Kara." Sophie gave Kara a smile. "You are going to save people's lives on this one. You know that, don't you?"

Kara shrugged off the praise. "Having these results puts us in a bind. I cannot ethically delay reporting this information to the county and state health departments or to the people

whose wells the contaminated water was drawn from. But
the moment I report the contamination and its ostensible
source, the fine folks at Northrup will be on to me."

If they aren't already.

"That's when the real fun begins." Matt shot her a conspiratorial adrenaline-junkie grin.

Kara took a deep breath and spoke the words casually and
with finality, just as she'd rehearsed them. "Just FYI, I won't
be available tomorrow morning. I'm chaperoning a field trip
for my son's preschool class."

The good mood permeating the room vanished.

Matt coughed. Tessa sipped her latte. Syd stopped punch-
ing numbers into her calculator and looked up.

"Okay." Tom nodded. "Do you feel comfortable leaving
the Northrup story untended for a day?"

Resolved to stand up for herself, Kara met Tom's gaze.
"It's not even a full half-day. I doubt anything earthshaking
will occur during the three hours I'm away. I'll have my cell
phone just in case. Even reporters are entitled to time off."

"It's more an issue of commitment than a question of
what you're entitled to, McMillan." His voice carried a clear
note of disappointment.

Matt coughed again.

Kara sat up straighter and tried to look outraged instead
of intimidated. "Are you questioning my commitment,
Tom?"

He waved her query away with an impatient swipe of his
hand. "Of course not. By all means, take the morning off."

But the cold shoulder he gave her for the rest of the meeting proved he was far from happy with her decision.

REECE SNIFFED his shirt and relished the homey scent of
the fabric softener. He was used to the dull industrial smell
of dry cleaning on his clothes, and it surprised him how
much he appreciated the difference. Or perhaps it was just
the fact that Kara had personally washed this shirt that was

getting to him. He'd been about to hang it in his closet last night when he'd decided instead to wear it again.

This fact would, of course, remain forever his secret. If he ever told any of his male friends this, they would write him off. "Whipped," they would say.

He turned his mind back to the session. A senator from the Western Slope was making a passionate appeal for changes in the way marketing for the fruit industry was regulated. Reece couldn't figure out *why* state law regulated the marketing of fruit in the first place and listened closely, taking notes, until his cell phone vibrated in his pocket. A glance at the display showed him it was a call from the police department.

He stood and hurried from the Senate chamber into the hallway. "This is Sheridan. Go ahead."

"I checked files dating back five years, Senator. Found nothing. If she filed a report, there's no record of it."

"Is it standard operating procedure to keep reports on file?"

"Yes. Are you sure she filed an official report?"

"Believe me, Chief Irving, if she did anything, she did it officially and by the book."

"That's damned peculiar."

"Is it possible that whoever took the report didn't take it seriously and just threw it away?"

"It's possible, but I think it's more likely that it got lost."

"You just said you looked through all the records and found nothing."

"Yes, but—"

"So where else could it be?"

"I don't know."

"Here's what concerns me, Chief. Kara McMillan has ruffled a lot of feathers in this city. What if someone deliberately ignored her report and left her open to danger because he just didn't like her?"

Chief Irving hesitated for a moment. "None of my detectives would do that."

"I'm glad to hear that, because we are all guaranteed equal protection under the law. Unfortunately, Ms. McMillan is so convinced the police department won't help her that she hasn't reported a recent incident in which her life was blatantly threatened."

"I don't like to hear that. Give her my number, Senator, and I assure you I'll handle the case personally. In the meantime, I'll ask our officers to put in extra patrols on her street."

"Thank you, Chief. I'd appreciate that. I'll pass your number along."

Reece disconnected the call and glanced at his watch. He needed to leave soon if he was going to make it to the little wine shop on 16th Street before it closed. There were also groceries to buy, flowers to order, sheets to wash, and a condo to clean.

When had he last gone to this kind of effort for a woman? He didn't know. He didn't care. All he knew for sure was that he had a lot to do to make his home sex-ready for tomorrow night—and that Kara would be worth every rubber-glove minute of it.

KARA NOTIFIED the people who'd let her take samples from their wells and heard the shock, rage, and fear in their voices. She couldn't tell them where the contamination was coming from because she wasn't 100-percent certain herself. But at least they knew not to drink it or give it to their livestock. She passed on the phone numbers for the county, state, and EPA water-quality offices and asked them to call her if anything developed.

"You got it, honey," said Moira Farnsworth. "Without you'd we'd be drinking the damned stuff."

She reached Mr. Marsh late in the afternoon and was relieved to hear he was doing well.

"I've got something for you," he said, his voice betraying excitement.

"You do? What?"

"Videotape."

She was so stunned it took her a moment to react. "Videotape?"

"Yeah. I hid one of them little video cameras in my gear and got footage from everything inside the plant."

Kara wanted that footage, and she wanted it now. "That's very daring of you, Mr. Marsh. Do you think anyone might have seen you taping?"

"No way. I made certain no one else was around. Besides, I kept the camera hid."

"That's good. When can I see it?"

"Let's meet at the usual place tomorrow at noon."

"See you there."

"Video-frigging-tape!" she crowed to the rest of the I-team. "Does it get any sweeter than that?"

She was so excited about the video footage that she completely forgot about her problem with Tom. She'd known his words in the meeting weren't the end of it. The other shoe dropped just as Kara was preparing to leave for the day.

"McMillan!" Tom's voice poured out of the speaker on her phone. "Step into my office, please."

"We're with you, Kara." Sophie gave her a hopeful smile.

Tessa shook her head. "He's lucky you don't sue his ass, girl."

"Thanks." Kara took a deep breath and walked off to face her doom.

Tom was bent over his computer reading some report on the Internet. He didn't look at her when she walked in. "Is this going to be a regular thing, McMillan?"

She felt her pulse quicken. God, how she hated being intimidated! Why did she let Tom do this to her? "No. They were short on chaperones and would have had to cancel—"

"I'm glad to hear that." Then Tom turned to face her and gave her a version of the "watchdogs of freedom" speech he saved for when he wanted to make someone feel guilty for having any life beyond the newsroom.

Kara listened, her fear of him gradually turning to anger. She tried not to roll her eyes, tried not to heave a bored sigh. God, the man could be a dick!

Keep your mouth shut, McMillan. You need the regular paycheck, remember?

"The bottom line, McMillan, is that we are the watchdogs of freedom, the Fourth Estate. We guard the future. It's a big responsibility, one that demands a total commitment. You already leave early every day to pick up your kid. You take time off when he's sick. And now you're taking time off to take him to a museum. Yes, I know you're entitled to time off, but it's not a matter of what you're entitled to or how much comp time you have. It's a question of drive, McMillan. I need to know your heart is in this."

She couldn't believe what he'd just said, felt her guts begin to simmer with rage. "Of course my heart is in this, Tom! I have been since the day I walked through the door."

He measured her through eyes that seemed to lack compassion, then apparently having finished bullying her, he motioned her out of the door.

Kara turned to leave, but rather than feeling relief that it was over, she felt white-hot rage. She turned to face him, and the words left her mouth before she could stop them. "You are so full of crap, Tom! I don't leave early every day. I leave after a full eight-hour day and then put in a couple hours every night. I work at home on the weekends. I work my ass off precisely because I know how important a free press is. I don't need your sermonizing to tell me that!"

He looked up at her, his face devoid of emotion. "Shut the door, McMillan."

"Why? There isn't a person who works in this newsroom who hasn't felt what I'm feeling right now. You begrudged Matt time off for his wedding. You begrudged Syd time off for her father's frigging funeral. You begrudged me maternity leave. And now you bully me because I want a few hours off to spend with my son?" She was so angry her voice trembled. "The truth is this paper owes me so much comp time there's no way I could take it all. If I want to take a few hours to be a responsible parent to my son, then, damn it, I'm going to take a few hours, and you're not going to get away with giving me a guilt trip about it!"

He looked genuinely surprised now. "Are you through?"

Shut up, McMillan. Shut frigging up!

But Kara's blood was at a full boil now, and she was going to say it all. "You always say that we journalists 'guard the future.' What is that future, Tom? Have you ever stopped working long enough to ask yourself that question? Well, my son is my future. He's a human being, and he depends on me for everything. He is my first responsibility, and I'm not going to apologize to you for trying to give him the love and care he deserves! If you don't like that, take it up with Human Resources, because I'm through putting up with this crap! I am entitled to a fucking life!"

Then she turned, and, all but oblivious to the cheers and applause from her newsroom colleagues, grabbed her briefcase and stormed down the hallway toward the exit.

KARA WAS so distracted pondering the consequences of her outburst that she was on autopilot through dinner, bath time, and bedtime stories. So much for being a good mother.

She had no idea what Tom would do. Perhaps she'd be written up. Or maybe he'd take the Northrup story away from her and give it to someone who wasn't on his shit list. Maybe she'd find a check in her box tomorrow along with an invitation to turn in her keys and get lost.

"Read another one, Mommy." Connor held out yet another dinosaur book.

"Not tonight, pumpkin. But tomorrow we go to the museum to see real fossils. Won't that be fun?"

He nodded, crawled beneath the covers, and smiled up at her, innocent adoration in his eyes. In that moment, she felt terribly unworthy of that much love.

Fighting tears, she sat, running her fingers through his

silky brown hair. The scent of baby shampoo, one of her favorite smells, tickled her nose. "I love you, Connor. You're a wonderful boy, and I love you. No matter what, you remember that, okay?"

He nodded.

She kissed his cheek and tucked the covers up to his chin. "Good night."

"Good night, Mommy."

He called just as she shut off Connor's light. Overwhelmed by her confrontation with Tom, she had forgotten all about him.

This time she hit record.

"Stupid bitch! Back off now, or your son is going to grow up without a mother. Do you understand me?"

Kara's pulse pounded, and her mind raced for some way to get him to reveal who he was or at least to confirm his connection with Northrup. "I think you have the wrong number."

Slick, McMillan! Bet that one's in the FBI training manual.

"I know exactly who I'm talking to, Kara McMillan. And you'd best do as you're told."

"What do you want me to back off from? What am I supposed to—"

But the line was already dead.

KARA HADN'T been able to sleep all night, but as she slipped a new dinosaur T-shirt over Connor's head and made his oatmeal, she did her best to act like a mother who had nothing on her mind but a delightful day at the museum with her child. She added apples to the oatmeal, packed chocolate milk with his lunch, and even growled with him, as they displayed their six-inch-long serrated T-rex teeth—hidden by foamy toothpaste—in the bathroom mirror.

It was a sunny day, one of those strange Colorado winter days where it's so warm people walk down the street in shorts and sandals against a backdrop of snowy, white mountains.

Kara helped Connor into his car seat and then slipped into the driver's seat. "Let's go see some fossils!"

The other preschoolers were likewise full of growls and extra bounce, and Kara found herself laughing at their Pleistocene antics despite her other stresses.

She got the call just as they were climbing aboard the school bus that would take them across town.

"Kara McMillan?" The voice was unfamiliar.

"Yes."

"I'm Scott Hammond. I'm an inspector with the state health department. Can we talk off the record?"

Kara settled into her bus seat beside Connor and tucked her purse between her thighs. "Actually, now isn't a good time, but I would love to speak with you. Can I call you back later today?"

"No, this is important. Northrup is crawling all over this place. They've been here since Monday. You need to get down here. Their attorneys are scouring through our records, telling the state attorney which documents they can include in your open-records request and which they can't."

Kara felt a surge of fury. "That's illegal. They can't get away with that."

"It's worse than that. They know about Henry Marsh. He came to me a few months ago, gave me photos, told me what was going on out there. I made official records of it but kept his name hidden in my own personal files. When I arrived this morning, those files had been taken. Based on what you asked for in your open-records request, I figure he's been speaking with you, too."

Kara couldn't believe what she was hearing and chose her words carefully. What if this were just some clever ploy to get her to admit the whistleblower's identity? "I can't discuss my investigation, Mr. Hammond. I can't even be certain you're who you say you are."

"I understand. But please hear me when I say I'm afraid

for Mr. Marsh's safety, ma'am." The man's voice got quieter as if he were afraid of being overheard. "And if you're seriously pursuing this story, I'm worried about you, too. These guys aren't going to write you a letter to the editor. They're going to beat the shit out of you with baseball bats."

CHAPTER 10

KARA'S MIND raced. And even as she tried to find a way around it, she knew she had no choice. She needed to get to the state health department immediately—and she needed to warn Mr. Marsh.

How in the bloody hell had this happened?

"Mr. Hammond, would you be willing to talk with me off the record when you're someplace where you can speak freely?"

"Yes. I'm in the phone book. Call me at home later. I have to go. I'm in over my head as it is." Then he hung up.

Kara looked down at Connor, who was playing with a plastic stegosaurus and knew she was going to break his heart. "Connor, I just got some very bad news. I need to go into the paper right away."

He stopped playing and looked up at her, a child's disbelief in his brown eyes. "Why, Mommy? You said you were coming with me to the museum."

"I know, Connor, and I'm so, so sorry, but there are some bad men, and they might hurt someone if I don't go warn him."

"Can someone else warn him?"

Kara reconsidered it for a moment, shook her head. "I'm the only one who knows who he is and how to reach him. I promised him I wouldn't tell anyone his name."

"You promised to come with me to the museum."

"You're right. I did. But now I find I can't keep that promise, and I feel terrible about it. I'm sorry, pumpkin. I'll try to make it up to you somehow." Kara climbed out of the seat, leaned over, and gave Connor a kiss on the cheek. "Make sure you get a good look at the T-rex so you can draw me a picture, okay?"

Connor's chin quivered and tears gathered in his eyes.

Kara hugged him against her. "I love you more than anything, Connor. I hope some day you'll understand. I'll come get you as soon as I can today."

She turned and scooted down the narrow aisle, ready for what was certain to be a horrible confrontation with Janice.

Connor's teacher took the news better than Kara had anticipated. The older woman listened, a disapproving I-told-you-so look in her eyes. "Well, I wasn't entirely sure you'd remember, so I signed up one extra parent just in case."

Janice's words felt like a slap across the face, but Kara bit back her anger. "It breaks my heart to disappoint Connor this way, but, truly, there is more at stake than I can explain. I'm sorry."

As the bus drove away, Kara spotted Connor staring sadly at her out the window. Regret lanced through her gut, knife-sharp. Through her tears, she smiled and blew him a kiss.

FEELING ALMOST sick and beyond furious, Kara reached the state health department in less than twenty minutes and found Joaquin already waiting for her, his camera at the ready. She'd already called Tom and demanded in her best don't-screw-with-me voice that he contact the press association attorney and send a shooter right away. She didn't have the time or the patience for a rehash of yesterday. Apparently he got the message, because he said nothing about her outburst but promised to do as she asked.

"Hey, Karalita. What's going on?"

She filled Joaquin in quickly. "My guess is they're shredding everything they can and just hoarding the rest. My goal is to get my hands on as many documents as I can and figure out whether they did leak the whistleblower's identity and how in the hell they got a hold of it to begin with. I'd like you to just start shooting and not stop."

Joaquin grinned, his white teeth a sharp contrast to his coffee-brown skin. "Are you asking me to intimidate them with my camera?"

Kara nodded. "And, Joaquin, it could get ugly. If they call the cops or threaten to arrest us, do what you feel you need to do."

"Hey, they bust you, they bust me."

"Let's go." Too angry to feel nervous, Kara led Joaquin to the locked security doors at the rear of the building, waited until someone exited, and grabbed the doors before they could click shut again.

They walked through a labyrinth of hallways toward the air- and water-quality division.

"This place is *loco*. It's a maze," he muttered.

"Are you dropping breadcrumbs in case we need to make a hasty exit?"

They came to the right set of double glass doors, and she took a few moments to look the room over. A sea of beige cubicles stretched from one side of the room to the other, one decorated garishly for the approach of Valentine's Day—clearly the desk of the older middle-aged woman who played the role of Office Mommy. Every office had one. They were the ones who brought candy, remembered everyone's birthdays, and were always happy to hear news about other people's kids and grandkids.

A copy machine stood idle in the far right corner, while the left wall was lined with glass-walled offices. In the corner office—Director Owens's office—she saw what she was looking for: a collection of suits.

"Just act like you own the place," she told Joaquin. Then she turned on her digital recorder, dropped it in her pocket, and opened the door.

She carved a direct path for the director's office, Joaquin

behind her. The men in suits noticed her a second before she opened the glass door and entered.

"Who—?"

"Mr. Owens, you've given Northrup officials access to documents requested by the *Denver Independent* under state open-records laws. I want an explanation. And this is on the record."

For a moment no one said anything but stared at her in silent astonishment, the only sound the persistent click of Joaquin's camera.

Then Owens stepped forward, a bland smile on his face, and motioned her toward the door. "You can't just barge in here, Miss McMillan. You have to sign in with the security desk. I'll escort you both up front, and perhaps I can answer some of your questions."

"I'm not going anywhere until I have the documents I requested—and a list of every single document you've redacted at Northrup's request."

Owens laughed and put an arm around her shoulder as if to turn her toward the door. "I'm afraid that's just not possible, Miss McMillan. First you have to sign in—standard operating procedure, you understand—and then we'll sit down and discuss this."

Kara shrugged off his touch. "I'm not leaving without those documents and the list."

The men looked at one another, clearly not used to having anyone defy them. Then a tall balding man in an exquisitely tailored suit stepped forward.

Galen.

She felt the blood drain from her face and fought to keep her expression neutral.

"Allowing my client access to these documents before making them public is completely within the bounds of the law, Ms. McMillan. According to Colorado Revised Statutes—"

Ms. McMillan. You had his baby, and he calls you Ms. McMillan.

Cold rage flared in her belly, and she exploded. "Listen,

lawyer boy, don't quote statute at me. I know open-records law inside and out, and there is no provision that entitles a corporation to pick and choose which public documents the public gets to see. Public records are public. Period."

Galen looked stunned and sputtered.

I'm not the naive college grad you screwed and dumped, am I?

"I'm calling security." A man dressed in a brown suit moved toward the phone.

"Go right ahead. And while you're at it, call the cops." Kara laughed. "It will make a great front-page story: 'Reporter arrested while trying to pick up Northrup documents at State Health Department. Northrup officials involved.' That kind of controversy is solid gold for us. I suspect it's not so good for you, though. Then there's the fact that the paper will sue your ass."

The man in the brown suit put down the receiver.

Galen looked over his shoulder to a silver-haired man dressed impeccably in a sleek gray suit. The two seemed to communicate something with a glance. Then the older man turned his head and met Kara's gaze. He had the coldest eyes she'd ever seen—ice-blue eyes. Arctic.

A short man with greasy brown hair and wearing a brown turtleneck sweater took a few tentative steps in her direction. A pair of thick glasses weighed down his pale face. He reminded Kara of a turtle.

"Ms. McMillan, I'm Ernie Harris, the state's attorney. If you can give us some time, we'll get your documents ready." He looked sheepishly at the taller men around him. "I don't think we have a choice here."

The man in the brown suit threw up his arms.

Owens looked nervous and spoke to the silver-haired man. "If that's what the state's attorney says, I've got to go along with him."

The man with the perfectly styled silver hair gave Kara a chilling look and then turned toward the door, several manila folders in his hand.

She blocked his path. "If those are public documents you've got, you're not leaving until they've been catalogued and photocopied."

The man's nostrils flared. His face turned red. He turned, hurled the folders onto Owens's desk, and then stormed out the door, Galen behind him.

The man in the brown suit swore under his breath. "Would someone please get rid of that goddamned camera!"

Two hours later, Joaquin loaded the last box of documents into the trunk of Kara's car. "That's it."

"Thanks, Joaquin. You were great."

"My pleasure. But do me a favor?"

"Sure."

"Remind me never to piss you off."

Despite the tension headache that was making her skull feel like a bombing range, Kara laughed. "You got it."

As Joaquin climbed into his truck, Kara glanced at her watch. She had fifteen minutes to reach Quebec and Smith, where she'd be giving Mr. Marsh some very bad news.

HE TOOK it pretty well. "I guess that's my fault. I should have told you I'd talked to Scott Hammond before I called you. He's a good guy. I know he didn't mean for this to happen."

Kara drove through Denver's streets, making random turns, Mr. Marsh's six-foot-plus frame folded into the passenger seat. "He's afraid something could happen to you or your family."

He gave a nervous laugh. "Yeah. Me, too."

"I think you should leave town for a while."

"I've been thinking of sending my wife and daughter to her mom's house in Tennessee."

"Good idea. Any chance you can join her?"

For a moment he said nothing. "I'd lose my job."

She knew that meant more than losing a paycheck. It meant losing health insurance. It meant losing their home. It meant leaving friends behind with no explanation, no forwarding address. "I feel sick about this, Mr. Marsh. This isn't how things are supposed to turn out."

"It ain't your fault. You done all you could." He paused for a moment, clenching and unclenching his big, calloused hands in his lap. "Well, I guess I hated working for those bastards anyway."

"Does that mean you'll leave town?"

"I've never walked off the job before in my life. I don't feel good about it. But I guess it beats ending up dead in a ditch somewhere."

"It sure does." Kara made a right turn, started heading back toward Quebec and Smith. "So tell me about these videotapes. How in the hell did you sneak a camera into the plant?"

BY THE time she pulled into the newspaper's parking lot, her headache was on the brink of becoming a migraine. She enlisted the help of the security guard in loading the boxes on a dolly and hauling them up to the newsroom. She stepped out of the elevator and saw her coworkers' faces turn her way.

"Heard you kicked butt today, McMillan."

"You're a bad-ass, McMillan. Yesterday Tom, today the state health department."

"McMillan's kicking ass and taking names."

"Thanks, but Joaquin was there, too, you know." Kara directed the security guard to her desk, thanked him, and then unloaded the boxes off the dolly. There were four of them—an estimated 7,500 pages of documents, Northrup's inspection and complaint records dating back thirty years.

"A little light reading, McMillan?" Tom's voice startled her from behind.

She turned to face him, saw he was smiling. "I thought I might get bored over the weekend."

Then Tom raised his voice and spoke to the entire newsroom. "I believe Ramirez has a slide show of sorts for us all in the conference room."

"Oh, no!" Kara rolled her eyes, but allowed herself to be herded down the hallway.

She shared the task of narration with Joaquin as he ran through the photos he'd taken that morning, recalling what Owens and the others had said. Her coworkers howled with laughter at the shocked expressions on the men's faces.

Joaquin flashed to the next image, a shot of Galen looking stunned. "So this guy steps forward in his Armani suit and starts trying to tell her that what they're doing is legal, and she shouts at him, 'Listen, lawyer boy, don't quote statute at me.'"

The room erupted with hoots and cackles, but Kara barely heard them, her gaze fixed on Galen's face. He'd lost a lot of hair and looked much older than she'd imagined he would. His clothes were still slick. Well, he'd always been a shopper, always made the mistake of thinking that the clothes made the man. No one but Holly knew he was Connor's father, and Kara had no intention of telling anyone. Staring at the photograph of him, red-face and speechless, she couldn't fathom why she'd ever been attracted to him. How could she have had sex with him? How could anything of him exist inside the little boy she loved so much?

She hadn't seen him for almost five years, not since the week she'd found out she was pregnant. She'd hoped never to see him again.

Something bit into her palms. Her own fingernails.

She forced herself to relax, to breathe. Seeing Galen again had shaken her up more than she'd realized. She was grateful when Joaquin switched to the next shot.

When the lights came up, her coworkers clapped, even Tom.

She shook her head and waved off the compliments, feeling embarrassed. So many things had gone wrong today. She missed Connor's field trip, living up to his teacher's worst expectations. The whistleblower's identity was out, his life in a shambles. Northrup knew she was on to them. Yet her coworkers were cheering for her.

Determined to find some aspirin and caffeine, she thanked

Joaquin for his help, and then started down the hallway toward the break room. She wanted to leave to pick up Connor early, but she needed to get the documents safely stowed, put a call into OSHA on Mr. Marsh's behalf, and talk to the guys in IT to find out what kind of database they would be able to set up for her. She couldn't be expected to manage 7,500 pages of documents with sticky notes. She would take the videos home and watch them this weekend during one of Connor's naps, and if she—

"McMillan!"

It was Tom again.

She stopped and turned back to face him, head throbbing.

"For what it's worth, I'm sorry you missed your son's trip. But you did the right thing."

"Did I?" She turned away, the image of Connor looking forlorn and abandoned in her mind. How was she going to make this up to him? How could she make him understand? All he knew was that she had promised him, and she had broken her promise.

She would cook him a batch of spaghetti, give him a nice bubble bath, and then curl up with him to read stories and listen to his adventures. She would even let him stay up late, and maybe they'd watch *Star Wars*. Then tomorrow she would take him back to the museum so they could enjoy together what they hadn't been able to share today.

And then she remembered.

She was supposed to have dinner with Reece tonight at his place.

There was no way. She was too damned tired. She was too grouchy. She wasn't remotely in the mood for romance or sex. Today had proved she couldn't balance her life as it was. She had no time or room for a man. She hated to cancel on him at the last minute, but she needed to focus on her priorities.

She'd just swallowed two Excedrin when Tessa and Sophie came up behind her.

"I just heard Tom apologize to you, bless his heart." Tessa slipped an arm around Kara's shoulder.

"Yeah, I guess so. Sort of."

Sophie dropped four quarters in the soda machine. "That must be because Human Resources got wind of your little exchange with him yesterday and came down on him with both feet. You missed a good show."

"Really?" That was the best news she'd heard all day.

REECE LEFT session early and headed home through rush-hour traffic, stopping to buy fresh flowers along the way. The day had crept by more slowly than any he could remember. In fact, he wouldn't have been surprised to learn that time was moving backward. But now it was over, and the stage was set for seduction.

Not that he actually planned to seduce Kara. There was always the chance she would refuse him—she had gone out of her way to avoid getting too close to him Wednesday night. Still, he knew from the one and only true kiss they'd shared that there was fire beneath her aloof exterior. She was a passionate woman, and he intended to give her every chance to let that passion loose on him.

He'd kept the menu light—tomatoes with mozzarella, fresh basil, and olive oil as an appetizer; a salad of mixed greens; fresh steamed asparagus; and chicken marsala for the entrée with crème brûlée for dessert. Dessert was already made, and the rest would be easy. Extraordinary food didn't necessarily require extraordinary effort—something he'd learned from his father.

He'd just pulled into his parking lot when his cell phone buzzed. "Reece Sheridan."

"Hi, Reece. It's Kara. I hate to do this to you, but I can't come over tonight."

Somehow, he managed not to groan out loud despite the bitter disappointment and irritation he felt. "Is something wrong?"

For a moment she said nothing. "I've had a terrible day and wouldn't be good company."

"I'm sorry to hear that. Is there anything I can do to help?"

"No." Her voice quavered. Was she crying? "In the past two days I've come close to losing my job, getting arrested, and winning the Worst Mother of the Year Award."

"I'm sure it's not that bad."

"No, really, it is." Then she told him how she'd ended up shouting at her editor over taking the morning off to chaperone her son's field trip to the museum—only to have all hell break loose at the paper, forcing her to miss the trip. "I promised him I'd go with him, and I broke that promise, and after spending two days screaming at people, I just don't have the energy to be charming or to wear pantyhose. I'm really sorry."

He could hear the exhaustion in her voice and beneath it a note of despair and was relieved to realize she wasn't just trying to pull back from him again. He turned into his parking space and shut off the engine. "So am I."

Major damned understatement.

"It's probably best this way. Between my job at the paper and raising Connor, I have no business getting involved with anyone."

Now she was pulling back from him. "I have a better idea. Rather than scratching me off your overly long to-do list, how about you kick back in your sweatpants and spend time with Connor, while I bring over the groceries I bought and cook dinner for the three of us. That way the food won't go to waste, and you won't have to cook. I'll even help with the dishes."

For a moment she said nothing. "You would really do that?"

"Sweetheart, I'm already on my way over."

CHAPTER 11

"I CAN'T believe you're doing this." Kara watched as Reece carried three paper grocery sacks full of food into the kitchen. He was dressed in well-worn jeans and a silky black T-shirt that looked like it had been painted over his muscles. It was the first time she'd ever seen him in jeans, and she found it hard to take her eyes off him. What was it about a man's ass in denim?

"I guess no man has ever gone out of his way to spoil you before." He set the bags down on the table, ducked down, and touched a quick kiss to her forehead. "Well, get used to it. Would you like some wine?"

Soon she was settled on the couch, sipping Chardonnay and snuggling with Connor in front of *Sponge Bob,* while Reece sliced tomatoes in the kitchen. She had tried to help, but he had shooed her out and told her she wasn't allowed to lift so much as a paring knife. It was strange thing to have a man in her house, let alone cooking for her. She wasn't sure how she felt about it.

She awoke with a start to the sound of Connor's giggles and the tantalizing scent of something cooking. She lay on the couch, her grandmother's quilt pulled up to her chin. She hadn't realized she'd fallen asleep.

"Okay, buddy, now pour the lemon juice in while I stir in the wine. Just like that. Perfect!"

Still groggy, she stretched and then stood and walked into

the kitchen. Reece stood next to Connor, who was perched on a kitchen chair in front of the stove, a tea towel tied behind his neck to make a sort of apron.

"Can I stir it?"

"Sure, but you have to be careful not to splash it out of the pan. Remember, it's very hot." Reece handed the wooden spoon to Connor, who stirred very slowly, a look of intense concentration on his little face. "Good job!"

The lump that swelled in Kara's throat took her completely by surprise. She knew Connor needed male role models, knew he needed more than she alone could give him. And here was proof—the adoration in his eyes as he watched Reece scrape the bottom of the sauté pan with a spatula, the way he leaned into Reece's chest, the delight on his face when Reece praised him.

"Your pretty mommy is awake." Reece winked at her. "Show her how you set the table."

Kara's attention had been so focused on the sight of her son with Reece that she hadn't noticed anything else. Three placemats sat on the table, each with a place setting of her grandmother's china, her holiday silver, and crystal wineglasses. On top of each plate stood a white linen napkin folded like a fan. On one plate lay a single red rose.

Some little romantic part of Kara—a part of her she'd thought long dead—sighed in feminine delight. She told it to shut up, but it didn't. In fact, it called her a slob. She was dressed in the same sweatpants and flannel shirt she'd been wearing the last time he'd been over.

You could have at least worn a different shirt!

Connor clambered down from the chair, took her hand, and led her around the table, explaining exactly what they'd done. "I helped Reece find the pretty plates, but he washed them because he said we had to be real quiet so we didn't wake you up. He let me put them on the table, and he showed me how to fold the napkins. Do you want to see?"

"You folded these?" She gaped at Connor, her amazement not feigned.

He nodded. "Reece, can we show Mommy how I fold these?"

"Hang on just one second." Reece lowered the flame on the sauce he was making, then walked over to the table, sat, and lifted Connor onto his lap. He took one of the napkins and shook it out. "Are you ready?"

And Kara saw exactly how Connor did it—with Reece's large hands guiding his small ones. She couldn't help sharing a conspiratorial grin with Reece. "That's terrific, pumpkin. They look so fancy!"

Within ten minutes dinner was on the table—and it was delicious beyond her expectations. Tangy tomatoes with fresh basil that exploded like summer in her mouth. Steamed asparagus with just a touch of butter. Boiled red potatoes glazed with butter and parsley. Chicken medallions flavored with wine sauce that were so tender they melted on her tongue. Wine that blushed against her taste buds and smoothed the edges off her rough day.

And dessert.

A culinary orgasm.

Kara could do nothing but watch, enchanted, as Reece kept Connor the center of attention throughout the meal.

"I heard you went to see the dinosaurs at the museum today. Which fossil was your favorite?"

"The T-rex!" Connor roared and then, between bites of potato, told Reece how long its teeth were, how big its feet were, and how tall it was. "A whole boy could stand up in its tummy."

"A whole boy?" Reece took a sip of wine, looked suitably impressed. "That's one big tummy, isn't it?"

Then Kara remembered. Reece was a teacher by profession. No wonder he was so good with Connor. But at that moment, his gaze met hers, the heat in his eyes sending a distinctly adult message.

She sucked in a quick breath and felt her pulse leap. "Okay, Connor, time to wash your hands."

Conner hopped down from his booster chair and dashed

down the hallway toward the bathroom, leaving her alone with Reece.

He spoke first. "He's an incredible little boy."

"Thanks. He means everything to me."

Reece nodded. "He knows that, Kara."

Without warning, tears blurred her vision. Embarrassed, she turned away and tried to blink them back. "God, I hope so."

Reece's strong arms drew her back against him. His breath was warm on her temple. "He knows. And he's proud of you. Do you know what he told me? He said, 'My mommy saves people, and sometimes it makes her sad.' That's what he said. You've done a great job with him."

"There are so many days I fall short."

It was her deepest fear, her biggest regret. Why had she shared it with Reece? Perhaps for the same reason that she leaned her head back against his shoulder now. She was simply not strong enough tonight to resist the comfort he offered.

"It's no small task to raise a child alone. Do you mind if I ask where his father is?"

Kara did mind, but she didn't say so. She could answer his question without telling him everything. "He wanted me to have an abortion and refused to have anything to do with me when I told him I was keeping the baby. He's never even asked to see Connor."

"He pays child support, doesn't he? Whether he's involved in Connor's life or not, the law entitles you—"

"I want nothing from him. Can we please not talk about this?" She pulled away from him and picked up the dirty plates off the table.

He took the plates from her. "I didn't mean to upset you."

She forced a smile. "I know. And thanks, Reece. For everything. Dinner was amazing. You're quite talented in the kitchen."

He leaned down, brushed a kiss across her lips, and gave her a wicked grin. "You ought to try me in the bedroom."

* * *

Reece clamped the new lock into place on the sliding glass door while Kara read one last bedtime story to her son, her sweet voice drifting into the kitchen and soft with a mother's love. He knew himself well enough to know where the dull ache in his chest came from. He'd spent very little time with his mother after his parents divorced. He'd never gotten enough of his own mother's affection.

But at least he'd known who his mother was, where she lived, and why she'd left. Connor had never seen his father, had no idea who his father was.

The man ought to be rotting in a jail cell. Deadbeat dad didn't even begin to describe him. Reece couldn't imagine himself abandoning a woman to bear and raise his child entirely alone. Even if he didn't have feelings for the mother—even if he loathed her as he did Alexis Ryan—he would have been a father to the child he helped create. Every child deserved a father, deserved the financial security, affection, and guidance of two parents, even if those parents never married. What Connor's father had done was despicable.

This certainly explained Kara's reluctance to trust or get close to a man. She'd gotten close to someone once—at least physically close—and had paid a high price for it. Now she worked too hard and worried too much, as the dark circles beneath her eyes proved. She hadn't even stirred earlier this evening when he'd found her sleeping and laid a quilt over her.

He stepped back, tested the door, and was gratified to see that it didn't budge. There was no way for an intruder to break in through this door except to smash the thick pane of tempered glass—not an easy task and very noisy.

Her voice startled him. "What are you doing?"

He turned and pointed to the new lock. "I picked it up yesterday. Let me show you how it works."

"You didn't have to do this."

"I know. I wanted to do it." Then he showed her how to

loosen the lock so the door would slide open and how to make certain it was secure.

"Thanks, Reece. I appreciate it."

"You're welcome." He wasn't so certain she'd be grateful about the next thing he had to tell her. "I spoke with Police Chief Irving about the calls you received. He promised me that he'd handle your case personally—if you call in a report."

She frowned. "You really shouldn't have done that."

"Has he called back?"

The shadow that passed over her face gave Reece his answer before she did. "Yes."

Reece took Chief Irving's card out of his pocket and placed it on the table. "Please call him."

"I don't like being manipulated, Reece. I don't want to give that bastard the satisfaction of affecting my life."

He rested his hands on her shoulders. "I understand that, Kara, but I don't want to see anything happen to either of you."

She glanced down at Irving's card. "I'll think about it."

Soon they were seated on the couch, glasses of Chardonnay on the coffee table before them.

"Connor was asleep before I left his room. Between the museum and the excitement of having you here, he was worn out."

From the soft look on her face he'd known she was thinking of her son before she'd spoken. "And how is his mother doing?"

She looked over at him, a faint smile on her sexy lips. "Better."

"Good." He bent down, took her feet in his hands, and turned her so they rested in his lap.

"What—?"

"Relax." He pulled off her fuzzy blue socks, tossed them on the floor, and massaged the soles of her feet. Her toes were dainty, feminine, and her toenails were painted a frosty light pink. He resisted the urge to lick them. "I'm giving you a foot massage."

For a moment she stared at him as if he'd sprouted antlers. Then he pressed his thumbs deeply into her arches, and she gave a little sigh.

"Does that feel good?"

Kara couldn't lie. She closed her eyes. "Yes."

"You know, I'm guessing that a woman who spends her days saving people and taking care of her son all by herself might have her own needs."

She opened her eyes, not sure she liked where he was going with this. "Maybe."

"Who meets your needs, Kara?"

She didn't know what to make of his question. Was he speaking sexually? If so, he knew the answer to the question already: it was purple and took two AA batteries. "I can take care of myself."

"I'm sure you can." He didn't sound convinced. "Most of the time."

What he was doing to her feet felt so good she didn't want to argue with him. "Almost all the time."

"I think you need someone in your life you can depend on, someone you can confide in when things go to hell at work, someone to massage your tired feet and your stiff shoulders, someone to bring you tea and cook a meal once in a while. Someone to be there for you."

Because he struck too near the truth of her loneliness, she made light of his words. "Are you saying I need a wife?"

"You need a man, Kara. A man you can open up to. A man whose passion for life matches yours. A man who grabs your hair in big fistfuls and twists and pulls it when he's fucking you. A man willing to walk the wire for you."

Kara couldn't speak. She stared into his blue eyes, too stunned to be angry. Her heartbeat tripped, faltered. The breath left her body in a shudder, and heat flared low in her belly.

"Your skin is so soft. I don't know what that scent is, but you smell good enough to eat." His voice was a deep, seductive rumble.

"It's lavender." She wasn't aware she'd spoken.

"It makes me want to kiss you everywhere." His hands had left her feet and now deftly massaged the muscles of her left calf, sliding beneath the fabric of her sweatpants until they reached the sensitive bend of her knee.

She shivered. "Mmm."

And then his hands were on the drawstrings at her waist, untying them, sliding beneath the fabric, beneath her panties, cupping her. The heel of his hand pressed against her mound, moving in slow, deep circles, unleashing a surge of wet heat. She knew she should stop him. She couldn't stop him. She didn't want to stop him.

She moaned, lifted her hips instinctively to meet his touch, and reached up to grasp his shoulders. "Oh! What are—?"

"Shh! Just enjoy it." He was leaning over her now, one knee thrust between her parted thighs, the other on the floor, the spicy scent of him surrounding her. The fingers of his free hand threaded through her hair and pulled her head back, exposing her throat to his kisses and the scrape of his five-o'clock shadow, while the hand inside her panties kept up a relentless rhythm.

She had to touch him, had to feel him. Her hands slid over the silky fabric of his shirt, grasped hungrily at the shifting muscles beneath, and fought with the buttons of his fly. But then his fingers found her clitoris, and she could do nothing but cling to him.

Never had it come upon her this fast, this intense. In an instant, she hovered on the iridescent edge of an orgasm. "Oh, jeez, I'm going to come!"

His voice was rough. "Goddamn straight you are!"

He pushed a finger deep inside her, and the shimmering heat exploded.

Her cries might have awoken Connor, had Reece not thrust his tongue into her mouth, taken them into his lungs. And even as his skilled fingers prolonged her climax, they drove her to a second shattering peak.

She gasped in surprise, arched against him, and shuddered as the jagged pleasure of it washed through her and left her weak. For a moment, she lay still, her eyes closed, and listened to the sound of their combined breathing. Then she opened her eyes and found him gazing down at her, a smile on his face.

"You're incredibly sexy when you come." He withdrew his hand and ran a finger slick with her own musky juices across her lower lip.

The ringing phone brought her upright with a jolt.

Reece saw the fear on her face and bit back several four-letter words. He stood and adjusted his rather painful erection. "Do you want me to answer it?"

She shook her head, popped off the couch and, tying her sweatpants as she went, hurried to the phone. "Hello?"

Her face blanched, and her finger flew to the record button.

A raspy male whisper came out of the answering machine's speakers. "—listen very well, do you? This is your last warning, bitch. The ride gets rough from here. Hurt us, and we will destroy you, got that?"

"Who is 'us'?"

But the caller had hung up.

"Dammit!" She slammed the receiver down.

Reece picked it up and held it out to her. "Call Chief Irving. Now."

Chief Irving arrived in less than ten minutes. He was a big, beefy man with a beer gut that made him look eleven or twelve months pregnant. His white hair was cropped short and stood almost on end, giving him the look of someone who'd recently gotten an electrical shock. But the pale blue eyes that gazed out at them from beneath bushy white eyebrows were intelligent, appraising—the eyes of a lifelong cop.

Reece watched while the officer questioned Kara about the calls and listened to the recordings, anger brewing in his gut—anger at Kara, at the cops, at the bastard who had threatened her and put the shadows in her green-gold eyes. She refused to discuss the story she was working on and told Irving only that it involved serious environmental crimes and a corporate whistleblower. She also told him that a state government source had contacted her this morning to warn her that both her life and that of the whistleblower might be in danger—a significant bit of information that worried Reece even more.

The whistleblower was leaving town. Kara was not.

"Can you give me the name of the company? Or how about the whistleblower's contact information?"

She eyed Irving suspiciously and shook her head. "Not without asking permission."

"How about the government source?"

She shook her head again. "Again, I'd have to ask first."

Reece gritted his teeth, torn between admiration and anger. His rational mind knew Kara wasn't withholding the information to be difficult. She had promised to protect people's identities, and she was trying to keep her word. He couldn't fault her for that; her strong sense of ethics was one of the things that attracted him to her. But his gut didn't give a damn about anyone else at the moment. He wanted to know Kara and Connor were safe.

"Well, Ms. McMillan, I'm afraid there's not a lot we can do with the information you've given us. If I could talk to the others—the whistleblower and the state government source—then we'd have something to work with. I know secrecy is important in your work, but your life is important, too. Whoever this guy is, he's persistent, and that bugs the shit out of me."

"I understand. I'll talk to my sources and see if they're willing to speak with you. I'll talk to my editor, too, and see what he says about divulging the name of the company and nature of the story. If he approves it, I'll call you."

"I suggest you get a new unlisted number." Irving reached into his briefcase and pulled out a small device that resembled a cell phone. Instead of a number pad it had only a large, red button. "And until this is over, I'd like to set you up with this."

"What is it?"

"It's a panic button." He drew out another device, this one with a long electrical cord. "Set the charger up next to your bed so it's beside you at night, and carry it with you during the day. If anyone tries to carry out this guy's threats, you just push the red button. The signal is relayed straight into dispatch, and units will be on their way immediately."

Kara frowned, turned the device over in her hands, and for a moment Reece thought she was going to refuse to take it. Then she set it down on the coffee table. "Thanks for coming out so late, Chief Irving. Sorry I can't be more helpful. I feel like I've wasted your time."

"Call me with any new information." Irving pointed at the panic button. "And push that sooner rather than later. I'd rather have a false alarm than a dead body."

Reece followed Irving toward the door. "I'll walk you back to your car."

Irving, it turns out, drove an ordinary car of the sort used for plain-clothes work. Reece opened the driver's side door. "If you come up with anything, could you let me know?"

"Sure, Senator. But I really wish she'd just tell us what we need to know."

So did Reece. "She's trying to uphold the ethical standards of her profession. She's made promises to people, and she's trying to keep them."

Irving tossed his briefcase in and squeezed his gut in behind the wheel. "I guess I can respect her for that. I just hope it doesn't get her killed."

Reece watched Irving's tail lights disappear down the street. "That makes two of us."

CHAPTER 12

KARA LIFTED Connor so he could drop a quarter into the saber-toothed tiger's gaping mouth. The grimacing beast gave a ferocious, mechanical growl, the same growl it had been dispensing to museum visitors for donations of spare change since she'd been a little girl.

Connor giggled with delight. "Another one, Mommy!"

His laughter had always felt magical to her, as rare and precious as the tinkling of fairy bells. It made her happy just to see him smile. It was one of many things about being a mother that had completely taken her by surprise.

Holding him up with one arm, she dug into her purse and felt her fingers brush up against something unfamiliar—the panic button. She batted it aside, scraped along the bottom of her purse, and pulled out a couple of loose dimes and a penny. "Here you go."

Three more gratifying growls.

Kara set Connor back on his feet, took his hand, and led him toward the exit.

"Can we come back again?" He looked up at her through expectant brown eyes and then yawned. He'd probably fall asleep in the car on their way home.

"I'd like that."

They walked out the big glass doors toward the crowded parking lot, passing Saturday's skateboarders, stressed-out parents with strollers, and gaggles of geese that lived in nearby City Park and suffocated the museum's lawn with their fertilizer. Watching the geese waddle, it was hard to imagine that their ancestors might have been the enormous, ferocious creatures whose bones she'd just seen.

Not that Kara had been paying that much attention to the museum's educational displays. Like a song playing over and over again in her mind, thoughts of Reece followed her everywhere. His thoughtfulness in making dinner, covering her with the quilt, installing the new lock. His gentle indulgence of Connor. His expertise with his lips and hands.

Good lord! She got turned on just remembering it.

He'd brought her over the edge so hard and fast she'd barely had time to breathe. And it had seemed important to him that she really enjoy it—she'd felt it in the heat of his kisses, heard it in his voice, and sensed it in the way he'd focused so intently on her response.

Goddamn straight you are!

They barely knew each other, and yet he seemed to understand so much about her, anticipating her needs and respecting her feelings in a way no one ever had. How could that be? And what did he want from her? He was going to an awful lot of effort just to get laid, if that's all he wanted. Besides, he'd had more than one chance to push sex with her, and he hadn't. He wanted more than sex, but the question was how much more.

Had Galen ever treated her with this same consideration? No, he hadn't. Oh, certainly, he'd done thoughtful things like buy her roses or surprise her with dinner at a fancy restaurant. But every gesture, every word had been predictable, almost mechanical, as if he knew what was expected of a lover and was determined to fulfill those obligations.

Nothing Reece did was ever predictable.

If she'd been with Galen last night, he would have expressed his concern for her safety in a few articulate sentences, then hurried her into bed so he could have his orgasm, too. But not once had Reece brought up the fact that she had come and he had not. Nor had he tried to bring them back to the place they'd been before the phone had rung. Instead, bristling with anger she didn't understand, he had checked every door and window to make certain they were all locked tight and then offered to sleep on the couch. When she'd told him she would be fine, he'd given her a good night kiss, promised to call her, and reminded her to lock the door behind him.

I guess no man has ever gone out of his way to spoil you before. Well, get used to it.

She wasn't sure she *could* get used to it.

Of course, it wasn't just a matter of what Reece wanted, she reminded herself. This was her life. It was what she wanted for herself and for Connor that counted.

So what did she want?

A man who grabs your hair in big fistfuls and twists and pulls it when he's fucking you.

A bolt of heat shot through her belly.

Oh, stop it! Just because he's sexy enough to thaw nuclear winter and pretty much frigging perfect doesn't mean you have to obsess over him!

She fished her keys out of her purse, unlocked the doors, and lifted a very sleepy Connor into his car seat, determined to put Reece out of her mind for at least the next five minutes. "Let's buckle you up. There you go, sweetie."

A shadow fell across the car from behind her.

She whirled about and found herself face-to-face with a ragged man in dirty clothes.

"Spare change, lady?"

Heart racing, she groped in her purse, grabbed some loose coins, dropped them into his filthy upturned palm.

Get a grip, McMillan! Since when do homeless people scare you?

"God bless, ma'am." He gave a little bow and walked off to work the crowd.

Only after she'd turned onto Colorado Avenue and her heartbeat had returned to normal did she realize that she'd completely forgotten about the panic button.

* * *

"PUSH IT! Push it! Eleven! One more."

Reece ignored the screaming of his pecs and triceps, brought the bar down almost level with his chest, and then pushed with every shred of his remaining upper-body strength. His muscles shook and felt paralyzed under the crushing weight, but he inched the bar upward.

"Come on! Push it! Push it! Twelve!" Miguel took the barbell's weight from him and lifted it into its rest. "Three-ten. That's your new best, *amigo*. You are cookin' today."

Reece sat up, caught his breath, and toweled the sweat off his face with arms that would barely bend. "Thanks, Miguel."

"You haven't mentioned her name once, but I can tell she's all you're thinking about." Miguel's voice held a prying tone as he removed two twenty-five-pound weights from the barbell for his own sets.

"It's that obvious?" Reece stood, grabbed his water, and shot the cool liquid down his throat.

"Definitely."

The amused look on Miguel's face only worsened Reece's already black mood. "Did you come here to lift steel or to chitchat?"

Miguel settled back onto the bench to start his sets. "Start counting."

Reece spotted his friend through three sets of twelve, but his mind was exactly where Miguel had said it was—all over Kara.

He'd done his damned best to get a good night's sleep—a stack of boring reading from the Capitol, a cold shower, his right hand. But every time he had closed his eyes, he'd seen the look of shattering bliss on her sweet face as she'd come, caught the delectable scent of her skin and the musk of her arousal, and heard her astonished gasp—that little feminine cry—when she'd come again. The knowledge that he'd been able to do that for her more than made up for the fact he hadn't even gotten out of his jeans, much less into her.

While grappling with his ravenous appetite for her all night long had been tough enough, worrying about her safety had been far worse. Time and again he'd heard that harsh, hate-filled voice in his mind. It had made his skin itch, made him want to hit someone.

Hurt us, and we'll destroy you.

The man's words and his voice had niggled at Reece, had eaten at him, had jabbed at his mind like a splinter.

"Hey, man, can't you count?" Miguel glared up at him, his dark face red from exertion and covered in sweat.

"Whiner." Reece lifted the barbell into its rest and bent down to retrieve his water.

Miguel sat up, reached for his towel. "Man, she really has you tied up. I've never seen you this bad before."

"Yeah." It was the truth.

But where was it all going? Reece had no idea. His feelings for her were running hot and thick and fast, but he had no clue where they were leading him and no idea what she felt for him. It was like racing down a winding mountain road at night—without headlights.

"Are you sure you should be getting involved with her? Maybe she's more trouble than she's worth."

"She hasn't had very good experiences with men, Miguel. The man who fathered her son dumped her when he found out she was pregnant. She has trouble accepting anything from me. She thinks she has to handle everything on her own."

Miguel shook his head. "You deserve someone without so much baggage. I'd hate to see you get hurt."

Reece tried not to feel irritated with his friend and changed the subject. "Ready for another set?"

"I need to hit the showers. My niece is celebrating her *quinceañera* next weekend at our place, and my wife wants me home to fix every damned thing in the house before relatives start arriving. Thanks for the workout." Miguel was a family man with an enormous extended family, and Reece had always admired the way he put his wife, children, brothers, sisters, and cousins first in his life. Hardly a weekend went by where something wasn't happening at the de la Peña home.

"Same to you."

Miguel turned to go but then stopped. "You want to come help out? It will be better for you than skulking at the Capitol or living like a hermit up at your cabin. It will take your mind off her, and I bet you can talk Hilaria into making her enchiladas."

Reece was about to accept when the idea came to him.

His cabin.

He yanked off his gloves and headed straight for his locker and his cell phone. "Miguel, you're a damned genius."

KARA TIGHTENED the screws that held the hook in place on her deck. "Okay, pumpkin. I think it's ready. Now we get to pour the seed in."

After Connor had awoken from his nap, they'd made a trip to the Wild Bird Center and bought a couple bird feeders and seeds so they could watch birds from the kitchen table. Connor seemed just as amazed as Kara to learn that birds might well be the direct descendents of dinosaurs, and Kara had thought it a great opportunity to introduce him to something new. She'd had enough room on her credit card to buy a child's guide to birding that had bold, colorful photos of common backyard species in Colorado. With any luck, the topic would hold his attention for at least a week.

She lifted the plastic five-pound bag of mixed seeds and tore a little opening in one corner. "I'll hold the bag, and you pour."

Connor grasped the bag with his small hands and tilted it so seed skittered down the acrylic tube of the feeder. "Is this what birdies like for breakfast, Mommy?"

"That's what the man at the store told me. I guess we'll have to see."

They'd just hung the feeder on its hook when the phone rang.

Kara tried to ignore the way the sound made her heart lurch and her stomach drop to the floor. That bastard had no power over her. None.

She'd called customer service at the phone company first thing this morning, but her new number wouldn't be in operation until Monday. Until then, she'd let her answering machine take her calls. She'd be damned if she'd give him another chance to frighten her.

"Now we wait and see which birds come to feed here. Do you have your book?" She opened the sliding glass door and heard a man's deep voice leaving a message.

Reece.

Connor heard him, too. "When is Reece coming over again?"

"I don't know, sweetie." She forced herself to walk calmly to the phone, lifted the receiver, and turned off the machine. "Hi, Reece."

"You're screening your calls. Good." The protective tone of his voice wrapped itself around her like a warm blanket.

"The guy isn't much of a conversationalist anyway." She tried to make light of it, but the joke fell flat.

"How are you and Connor doing?"

"We're fine. We went to see the dinosaurs this morning, and Connor was my tour guide."

"That sounds like fun for both of you. Does that mean you'll quit beating yourself up for missing the trip yesterday?"

How did he always manage to zero in on her sore spots? "Maybe."

"You're a wonderful mother, Kara."

"Thanks." She didn't know what else to say. Only she knew how often she fell short.

"I've got something to ask you, and I'd like you to listen to everything I have to say before you answer me." Did he sound nervous?

"Okay." What in the world was this about?

"My father and I built a cabin up above Estes Park. It's

surrounded by aspen. There's a little creek running through the property. There's no phone, no television, no fax machine, but there's running water, two fireplaces, and most of the time even electricity."

"Sounds wonderful." It did sound wonderful, but why was he telling her this?

"It's my little corner of paradise, and I'd love to take you there. President's Day is a week from Monday, and I'd love to spend the three-day weekend with you at my cabin. You seem like you could use a little time away from it all, and so could I. But more than that, I need to spend time with you."

He wanted her to go away with him for a weekend. He wanted—no, he'd said he *needed*—to spend time with her. They would be alone in the mountains, no distractions. They would end up having sex. Oh, yes, they would. Given what just being near him did to her, it would be inevitable, unavoidable, like the force of gravity.

Is that what she wanted? And if she agreed to go with him, what would come of it? Her life was full as it was. What he described sounded suspiciously like getting involved, and with the Northrup story getting hotter she didn't have time to be involved with anyone right now.

That was what her brain said.

But what her mouth said was, "I'd love to."

"You're welcome to bring Connor. Of course, if you want me all to yourself, I'll understand."

KARA MADE the phone call immediately. "Hi, Mom. Please tell me you're free next weekend. I really need you to watch Connor for a few days."

"Well, I had planned to attend a workshop on spirit-centered aging at Naropa. What's going on? Is everything all right?"

"I've been invited up to a friend's cabin for the weekend." She might as well tell her mother the truth. "Actually, it's not a friend. It's a man."

"A man? It's not that gay guy you were pretending to date for a while, is it?"

"No, Mom." Between her mother and Holly, Kara would never be allowed to live that down.

"Well, who is it? Do I know him?"

"You might have seen him in the paper. It's Senator Reece Sheridan."

"Oh! Oh, God! I'll cancel everything."

KARA HIT stop on the remote and flicked on the conference room lights. "That's it."

Syd spoke first. "Jesus Christ."

"How did the source manage to get this footage?" Joaquin's face showed the same astonishment and disgust Kara had felt Sunday afternoon when she'd finally taken time to watch the tapes.

"The source carved a hole in the bottom of a plastic thermos, tucked a video camera inside, and aimed the lens out the hole."

Joaquin shook his head. "Man, that took *cajones*."

Tessa flashed her trademark smile, though she looked tired. And no wonder. She'd been up all night covering a S.W.A.T. raid. "At least now we know where the dust is coming from."

Kara nodded. "Everywhere."

The videos, taped over a period of days, seemed to show the entire plant, inside and out. No matter where the whistle-blower had pointed his lens, there was dust. Piles of choking, caustic CKD that blocked catwalks; clung to railings and ceiling girders; and gathered beneath stairs, on top of machinery, in doorways. In some places it looked to be almost four feet deep. As the video showed, all it took was a gust of wind to pick the stuff up and carry it out the door and off-site to places where people were farming, raising children, breathing.

And then there was oil. Oil leaking from machinery into

pools on the floor. Oil sitting in abandoned drums in corners. Oil drums rusting in the irrigation ditch, floating in a dark, iridescent scum.

"Is there any chance the whistleblower could be arrested for filming this?"

"Possibly, if they want to claim he was giving away trade secrets. But I doubt Northrup will take it that far. It would only give the company more negative publicity. For now the source is resettled out of state, hopefully far from any harm caused by the health department leak."

"What else have you got?" Tom thumped his pencil impatiently on a copy of today's newspaper. Leave it to him to find discussing a human being's safety tedious.

"I've started sorting through the documents I picked up on Friday. IT has put together a spreadsheet that will enable me to sort them by date, type of document, author, recipient, and certain keywords. I can log in from home, so I'll be able to work on it in the evenings and on weekends. Even so, the trick is going to be cataloging them all quickly enough to keep the story moving forward. Seven thousand pages is a lot of reading."

Tom frowned. "You need an intern."

"I don't trust interns. I need someone I can rely on."

Tessa raised her hand. "I'll help."

"I really appreciate the offer, but your plate is already full enough, Tess."

"It's nothing a gallon of coffee won't cure."

"Count me in," said Matt.

Sophie smiled. "Me, too. Show us what you want, and we'll be all over it."

"McMillan, it looks like you've got yourself a crew. How about your state source?"

"I called several times this weekend, left several messages. I think someone has cold feet. Still I'm grateful for the warning. Without this person's help, Northrup would have gotten away with handpicking which documents we received, and the whistleblower might be exposed to danger."

Tom's pencil tapped. "Anything else?"

Kara took a deep breath and looked Tom straight in the eye. He was going to love this. "Yeah. I don't want to make more of this than it is, but someone keeps threatening to kill me, and I'm pretty certain it's someone associated with Northrup."

Kara recounted the history of the phone calls she'd received and how they'd started after she'd filed her open-records request with the state, which, she now knew, had contacted Northrup right away. Leaving out any mention of Reece, she also told them about how the calls had escalated until she'd called the police and how she hadn't been able to give them any useful information.

Tom interrupted her. "You were right to keep it to yourself. If the cops starting making phone calls to Northrup, it opens the door for Northrup's CEOs to find out exactly what you know and where this investigation is leading. And it will generate police reports, and the two big papers get a hold of it and will unleash their armies. You'll be in a race to break your own story."

"Then again, you can't break a story if you're dead." Tessa glared at Tom.

Kara could have hugged her.

Tom's retort was razor sharp. "Novak, you know these threats never amount to anything. McMillan has just allowed this guy to get under her skin. The last journalist killed in Colorado was exposing lunatic white supremacists, not greedy businessmen. No one with half a brain would attack a journalist. McMillan knows that." Then his gaze shifted to her. "But if it makes you feel safer, McMillan, talk to security."

Kara had known he would make her feel like a fool. "No. That won't be necessary."

CHAPTER 13

Kara hurried to her desk, juggling a dozen file folders, a turkey sandwich, her cell phone, and a fresh cup of tea. It was two in the afternoon already. In four hours, Reece was coming to take her to his cabin for three days. And right now all she could think about was lunch. "So a bag house filters the air to keep dust from being released into the environment?"

Mr. Marsh's voice crackled with static, but she could still make out his answer. "That's right. So if it's not working, the dust escapes."

"It looks like it hasn't been working for quite a while."

"That's right. It wasn't running right the whole time I was there—more than two years."

"I really appreciate your answering all my questions. You've been a big help. Are you and your family feeling safe and settled?"

"Yeah. My wife is happy to be back in her hometown, but I don't like it when I'm between jobs like this. Makes a man feel useless when he can't provide for his family."

She could hear the frustration in his voice and searched for the right words. "If it helps, what you've done here will probably save lives. If that's not the work of a real man, I don't know what is. You're a hero, Mr. Marsh."

For a moment he was silent. "Thank you, ma'am."

"Talk to you again soon." She ended the call, dropped the folders onto her desk and, unfortunately, her cup of tea with them. "Shit!"

"Potty mouth." Holly came up behind her, wearing a dress of bloody Valentine's red. "Oh, you have made a mess, haven't you?"

Kara pushed past her, hurried to the paper towel dispenser above the drinking fountain, and thrust several paper towels into Holly's hands. "You going to help or just stand there?"

A few dozen paper towels and five minutes later, the mess was cleaned up.

Kara opened the tea-stained folder that had taken the worst hit and held up dry pages. "At least it didn't ruin the documents." She looked up to find Holly staring at her, a piece of paper in her hand. "What?"

"A Depo Provera shot?" Then Holly's lips curved in a knowing smile. "Who is he?"

Kara grabbed the receipt from the women's clinic out of Holly's hand, crumpled it, and tossed it in the trash. She'd stopped by the clinic over her lunch break on Tuesday, determined not to make the same mistake twice. Apparently, she'd left the receipt on her desk. "None of your business."

Holly put her hands on her hips. "Oh, come on! I tell you everything!"

Kara sat and tore the plastic wrap off her sandwich, so hungry she felt shaky. "Yes, you do, and I wish you didn't. Don't expect me to do the same."

Holly looked stricken. "Well, if you don't want to know about my life, just say so."

Kara hadn't meant to hurt her. "I'm sorry, Holly. Really. You know I didn't mean it that way. I'm just more private than you are. Can you keep a secret?"

Holly glared at her. "Of course."

"Let me at least get a few bites of this sandwich in my stomach, and I'll tell you."

* * *

REECE CLOSED his office door and locked it. "Tell me what you've got."

Carol plopped several file folders on his desk, sat, and took a deep breath. "It's a damned mess, Senator. As far as I can tell, we've got a handful of senators who are deliberately overcharging the taxpayers."

"How so?" Reece rounded his desk, sat down, and grabbed his notepad and a pen.

"Well, you all get paid your salary, and you all receive a per diem for every day the Senate is in session, which is January through May, and for each day business calls you in to the Capitol outside of session."

"Right. The per diem is supposed to help compensate for travel and other expenses."

Carol fixed him with a serious look above her wire-rim bifocals. "But a handful of senators, including our Senate president, seem to be charging a per diem as if it were part of a full-time salary."

"How can they get away with that?"

"Basically, they just claim to have been here and they get paid for it. The forms aren't part of any permanent record, so there's no paper trail to prove who has claimed what or whether they were truly here on business or not."

"And someone like Devlin, who lives in Aurora, can simply turn the Capitol into an extension of his living room and make lots of extra money at the taxpayers' expense without anyone being able to prove anything."

Carol nodded. "That's it exactly."

He glanced at his watch and leaned back in his seat. His education bill was scheduled for first reading on the Senate floor in forty minutes. "Well, hell, Carol. If we can't prove anything, I guess that leaves us with fixing the system to prevent this from continuing. If I'm not mistaken, that will require a change in state law. Someone will have to introduce a bill."

The older woman smiled, a devilish gleam in her eyes. "Devlin will crucify you, sir."

Reece grinned. "He'll try."

KARA RUBBED the kink in her neck, her eyes on the page. When her phone rang, she picked it up without thinking. "Kara McMillan."

"You think changing your number makes any difference to us, little girl?"

She clicked record, but she was at work now, not at home. It wasn't fear she felt, but anger. "You know, on top of being an annoying asshole, you're a sexist pig, aren't you? Do your bosses at Northrup know you treat women like this?"

For a moment she thought he'd hung up, but then she heard his breathing. So her rage had taken him by surprise.

"You've been warned, bitch."

"Oh, that's original."

He hung up.

"Dammit!" She slammed down the phone and stood.

"Him again?" Matt looked up from his computer screen. "Sounds like a sicko."

"Yeah." She glanced at the clock. She had thirty minutes until she needed to pick up Connor. She grabbed her water bottle and headed for the water cooler.

She'd gotten through almost eight hundred pages since Monday—a drop in the bucket. Tessa and Sophie had been taking a few files each at night and working from home. Matt had slipped in a few hours of data entry yesterday. Between the four of them, they'd made it through about one third of the total.

It had been slow going at first, while she worked her way through the jargon and the abbreviations. She wasn't a mining or cement-manufacturing expert, and she had no idea what a "bag house" or a "nine belt" was. With the whistleblower's help, she'd be able to move through the material more quickly now. She'd been relieved to hear he and his family were safe and sound. That was one less thing for her to worry about.

She reached the water cooler, bent down to fill her bottle, and found herself looking down at three pairs of women's shoes in addition to her own. She looked up and found herself surrounded by Tessa, Sophie, and Holly, who all smiled at her with that unmistakable look of women who know a secret. "Holly!"

"I didn't tell them anything!"

Kara stood upright and glared at her friend.

Sophie slipped an arm around Kara's shoulders. "Don't blame her, Kara. We're investigative reporters. We've known something's going on for a while."

"Oh, bless her heart!" Tessa's voice dripped with sweetened southern sarcasm. "She wants to claw our eyes out!"

Realizing she wouldn't make it back to her desk alive, Kara gave in, feeling very much like she was in high school again. "I'm spending the weekend with Reece Sheridan at his cabin above Estes Park."

"*Senator* Reece Sheridan?" Sophie gaped at her.

Tessa looked amazed. "Oh my God! I had to interview him once. He was such a sweetheart—and sexy as original sin."

Sophie leaned closer. "How long have you been seeing—?"

"What's going on?" Matt walked up behind them.

Tessa glared at him. "You thirsty, Matt? No? Then scoot. We're women. We gossip."

Kara saw her chance and took it. "That's all for now. I have work to do."

Three disappointed groans turned to excited whispers as Kara pushed her way through them and made her way back to her desk. But her pulse was beating a bit faster.

Sexy as original sin.

And Kara would be spending the next three days with him.

* * *

REECE LIFTED his duffle bag into the back of the Jeep, running through a mental list of preparations. He'd driven up with groceries, flowers, and an extra load of firewood yesterday after getting out of session. Then he'd spent a few hours tidying the place up. He'd remembered everything.

Except condoms.

"Damn!" He unlocked the door, climbed into the driver's seat, and glanced at his watch.

If he hurried and mid-town traffic wasn't too bad, he'd be able to swing by the drugstore and be only a few minutes late. Either way, he had no choice. He needed to buy condoms—the biggest box of condoms he could find.

KARA THREW an assortment of long johns, turtlenecks, and sweaters in her bag, not sure what she should take. How cold was it up there? Would he expect to go hiking around or cross-country skiing? What should she bring to sleep in— her old flannel granny gown or something sexy?

Unable to decide, she threw them both in, together with five pairs of her warmest socks, a pair of slippers, two pairs of mittens, her laptop, and the files she'd brought home from the office.

"Mommy, when is Lily coming?"

Kara looked at her alarm clock. Her mother was running late. "She ought to have been here by now. Are you all packed and ready to go?"

Connor nodded and pointed to his little suitcase, which sat by the door, his favorite teddy bear on top.

"Why don't you watch a little *Sponge Bob* until she gets here?"

Kara settled him in front of the TV, finished packing, and then slipped into the bathroom to have one last glance in the mirror. She'd gotten home a bit early, jumped in the shower, shaved her legs, and gone over her skin with the lavender sugar scrub Reece seemed to like so much until her skin was bright pink and silky smooth. Then she'd blown her hair dry, put on her makeup from scratch, and dressed in jeans and a burgundy-colored turtleneck. For a treat, she'd worn a lacy black thong and matching bra—something she hadn't done in ages.

It had been so long. So long.

Was that fear she saw in her own eyes? She supposed it was. Could she really blame herself for feeling nervous, even afraid?

She knew Reece well enough to know he would go out of his way to make this weekend enjoyable for her. What she didn't know was what that would do to her. She couldn't afford to lose herself over a man again, couldn't afford to lose her balance. Not this time.

She had just zipped her bag and was carrying it down the hallway when the front door opened and her mother's voice rang through the house.

"Where's Connor?"

"Lily!" *Sponge Bob* forgotten, Connor ran to his grandmother.

Kara watched them hug. Despite her eccentricities, Lily McMillan loved her grandson.

"Look how much you've grown! My goodness, you're growing before my eyes!"

"We went to see the dinosaurs at the museum, and I saw the T-rex!"

"You'll have to tell me all about that."

"Thanks, Mom. I really appreciate it."

"I'm happy to help out." Her mother leaned in closer, whispered. "Especially if it means you're going to get laid. Where is this man? I want to meet him."

Kara felt a rush of horror. "Oh, no! God, no! No. I'm not ready for that yet. Connor, do you have everything? Let's get your coat."

Her mother raised a finely penciled eyebrow. "So you're going to hustle me out the door?"

Kara met her gaze, feeling both guilty and determined.

"Yes, I am. I don't want you to read his aura or align his second chakra or probe his past lives. I don't know what he'd think about that, and I don't want to find out."

When the doorbell rang, Kara almost moaned out loud.

Her mother shot her a look of triumph and marched straight toward the door.

Kara beat her to it. "I'll get it."

She opened the door, and the butterflies in her stomach collided. He wore Levis and a black cable-knit sweater that contrasted sharply with his blond hair. The faintest whiff of aftershave preceded him through the doorway.

"Kara." He ducked down and brushed his lips over hers.

The kiss made her lips tingle, but with her mother watching, Kara couldn't help but feel self-conscious. "Reece."

"Reece!" Connor dashed across the room, his face bright like sunshine.

Reece scooped him up. "Hey, buddy. I hear you went to see the dinosaurs a second time."

Connor nodded. "Mommy let me put money in the saber-tooth tiger's mouth, and he growled at me."

"Did it scare you?"

Connor shook his head. "It's a fake saber-tooth."

"You're a smart boy."

"Mom, I'd like to introduce Reece Sheridan." Kara shot her mother a warning look. "Reece, this is my mother, Lily McMillan."

But her mother wasn't watching Kara, her gaze focused instead entirely on Reece. "It's a pleasure to meet you, Senator."

Reece leaned down, Connor still in his arms, gave her mother a kiss on the cheek. "The pleasure is mine. And please—just call me Reece."

Kara could feel her mother's hot flash standing four feet away. "They were just leaving, weren't you, Mom?"

THE DRIVE to Estes Park lasted a little over an hour and took them up a winding canyon of evergreens, red rock formations, and little cabin-style inns. Kara had expected the drive to be awkward. But nothing was ever awkward with Reece.

At first they talked about skiing, both confessing to a secret passion for Telluride. Then they talked about how Reece had learned to cook from his father, who had insisted that a man without a wife was not consigned to a life of TV dinners. Then they talked about her mother, who had at the last minute asked Reece his sign. His answer—Scorpio—had clearly made her quite happy.

"Kara is a Cancer, you know," she'd said, before Kara could shut the car door.

Kara had been mortified. But it didn't seem to bother Reece at all.

"I think she was just trying to tell me that you and I are sexually compatible," he said, taking his eyes off the road long enough to fix her with one of his lethal smiles. "But I already know that."

Kara found it hard to breathe and felt warmth flood her body. "So sure of that, are you?"

"Oh, yeah."

"Sorry about last Friday."

He glanced over at her. "Sorry for what?"

Didn't he know? "Well, you . . . I . . . I enjoyed myself, but you didn't."

He chuckled. "That wasn't your fault. And, sweetheart, if you think I didn't enjoy myself, you're wrong."

They drove in silence through Estes Park, past gingerbread cottages and log cabins, past the Stanley Hotel with its alleged ghosts, toward Rocky Mountain National Park with its snow-covered peaks that rose like apparitions out of the darkness.

"Our property is bordered by the park on two sides, so it's sort of like having the entire park as our backyard," Reece explained as he slowed and turned onto a steep dirt road. "Hang on, darlin'."

Kara understood now why he drove a Jeep. Even padded with snow, the road was rutted and rough. Her car would have gotten stuck or slid backward to the bottom of the hill. But Reece drove with confidence, carrying them up the hill with no trouble at all.

Abruptly the ground leveled, and Kara found herself in a glade of bare aspen in front of what looked like a very large log cabin. Firewood stood chopped and neatly stacked beneath a tarp next to the front door. A wooden deck wrapped itself around the side of the house toward the back. A stone chimney rose from the roof on both ends of the cabin.

"Here we are." He stopped the vehicle, hopped out, and came around to help her to the ground.

The air tingled with cold and smelled of ponderosa pine, wood smoke, and snow. Beyond the branches of the aspen, stars glittered like ice chips in a clear velvet sky.

"It's beautiful, Reece."

"Thanks. Like I said, it's my little slice of paradise." He walked to the back of the Jeep, lowered the tailgate, and grabbed their bags. "It's where I come to get away from the chaos of the Capitol."

Kara hurried over to him. "I can carry that."

He smiled, his teeth flashing white. "You can, but I'm not going to let you."

He carried the bags to the door, unlocked it, flipped on the light, and then stepped back to let her enter.

If the cabin had been impressive from the outside, that was nothing compared to the inside. Kara gaped at her surroundings. "You built *this*?"

The wall to her right was of hand-hewn flagstone with a large glass-front woodstove built into it. Polished wood floors were covered by sheepskin rugs, the white fleece a sharp contrast to the dark of the gleaming wood. The space was divided between a sunken living room, with full bookshelves, a blocky sofa of butter-soft leather, a couple lamps, and a coffee table that looked hand-carved, and a dining room with a polished pine table and chairs. A bouquet of two dozen red roses sat in a crystal vase on the table, a gift for her.

"Yeah. My father and I built it over a period of years while I was in college." The look on his face was one of unmistakable pride. He crossed the room, grabbed a box of matches, opened the black steel door of the woodstove, and set the flame to old newspaper. In a matter of seconds, wood crackled and flames danced. "Make yourself at home. There's champagne in the fridge. I'll just carry our bags back to the bedroom."

Something inside Kara clutched at the word *bedroom*. Feeling nervous, she slipped out of her shoes so as not to track in snow and mud, then wandered into the kitchen, retrieved the champagne, and began to search for glasses.

"To the left of the sink." His voice startled her.

She gasped, whirled about, champagne in hand, and found him leaning against the doorjamb, arms crossed over his chest.

"Don't tell me you're nervous." He closed the distance between them, took the bottle from her, and set it down on the counter.

She started to answer, but his lips had already closed over hers.

CHAPTER 14

SHE TASTED sweet, her lips soft and pliant. But it was the little feminine sound she made in her throat—something between a sigh and a squeak—that sent a jolt of lust shearing through his gut and pushed him over the edge. He took one shuddering breath, inhaled her scent, and when his mouth came down on hers again, the kiss was hard and hot.

Blood roared in his head as he crushed her against him, forced his tongue deep into her mouth, and pressed her back against the kitchen counter. Already her impatient hands groped beneath his sweater, tugging at his T-shirt, pulling it out of his jeans, seeking his skin. He returned the favor, sliding his hands beneath her shirt over the silk of her skin to cup her breasts through the irritating lace of her bra.

Not good enough.

"Damn!" He broke the kiss, sought the clasp of her bra, found it between her breasts, and released it, taking the soft weight of her breasts into his hands. Her nipples were already hard and pressed greedily into his palms. He circled them with his thumbs, felt her body jerk, then ducked his head and took one puckered bud into his mouth.

Her hands clenched in his hair, and she gasped, a sound that sent a pulse of ragged heat to his already rigid cock.

He slid his hands down the smooth skin of her belly, unbuttoned her jeans, then slipped his hands beneath the denim, expecting to feel the silk of panties. To his delight there was only the bare satin of her skin. She was wearing a thong. "Jesus, Kara!"

Cupping and kneading her bare ass, he trailed kisses from her breasts down her belly, then dropped to his knees, her hands still twined in his hair. Black lace covered the dark triangle between her thighs, the musk of her arousal an irresistible invitation.

A dozen thoughts collided in his mind of all the things he wanted to do to her, but one stood above the rest. He yanked her jeans down her legs, tossed them aside, then nudged her trembling thighs apart.

Kara was under a full-scale sensual assault, unable to think, barely able to keep up with the onslaught that was Reece. Knees weak as jelly, she felt the humid warmth of his breath on her inner thighs, then cried out in shock as he ripped off her thong and the slick heat of his mouth closed over her.

"Oh, Reece! Oh, God!"

His strong hands clasped her buttocks and forced her hips forward, as his tongue tormented her, painting slick circles, probing, penetrating. The sensation stunned her, and for a moment she struggled to stay in control. But then his lips closed over her clitoris, and he suckled her.

She cried out his name, her breath coming in ragged pants. She was drowning in sensation, unable to keep her head above water, unable to do anything but ride with the intensity of it. Then, somewhere between bliss and oblivion, she felt him push a finger, then two, inside her slippery heat and stroke her aching center, thrusting deeply.

Orgasm flooded through her like a riptide, one brutal rush of ruthless ecstasy, tearing a shocked cry from her throat, plunging her helplessly into the abyss, leaving her to float, breathless, in a warm, liquid sea.

There was no doubt that if Reece hadn't been supporting her from beneath she would have fallen to the floor. She felt him slide up the front of her body, felt his fingers twine in her hair to force her head back.

"Open your eyes, Kara. Look at me." His voice was rough.

She did as he asked and saw an expression akin to pain on his face.

"Now taste yourself!" His lips, wet with her passion, closed over hers in a violent kiss, his tongue carrying her taste into her own mouth. Musky. Primal. Erotic.

He had remembered.

Instantly, she was on the edge again, hot, hungry, desperate for him.

They staggered like drunks out of the kitchen, locked together in a kiss, she wearing only her turtleneck and loosened bra, he still fully dressed. Then Kara felt the softness of sheep's wool beneath her feet. They sank to the rug, still plundering one another with tongue and lips. She grappled with the infuriating buttons of his jeans as he forced her back, stretching himself out above her.

Then his hand pushed hers aside, leaving her to feast on the feel of his chest while he freed himself. His voice was a rough whisper. "I need you, Kara! I need to fuck you fast and hard!" Then he froze, groaned. "Damn! I need to go grab a condom."

"No, you don't. I'm protected. And I want you now!" She wrapped her legs around his waist.

He hesitated for just a moment, his gaze locked with hers, then drove himself into her with one slow thrust that almost made her scream. It had been so long since a man had been inside her, and it took a moment for her body to adjust to the thick, hard feel of him. And then he was moving, pushing himself in and out of her, the sweet, slippery friction already blossoming into gold.

Reece's mind and body buzzed with lust. She felt so good—hot and wet and tight and perfect. "Sweet Jesus!"

Her eyes were squeezed shut, her dark hair fanned out across the white sheepskin beneath her. Little moans rolled from her lungs with each panting breath, moans that sounded like his name, like pain, like the raw ache of sex.

Her scent, her taste was all around him, on him, in his mouth, her nails cutting into his bare shoulders beneath his sweater, her legs locking him tightly in place.

He balanced his weight on his left forearm, reached down with his right hand to cup her ass, and plunged into her again and again. He was on the brink, the claws of an orgasm already dragging at him. But first he wanted to see her face again, wanted to watch pleasure dance across it as she came, wanted to feel her climax against his cock. Holding onto the tatters of his control, he buried himself deep in her heat and ground himself in circles against her.

Her response was immediate. She arched beneath him, her moans frantic. "Oh, my God, Reece!"

And then she gasped, delight like a sunrise on her beautiful face, her inner muscles clenching him like a vise as she came.

With a groan, he rammed himself into her, his control gone. He couldn't stop, couldn't think, could only feel. And then he exploded. Climax scorched through him, white hot and blistering, burning him to ashes that hung for a moment in the stratosphere, and then drifted slowly back to Earth.

He had no idea how much time had passed as he lay on top of her, fighting to catch his breath, his mind blissfully blank. Slowly he rolled off of her, out of her, pulling her with him so her head lay on his chest. It felt good to hold her, to stroke her hair. "You hungry?"

After a few moments of silence, her voice drifted back to him. "Starving."

THEY ATE dinner in front of the fire, lying on cushions like decadent Romans, Kara in her white silk bathrobe, Reece in a pair of black boxer briefs that left the rest of his gorgeous, muscular body open to her view. If she hadn't been so hungry she doubted she would have been able to do anything but stare at him. But sex had left her ravenous.

Fortunately, Reece had planned for that.

Filet mignon. Roasted potatoes and fennel. Field greens with fresh feta. Raspberry mousse. Champagne.

Kara swallowed her last sweet-sour bite of mousse and moaned in appreciation. "This is incredible. You should open a restaurant. Chez Reece."

"I prefer a more select clientele than I'm likely to get off the streets." He picked up his champagne flute, his blue eyes smoky, his lips curving in a smile that sent her pulse skittering. Then he drank.

She felt the heat rise in her cheeks and shifted, almost uncomfortable under his sultry gaze. "Well, thank you for sharing your extraordinary culinary skills with me."

He set the empty flute aside. "There's more than one way of making love to a woman."

Making love.

Is that what he thought they were doing?

Certainly, sex with Reece was like nothing she'd ever experienced. He demanded and gave everything, leaving her far beyond satisfied. When he touched her, his attention was focused, and his focus was total. He seemed to be right with her, through every breath, every touch, every tremor, as if he could feel what she felt, as if what she felt mattered more to him in that moment than anything else. That in itself was unnerving.

But not as unnerving as notions of love. The last time— the only time—she'd been in love, she had paid for it bitterly.

Reece pushed the tray that held their dishes aside, moved closer, and pulled her against his bare chest. "What did I say to make you frown?"

Was she so transparent? "Nothing. I—"

"Liar." He kissed her forehead, one hand reaching inside her bathrobe to cup her breast, this thumb tracing insistent circles over her already puckered nipple. "I'm not like him, Kara. Whoever he is, I'm not like him."

She ran a hand over his chest with its mat of golden curls and teased one flat brown nipple, desire already running hot in her veins. "No. No, you're not."

Then his mouth closed over hers, and she forgot everything but him.

HE HADN'T been able to get in through the sliding glass door, so he'd had to break a window. The bitch didn't have an alarm system, so that made it easy. He'd busted the glass, unlocked the window, and then forced it open and crawled inside, his crotch itching with anticipation.

She was supposed to be home with her brat. They'd told him she was always home at night. But she wasn't home tonight. That put a kink in things.

He was supposed to break in and force her to hand over the documents and tapes. The boss man didn't care if he roughed her up a bit, and that was fine. He'd been looking forward to it. He liked hurting women, liked it when fear filled their eyes and they started to cry, loved it when they begged him not to hurt them, and cherished that moment when they realized their begging wasn't going to stop him.

He rubbed the bulge in his pants, angry that he had missed his chance. Then he settled down to wait.

THEY LAY on the bed, limbs tangled, bodies languid, skin covered with a sheen of sweat, as orgasm faded into sleep. A fire roared in the glass-front woodstove and cast a warm glow through the bedroom.

Her head on his shoulder, Kara ran a finger down the furrow at the center of his chest, his breath warm against her temple. "Are you real?"

His hand skimmed over the curve of her hip. "Yeah. You?"

KARA AWOKE, her face buried in Reece's chest. His heart beat steadily in her ear, a strong, soothing sound. She rolled onto her back, the hard bulge of his bicep in the crook of her neck, and stretched, feeling as warm and lazy as a house cat.

"Good morning, beautiful." His voice was deep and rumbling with just a touch of sleep.

She rolled onto her stomach, looked into his face, and felt her heartbeat hitch. He was so damned gorgeous. "Good morning, Senator."

It was then she noticed the bed. It had been dark last night, and she'd been so lost in Reece that she hadn't even looked at it. Its four posters were hewn from what had clearly once been aspen trees. The headboard and footboard were made of smaller branches interlaced and woven together. It was both rugged and beautiful—an apt reflection of its owner.

She reached out and ran her finger over one smooth woven branch. "Where did you find this? It's beautiful."

"I made it." He rolled onto his side and rested his hand on the small of her back. "We had to clear some trees off the plot before we could break ground. It seemed a shame to waste them. I took four big trunks for the main supports and the smaller, suppler branches for the headboard. It took me most of a summer to get it right."

"Is there anything you can't do?"

He pressed his lips into her shoulder, and his hand closed over her derriere. "Well, right now I can't keep my hands off your ass."

They had sex in the shower, hands sliding over slick, soapy skin, then dried off before the fire. Reece made omelets with hash browns for breakfast, along with a bowl of sweet strawberries and a pot of freshly ground coffee. While Kara did the dishes, he went outside and chopped wood—which Kara watched surreptitiously through the kitchen window. What was it about a man doing manly things that put a woman's hormones in a whirl?

Then, after pouring coffee into a thermos and packing some snacks into a backpack, Reece took her out to show her the property. The snow was deep enough to require snowshoes, which Reece had in a storage shed behind the cabin.

Kara quickly grew accustomed to walking in them and had no trouble following Reece through the trees.

The sun was shining, and the air was fresh and biting cold. Tall bare aspen thrust white trunks out of the snow, their branches a lacy froth against the blue sky. In the distance the fourteen-thousand-foot-high peaks that made up the backbone of the Rockies glittered white in the sunlight.

He showed her the natural hot springs that bubbled up from deep in the earth into a pool carved into rock by millennia of erosion. He showed her the wild raspberry patch that yielded its harvest to chipmunks and hungry bears every summer. And he showed her his father's grave, the headstone half buried in snow.

As they walked, Reece told her how they'd found the property through the friend of a friend, who was trying to unload it before moving back to Texas. They'd spent the next summer camping in a tent by night and building by day. Over the years, they'd finished the interior and made or purchased furnishings.

"We spent every summer for fifteen years making the cabin better, more comfortable, caring for the property." There was both grief and pride in his voice as he spoke.

"It shows. When you said 'cabin,' I was expecting some drafty pile of logs decorated with antlers and stuffed animal heads."

Reece grinned from beneath his sunglasses. "Disappointed are you? I could shoot a few things and hang them on the wall if you like."

"No thanks. Let the critters keep their heads."

They drank coffee on top of a large outcropping of rocks that looked out over a valley of snowy white. A herd of elk moved like brown dots in the distance, pawing for forage beneath the snow, nibbling bark off the trees.

Kara felt herself relax, let her gaze wander across the landscape—a landscape so wide and open that it kindled a strange ache in her soul. "It's so peaceful here, so quiet."

He pulled her back to rest against him, kissed her hair.

"My father had planned to live up here after he retired."

"I'm sorry he never got the chance."

"Me, too."

"You must miss him terribly."

"Yeah."

They were almost back to the cabin when Reece motioned for her to stop and crouched down to look at the snow. "Mountain lion tracks."

"Really?" Startled, Kara looked around her, and then stared down at the paw prints in the snow. "Have you ever seen them here before?"

He chuckled. "All the time. There's an old male who counts this as part of his territory. I've seen him a few times—a big cat. Probably one hundred and eighty pounds. Every once in a while I come across the carcass of a mule deer he's brought down."

A shiver ran down Kara's spine. Apart from skiing and the occasional hike, she was strictly a city person. Wildlife to her meant squirrels. "Has it ever tried to attack you?"

He shook his head. "Mountain lions aren't interested in people. They do everything they can to stay out of our way."

"How do you know all this? Oh, that's right. You're the environmental senator, the tree-hugger. How could I forget? You've probably studied all of Colorado's wildlife."

"That's right. I've read about their habitat needs, their hunting habits—their mating habits."

"Mating habits?"

"Yes, mating habits." He stood and circled her like a predator, his voice dropping to a growl. "The male mountain lion finds the female by scent."

Kara heard snow crunch behind her and felt the thrill of being stalked. His hand slid beneath her coat and inside her jeans, his cold fingers drawing a gasp as they touched her skin and again when they sought and found her most sensitive spot.

"He knows when she's primed to mate, knows when she's ready for him."

Kara was ready for him now. She pressed her behind into him and knew from the iron bulge in his pants that he was ready, too.

"The male outweighs her by a good seventy pounds." He jerked down her jeans, kicked off her snowshoes, nipped the side of her throat with his teeth. "When he finds her, he bites her neck and forces her head to the ground."

With a moan of anticipation, she let him force her to her knees, her gloved hands sinking to the wrists in the snow. Behind her came the sound of metal buttons being wrenched out of denim buttonholes.

"Then he mounts her from behind, fast and rough." His hands grasped her hips, and he sank into her with a single, powerful thrust.

Words became gasps and moans and whimpers as he hammered himself into her, his balls slapping against the chilled skin of her bare ass.

Kara had never climaxed like this before, so the power of it when it hit her took her by surprise. A wild cry tore itself from her throat, followed by his deep groan as he came inside her, both sounds swallowed by the vastness of the Colorado winter.

Kara lost track of the number of times they had sex over the next two days. On the couch, in the shower, on the bedroom floor, on the kitchen table, in the hot springs. She kept expecting the fierceness of her need for him to die down to something manageable. But it didn't. All he had to do was touch her. Sometimes he didn't even have to do that.

It wasn't until Sunday night as they lazed naked in the steaming waters of the hot springs that she realized that she hadn't once hooked up her laptop, checked cell phone messages, or checked her e-mail. She'd called her mother to check on Connor only once.

Now it was almost over. By tomorrow evening, she and Reece would be back in Denver, where real life waited for them. And then what?

She didn't want to think about that.

She snuggled into him, watched fat snowflakes drift idly from the dark sky and melt on the surface of the water, her body replete and relaxed as warm honey from their latest bout of crazed sex. His strong arm fit so naturally beneath her breasts. Her head felt so at home on his shoulder. Why couldn't they stay like this forever?

"Reece."

He kissed her hair, which was damp from the steam. "Mmm."

"Thank you. For all of this. I can't remember when I've ever had a better time."

He held her a bit closer and nuzzled her ear. "You're welcome."

"Whatever happens, I want you to know that I'll always remember this."

"I'm counting on it."

BY THE time they hit the outskirts of Denver, Kara felt the tension begin to return. Her mind began to fill with all the things she needed to do when she got back to the paper tomorrow, each task like an irritating grain of sand.

Reece took her hand and gave it a reassuring squeeze. "What's on your mind?"

"Work."

"Can you talk about it?"

She shook her head. "Not yet."

"You're damned good at what you do."

The compliment was unexpected. "Thanks."

"I hope you'll find time to squeeze me in. I want to see more of you, Kara. I don't know exactly what's happening between us or where it will lead, but I do know I want to be with you."

This was the conversation she'd been dreading. "It's not just my job. There's Connor. I don't want him to get the wrong idea."

"And what idea is that?"

She searched for the words. "He's a vulnerable little boy. With no father . . . I don't want him to get hurt. If we become involved—"

"We're not involved now?"

"Not like that."

"Then what were these past three days?" There was an edge to his voice now.

"A weekend."

"That's all it was to you? A weekend?"

She couldn't lie. "No. It was more than that, Reece. It was . . . wonderful."

"Then what's the problem?"

"The problem is that I have a son who will be crushed when you decide you've had enough of the two of us and vanish."

"I see." Anger churned in Reece's gut. She was pushing him away. Already she was pushing him away.

"I'm not sure you do. I can't let my needs or desires hurt my son. That's all. I don't want to be the kind of single mom who has a revolving door on her bedroom."

He took a deep breath, determined not to let their time together end with an argument. "You're not that kind of woman, Kara. Spending a weekend with me doesn't make you that kind of woman. You deserve a life, you know."

They finished the drive in silence, Reece biting back his frustration. He pulled into her driveway, the sun already starting to set over the mountains, now a purple outline on the western horizon. They met at the back of the Jeep. But rather than opening the tailgate and removing her bag, he pulled her into his arms.

"I'm not going anywhere, Kara. And I won't let you push me out of your life just because you're afraid." He silenced her objections with a kiss and felt her response as she softened in his arms and kissed him back.

No, he wasn't going anywhere.

"I don't suppose you're going to let me carry my own bag, are you?"

"Nope."

She led the way to the door, slid in her key, unlocked it, pushed it open.

And froze.

CHAPTER 15

REECE HEARD Kara's gasp and saw the shocked disbelief on her face. Beyond her, he saw the cause.

"Oh, my God!" She took a step to go inside.

He slipped an arm around her waist and restrained her. "No, Kara! Whoever did this might still be in there. Back inside the Jeep. Come on."

He guided her back to his vehicle, tossed her bag in the back, and then called 911 on his cell phone. "Break-in and possible burglary at 1105 Corona. We're not sure if the intruder is still here. We just arrived to find the place trashed."

He started the engine, backed the car out of the driveway, and parked a few houses down the street. If someone was in there, someone who wanted to hurt Kara, Reece was going to make damn sure she didn't present an easy target.

Kara heard Reece speaking with police dispatch, but his words barely registered. Her mind raced, fragmented thoughts shooting rapid-fire through her mind as if in time to her pulse. Someone had torn her home apart. Someone had broken in and destroyed it. They had intruded into her life, into her home. They had probably taken her TV and stereo. Well, those she could replace. At least no one was hurt. Yes, she could replace everything. Her insurance would cover it. It would be all right. She would clean the place up, file an insurance claim, and it would be fine.

Even as she tried to come to grips with it, tried to soothe

herself, a clammy finger drew itself down her spine. What if *he* had done this? What if he had been trying to make good on his threats?

"It will be okay, Kara." Reece gave her hand a squeeze, his blue eyes full of concern. "They're on their way."

By the time the three squad cars arrived, lights flashing, Kara had gone from being shocked to boiling mad. She paced the sidewalk while they cleared the house. "I want to punch someone!"

Reece stepped into her path and presented his torso as a target. "Okay, but not too hard. I bruise easily."

The absurdity of his pretending that she could physically hurt him stopped her in her tracks and broke through some of her rage. "I don't want to hit *you*. Damn it!"

He took her in his arms. "I know, sweetheart."

A drab olive-green car pulled to the curb, and she recognized Chief Irving. He hoisted his girth out from behind the steering wheel and strode over to them, notepad in hand. "Senator. Ms. McMillan. Sorry to be meeting with you under these circumstances. Can you bring me up to date?"

Omitting certain details, Kara described how she'd gone away Friday night and had just arrived home to find that someone had broken in. She told him how Reece had prevented her from entering the house.

"But I'd really like to go inside as soon as I can, Chief Irving. It's my home."

Chief Irving nodded. "I understand, Ms. McMillan, but right now your home is a crime scene. When we're done, you'll be free to go inside. And quick thinking, Senator. You never want to enter a home that's been burglarized until after the police have cleared it. People end up dead that way. Now let me see what our boys have found."

The minutes seemed to stretch into hours as Kara waited, Reece beside her. She called her mother on her cell and asked her to keep Connor one more night to give her time to make her house safe again.

Her mother agreed and offered Kara her couch for the

night. "You don't want to sleep there, Kara. All that bad juju won't be good for you."

"Thanks, Mom, but it's going to take all night to clean this place up. I'll probably be too tired to make it to Boulder."

"Then make sure you burn some sage or something."

Kara saw Chief Irving walk out her front door, headed in her direction. "Burn sage. Got it. Thanks, Mom." She hung up, found Reece smiling at her. "What?"

"Your mom really loves you, you know."

"Yeah. She's just a bit crazy."

Chief Irving flipped to the next page in his notepad. "Well, Ms. McMillan, we'll need you to comb through the place and tell us if anything was stolen."

"So it looks like a routine burglary to you?" She'd probably overreacted earlier when her imagination had tried to tie it to the phone calls.

Chief Irving met her gaze. "I didn't say that. But come on in and tell us if you find anything missing. And be prepared for a mess."

The chief's warning did nothing to prepare Kara for the shock of seeing so much of what she owned broken and in a shambles. The television lay in shattered pieces on top of broken picture frames, shredded books, and cracked CDs. Her VCR, DVD player, and stereo were reduced to components and snapped wires. Papers and newspaper clippings from her filing cabinet were strewn everywhere, the contents of her desk drawers beside them. Wads of fluffy white stuffing from her couch lay like snow across this landscape of destruction.

The kitchen was a bit better than the living room. The window above the sink was shattered and pried open, glass littering the floor. And although some dishes lay broken, the intruder hadn't opened her cupboards to smash all of them. An ice cream container sat empty on the counter next to the refrigerator.

She stared into the darkness of her backyard through the

open hole that used to be a window. "Well, I guess that new lock worked. He didn't get in through the sliding glass door."

Down the hall, she found her bedroom ransacked, as if someone had gone through every drawer looking for something. Clothes from her closet lay strewn across the floor. Her mattress was slashed open and lay sideways, half on the floor and half on the box springs. Her jewelry box, which had held nothing but earrings and a clip of baby hair from Connor's first haircut, lay open on the carpet. The panic button, which she'd left behind, sat oddly untouched amid the chaos.

Then she spied purple. Humiliated, she kicked a sweater on top of her vibrator and prayed neither Reece nor the cops had seen it.

Reece's voice startled her. "Whoever did this left Connor's room alone. Have you found anything missing?"

She shook her head. "No. Nothing."

She didn't have to be a detective to realize what that meant. This was anything but a routine burglary. This was personal.

Chief Irving was waiting for them downstairs in the kitchen. One gloved officer was busy dusting for fingerprints, the black dust like ink blotches on the window, the refrigerator, the ice cream container.

"Why don't you have a seat, Ms. McMillan? Can we get you anything? Something to drink?"

Kara swallowed and met the detective's gaze. "I'm fine standing."

"Here's the way I see it, Ms. McMillan. Our guy shows up while you're gone. He can't get in through the sliding glass door so he breaks the window. He doesn't steal anything. In fact, he makes himself at home—sits down with a pint of Ben & Jerry's, eats a few granola bars, a bag of tortilla chips, perhaps watches some television, maybe even takes a piss. You don't leave the seat up, do you? Then he decides to break stuff. And when he's done breaking stuff, he leaves. Now why does he do that, Ms. McMillan?"

Kara noticed the granola bar wrappers and the empty bag of chips on the floor and wondered why she hadn't noticed them earlier. *Think, McMillan! You're an investigative reporter, remember?* "He was searching for something and got hungry. He must have felt he had time enough to eat. Then, when he couldn't find what he was looking for, he got angry and destroyed my belongings."

"What would he be looking for, Ms. McMillan?"

"Whistleblower videotapes. State health department documents."

Then Reece spoke. "Or maybe he hung around so long because he was waiting."

"Waiting for what?"

His hands cupped her shoulders. "For you."

IT WAS almost midnight. The police had gone. The insurance adjustor had come and gone, promising a check by mid-week. Only Reece remained.

He'd stayed with her to help her clean up the place. Now the trash can outside was full to overflowing with the shattered remains of Kara's belongings, several trash bags that didn't fit sitting beside it. The couch and her mattress sat on the curb awaiting pickup by the city. Her clothes had been folded and put away or hung back in the closet. The floor had been swept and the kitchen floor mopped to remove glass slivers.

Behind Kara, Reece used his electric drill to tighten a bolt that held a sheet of wood in place over the broken kitchen window. "It's not pretty, but it will keep out both thugs and cold air until the glass is replaced."

She wrapped her arms around herself, feeling strangely dull and chilled. "Thanks."

Reece unplugged the drill and turned to find Kara standing in the middle of her almost empty living room, arms hugged tightly around herself, dark ponytail hanging down her back. She looked vulnerable, despondent. Apart from her bout of temper while she was waiting for the police to let her into her own home, she had shown almost no emotion. It had been hard enough for him to see what the son of a bitch had done to her belongings. He'd felt enraged. If she and Connor had been home when the bastard had struck . . . He didn't want to think about it.

He couldn't imagine how she must be feeling. He knew that holding onto her emotions was her way of trying to be strong. But he also he knew he couldn't leave her alone with this.

He packed the last of his tools away and clicked the toolbox shut. Then he crossed the room and wrapped his arms around her. "I'm so sorry this happened, Kara."

She gave a weak little laugh. "Me, too."

He turned her to face him and pulled her against his chest. She felt small and soft, and a surge of protectiveness shot from his gut. "Get whatever you need for work tomorrow. You're coming to my place for the night. You can follow me in your car."

She stepped back from him and shook her head. "I can't, Reece. I'm not going to let whoever did this intimidate me or drive me out of my own home. I have to stay."

"I admire your courage, but I'm not leaving you here alone. Besides, you've been brave enough for one day. What you need is a good night's sleep, and we both know you're not going to get that here." He could tell from her eyes that he was making inroads.

"I'll just be running away. I need to stay and face it. That's the only way I'm going to get over this."

"Okay. I'll get our bags and be right back." He started for the door.

"What do you mean 'our bags'?"

"I told you I'm not leaving you here alone. If you stay, I stay."

"But there's no place for anyone to sleep except Connor's bed, and it's a twin."

"I'll take the living room floor."

She gaped at him for a moment, then stomped off toward her bedroom. "Fine. Have it your way. But I'm only going with you because I can't stand the thought of you sleeping on my floor."

"Whatever works." He picked up his toolbox, flicked out the kitchen light, and grinned.

When Kara pulled into the parking lot at the newspaper the next morning, she was in a strangely good mood given what had happened last night. Maybe it was the fact that she would get to see Connor later today. She missed him terribly. Or maybe it was the delicious breakfast of blueberry crepes Reece had somehow whipped up while putting on his senator costume—starched shirt, silk tie, and tailored trousers that draped perfectly over his scrumptious butt. Or maybe it was the way he'd put her to sleep last night and woken her up this morning—one slow, sweet climax after the next.

Okay, that was definitely it. Even if her brain had a few cobwebs in it from lack of sleep, her body felt like spun silk.

She parked, grabbed her briefcase, and got buzzed through security. She hadn't made any headway on the health department records over the weekend, of course, so she needed to catch up on that today. She also needed to get in touch with Scott Hammond at the state health department and find out how much he was willing to tell her. If Northrup really was behind the calls and the break-in, she needed to finish the story quickly.

Ink was a journalist's best defense.

Somehow it felt easier to face what had happened to her house by the light of day. Though she hadn't told Reece, she was grateful he had manipulated her into staying with him. She doubted she'd have been able to close her eyes alone in her strangely empty house. She knew what her mother meant now by "bad juju." She hadn't been able to shake the sense of malevolence she'd felt. She had arranged to stay at her mother's place for the next few days until the insurance check came. She didn't want Connor to see his home this way.

She found her desk buried in press releases, her e-mail crammed with spam, and seven messages on her voicemail. Her morning got even brighter when none of the seven messages was a whispering voice threatening dire consequences. She'd just left another message on Mr. Hammond's home voicemail when she spied Tessa making straight toward her, documents in her hand and a worried look on her face.

"We've got a problem, Kara." Tessa handed her the documents.

Kara's good mood evaporated.

It was a police report. It was date-stamped for last night. And right there on the first page was her name—and Reece's. "Damn! Damn! Damn!"

The report detailed accurately what had happened, including the fact that the victim and the witness had been away for the weekend.

Tom was going to be furious. But how would Reece feel? It was his name, after all, and not hers that would catch reporters' attention. He was likely to find himself getting phone calls from media eager to speculate on his love life— and any political advantage he was deriving from it.

How could Kara have gotten so sloppy? She was a reporter, for God's sake! She knew what a police report entailed, what was likely to be included. Why hadn't she anticipated this and done something to prevent it?

You were scared and angry, and you weren't thinking. Not thinking being the key factor.

Tessa gave a heavy sigh and shook her blond mane. "I don't see how we can hide this from Tom. If any of the other papers pick it up first—"

"He'll kill me."

Tessa nodded. "If you're lucky."

"Thanks, Tessa. I guess I've got twenty minutes to figure out how to handle this. I need to warn Reece."

Tessa leaned closer and whispered. "Did you at least have a good time?"

Kara couldn't help the dreamy smile that spread across her face.

"I thought you would."

She waited until the end of the meeting to bring it up. "Someone broke into my home over the weekend. Nothing was stolen, but most of what I owned was destroyed. The police have determined that it wasn't a routine burglary. My theory is that someone wants the whistleblower videotapes and state documents. Here's the police report."

She tossed it to Tom, who spent a moment skimming it, then looked up at her through emotionless blue eyes. "Got a thing going on with a state senator, I see."

Matt's head whipped around so fast she was surprised he didn't give himself whiplash. Syd looked up from her calculator. Joaquin's eyebrows shot upward. Sophie gave her knee a reassuring squeeze under the conference table. Tessa rolled her eyes.

Kara met Tom's gaze. "Reece . . . That is, Senator Sheridan and I only recently—"

Tom tossed the report back to her. "I don't care whom you fuck, McMillan, as long as it doesn't compromise this newspaper. Novak, get a blurb on this in our police blotter. I don't want the other papers thinking we're trying to bury our own shit. If you're not in a sexual swoon, McMillan, get copies made of those tapes and documents. They're too important to lose."

Reece glanced at his watch and motioned for Brooke to grab his file on the tire-burning bill. He was due on the Senate floor five minutes ago. "I think what we've got is workable and responsible. Lawmakers will hate it, but the taxpayers will love it, which is one way to know for certain it's a good bill. I really appreciate your help."

He'd spent most of the morning on the phone with legal,

working out the details of his new bill, which would change the way the state tracked money paid to lawmakers. If it passed, no one would be able to hide a dime earned at the taxpayers' expense. Devlin was going to hate him.

Reece scrolled through the missed calls on his cell phone and saw that Kara had tried to reach him. "While I have you on the phone, I've got one other question. If I wanted a comprehensive list of open-records requests made over the past six months by a specific reporter, would the state's attorney be able to produce that list?"

State health department documents, she'd said, but she couldn't tell him anything more. But as a member of the Legislative Audit Committee, he wasn't without resources. If someone within state government was threatening her or had any idea who might be behind the phone calls and the break-in, it was within the scope of Reece's position to find out who it was—and to do something about it. It wasn't an abuse of his authority; it was his job, even if there was a personal angle to it.

"That would be great. Thanks. The reporter's name is Kara McMillan."

CHAPTER 16

KARA LAY back, eyes closed, and let the hot water engulf her. One of the perks of staying at her mother's house was the huge sunken tub off the master bedroom. Her favorite lavender bath salts, a dozen candles, and it was the perfect place for Kara to relax and to think. As her mother was reading Connor a bedtime story—a child's book about the prince who ran away from home, i.e., the Buddha—she actually had time to relax and think.

She'd read through a mountain of documents so far this week, so many pages that her shoulders ached and she dreamed in charts. What she and the others had found was a long trail of complaints from Northrup's neighbors, including Ed and Moira Farnsworth and Dottie and Carl Perkins. There were also dozens upon dozens of copies of complaints that had been filed with the county health department and then passed on to the state. Talk about passing the buck.

There were also state inspection reports showing numerous violations of state air-quality laws, some relating to the plant's smokestacks, the rest relating to dust emissions. In more than one case, the state inspector had caught Northrup employees doing funky math to make their toxic emissions fall below state limits—a serious crime. The odd thing was that if she followed the mountain of paperwork resulting from the inspections, she always ended up with nothing. No penalties. No major fines. The steepest fine she'd uncovered so far was for six thousand dollars—hardly a drop in the bucket for a company that raked in ten billion each year.

How could that be? Why would inspectors from the state health department, whose job it was to protect public health, go to the trouble of double-checking Northrup's math if the department had no intention of prosecuting the company for breaking the law? It made no sense.

She knew exactly who could answer this question. But he didn't seem to want to speak with her. After warning her that she and the whistleblower might be in danger, he had suddenly gone quiet, refusing to return her phone calls. But Mr. Hammond had done those inspections. He had checked the math. He'd caught them falsifying their reports to the state. He would know why Northrup had never been prosecuted. It was time to quit waiting for him to call back and to try a different way of making contact.

Kara stretched, wiggled her toes in the water, and wondered absently if there was any way to put a gigantic, sunken bathtub in her tiny bathroom. Tonight was her last night at her mother's house. The insurance check had come yesterday, and the three of them had spent last evening shopping—mattress, couch, TV, stereo, DVD player, and *Sponge Bob* galore. The furniture and television had been delivered today, and Kara had used her lunch hour to rush home and arrange things. Tomorrow, she and Connor would go to a slightly different but familiar home. They would refill the bird feeder, which was surely empty by now, eat spaghetti for dinner, and snuggle together with a stack of books. Life would go back to normal.

Or maybe it wouldn't.

What was she going to do about Reece? All she had to do was think of him and her body started to glow. Senator Reece Sheridan was devastating in bed. That much was for certain. He was pretty damned wonderful out of it, too. But this was moving too fast. Kara was thinking of him constantly, wishing she were with him, wanting to talk with him, to hear his voice, to touch him, to feel his hands and lips on her skin. She was like an addict, and he was her fix.

It was one thing to like a man and to enjoy having sex with him. It was quite another to become enmeshed with him, to feel like her day wasn't complete without him, to *need* him. And no way, *no way* was she going to let herself fall in love with him. Not if she could help it.

And what happens if you can't help it, McMillan?

The very thought had her eyes flying open, her heart racing.

It was time for her to get her life on an even keel again, to put the Northrup story to bed and focus on raising her son. She couldn't afford to get this lost in a man. Was she so pathetically horny that she couldn't do without him for a while?

The door handle turned, and her mother stepped inside. "He's sound asleep. What a wonderful boy he is, Kara! Such an old soul!"

Kara sat up, feeling awkward. She wasn't body shy, particularly not around her mother, but she wasn't used to lounging naked in the tub with an audience. "I'll get out if you need to use the bathroom."

Her mother waved off her offer and sat on the carpeted floor. "Hush! Just keep soaking. I thought we could chat. We rarely get time alone."

Irritated that her privacy had just been obliterated, Kara leaned back and closed her eyes. "What do you want to talk about?"

"Reece."

Kara felt a jolt rush through her, but she kept her eyes closed. "You don't waste time, do you?"

"Connor adores him, you know."

"Yeah."

"And I can tell he's good for you."

"Is my aura full of smiley faces or something?"

"You seem happier, more relaxed—probably because all that pent-up sexual energy has finally been released."

Kara said nothing, knowing that any objection would be a lie.

"And when you're with him, there's something in your eyes I haven't seen since before Connor was born." Her mother never mentioned Galen by name. "I'm really happy for you, Kara, and I don't want to see you screw this up."

Kara sat up, eyes open. "You're hardly the one to give advice on relationships, Mom."

"If by that you mean I've slept with every guru, shaman, and warlock on this side of the Rockies and am still alone, you're right. But you'd be wrong if you thought this is how I wanted my life to be."

"You always said my father's leaving was the best thing that ever happened to you." Kara hadn't heard her mother speak this seriously about anything in a long time.

"I only said that because I was hurt and angry. A man I thought loved me woke up one morning and decided he'd rather be someplace else. At first I was crushed. Then I was enraged, so furious that I wanted to tear his world apart."

Kara knew that kind of rage. She'd felt it when she'd lain alone in a hospital room swamped with contractions, the pain tearing her body apart. She'd felt it when she'd had to turn her precious eight-week-old son over to day care and return to work. She'd felt it when she'd been up all night with a crying baby, only to head to work early in the morning. And she felt it every time Connor asked about his daddy.

"Trouble was I couldn't hurt your father. He was gone. So I ended up tearing my own life apart. But you don't have to do that, Kara. Don't punish Reece for the sins of another man. Don't let your fear of being hurt again turn you away from a man who truly loves you."

As her mother rose and walked out of the bathroom, Kara was surprised to find tears streaming down her cheeks.

SESSION HAD just adjourned for a lunch break when Reece saw her walking toward him. She was dressed for business, but she looked like sex—a tailored black suit that hugged the curves of her body, her slender legs in black hose, her long hair hanging dark and sleek over her shoulders, her blouse buttoned one button too low. She walked straight toward him down the hallway, which was crowded with senators, aides, lobbyists, press, and assorted bottom-feeders.

He tossed his jacket over his shoulder and met her halfway. "Ms. McMillan. The *Denver Independent,* right?"

Her lips curved in a naughty smile. "Senator Sheridan. I was hoping you might have a few minutes. I have some questions."

He glanced at his watch and pretended to consider it. "Session resumes in about an hour, so I've got a few minutes. Would my office work?"

The elevator ride and the walk down the hallway almost killed him. He wanted to touch her, but he didn't dare. They made small talk, though Reese was hardly aware of a word they said. No sooner had he shut and locked his office door than they were on each other, kissing, their hands seeking the fastest way past clothing to skin. Reece opened a few buttons and found her breasts, while she yanked down his zipper and slipped her hand inside his boxers.

Her hand surrounded his erection, and she arched her breasts into his hands. "Now! Oh, God, now!"

He backed her against his desk, turned her so she faced away from him, lifted her skirt, and felt his lungs implode.

She was wearing stockings, garters, and *no panties.*

"Jesus Christ, Kara!" He bent her over, ran his hands over the bare curve of her ass, and savored the view and the feel of her. Then he nudged her thighs apart and, spurred by her impatient pleading, nudged his cock into her, his hands gripping her hips.

She was already wet, and she closed around him like a fist. He fought to stay with her, to make sure she enjoyed it, too. But the sight of her bowed over his desk, her bare ass exposed, his cock pounding into her, brought him hurtling toward the edge.

Quickly, he reached around, sought between her slick folds for her pert little clitoris, and stroked it. In a matter of moments, her breathing was ragged, each exhalation catching in her throat, threatening to become a full-fledged moan that could be heard in the hallway beyond. Her hands bunched into fists, crumpled paper, beat against the wood.

Faster, harder. She felt so damned good. Slick. Tight. Like heaven.

He felt the tension inside her peak and break. Her breath caught, and for a moment he was thought she was going to scream. But all that escaped was a long, shuddering sigh as her body shook with release. And then he was thrusting into her like a madman, lost in the hot rush of orgasm.

For a moment, they remained as they were, Reece still pulsing inside her, her body quivering around him. Then his phone rang, and he remembered exactly where they were. Slowly, reluctantly, he withdrew, turned her, and pulled her against him.

"Now, that's what I call a lunch break." He kissed her forehead and felt a surge of warmth when she rested her head against his chest and laughed.

"I can't believe we just did this! What if someone had walked in?"

"It would have been Monica's blue dress all over again. Speaking of which"—he reached for a box of tissues and handed her a few—"here."

In a few minutes, their clothes were back on straight, the scent of sex in the air the only sign that what had transpired wasn't an interview.

That and the stupid grin on your face, Sheridan.

Reece pulled her close, slipped a hand beneath her skirt, and cupped her bare buttocks. "Is this what you normally wear to the office? If it is, I'm going to have one hell of a time getting through the work day."

Kara looked up at him from beneath absurdly feminine lashes. "I actually only stopped by to ask if you'd like to come by tonight—say nine-thirty? The garters were just supposed to be incentive."

"That they were, sweetheart. If I'd have known what was

underneath your skirt, you'd have never made it out of the elevator, and the guys who staff the security cameras would have gotten a glimpse of the sweetest derriere on Earth."

That made her blush. "I need to go."

"I know." He ducked his head, took her mouth in a long, deep kiss, and then released her. "Nine-thirty. And wear the garters."

Not trusting himself to keep his hand off her, he waited until she'd gone to step out of his office. He found Galen Prentice threading toward him through the crowd. His tire-burning bill was up for second reading today. No doubt Prentice wanted to go over some of the objections that had arisen during first reading.

"Was that Kara McMillan who just walked out of your office?"

Instantly Reece was on guard. "She had some questions about one of my bills."

"Yeah. I know her—if you take my meaning." Prentice nodded, a self-satisfied smirk spreading across his face. "Watch out for her. She's a hot piece of ass, for sure, but she's not worth it. All she wants is to snag herself a successful husband. She tried trapping me a few years back. Got knocked up, then looked at me like I was supposed to marry her or some damned thing. I made it real clear I wasn't going to fall for that old trick, and—"

"You're the bastard who got her pregnant and left her!" Rage blazing white-hot in his gut, Reece grabbed the lapels of Prentice's pricey double-breasted jacket and backed him against the wall. "You ought to be rotting in a jail cell!"

Prentice's face turned red, and he tried to dislodge Reece with a shove. "Back off, Sheridan! Are you crazy?"

But blood hammered in Reece's ears. "It's against the law to desert your own child, Prentice!"

"It's not mine! I never wanted it!"

"That's not how the law works, and you know it!" Hearing Prentice refer to Connor as "it" did nothing to cool Reece's temper. He leaned forward until he was shouting into the man's face. "Maybe you didn't want a child, but you sure as hell were enthusiastic about fucking her, weren't you? A pretty young woman right out of college looks good to a middle-aged lawyer. Did you enjoy her? Did you brag to your friends how clever you were when you abandoned her?"

Prentice was sweating now, oily beads of perspiration on his balding head and upper lip. "Get away from me, or I'm going to press assault charges!"

With a jolt, Reece realized a crowd had gathered around them. He let go of Prentice's jacket but gave the man no room. "Watch what you say about her, Prentice. Think very hard before you open your mouth."

"Or what, Senator? You'll punch me?" Prentice slid sideways along the wall, his voice high pitched and panicky.

"She deserves better than you. They both do. Come to think of it, you did them both a favor."

There was a murmur in the crowd, and Reece heard Alan, the sergeant-at-arms, asking people to step aside. "What's going on, Senator? Is this man bothering you?"

"No, Alan, he was just leaving."

Prentice's nostrils flared, and his sweaty face turned red. "I have every right to be here! I wasn't bothering you! You attacked me!"

"Stay away from me, Prentice." Then Reece turned back toward his office, not noticing the reporter who stood nearby with her recorder, a look of excitement on her face.

KARA GLANCED at her watch—5:04.

She'd spent an hour at the DMV doing a bit of research and now sat parked across the street from the most recent address on file for Mr. Scott Hammond. For two weeks now, he'd been ignoring her messages, screening his calls. But he couldn't shake her off that easily. He had answers to some very important questions rattling around in that brain of his, and she needed to get at them.

She was watching for a 2001 silver Toyota Corolla with Colorado plates F1J-2390. By her estimates it was at least a twenty-minute commute from the state health department's offices to Hammond's home, a little '70s ranch-style house with a carport. But if Hammond were like most government employees, he'd left work early. It was Friday, after all. As every reporter knew, you didn't stand a prayer of reaching anyone in a government office after four-thirty on a Friday.

She sat back, her gaze on passing cars, her body still purring from her lunch tryst with Reece. She'd never done anything like that before. She'd gone to bed with her mother's disturbing words in her mind, but she'd woken up with the rudiments of a silly plan. The idea had been to pay Reece a quick visit, lift her skirt, and show him what he wasn't getting any of until later that night—if he was very lucky. She'd meant to turn him on, but walking around the office with the lace abrading her thighs, her privates bare, had made her blood burn. She'd been so turned on by the time she'd reached the Capitol that it had taken every ounce of self-control she possessed not to maul Reece in public. But the wait and the frustration had been worth it. When he'd bent her over his desk and pushed himself inside her, it had been absolute screaming heaven.

God, she got hot again just remembering it—and the fact that he was coming over tonight. It would be their first night together since Monday. Strange that four days without sex seemed like an eternity when she'd gone five years.

Headlights rounded the corner, momentarily blinding her. Then the car turned into Mr. Hammond's driveway and slid under the carport. A silver Toyota Corolla. It was 5:07.

"Your tax dollars at work." Kara slipped her digital recorder into the front pocket of her suit jacket, opened the car door, and met Mr. Hammond on his own front porch. He was a short man with thinning brown hair and the posture of someone who spent too much time hunched over a desk. "You're a hard man to get a hold of."

He gaped at her in astonishment and then looked around

as if to see who else might be there. "What are you doing here? You're going to get me fired—or worse!"

"There's no one here but me, Mr. Hammond. And I have some questions that need answers. You're the only one who can help me."

He looked at her, fear written on his face as plainly as words on a page. He pushed past her and stuck his key in the deadbolt. "I can't help. I'm sorry. Really, I am."

"I've seen your inspection reports, Mr. Hammond. I know you're a man who takes his job seriously. You want to protect people. You double-checked Northrup's math, caught them faking the numbers. Why weren't they prosecuted?"

He stepped through his front door and turned to face her. "I wish I could help you. I really do. But I've got a wife and two kids to feed. They'll be home any minute. I need you to leave now."

"Whistleblowers get federal protection, Mr. Hammond."

"Not when they're dead they don't."

CHAPTER 17

MR. HAMMOND tried to shut the door, but she stuck her foot in and blocked him.

"Off the record. Please, Mr. Hammond! Think of the whistleblower. He has kids, too. What happens to him if Northrup isn't held accountable? What happens to me? They may have broken into my house last weekend. I've got a son."

He met her gaze through brown eyes that held both compassion and great misgiving. "All right. But only five minutes. And everything is strictly background. Off the record."

"Agreed." She slipped inside before he could change his mind and noticed that he pulled the curtains shut before he turned the lights on. "I've read through about half of the documents so far, and I've found dozens of inspection reports that have your name on them. What I haven't found are successful prosecutions or even high fines. Tell me who's protecting Northrup."

He sat down on the overstuffed sofa, buried his face in his hands, and gave a nervous little laugh. "I suppose you want names. It's not that easy. All I know is that I do the inspections, turn in the reports, and after I'm thanked for doing a good job, it all disappears. State bureaucracy, Ms. McMillan."

"Don't try to tell me it's the system, Mr. Hammond. I don't buy that. Decisions are made by people. People have names."

"Start at the top. The governor, who gets big campaign donations from Northrup, tells my boss that he's gotten a complaint from Northrup that inspectors are picking on them. The director of the health department knows his ass is on the line because he was appointed by the governor, so he tells me to back off. How's that for starters?"

"You're saying the governor is in Northrup's pocket and is exerting pressure on your department to go easy on them?"

He gave another nervous laugh. "Yeah. That's part of it."

"Tell me the rest. How can major violations of state and federal environmental laws just disappear? Not even the governor can accomplish that, can he?"

Mr. Hammond looked at the floor and then met her gaze. "What is the single most powerful governmental body in the state?"

"The state legislature."

"Think smaller."

There was only one governmental body that held authority over the legislature. "The Legislative Audit Committee."

"Find the memo from the LAC, and you'll have your answer." He stood. "Now please leave. And please don't contact me again."

"It can't be the whole committee, Mr. Hammond. They would never act unanimously to protect a polluter."

He herded her toward the door. "Please go! Please. I'm sorry I can't help you more. And be careful."

"Why should I be careful, Mr. Hammond? Who wants to hurt me?"

But he had already shut the door.

KARA EXAMINED herself in the mirror. She wore the same thing she'd worn to work, but rather than a blouse beneath her jacket, she wore nothing, leaving her cleavage exposed from neck to navel. Her hair was coiled on top of her head. Lipstick as red as lust colored her lips. Scent was dabbed on her wrists, between her breasts, and onto her pubic hair. She was ready for him.

God, was she ready for him. It had taken no small amount of effort to make her way through dinner, bath time, and *Fox in Sox* tonight. Fortunately, Connor had exhausted himself playing dinosaurs at day care and fell asleep quickly, leaving her free to take a hot bath and prepare for Reece. She'd put fresh sheets on the bed, turned down the covers, and set candles around the room, candles she'd already lit. White wine chilled in the refrigerator, something Italian the wine store clerk had chosen for her when she'd pleaded for help. She'd sliced cheese and fruit to go with it, knowing they would be hungry afterward. It was the first time Reece would be spending time in her bed, and she wanted it to be just right.

Why it was so important that everything be perfect she couldn't say. She didn't want to think about that just now. All she knew was that she wanted him. She wanted him so badly that she ached with it. For tonight she wouldn't analyze it. She would just enjoy it.

She had just gone to check on Connor when she heard Reece's quiet knock on the door. Looking through the peephole to make certain it was he, she unlocked and opened the door. "Senator."

His face was lined with stress, but he smiled, his gaze raking over her. "Ms. McMillan."

Reece stepped inside and shut and locked the door behind him, all thoughts of his confrontation with Prentice dissipating at the sight of her. She was dressed much as she had been this afternoon—but with a few very noticeable differences. "You look incredible."

The smile she gave him was both shy and seductive. "Have you eaten supper yet?"

He tossed his jacket onto the new couch and pulled her against him, intent on smearing that obscenely red lipstick all over her mouth. "Who needs food?"

They kissed their way recklessly to the bedroom. Tongues invaded, twined, stroked. Teeth nipped, bit, bruised.

Hands fisted in hair, tore at clothing, fought to find skin.

Reece forced himself to let go of her and shut the door behind them. "Undress—everything but the garters and stockings."

Her pupils were dilated, her breathing unsteady. Her gaze never left his as she did as he asked, peeling off the jacket he'd already unbuttoned, unzipping her skirt, letting it fall to the floor. And then she stood before him, all but naked, the bared curves of her hips and ass and the lush triangle between her thighs framed by the black lace garters.

He felt the same rush of air from his lungs. But this time he was determined to go slowly. She was a banquet, and he was going to savor every bite. He let his gaze wander over her, let her hunger—and his—build. "Lie down."

She took two steps backward and lay down on her bed, her thighs parting just enough to give him a glimpse of paradise.

He took off his already loosened tie, knelt beside her, and heard her surprised intake of breath as she realized what he was going to do. He bound her wrists and tied them to one of the slats in her headboard. Then he yanked the pillow out from beneath her head—and slipped it beneath her hips.

Her breathing was fast, erratic, her nipples already hard and beaded. "Oh, Reece, now!"

"No." He let his hands enjoy the feel of her—the firmness of her breasts, the satin curve of her belly, the flare of her hips. He parted her thighs and drank in the sight of her, the scent of her. He slid his fingers lazily over her already damp cleft, then gave her swollen clitoris an idle flick.

Her body jerked, and she whimpered. "Now! Please!"

"No." She had taken him by surprise at the Capitol today. It was his turn to surprise her. "I hope you don't mind if I brought a friend. I thought we could have a little threesome tonight."

She gaped at him. "Wh-what?"

"I thought we'd try a little ménage à trois. You're much too hot for me to keep to myself. You're okay with that, aren't you?" He made an educated guess and reached over to open the drawer of her small bedside dresser, then pulled the purple device out of a frothy pile of panties. "It's just you, me—and Mr. Jiggle Stick."

She gasped and tried to sit up, but with her wrists tied, she could only writhe. It was sexy as hell. "Oh, no, Reece, you can't—!"

"Yes, I can. And there's nothing you can do to stop me." His cock strained rudely against his trousers, eager to get inside her. But he had other plans.

He turned on the vibrator, stretched out beside her, and chuckled at the embarrassed look on her face. Then he kissed her. While his tongue took her mouth, hard and deep, Mr. Jiggle Stick buzzed against her puckered nipples.

Her body jerked again, and she whimpered into his mouth, her hips rising off the pillow in search of release. But she would have to wait, to endure it, because he wasn't finished yet.

Where the vibrator went, Reece let his lips and tongue follow—over her nipples, down her belly, across her inner thighs. He savored the taste of her, his mind reeling with urgent, aching lust.

Kara forgot to feel embarrassed, forgot to think, forgot to breathe. Her skin was hypersensitive, every nerve awakened by the soft vibrations, so that the kisses, licks, and nips that followed were almost unbearable. She heard the unmistakable sounds of a woman lost in the bliss of sex, and her arousal rose a notch when she realized the sounds were coming from her own throat.

Then he touched the vibrator lightly to her clitoris.

She all but screamed.

But as she lifted her hips for more, he moved it away. "Uh-uh. Hold still."

"I can't!"

"Yes, you can." He moved the vibrator until it was a fraction of an inch away from her swollen flesh and held it there.

She bit her lip and fought to hold still, burning, aching, waiting.

When he let it touch her again, it was all she could do to keep from bucking against it. He rubbed it over her lightly, the vibrations making her inner muscles clench with pleasure so intense it almost hurt. Then he slipped a finger inside her and stroked her hard, until she was panting, pleading, begging.

Abruptly, the sensation stopped, and she moaned in desperation. She felt the mattress shift and opened her eyes to find him kneeling over her, a wicked grin on his face. "Now, Reece, please!"

"Mr. Jiggle Stick and I talked it over, and he gets to take you first." Then his hands clasped her already parted thighs, and he pushed her legs apart and back, opening her to him completely. "But when he's done with you, I'm going to fuck you long and hard."

She watched almost in disbelicf as he sank between her thighs, the buzzing vibrator in one hand. She realized what he meant to do seconds before he did it. "Oh, jeez!"

"Don't be afraid. I won't let him hurt you." He nudged the vibrator into her, one slow inch at a time, until she whimpered with impatience. When its length was deep inside her, he turned it on high. Then his mouth lowered and closed over her.

"Oh! Oh, my God! Reece!" They werc the last intelligible words she spoke. It was too much, too much. The vibrator gliding slowly, slickly, in and out of her, hard and pulsing. Reece's tongue and lips torturing her swollen flesh. The sound of his aroused groans.

It didn't seem possible that anything could feel this good. She was lost in pleasure, lost in lust, lost in her body's need. Overwhelmed, she tried to fight back the climax that surged toward her, to ride the crest. But he was relentless. Before shc could climb on top of the current, before she had any chance to control it, the wave overtook her and plunged her into ecstasy.

The strangled scream that came out of her throat sounded wild, almost more animal than human. Only the weight of his arm, thrown across her hips at the last second, kept her from coming off the pillow. Holding her down, he kept up his assault and forced her to ride out the pleasure until she lay weak and trembling, bliss lapping at her like quiet surf.

She shuddered when he withdrew the vibrator, and her eyes snapped open when she heard the zipper on his trousers. He knelt between her thighs, his shirt unbuttoned to reveal luscious muscles she couldn't touch, his erection jutting from his pants, demanding and erotic.

His voice was rough. "He's had you. Now it's my turn." He grasped her hips, and with one slow thrust he was deep inside her, thick and hard.

"Oh, yes, Reece, yes!"

And as his sure strokes drove her once more over the brink and he emptied himself inside her, there was nothing in the world for her—nothing—but him.

REECE WAS deep asleep, Kara's naked body pressed against his, when he heard it. A thud. Unmistakable, it jerked him from dreams to wakefulness.

He sat up, listened.

Other than Kara's murmur as she snuggled into him, he heard only silence. He had just started to lie down again when it came again, much louder this time.

Kara bolted upright, eyes wide, sheet clutched to her breasts. "Someone's out there! On the deck!"

The fear on her face sent tentacles of anger twining through his gut. Reece got out of bed and, still naked, strode toward the bedroom door. "Stay here. If anything happens, push the panic button."

"But I should be the one to check! It's my house, and you shouldn't have to do it just because you're the man."

He cast her a withering glance that was probably lost in the darkness. "Burn a bra if you want, but don't be ridiculous!"

"Reece!"

"What?"

"Be careful!"

His heart gave an extra beat. So she was worried about him. He liked that. "I will. Now stay here."

Kara watched him disappear down the hallway, her heart pounding deafeningly in her ears. She felt stupid cowering in her bed while he went to face danger alone. She had just climbed out of bed and wrapped the sheet around herself when she heard him call for her in a loud whisper.

"Kara, come see your night prowlers."

She hurried down the hallway and found him staring out the sliding glass door, the porch light casting the valleys and ridges of his naked body in high relief.

He held out his hand. "It's okay. You'll see."

She took his hand, looked out the door, and saw three masked intruders. "The thieving, little pigs! That's who's been eating the bird food. Don't they need to go hibernate or something?"

"Raccoons aren't true hibernators. When it gets warm, they come out to forage."

She couldn't help but laugh as they cast her guilty looks and kept eating. "I can't believe they climbed up there. They look ridiculous!"

"They have opposable thumbs, you know."

Where did he learn this stuff? "Thanks, Dr. Doolittle."

Then she turned and found herself staring at his naked body in all its glory. He looked like a classical statue—except for the part of him that was steadily growing thicker, harder, and longer. She met his gaze and smiled.

He shook his head. "It's two in the morning, Kara. We have to get up in three hours, remember?"

"Last one in bed gives head." She turned and ran, stifling giggles, back toward the bedroom, Reece one step behind her.

IT WAS only later, after she'd given him the blowjob of his life and lay asleep beside him, that Reece realized he'd forgotten to tell her about his confrontation with Prentice.

* * *

HE DIDN'T tell her in the morning either. Somehow, Kara's alarm didn't go off, and the two of them were awakened by a curious four-year-old, who climbed into bed between them, looked Reece in the eye, and asked, "Are you having sex with my mommy?"

Still half asleep and unsure what Kara would want him to say, Reece mumbled, "Not at the moment." Then he nudged Kara awake.

In the mad rush to get everyone presentable and off to the office and day care on time, he'd quite simply forgotten. But when he got to the Capitol and picked up the papers he realized what a huge mistake that was.

There on the front page of the state section in full color was a photograph of him face-to-face with Prentice above an article with the headline, "Senator Sheridan, local attorney come close to blows: Woman at heart of dispute."

Coffee turned to lead in his stomach as he read an almost verbatim account of his encounter with Prentice. "Sheridan then shouted, 'Maybe you didn't want a child, but you sure as hell were enthusiastic about [expletive deleted] her, weren't you? A pretty young woman right out of college looks good to a middle-aged lawyer. Did you enjoy her? Did you brag to your friends how clever you were when you abandoned her?' "

But it was the second-to-last paragraph that clinched it. "The identity of the woman in question is uncertain, but a recent police report linked Sheridan with Kara McMillan, an investigative reporter and columnist with the *Denver Independent*. McMillan, a single mother, and Sheridan, who is also unmarried, were not available for comment Thursday evening."

He buried his face in his hands and cursed his own stupidity.

Way to fuck it all up, buddy. The voters will think you're a psychopath, and you'll be lucky if Kara ever speaks with you again.

He took a deep breath, reached for the phone, and dialed, hoping he would reach her before the newspaper did.

KARA FELT her cell phone vibrate but barely noticed it as she read to the bottom of the article. Blood thrummed in her ears. The floor seemed to tilt. How could this have happened? Why hadn't Reece warned her?

The identity of the woman in question is uncertain, but a recent police report linked Sheridan with Kara McMillan, an investigative reporter and columnist with the Denver Independent.

Tom had called her into his office the moment she'd stepped into the office and tossed the paper in her face. Now he sat staring up at her through those flat eyes of his.

She dropped the paper back on his desk and fought to smooth over her shock. "I knew nothing about this, nor was I there. I'm sorry the newspaper was mentioned in the article, but it was hardly my fault."

"Reporters are not supposed to lead lives that become the subject of public speculation, McMillan."

"No, they're not." There was no way around that.

"Your boytoy is a state senator, a controversial public figure."

She winced at his choice of words and felt shock flare into temper. "He's hardly my boytoy. Senator Sheridan is a close—"

"I don't care what he is!" Tom's voice boomed through the office. "You're fucking a state senator, and it's making news! At least if you were plying him for information, getting him to spill insider secrets, I could respect it! But I can't put up with a member of my staff sleeping with the enemy and compromising this newspaper!"

Kara gaped at him in disgust, turned her back on him, and jerked open his office door.

"I didn't give you permission to leave!"

She spun around in the open doorway and faced him,

beyond fury. "Tom, you are such a dick! Does anyone here question you when you choose to screw members of your own staff? That's worse than sleeping with the enemy. That's a lawsuit! Talk about compromising the newspaper!"

The stony mask slipped from his face, and he glared at her. "You are crossing the line, McMillan."

"*You* crossed the line, Tom. I'm damn good at my job, and I'm tired of your bullshit! If it's not who I have sex with, then it's the fact that I'm a mother. Has anything ever compromised my ability to do my job? No! So quit your goddamned yelling and talk to me with some measure of respect, or I'll quit and take this story across town!"

"I'm writing you up for this."

"You do that." Shaking with anger and sure she was about to cry, she turned and walked into a stunned and silent newsroom.

CHAPTER 18

Kara was sitting at her desk, trying hard to focus on the documents in front of her, when the roses arrived. Two dozen blood-red, long-stem roses in a vase of Orrefors crystal. She ignored Matt's whistles and taunts as the delivery woman placed the flowers on her desk. She also ignored the little card that came with the flowers. She knew who'd sent them.

She'd gotten the message Reece had left on her cell and had heard his version of the story, or at least part of it: Galen had seen her leaving Reece's office and had taken it upon himself to reveal her past and to say unflattering things about her to Reece, who'd leapt to her defense, not knowing a reporter was standing only feet away. His message said he'd meant to tell her about the confrontation last night but had gotten distracted.

How could she have been so stupid? She'd known from the beginning that getting involved with a politician was a bad idea. She'd known it would put her job at risk. She'd known it had the potential to shatter the fragile china-doll balance of her life. She'd walked into it with her eyes open. She'd even gone to his place of work and had sex on his desk, for God's sake! Now Reece was getting bad ink, and she'd been written up for the first time in her career.

Worse than that—far worse than that—anyone who knew her and had read the article could now speculate that Galen was Connor's father. It was a secret she'd kept from everyone except her mother and Holly. Galen's name wasn't even on Connor's birth certificate. Somehow it had seemed kinder to allow Connor to wonder who his father was than to give him the name of a man who didn't care that he even existed. And if she were honest with herself, it had taken some of the pain out of Galen's rejection and his accusations to simply deny his involvement with her child.

But now that fact was a matter of cheap gossip.

Well done, McMillan. Frigging brilliant.

Anger seethed in her belly. Anger at Tom, at Galen, at Reece. Anger at herself.

Pretending the roses weren't sitting there, she forced her gaze back onto the folder in her hands. Mr. Hammond had told her to look for the memo from the Legislative Audit Committee, and that's what she was doing. No one had yet entered it into the database, so she was now going page by page through the thousand or so pages that had yet to be documented. If it was here, she would find it. If it wasn't, she would drive over to the health department and raise hell.

"Damn it!" She dropped the folder onto her desk and faced the roses.

They were truly lovely, their scent heady enough to rise above the office odors of stale newsprint, cleaning products, and coffee. She reached for the card and tore open the envelope. On a card of plain white was an apology.

I am sorry to the bottom of my heart. Reece.

He'd signed it himself. She recognized his handwriting.

"What does it say?"

She turned to find Tessa and Sophie standing behind her. She tossed them the card and went back to her work.

"Bless his heart!" That was Tessa's standard southern belle response to everything, so Kara ignored it. "I like this guy more and more every day."

Sophie rolled a spare chair up next to her, making it clear this invasion of space wasn't over yet. "Kara, I think it's time we had a girls' night out. It's been ages."

Kara set the papers aside and turned to her friends. "I know you both mean well, but right now all I want to do is get the Northrup story and this entire damned day behind me. I don't want to talk. I don't want sympathy. I don't want advice."

"Which is why you need it," Sophie insisted. "It will be great—you, me, Tess, Holly, and Connor. We'll go to Red Robin. Connor will be so distracted by the fries and balloons he won't realize what we're talking about."

Kara moaned and buried her face in her hands, remembering Connor's words this morning.

Are you having sex with my mommy?

"Oh, lord!" They were supposed to have woken up early enough for Reece to leave before Connor got out of bed. But Kara had somehow turned off the alarm in her sleep—or been so preoccupied that she'd forgotten to set it.

"Ah, poor baby!" Tessa cooed. "Look at her! She's a damned wreck. I could kick Tom's ass."

"You'll have to beat me to it, Tess." Sophie put a hand on Kara's shoulder and gave her a squeeze. "You're not squeaking out of this, kid. If you try, we'll show up at your front door with a bottle of tequila."

"Beautiful." Kara knew better than to think Sophie was bluffing. "All right. You win. Red Robin at six."

SHE HADN'T returned his calls. He knew she'd gotten the roses, because he'd called the florist to make certain. Clearly, she was furious with him. Hell, he was furious with himself. While Prentice certainly deserved everything he'd gotten and more, Reece had let his temper get the best of him and, in trying to stand up for Kara, he'd dragged her into the mud. He'd handled the situation poorly, and she was paying the price.

Certainly, the incident wasn't likely to boost his political career. But it wasn't likely to hurt him, either. It would die down once the press found some other morsel to chew on.

No one was going to fire him. If something like this was enough to keep him from getting elected for a second term then he probably wasn't pleasing his constituents in the first place. Besides, teaching, not politics, was his job.

He picked up the phone, intending to call legislative legal and get an update on his request for a list of all open-records requests Kara had filed, when his fingers dialed the *Independent*. "Kara McMillan, please."

To his surprise, she was at her desk and took the call. He heard ice slide into her voice when she realized it was he. "I can't talk now."

"I'll come by tonight. We can talk then."

"I won't be home." She said it with finality.

"You're angry, and I don't blame you."

"I came close to losing my job today, and the entire newsroom is now speculating on my love life and Connor's paternity. You bet I'm angry!" A quaver in her voice hinted at tears.

The jagged edge of regret pressed into his gut. "God, I'm sorry, Kara. He said things . . . There's no excuse. I lost my temper."

"That part of my life is private." Her voice was a strained whisper, and he knew she was trying to keep from being overheard. "You had no right getting involved, no matter what he said!"

"I shouldn't have lost control. But hell, Kara, I had just made love with you and then he came along." How could he explain what it was like to still have the scent of a woman on your skin and then have to listen while another man bragged about abusing her? But Reece was making excuses. There were no excuses—except perhaps one. "I care about you, Kara. And I care about Connor, too."

She gave a joyless laugh. "We need to talk about that."

He could tell where this was headed. "Don't try to shut me out, Kara. We both know there's more to this relationship than sex."

He could hear the hesitation in her silence. "I have to go."

So did he. He needed to call legislative legal, and he was due on the Senate floor in forty-five minutes. "I know. I'll call."

Then, with so many things still left unspoken between them, he hung up the phone.

IT WAS late afternoon when Kara found it. An innocuous-looking memo, it was dated last November and stamped "CONFIDENTIAL" in big, red letters. She read through it quickly, shaking her head in disgust.

Mr. Hammond's continual pursuit of Northrup raises disturbing questions about his objectivity and his ability to conduct his duties in a rational manner. After reviewing his inspection reports, it is clear that there are improprieties in his conduct and the manner in which this inspection was carried out. Further harassment of Northrup could result in a performance audit of the air-quality division.

The threat was clear. Leave Northrup alone, or heads will roll. The signature on the document was blacked out with heavy marker. But the letter had been written on Legislative Audit Committee letterhead. Clearly, someone on the committee was in Northrup's pocket and was using his or her authority to derail the health department's enforcement efforts by threatening people's jobs. It was her job to figure out who had sent the memo.

What fun it was going to be to interview the committee's members one by one with this tidbit in her arsenal. By the time she was done with them, they would probably hate her, but that went with the job. She would write up an open-records request for each one of them, scrutinize their e-mails, their bills past and present, their campaign accounts. She would find out where their relatives worked, where they owned stock, where they'd worked before going into politics. She would find out which one of them had ties to Northrup, and she would give that person front-page exposure.

She turned to her computer, called up the state legislature's home page, and clicked on Legislative Audit Committee. It had eight members—four from each party—their photographs arranged in alphabetical order. Last on the page gazing back at her with that familiar sexy smile was Senator Reece Sheridan.

KARA WIPED ketchup from Connor's shirt with a spare napkin and set the remainder of his hamburger back on his plate. "There you go, pumpkin."

Across from her Tessa sipped her iced tea daintily and nibbled on her cheeseburger. "If you ask me—and I know you haven't—you should be baking you-know-who a nice cake, not giving him a hard time. He's the one whose picture's in the paper."

"That's your advice? Bake him a cake?" Kara rolled her eyes.

Sophie leaned forward as if imparting a secret. "He thought he was protecting you. He got all angry and male for you. He went to the mat for you, Kara."

Holly groaned. "If you weren't so damned afraid of men you'd see that. And that creep finally got a bit of what he deserves. I think you-know-who is a hero."

Kara eyed Holly's scant dinner of a side salad and a Diet Coke and tried again to change the subject. "And if you didn't starve yourself to death you wouldn't be so grouchy."

"Well, if you don't appreciate him, I do. I like good, strong men. Can I have his phone number?" Tessa popped a fry in her mouth and met Kara's glare with innocent blue eyes.

"You'll have to arm wrestle me, Tess," said Sophie. "I was going to try to seduce him into having an affair with me behind Kara's back, but if she's going to end it—"

"Arm wrestle? Hell, I'll just hit you on the head with a brick when you're not looking. I keep one in my purse for just such an occasion." Tessa smiled sweetly, then bent over to kiss Connor on the head. "Is that tasty, sugar?"

"You two forget that I've already met him." Holly winked at Kara. "If Kara dumps him, he's mine."

"You all act like he and I are about ready to register for gifts or something. It's not like that. There's no way he and I could ever have a long-term relationship." *Especially now.*

Kara had written up eight comprehensive open-records requests before leaving work today. They were the most thorough, far-reaching requests she'd ever written, and one of them had Reece's name on it. Even if they were able to work past what had happened today, she couldn't date a man she was investigating.

"Now you sound like Tom." Tessa made a decidedly unladylike face. "Oh, sometimes I hate that man!"

"You said it, Tess. I can't believe he asked about the safety of the whistleblower videotapes but had nothing to say about the fact that someone had trashed your home, Kara. You're more important than frigging tapes. He's such an insensitive S.O.B.!"

Holly finished her lettuce and gazed longingly at everyone's fries. "I heard you called him a D-I-C-K. Wish I'd been there to hear it."

"Yeah, I got myself written up. It was great." Kara shoved the rest of her guacamole burger aside. She wasn't hungry tonight. "Tom's an amazing journalist, you know."

Tessa popped another fry into her mouth. "Yeah? Well, too bad he's such a rotten human being."

"Mommy, can I go see the race car?" Connor fidgeted impatiently in his booster chair.

"Are you full?"

"Yes, he is." Holly stood and lifted him to the ground. "I've got a pocket full of quarters just for you, Connor. You and Auntie Holly are going to play with the arcade games while your mommy has a nice chat with her friends." Then Holly leaned in and whispered to Tess and Sophie loudly enough for Kara to hear. "Get details! I want to know what he's like in bed!"

Kara wished she could share in her friends' good humor,

but as she watched Holly lead Connor down the balloon-filled hallway, all she could feel was a dark hole in her chest.

REECE DROPPED the empty carton of Chinese takeout into the trash and glanced at his watch. It was almost eleven. Outside his window, the lights of Denver sparked white in the darkness, the streets almost empty. He could finish reading this last bill, head over to the twenty-four-hour gym for a hard workout, and make it home to bed by two. And maybe, if he was lucky, he'd be able to lie down in his bed, alone, and not think of Kara.

He needed the workout. He'd been a senator for two years now, and today was easily his most frustrating day in office. And not just because he'd ended up on the front page of the state section and hurt the woman who mattered most to him. His call to legislative legal had ended with stonewalling. The person who had promised so helpfully to track down a list of Kara's open-records requests had put him on hold for almost twenty minutes before telling him she'd made a mistake. It would be impossible for the state's attorney to give him that information because most requests didn't come through their office, she'd said. Reece knew a lame excuse when he heard one, and he'd realized immediately that he was getting the runaround. He'd asked to speak with the state attorney himself and gotten only voicemail.

Then he'd had to watch as his fellow senators had killed his urban-growth bill by a mere two votes. Devlin had lobbied hard against that one and had leered like a street thug when the final vote was counted. Reece doubted Devlin actually had anything against the bill itself, merely the senator who had proposed it. If Reece were to carry a bill declaring the earth round and the sky blue, the bastard would probably vote against it, too.

He glanced back down at the page, tried to concentrate on the words, and saw green-gold eyes. If all she wanted with him was sex, he wasn't interested. She meant too much to him for him to settle for them being mere sex buddies. But what were they then? They'd never had the relationship talk because she'd avoided it. He hadn't pushed because there'd been no reason to force the issue. And, truth be told, his feelings for her had taken him by surprise. He'd expected good conversation and good sex. What he hadn't expected was for her to move so quickly into the center of his universe.

But was he at the center of hers? No, that space was reserved for Connor, and he couldn't argue with that. Nor did it bother him that so far he'd had to do almost all of the giving. He knew she'd been badly hurt. He was more than willing to do more than his share and see where it took them. But what he couldn't tolerate was being shut out.

He looked out the window into the darkness and considered something that hadn't occurred to him before. Was it possible that he'd connected with her precisely because she shut him out? Was he still the hurt little boy whose mother had left him?

No, he decided. That was behind him.

He stood, tossed his tie and a stack of unread bill summaries into his briefcase, and clicked it shut. She was angry, and she had every right to be. He would call her tomorrow, and somehow they would work through this.

He locked up his office and walked down the empty hallway toward the elevators, his shoes making clicking sounds against the polished marble. When he rounded the corner, he saw Alexis standing there, dressed to win votes in a fitted suit of mauve silk. She was talking to one of the newer House members, her hand on his arm.

On second thought, Reece would take the stairs.

KARA STARED at the ceiling in her darkened bedroom, unable to sleep. She could smell him on the pillows, spice and man. She could smell both of them, the scent of sex lingering in sheets she hadn't had time to change. She glanced at her clock.

It was eleven-ten. He was still awake. She could call his cell, apologize for being so cold to him, and thank him for the flowers. It was true that what he'd done had hurt her, but she knew he hadn't meant things to turn out that way.

He went to the mat for you, Kara.

Sophie's words echoed in her mind, not for the first time since dinner. Had a man ever stood up for her like this before, risked anything for her before? Her father hadn't. Galen hadn't. Tom hadn't.

Kara flicked on her bedside light, picked the paper up off the floor where she'd dropped it, and read what they'd quoted Reece as saying.

Sheridan then shouted, "Maybe you didn't want a child, but you sure as hell were enthusiastic about [expletive deleted] her, weren't you? A pretty young woman right out of college looks good to a middle-aged lawyer. Did you enjoy her? Did you brag to your friends how clever you were when you abandoned her?"

It was almost painful to read the words, even more difficult to see the photograph of Reece glaring angrily into Galen's face—her present and her past colliding where everyone could see it, read about it.

But one thing was clear. Reece had stood up for her.

God, how she wanted to call him. But nothing changed the fact that he was now part of her investigation. And no matter what she felt for him, no matter how badly she wanted to be with him, she couldn't compromise the investigation.

She had just switched off her light when she heard the unmistakable sound of something moving on her deck. Her pulse skipped, and she found herself on her feet, staring down the dark hallway toward the kitchen, panic button in hand.

You're being silly, McMillan. It's just raccoons.

Irritated with herself, she went to shoo them away.

CHAPTER 19

KARA HURRIED down the hallway, past Connor's darkened room, past the bathroom with its reassuring nightlight, feeling strangely naked in her nightgown. The kitchen floor was cold against her feet as she stepped silently toward the sliding glass door.

Behind her the refrigerator kicked on and made her jump.

Outside, something was moving.

Raccoons, McMillan. Cute, furry garbage-eaters.

She hesitated for a moment, then swore at herself. She was letting the bastards get to her, allowing the threats and the break-in to make her afraid. She released the breath she hadn't realized she was holding, took one last step, and pushed the curtain aside.

Beyond the deck, two raccoons ran for the cover of darkness.

Kara heaved a sigh of relief and watched as their fat, ringed tails disappeared into the shadows beyond the range of the porch light. She would have to move the birdfeeders. She didn't want to deal with this silliness every night.

The man appeared out of nowhere. Dressed in black, he was just there, a dark shadow against the glass. As if in slow motion, he raised his hand.

A gun.

Kara's heart gave a violent lurch, one hard hammer stroke of terror. She dove for the cover of the cupboards on her right, a strangled scream in her throat, fear like poison in her veins. Then she remembered what she held in her hand, and she pressed the panic button once, twice, three times.

There was a loud pop and the sound of breaking glass. He was using bullets to break through the door. And when he got in he would use bullets on her.

She was on her feet and running before he fired the second shot, only one thought in her mind.

Connor. She had to protect Connor.

She could hear him crying, hear him calling for her. He stood in the hallway in his Power Ranger pajamas, teddy bear clutched in his arms. He started to run toward her.

She held out her hand to stop him. "No! Go back! Get under your bed, Connor! Go! Hide! Now! Run!"

"Mommy!" The fear and confusion on his face broke her heart.

"Connor, listen to me! There's a bad man! Get under your bed! Hide fast! Good boy! Quiet now! Stay there! Don't come out no matter what, do you hear me?"

Shattered glass fell like rain against the kitchen floor, followed by the heavy tread of booted feet. He was coming for her.

She had to fight him. She had to fight him to protect Connor. But she had nothing.

She jerked open the coat closet, grabbed Connor's little wooden baseball bat, then pressed herself up against the hallway wall, heartbeat thrumming sickeningly in her ears, her blood turned to ice.

"Come here, bitch, and I'll go easy on you." His voice was close, just around the corner by the refrigerator. "You might even like it."

She forced herself to wait, held her breath. And then she saw it. The tip of his boot. She leapt out and swung the bat as hard as she could toward his face. "Not in this lifetime, you bastard!"

He bellowed in outrage as the bat struck his bent arms and drove the gun against his nose. The gun flew from his grasp, slid out of sight under the kitchen table.

She swung again, aiming for his head.

But this time he was ready. One hand still pressed to his bleeding nose, he deflected the blow, yanked the bat from her arms, and threw it aside. He was a big man and outweighed her by a hundred pounds.

She ran for the front door, hoping to lure him outside, away from Connor.

But he was fast. She'd only just turned the deadbolt when he grabbed her hair and jerked her painfully backward.

His breath was hot and foul on her cheek. "Fucking bitch! You broke my nose!"

"Tell someone who cares!" She drove an elbow into his gut and encountered a wall of muscle.

Where were the police? What if the button hadn't worked?

He slammed her into the door as if she were a rag doll. "I want the tapes. I want the documents. And you're going to fetch them for me like a good little girl."

So it was Northrup. Anger swelled from inside her and blotted out her fear. "Go to hell!"

He hurled her across the room. "Stupid bitch, you don't get it, do you?"

She fell across the coffee table, heard bone break and felt the air leave her lungs in a painful rush. She rolled to the floor, tried to crawl away, but the toe of his boot caught her in the stomach and left her gasping in pain. She rolled onto her back, kicked at him, striking his knee and stomach.

He grunted and swore, blood still pouring heavily from his nose. Then his fist caught her cheek and sent a shockwave of light, of agony, through her brain.

She was only vaguely aware of the hands that lifted her nightgown, of the tears that trickled down her cheeks, of the knee that forced her thighs apart or the hands that encircled her throat and squeezed.

"When I'm done with you, you'll do anything I tell you to do. Or maybe I should let you die with me inside you."

Then the room exploded.

REECE SLIPPED a jazz mix into his CD player, turned east on Fourteenth, and headed toward the gym. He resisted the urge to turn left onto Corona, and instead let the street pass. She was probably asleep by now. If he showed up on her doorstep at eleven-fifteen at night, he would probably succeed only in scaring her. He needed to give her space, give her time to work through whatever she was feeling. A little time to think wouldn't hurt him, either. Or so he told himself.

Ahead of him, the blue-white-red of police lights flashed as two squad cars raced toward him, headed west. He pulled over to the side of the road. They were running silent, doing at least fifty. Then they slowed and, one by one, turned left onto Corona, their lights filling his rearview mirror.

Kara.

He waited until the last car had passed, then pulled an illegal U-turn and followed them, hoping to God he was wrong. But the squad cars had already pulled to a stop in front of her house, joining a third that was parked in her driveway. Two armed officers raced toward the front door, while two more circled toward the backyard.

"Damn it!" Reece pulled over, leapt from his Jeep, and ran.

"Stop where you are! Police!"

It took a moment for him to realize the command was meant for him. He stopped and raised his arms. "I'm Sen—"

Beefy hands slammed into his back. "Lie down on your stomach, hands behind your head! Now!"

Seething, Reece knew he had no choice unless he wanted holes in a few vital organs. He lay flat on the pavement and locked his hands behind his head. "I'm Senator Reece Sheridan. This is my girlfriend's house."

"Stay down!" A cop kicked his legs apart and began to pat him down.

"My ID is in my rear pocket. This is my girlfriend's house, and I need to know if she and her son are all right!"

The cop's hands roamed over his torso and then reached for his wallet. "I don't care who you are. Stay down!"

"Let the senator up, Fisher." It was Chief Irving's voice. "Sorry, Senator. The men are just doing their job."

Reece rose and took his wallet from the cop's hands. "Thanks. Where's Kara? What happened?"

A burst of static came over Chief Irving's radio. "Affirmative. We need an ambulance and a body bag. Someone needs to call out the medical examiner and Child Protective Services. There's a little kid in here scared to death."

Body bag. Medical examiner.

"Christ, Kara!" Reece ran, heedless of Chief Irving's shouts, heedless of the fact that everyone around him was armed. He pushed through the front door and then he saw her.

She lay on her back on the carpet, pale as death, the white of her nightgown stained with blood, her face bruised. Dark bruises ringed her throat. Her nightgown rode high on her thighs, as if she'd been raped.

But she was shivering. *She was alive.*

A mixture of relief and helpless rage surged through him, and he threaded his way past the uniforms to her side.

"Who the hell are you?" A cop grabbed his shoulder.

Reece brushed the hand away, knelt next to her, and cupped her cheek. "Kara, sweetheart, can you hear me? It's Reece."

Her head turned toward him, and her eyes fluttered open. Her voice was weak, her breathing erratic. "Reece?"

"I'm right here. You're going to be okay, Kara. An ambulance is on its way."

She shivered violently, clearly in shock. "Connor. Help him."

He gave her hand a squeeze, slipped out of his jacket, and covered her with it. "I'll watch over him." He turned to the cops. "Where's the boy?"

"He's under his bed, and he won't come out."

Reece started down the hallway but stopped when he saw the body sprawled on the kitchen floor in a pool of crimson.

"He dove for that piece." The cop nodded toward a Glock .45 auto that lay on the floor like an abandoned toy. "Now he's dead. Looks like she roughed him up some. Not his night."

"No." Reece turned his back on death and followed the sound of a child's crying. He found an officer crouched down next to Connor's bed, crooning to the boy, who called for his mother with a tiny, frightened voice. No doubt the officer's uniform and gun were doing little to soothe the child's fears. "Leave me alone with him, please."

"If you say so." The cop stood and walked off.

Outside, sirens signaled the arrival of the ambulance.

Reece knelt down and spied Connor backed into the far corner on his belly, teddy bear clutched to his face. "Connor, buddy, it's me. It's Reece. It's safe now. Your mommy sent me to find you."

Connor looked up, his eyes wide with fear, and he hiccupped. Then, as if his life depended on it, he crawled forward on his belly and threw himself into Reece's arms. He smelled like baby shampoo, and his little arms were wrapped tightly around Reece's neck.

Some unfamiliar and fierce emotion surged from Reece's gut. He hugged Connor tightly and whispered reassurances in his ear. "You were a very brave boy. Your mommy is going to be so happy to see you. But she's got to go see some doctors now."

"The b-bad m-man hurt her." The child was quaking like a leaf.

Reece found himself wishing he'd pulled the trigger that had brought that bastard down. "Yes, but he won't hurt anyone ever again."

"The p-policeman shot him."

Why did a child have to know any of this? Reece stroked his downy hair. "Yes, he did. They came to help you and your mommy. Now it's all over, and you're safe. Would you like to stay with me until your grandma comes?"

Connor nodded.

WHERE WAS Reece? He had been here. She was sure of it.

And where was Connor? Dear God, was Connor okay?

Kara's mind drifted between numbness and pain, oblivion and fear. It hurt to breathe. It hurt to open her eyes. It hurt to talk. But still she called for them.

She was cold, so cold.

A man in a white shirt put something over her mouth and shined a light in her eyes.

"Pupils responsive. BP is seventy over forty. She's going shocky. Let's get an IV started."

What had happened? "Reece!"

She felt hands reach inside her nightgown and tried to fight them off.

"It's okay, darlin'." The man's voice was soothing. "I'm just hooking you up to the monitor."

Monitor? Nothing made sense. "Reece!"

"Possible right pneumothorax. Possible skull fracture. Let's get her under transport."

She was hurt, and they were taking her to a hospital.

She felt herself being lifted and cried out against the pain.

"Sorry, darlin'. I know it hurts. Let's go."

Cold air brushed her face, then a warm hand.

"We'll be right behind you, Kara."

She opened her eyes and saw them—Reece and Connor. Reece had wrapped Connor in a blanket and was holding him.

She reached for her son, tried to smile, and winced as she took air into her lungs to speak. "I'll see you later, pumpkin. Reece, take care of him."

He kissed her hand. "You know I will."

When the darkness sucked her down again, she gave in to it, let herself go.

* * *

REECE SAT across from Lily McMillan in the hospital dining room and watched as she cut up her grandson's pancakes. It had been a long night for all of them. Connor at least had gotten some sleep, much of it on Reece's lap.

Reece had reached Lily on his cell, and she'd met them at University Hospital, her face white with worry for her daughter. He'd told her what he knew—that an armed man twice Kara's size had broken into her home and that she'd somehow fought him off long enough for the police to arrive and save her life and Connor's.

"Did he rape her?" Lily had asked, a woman's knowing fear in her eyes, eyes that reminded Reece so much of Kara's.

Rage had burned hot in his stomach. "I don't know. It looked like he at least tried to."

They'd whisked Kara off for a CT scan and X rays, giving Reece an hour or so to talk with Lily, who, beneath her granola exterior, had a sharp mind and loved her daughter fiercely. When the doctor had emerged, his face drawn with fatigue, she had slipped her hand through his—whether to offer support or seeking it, he wasn't sure. But he'd liked how it had felt.

The doctor had then explained that Kara had a concussion, two broken ribs, a collapsed lung, some trauma to her trachea, and dozens of scrapes and bruises. Though they'd feared she was bleeding internally, nothing had been picked up on the CT scan. The rape kit they'd performed on her was inconclusive. Although bruises between her thighs made it clear her attacker had tried to sexually assault her and they'd seen live sperm on the slide, there had been no visible ejaculate and no vaginal trauma.

"I'm inclined to think she had sex in the past couple of days and the sperm we found are hardy survivors."

Reece felt it was his responsibility to speak. "I was with her last night."

He felt Lily squeeze his hand, a gesture of unity.

The doctor nodded. "That makes perfect sense, then. I'm disinclined to believe she was raped. He was so rough in every other way, I can't believe that he could have penetrated her without causing tears or bruising."

Thank God. At least she had been spared that.

"She's going to be here for at least a few days, possibly a few weeks. With head injuries it's sometimes hard to know how a patient will be affected. The concussion is probably her most serious injury, though a bruised trachea is also serious."

Lily's voice had quavered slightly, just as Kara's did when she was fighting tears. "Bruised trachea?"

"He tried to strangle your daughter, ma'am. We're observing her closely to make certain her trachea doesn't swell and cut off her breathing. If it does, we'll have to intubate her or perform a tracheotomy. Right now, she's sleeping comfortably. We're giving her morphine. You can go see her if you'd like."

Lily had spent the night in Kara's room with Connor, sleeping on a cot, while Reece had paced angrily in the waiting room, waiting for dawn.

He drank his coffee and finished his breakfast, while Lily listened to Connor's retelling of his scary night.

"You were a very brave boy, Connor. Your momma is so proud of you!"

Connor smiled shyly, his lips curving beneath a milk mustache. Then as quickly as it appeared, his smile faded. "Why did the bad man hurt Mommy?"

Reece leaned down and met the boy's gaze. "I don't know, buddy, but come Monday, I'm going to find out."

HIS EXHAUSTION held at bay by anger and caffeine, Reece strode into the state attorney's office Monday morning, past the startled administrative assistant, and directly into his private office.

His head jerked up at Reece's intrusion. He was in the midst of a phone call and glared at Reece. "Can I put you on hold? I'm sorry." He clicked a button on his phone console. "Who are you, and what the hell do you think you're doing barging in here?"

"I don't believe we've been introduced. I'm Senator Reece Sheridan from the Legislative Audit Committee. I'm here for a list of all open-records requests made by reporter Kara McMillan over the past six months, and I'm not leaving until I have the information. Please, finish your call. I'll just make myself comfortable."

Tom was behind on tomorrow's editorial. The team had taken news of the attack on McMillan poorly, all but accusing him of not taking the threats against her seriously. But there was no proof Northrup was behind the attack, not yet. He'd tried to explain that newspapers deal in facts, only to have Novak and Alton storm out of the meeting.

They acted like he didn't care. But he did. McMillan was his best reporter, and it bothered him to know she'd been hurt. Smart, efficient, a great writer, she could digest complex information like most people digested their own spit. If he was hard on her it was only because he expected great things from her. When she won the Pulitzer, she would thank him.

He reassured himself of this fact and tried to force his mind back onto the words on his screen. He'd added another two hundred or so when Paula from HR stepped into his office, an incident report in her hand. He didn't have to ask what it was. He'd finished writing it just yesterday.

In her fifties, Paula hadn't let herself go the way some women did. From her carefully manicured fingernails to her carefully colored hair, she gave the impression of being in her forties. Regular trips to the gym kept her slim. When she wasn't babbling about her grandchildren, she was even intelligent. Of the women his age in the building, she was undoubtedly the most attractive. They'd had sex off and on for years, ever since she'd gotten divorced."

She glared at him. "What the hell is this?"

"An incident report."

"You're writing Kara McMillan up for insubordination?"

"That's correct." He turned back to his computer, effectively dismissing her.

"Look at me, Tom." She raised her voice a notch.

He faced her and said nothing.

"I've got half a dozen witnesses who said you berated Ms. McMillan for dating a state senator, using foul language, and—let me make sure I'm getting this right—calling her companion her 'boytoy.' As I understand it, you accused her of compromising the paper and told her you'd respect her if she were fucking him for secrets, is that correct?"

When he said nothing, she continued.

"It's my understanding Ms. McMillan became upset with you, called you a dick and said, and I quote, 'Does anyone here question you when you choose to screw members of your own staff? That's worse than sleeping with the enemy. That's a lawsuit. Talk about compromising the newspaper.'"

Tom felt the angry flush creep up his throat onto his face. His own staff was turning against him, quoting him to Human Resources. *Reporters!*

"At this point you told her you were writing her up, is that so? Answer me, Tom."

"That's essentially accurate."

"Why is none of that on this form? All it says here is that she was insubordinate, not that you provoked her, insulted her, and harassed her. You've taken her alleged insubordination out of context and placed it in her permanent file. Would you do that in a news story?"

She had him there. "No. But my sex life was not making headlines."

"Not yet, it hasn't. Wait till one of those nineteen-year-old interns you like so much decides to sue. Now hear me: I won't put this in McMillan's file! She's absolutely right. Until you quit screwing the help, you can forget criticizing anyone else's choice of bed partner. Got that?" Paula tore up the document and scattered the pieces on his desk.

"Got it."

"And while I'm here, you might want to explain why you knew she was being threatened but chose to do nothing to protect her. The publisher wants to know."

From out in the newsroom came the sound of cheers, whistles, and applause.

CHAPTER 20

KARA DRIFTED in a narcotic haze, beyond pain but not quite beyond nightmares. At times she could feel his hands around her throat or hear his voice. Then she would fight him only to open her eyes and find her mother or Reece beside her, holding her hand, stroking her hair.

Outside of her dreams, she knew she was alive. She knew Connor was safe. But everything else seemed to blur. Holly, Tessa, and Sophie had come to visit her, though she couldn't remember what they'd said—something about Tom getting in trouble with Human Resources. Then Tom had come to see her personally, and she thought she'd heard him say he was sorry—surely a drug-induced delusion.

The police had also come to visit. They'd asked her questions, and she had tried to answer. But with painkillers syruping through her veins, details from the attack were fuzzy. When they'd asked her about the story she was working on, she'd refused to speak and told them to talk to Tom.

More than once she'd awoken, sure there was something she needed to do, someone she needed to check on, but when she'd opened her eyes, all that remained was a niggling sense of urgency. *What was she supposed to do?*

"Sleep," Reece told her, then kissed her forehead. "Just sleep, sweetheart."

And so she slept.

* * *

REECE KISSED her cheek, pulled the blanket up over her shoulders, and watched her drift off. He hoped the last dose of pain medication she'd been given would last long enough to give her some hours of deep sleep. He could tell fear stalked her in her dreams, and he felt powerless to stop it.

He'd almost lost her. It had been so close. By the cops' estimation, another handful of seconds and the bastard would have succeeded in raping her. Another two minutes, and she'd have been dead. Who knows what would have happened to little Connor.

Reece knew without knowing that Kara had lasted as long as she had because she'd been fighting to keep her son safe. It touched him in a way he couldn't express, pushed a sore spot deep in his chest, perhaps because his own mother had never seemed to spare a thought for him, much less put her life on the line. It made Kara all the more precious in his eyes and gave him another in a long list of reasons to admire her. She loved her boy down to the last drop of her blood. It was as simple—and as beautiful—as that.

When he'd heard the call for a body bag and the medical examiner, a terrifying pain had lanced through him, the kind of pain he'd known only once before, when the state patrol had called to say his father had been killed. He'd run into her house, sure for a sharp string of seconds that she was dead. Then he'd seen her, battered and beaten, but alive. And a raging fury had pushed fear aside.

He was going to find out who was behind this, and if it was someone in the state government, Reece was going to use his authority as a member of the audit committee to make certain that person served a long prison term and never worked in government again.

No, it wasn't an abuse of power. It's what his authority was for in the first place.

He watched her sleep and felt an odd tenderness stir in his belly. He hadn't been searching for a relationship. He hadn't been looking for someone. But he'd found her just the same. How had she come to mean so much to him so quickly? He'd only known her for a month, and already she was essential. When she was healed and this was all over, they had a lot to talk about.

A middle-aged nurse dressed in blue scrubs stepped into the room and walked over to check the IV pump. "How's she doing?"

"I think she's having nightmares."

The nurse nodded and pushed a few buttons. "Poor thing. I'll be back with her next dose of pain meds in about three hours. In the meantime, you ought to try to get some sleep yourself."

"Yeah." Except for a few hours yesterday evening, he'd spent all his time these past few days either at the Capitol or at the hospital, and he knew he looked pretty ragged around the edges.

His sister had said as much when she'd dropped by earlier this evening. Melanie had seen the photo of him shouting in Prentice's face in the newspaper and had gotten worried about him. She'd tried to reach him at home that night. Of course, he hadn't gone home. Except for a quick shower and change of clothes, he hadn't been home since Kara was attacked.

Melanie had finally caught up with him on his cell and surprised him in Kara's room with Vietnamese take-out. "It's healthier than hospital cafeteria food," she'd said.

She'd stayed with him for a few hours, fussed over how tired he looked, admonished him for losing his temper with Prentice, and then contradicted herself by praising him for ripping Prentice's head off. Then she'd given him a hug and taken off to spend the evening with her new boyfriend. It was the most time they'd ever spent together outside of the holidays.

He wasn't used to having a sister around, but he thought he could get to like it.

Miguel had called, too, expressed his concern, and asked

Reece again if getting involved with Kara was such a good idea. "She seems to come with trouble."

This time Reece hadn't bothered to hide his irritation. "This wasn't her fault, Miguel."

The public had poured out its love for her, filling the room with flowers and cards wishing her a speedy recovery and expressing admiration. In fact, so many people had sent flowers, that they couldn't all fit in the room, and Lily had taken it upon herself to distribute a dozen or so bouquets to patients around the hospital who, according to the nursing staff, weren't getting visitors or flowers of their own—old people with no family, people dying of cancer, homeless people.

Reece brushed a strand of hair from Kara's bruised cheek, glanced at his watch, and saw that it was already past ten. He walked over to his briefcase and opened it, careful not to let his loaded nine-millimeter Sphinx semi-auto show in case a nurse came unexpectedly back in the room. Even with his concealed-carry permit, weapons weren't allowed in the hospital. But he'd be damned if he was willing to leave Kara undefended again.

Reece retrieved the folder file containing the documents the state attorney had given him yesterday and sat in the chair, determined to figure out who was behind this. The trouble was that Kara was damned good at her job, sticking her nose into everything like a conscientious reporter should. Over a six-month period, she'd filed thirty-seven open-records requests.

Videos and state health department documents.

That's what she'd told Chief Irving. Of course, as she handled the environmental beat, most of the requests she'd filed had been with the state health department. If he eliminated all but those, however, that cut it down to twenty-six. He'd take it in chronological order under the assumption that if someone wanted to kill Kara, she had to be pretty deep into the story.

He reached for the cup of lukewarm hospital swill that

was supposed to be coffee and settled in for another long night.

KARA STARED into the hospital bathroom mirror and tried to come to grips with the stranger she saw reflected there. Her eyes were dull from narcotics and nightmares. An IV tube ran from a plastic bag on a pole into the back of her left hand. Her hair was tousled, tangled from four days in bed. And there were bruises.

She ran her fingers over her left cheek and felt the crushing blow of his fist. The bruises were fading from purple to red and yellow, but the flesh was still swollen, giving her a slightly lopsided appearance. A ring of purple around her neck showed where hands had tried to choke the life from her—big hands, a killer's hands. They had squeezed so hard, squeezed until her lungs burned and the world had turned to black spots.

She slipped off the hospital gown and saw the dinner-plate-sized bruise where her ribs had struck against the coffee table, driving the breath from her body, collapsing her lung. A bandage covered the wound left by the chest tube they'd used to re-inflate her lung. A saucer-sized bruise marked where the toe of his boot had caught her belly.

But the hardest thing to see were the twin bruises on her inner thighs made when he'd slammed into her with his knee and forced her legs apart. Vague flashes of the ER doctor examining her came into her mind—her feet in stirrups, the cold stretch of a speculum, the doctor combing through her pubic hair for evidence, swabbing for semen. They'd done a rape kit on her, she realized—one last violation.

She would heal. She was alive, and Connor was safe, and that's what mattered. But even as these thoughts filled her mind, she began to tremble, nausea uncoiling like a snake in her stomach. She could still smell his breath, hear the hatred in his voice, feel his hands hurting her.

They said he didn't rape you, McMillan. He's dead. Pull yourself together!

She leaned against the sink and took deep, steadying breaths that hurt her ribs. Behind her was the shower. Before she could admit to herself what she was doing, she'd pulled the IV from her hand, dropped her hospital gown on the floor, stepped into the shower, and turned the water on as hot as she could stand.

How long she stood there under the spray, she didn't know. But gradually as the scalding water bathed her skin, her nausea and trembling subsided. She took up the courtesy soap, tore open the package, and began to wash herself, wincing as the water drove against her bruises with the force of a hammer. Finding little bottles of shampoo and conditioner, she washed her hair also, willing her terror and the darkness of her memories to slide down the drain with the suds. She was clean again. She was herself again.

It was only after she'd turned off the water and reached for the towel that the weakness set in. She found herself fighting dizziness as she dried off and slipped back into her hospital gown. By the time she'd brushed her teeth, she was forced to lean against the sink to keep from collapsing.

That's how Reece found her, her dark hair dripping wet, her face pale as death, and looking as if she were going to faint. Her IV dangled uselessly, dripping onto the floor. Steam covered the mirror, the walls, the faucet. She must have been in the shower for a long time. "You're not supposed to be out of bed."

She jumped at the sound of his voice, proof she hadn't heard him enter, hadn't heard him call for her, hadn't even heard him open the bathroom door. "I wanted . . . a shower. I . . ."

He scooped the sweet weight of her into his arms as her knees buckled and carried her back toward the bed. He understood why she had wanted the shower—she was reclaiming her body. But it still angered him that she had taken such a crazy risk. "If you fall, you're going to become a permanent resident, you know."

Her head rested against his shoulder. "You shouldn't be helping me."

"Why not?" He laid her gently down in the bed and tried to avoid putting any pressure on her broken ribs.

"I'm investigating you."

"I know." He pulled up the blankets, ignored the flicker of anger in his gut. "I'm getting the nurse."

He strode out of her room, down to the nurses' station, flagged one of the nurses, and then watched as she took Kara's vitals and inserted a new IV.

He'd found her open-records request this morning. It was crammed into his inbox with a stack of other neglected faxes that had come in over the past three days. He'd recognized immediately what it was, and it had hit him like a fist—not the fact that she had requested documents from him, but the fact that she hadn't trusted him enough to simply ask. He'd have been happy to give her or any other reporter any document in his possession, from his campaign finance records to a record of his cell phone calls, without anyone having to use legal muscle to get it. He wasn't a goddamned crook, and he had nothing to hide.

He'd known it was her way of keeping their relationship separate from their careers, but it had felt like a blow just the same. He'd read through it and tried to figure out what she was after.

Under Colorado Revised Statute § 24-72-202(3), I am requesting all documents written or received by you pertaining to the state health department and/or environmental enforcement actions at the state health department. These documents will include, but are not limited to: Legislative Audit Committee correspondence, letters, memorandums, e-mails, inquiries, reports, and requests for information, as well as notes from meetings or phone conversations.

He'd had to grin at her thoroughness. She wrote like a kick-ass lawyer. But did she truly believe he or someone else on the audit committee was interfering with the health department's ability to do its job?

The next sentence had jarred something in his mind.

I am also requesting any correspondence between you and any individual employed by or under contract with Northrup Mining, Inc., as well as any document of any kind that mentions Northrup Mining, Inc.

He'd seen the name Northrup before. But where?

He'd grabbed the folder with the state health department documents in it and searched through it until he found an open-records request dating back to January, the week after he'd met her. It was a request for any and all documents pertaining to Northrup Mining, Inc., dating back to the day the company opened operations in Adams County. In that instant, he'd known he'd found what he'd been looking for. Without meaning to, she'd given him the clue he'd needed.

It was a clue he was going to follow. He was meeting with the director of the state health department tomorrow. He'd take a look at Northrup's file himself.

"Next time you want to get out of bed, young lady, you buzz the nurse first. Are you in pain?"

Kara shook her head. "No more pills or shots. They make it hard to think."

"That's the concussion, honey. Let me know when you change your mind." Then the nurse walked out of the room and left them alone.

Kara felt his hand stroke her wet hair. She opened her eyes and forced herself to meet the gaze of the man who'd been at her bedside for the past four days, the man who'd comforted her son, the man who'd stood up for her against Galen. The man she was investigating. "I needed a shower. I needed to . . . be clean again."

"I understand." His eyes told her that he did, indeed, understand. "I just wish you'd waited until either I or your mother were with you."

"You shouldn't be here." She had to say it. Someone had to say it.

"Why not, Kara?"

"Because I'm investigating you. Because it's a conflict of

interests." She felt the hot sting of tears in her eyes and turned her face away from him. "Because it's not right for me to need you so damned much when all this stands between us."

"Do you need me?"

She hated herself for being so weak, so pathetic. She choked out the answer. "Yes."

His lips pressed warm against her forehead. "Then we'll worry about the rest later."

FOR KARA, later came sooner than she had expected.

Tom arrived after Reece had gone back to the Capitol, a file folder in hand and a stack of papers tucked into his armpit. "You're looking . . . better."

"Really? Holly told me I look like something off the cover of a tabloid." Kara couldn't help but smile at her friend's ill-chosen words. "OJ's latest girlfriend, I believe she said."

Tom cleared his throat, shifted awkwardly, and Kara realized how out of place he was outside a newsroom or a bar. "Yes, well, at least it's not permanent."

If her ribs hadn't hurt like hell, she might have laughed out loud.

"I saved the papers, figured you'd want to see the ink you've been getting." Tom tossed them onto her lap.

"INDY REPORTER ATTACKED" was the headline of Tessa's story—all caps and sixty-point type. The other papers hadn't played it up quite as much, though she'd still landed on the front page. "Reporter assaulted." "Reporter stable." "Journalist on the mend."

She skimmed quickly over Tessa's article and then the others. They had all interviewed Reece, who'd been very cautious in his comments, acknowledging only that he and Kara were friends and voicing his confidence that the police were handling the case competently and professionally. But while any other victim of an attempted sexual assault would've been granted anonymity, her name had run in every paper, together with details from the police reports. The logical part of her knew it was the price of being a public figure, but it still turned her stomach to see phrases like "no vaginal trauma" next to her name and head shot.

The man who'd tried to kill her had a name—John David Weaver.

She turned the papers over.

"The cops are threatening to charge me with obstruction of justice or some damned thing if I don't reveal to them the nature of your investigation. We've got legal working on it. We've got to wrap this up quickly, McMillan. Once the cops have it, everyone will have it. I've been doing a little research myself." He handed her the file folder. "Thought you'd want to see this."

Kara opened the file and saw the full printout for a bill. She read through it and saw that it would amend state law to allow the burning of tires as a fuel source for industry. She knew some people felt it was a better way to recycle tires, as it kept them out of landfills and decreased the need for coal mining. She glanced up at Tom, puzzled. "I see that Reece is the sponsor, but I don't see what this has to do with my investigation."

"Look on the last sheet."

She pulled the last page out and put it on top. It was a list of people slated to testify in committee on behalf of the bill. She read down the list, and her pulse began to pound in her ears. She didn't recognize the names, but under "Title/Place of Employment" two of the witnesses had listed Northrup Mining, Inc.

"This is circumstantial evidence."

"It could be coincidence, but it does tie him to Northrup. He's been a member of the Legislative Audit Committee for two years and has frequent contact with the health department."

"I'm in touch with the health department on a weekly basis. Does that mean I'm trying to corrupt them? Perhaps he's just doing his job." It couldn't be Reece. His environmental record was stronger than that of any other senator. Why would he protect a polluter? Kara's head began to throb.

"There's more. I got a phone call from a source in the state attorney's office today. It seems that about a week before you were attacked, Sheridan contacted them and demanded a comprehensive list of all open-records requests you'd made to the state over the past six months."

"What? Why would he do that? If he's in bed with Northrup, he'd already have a copy of my open-records request. He'd already know what I'm after."

"I have no idea what your politician is up to, McMillan, but I figure you'd best find out." He glanced at his watch. "Now when are they letting you out of here?"

CHAPTER 21

KARA SORTED impatiently through a pile of newspapers while she waited for the doctor. They were supposed to discharge her today. And it wouldn't be a moment too soon. She was tired of lying in bed like some hapless victim, tired of being afraid, tired of being away from Connor. She wanted her life back. She wanted to get back to work, to finish the investigation, to expose Northrup and whichever senator was playing dirty on Northrup's behalf. At least then she would be *doing* something. She wouldn't feel so damned helpless.

She'd lost so much time on the investigation. She'd snuck in a call on her cell phone to the whistleblower and had been relieved to know that he and his family were still safe. But she couldn't shake this growing sense of urgency. She needed to wrap this story fast.

Her mother had called to say she was coming over with Connor and a bag of clothes for Kara to wear home. Not that Kara was going to her own home. Although a crime-scene cleanup crew had removed the mess and her mother had seen to it that a new sliding glass door had been installed and the bullet holes in the wall had been repaired, Kara couldn't bear the thought of being in that space again—not yet.

Memories from that terrible night played in her mind like scenes from a video that wouldn't stop. She found herself jumping at unexpected noises, her adrenaline on full blast, her heart rocketing around her chest, fear whipping through her belly. The woman from the Denver PD's victim assistance program who'd come to visit her told her that was completely normal and had suggested she get counseling. But Kara didn't want frigging counseling—she wanted to find the bâstards who'd tried to have her killed and print their police mug shots on the front page of the paper. Then she'd be able to get on with her life.

A knock at her door had her bolting upright, then wincing at the shooting pain in her ribs and skull. Tom walked in—accompanied by Chief Irving.

"You can only tie this up in court so long." Chief Irving pointed an accusing finger at Tom's face. "This is bullshit, and you know it. Our guys put their lives on the line to save one of yours. This has nothing to do with First Amendment rights. It has to do with attempted murder!"

"We're all grateful the cops felt like doing their job that night, Irving, but we have our job to do, too. We can't share our sources with you, period. And we can't risk you giving information away to the other papers."

Kara watched the two big men argue and saw the door nudge open again. Her mother peered into the room, then stepped tentatively inside, followed by Connor. Tom and Chief Irving didn't seem to notice, not even when Connor crawled up onto the bed and into Kara's lap. They still stood face-to-face, both well over six feet tall, separated only by Chief Irving's protruding abdomen.

"How do I know one of your boys won't slip up and pass the info along to the other papers? We know how easy it is to loosen lips at the DPD."

"You saying my officers can't be trusted?"

Kara realized what her mother was going to do a second before she did it.

"Excuse me!" Her mother forced her five-foot-four self in between the two men. "If you two bulls would like to continue this territorial dispute, perhaps you could lock horns outside. Or perhaps you could urinate around your respective territories. Either way, this is a hospital, so if you want to stay in Kara's room, shut up!"

Kara had never seen Tom looking quite so astonished in all the years she'd known him. He glared down at her mother. "Who are you?"

"I'm Kara's mother, Lily McMillan."

To her horror, Kara watched as Tom's gaze dropped from her mother's face to her mother's . . . breasts. And she knew exactly what he was thinking. *The topless protest photo.*

"Good to meet you." Tom reached out his hand and continued to check out her mother, his gaze sliding over her as if she were the latest reporting intern. "I'm Tom Trent, edit—"

Her mother shook his hand, a look of disdain on her face. "I know who you are. Kara's told me what an ass you can be at times. I see it's true."

Tom flinched as if she'd hit him, and for the second time a look of complete astonishment crossed his face. He wasn't used to being dressed down.

Kara's stomach turned. "Thanks, Mom. Now I need a new job."

But no one seemed to hear her, except Connor, who looked up at her confused. She kissed the top of his head and gave him a reassuring squeeze.

"I'm Chief Irving, Lily. I apologize for disturbing your daughter, but it's her safety we've come here to discuss."

"Can't it wait until I get her home?"

Tom and Chief Irving looked at one another and shifted uncomfortably.

Tom spoke first. "We don't think she should go home with you."

Kara and her mother spoke at the exact same moment. "What?"

Tom placed what was ostensibly a reassuring hand on her mother's shoulder. "The newspaper is very concerned about McMill . . . about Kara's safety. I agree with Chief Irving here that she would only be putting all of you in danger if she were to stay with you."

Chief Irving cleared his throat, looked as if he were getting ready to drop a bomb. "Lily, it's probably best if you and Connor were to go out of town for a few weeks—"

"At the newspaper's expense, of course," Tom added.

"—until this is over. In the meantime, we'll put Kara up in a safehouse."

Kara felt fear roll over in her stomach, and she hugged Connor more tightly. She started to speak, but Tom cut her off before a single word made it past her lips.

"A safehouse? I thought we agreed on a secured hotel."

Chief Irving shook his head. "No, we agreed on a DPD safehouse."

As the men began to argue again, Kara met her mother's gaze and saw fear in her mother's eyes. What had she gotten them all into?

REECE CHECKED in at the security desk at the state health department, received his visitor tag, and was escorted back through a maze of hallways to the director's office by Director Owens himself. The man oozed friendliness that didn't manage to quite cover his nerves.

"We're glad you're here, Senator. We're proud of the work we do, and it's not often that we get to show it off."

"I'm here on specific business, Mr. Owens."

"Yes, I understand you've requested to view one particular file." The words were spoken with studied blandness.

"The Northrup file."

"I believe it's waiting for you on my desk. May I ask what your interest is in this particular mining operation?"

"It's related to my work with the Legislative Audit Committee." *In other words, no.*

The lines around Owens's eyes drew tighter. "I understand."

I bet you do.

Reece followed him through his office door, aware that everyone in the office was staring at him, and sat in the plush leather chair offered to him. Scenic photographs of Colorado's mountains decked the walls of the office, their cherry wood frames matching Owens's rather luxurious executive desk and bookshelves.

"Can I get you something to drink, Senator?"

"No, thank you. Just the file."

Owens smiled and handed him a file folder about an inch thick. "Here you go. I trust you'll find everything in order. We work hard with companies to balance the needs of the environment with the realities of business."

Reece opened the folder and met Owens's gaze. "And which is your priority, Mr. Owens—the environment or business?"

Owens seemed to strain to maintain his smile. "Obviously our job is to protect human health, which means enforcing environmental laws is our first priority."

"Glad to hear it. Where's your copy machine?"

An hour later, Reece's mild irritation with Owens had become full-fledged rage. Obviously, the man thought he was an idiot. To the untrained eye, the Northrup file might seem completely satisfactory. The annual inspection reports, air-quality tests, emissions licenses—everything seemed to be in perfect order. It showed Northrup getting snagged on some minor violations—a broken sprinkler system designed to keep down dust emissions, visible dust emissions on a high-wind day, one self-reported "upset" that resulted in a surge of pollutants from their smokestacks.

Every big industrial company had its mishaps. They all made mistakes. Northrup's file was as perfect as any industrial file was likely to get. Too perfect, in fact. There were no major enforcement actions, no fines, no complaints—nothing to interest a seasoned investigative reporter like Kara. Nothing that might catch the attention of a state senator or the audit committee. Nothing that might drive someone to kill.

The only explanation was that the file had been purged. The documents had either been shredded or pulled and hidden away somewhere. He'd bet on the former.

He walked back to Owens's office, a duplicate of Northrup's file under one arm, the original folder in his hand. He found the director in a meeting. Not bothering to knock, Reece strode in and dropped the folder onto Owens's desk, where it fell with a loud smack.

"I'm not an imbecile, Owens. Cut past the bullshit, and show me the real file. I want to see every single document in this office with Northrup's name on it—the ones journalist Kara McMillan managed to get from you."

IT WAS happening too fast. Kara wasn't ready for this, for any of this.

Struggling to hold back the tears, she sat on the chair because she was too dizzy to kneel. She held Connor close and kissed his hair. "You have fun at Disney World, and stay close to Lily at the beach, okay? I'll miss you."

Connor hugged her tightly. "Lily says we're gonna fly in an airplane. Are we gonna fly in an airplane, Mommy?"

Kara held him at arm's length where she could look into his sweet brown eyes. She forced herself to smile. "You sure are, pumpkin. You're going to get to see the tops of the clouds."

Excitement shone unmistakable in his eyes, and he smiled, a bright smile full of innocence. By sending him away, she was protecting that innocence. But knowing that didn't make it any less painful.

"Okay, Connor. Let's go. The taxi is waiting for us." Her mother's voice was filled with artificial cheer. She and her sister barely tolerated one another, so taking Connor to Florida for two weeks was a major sacrifice.

Kara gave her son one last kiss, then forced herself to let go. She stood and hugged her mother. "Thanks, Mom. I hope you and Aunt Martha get along."

"We will, or maybe I'll send her on to her next life." Her mother embraced her fiercely. "Stay safe, Kara, please! Put these bastards away. And be kind to Reece. He's a good man, and he's in love with you, whether either of you realize it or not."

These last words came as such a shock to Kara that she didn't burst into tears until after her mother and Connor had left her hospital room. Then she lay across the bed and wept, sobbing out the grief and pain of the past week until her ribs and head ached.

Knock it off, McMillan! They're safe, and that's what matters.

She sat up, blew her nose, and walked to the bathroom to rinse her face in cold water, trying not to trip on the three suitcases her mother had brought. She would be living out of these suitcases until her investigation was finished and the coast was clear—at least two weeks by her best guess. She had at least ten interviews to do, plus countless documents to research before she'd be ready to write the first of what was sure to be several stories. Until whoever was threatening her had been exposed and locked up, she was going to be under virtual house arrest.

She dried her face, walked to the window, and looked out over the city. She'd best get used to a bird's-eye view. The paper had reserved the top floor of an exclusive Denver hotel. The elevators would be restricted so only those with security keys would have access to her floor. The doors leading out from the stairwells would be locked from the inside, preventing anyone from gaining entrance to her floor in that way. The room itself was already set up with her computer, Internet access, a fax machine, and a blocked phone line rigged for recording and for automatic call trace. With security cameras in the elevators, it was as safe an environment as any the police could provide at a safehouse, and it had the benefit of being much more comfortable. Only Tom and Chief Irving knew exactly where she was going.

Chief Irving was supposed to come by at any moment to take her to her temporary prison, so when the knock came at her door, that's who she was expecting. She turned and felt her pulse pick up a notch. "Reece."

Just by looking at him, she could tell he was edgy, tense, angry. He crossed the room, stepping over suitcases, and ran his thumb over her cheek. "You've been crying."

She looked away, feeling sick inside. How could she want him so desperately even now, when she knew he'd gone behind her back? "You shouldn't be here."

"Probably not, but that hasn't stopped me so far." He pressed his lips to her hair. "Are you leaving on a trip or something?"

She stepped away from him and crossed her arms over her chest. "They're taking me to a safehouse of sorts. Connor just left for the airport with my mother. They're going out of state for a while."

"That explains the tears. I'm sorry, Kara. I know it has to be hard, but it's probably a good idea. The little guy's been through more than enough." He reached for her.

She stepped back. "Yeah. Thanks for all you did for him."

"Something else is bothering you."

Then she blurted it out. "What's your relationship to Northrup Mining, and why did you contact the state attorney's office about my open-records requests?"

"Has this turned into an official interview?"

"Not yet." Anger at Reece, anger at the man who'd attacked her, anger at Northrup roiled inside her. She crossed the room, took the digital recorder out of her purse, turned it on, then dropped it in her shirt pocket and turned to face him. "Now it's official."

"You're recording me?" A muscle ticked in his cheek.

"Yes. Normally the subject being interviewed wouldn't know I'm recording them. State law doesn't require disclosure, provided I'm a part of the conversation I'm recording."

"I see." He slipped out of his jacket and sat in the nearby chair. "Okay, Ms. McMillan, ask your questions."

She tried not to remember that he'd sat in that same chair for endless hours while she'd drifted in and out of consciousness, that he'd slept there when he hadn't been stroking her hair, giving her ice chips, or holding her hand.

He was a politician. She was a reporter. She had a job to do.

She sat on the edge of the bed, looked directly into his eyes, and wanted to weep at the cold fury she saw there. "What is your relationship with Northrup Mining, Inc.?"

"Northrup is one of several Colorado industries that signed on to testify in favor of a bill I am sponsoring. The bill would allow industries that burn coal to burn waste tires, provided burning tires doesn't produce a net increase in the number of pollutants being emitted from their stacks. I have no other connection to Northrup—no campaign donations, no soft money, no stock. Nothing."

She forced herself to focus, forced herself to ignore the pain she felt at having to question him as if he didn't matter to her. "Were you aware of Northrup's violations of environmental laws when they signed to testify on behalf of your bill?"

Reece fought to keep his temper in check, stung by her frigid professionalism and her lack of trust. "No. In fact, my examination of Northrup's file at the state health department today revealed a company with an above-average environmental record."

"You went to the health department and reviewed Northrup's file?"

He felt a short-lived burst of satisfaction at the surprise that crossed her face. "In light of your open-records request, it seemed in keeping with my duties as a member of the Legislative Audit Committee to look into Northrup myself."

"And you claim their environmental record is above average?"

"No. I said the file revealed a company with an above-average record. I have reason to believe the file has been purged." He reached into his briefcase, retrieved the folder of copies he'd made, and tossed it onto the bed beside her.

Curious, she grabbed the file and skimmed through it. Shaking her head, she turned to him. "Is this all they gave you?"

"Yes, ma'am. I told Director Owens that I believe he is withholding information, an allegation he denied."

She sat on the bed again. "Owens is a liar."

"So I deduced. I have filed a formal open-records request with his office, demanding all documents pertaining to Northrup, specifically those that were a part of your open-records request."

She looked stunned. "Had you ever seen Northrup's file before today?"

"No."

"Have you ever had contact with the state health department about Northrup or any enforcement action at Northrup prior to today?"

"No."

"Why did you ask the state attorney to provide you with a list of my open-records requests?"

He resisted the urge to go to her, to touch her. "The life of a woman I care very deeply about was in danger. For professional and ethical reasons, she couldn't tell me who she thought was behind the threats against her. But as I knew it involved state health department documents, it was within my purview as a member of the audit committee to start my own investigation."

"You're using your position for personal gain. You had no business getting involved."

"Like hell I didn't!" Anger had his ass out of the chair. He closed the space between them in two steps. "The time I spent making love with you actually meant something to me. I couldn't stand by and do nothing while some lunatic tried to murder you. Sorry if you don't like that, but it's who I am."

Her chin went up. "I don't need you looking out for me."

"Goddamn it, Kara, quit pushing me away! Is sex the only thing you're willing to accept from me? If that's all you want, then I'm not interested."

Her eyes were wide, and she looked as if he'd struck her. "I-I understand."

He wanted so much to pull her into his arms, to kiss her confusion and doubt away, but he stood his ground. "Do you?"

She nodded, two wooden jerks of her head. "It's probably best if we go our separate ways."

"Christ!" Now he *was* angry. "That's not what I said! How can you be willing to end our relationship without fighting for it first? How can you be so willing to let go when we both know that what we have together is special? Is that what you really want?"

She turned her face away from him, and her voice dropped to a whisper. "No."

There was a sharp rap at the door. "Ms. McMillan?" Chief Irving stuck his head inside and acknowledged Reece with a nod. "Are you ready to go?"

"Yes." She met his gaze.

Reece forced himself to step back from her. "How will I get a hold of you?"

"I'm afraid that won't be possible, Senator. We're taking her to a secret location until this is resolved, and no one, not even her mother, knows where it is. We can't give you the phone number for security reasons. However, Ms. McMillan will be able to contact you by her secure line. She won't have her cell phone."

If Reece hadn't felt so angry and so hurt, he might have acknowledged the desperation and sadness in her eyes. Instead, he gave her a cold smile. "I guess the ball's in your court, Kara."

Then, fists clenched, he turned his back on her and forced himself to walk away.

CHAPTER 22

THE LOEWS Hotel was a monolith of black glass against the clear afternoon sky. Detective Irving drove Kara to the security entrance used by movie stars and visiting dignitaries and whisked her inside. The manager, a tall dark-haired man whose otherwise handsome face was marred by old acne scars, met them there and sent a bellboy after her luggage. Then he guided them through a hallway, past the kitchens, to a private elevator that carried them swiftly up thirty floors to the Belle View Suite.

"President Gerald Ford, Sting, and Oprah Winfrey all stayed here," the manager boasted as he unlocked the double doors with his keycard.

A mechanical hum. A click.

The manager pushed the doors open and revealed not just a luxurious hotel room, but an enormous apartment. Kara knew she was supposed to react with "oohs" and "aahs," but everything that had happened this morning had left her feeling numb—saying good-bye to Connor and her mother, her disastrous confrontation with Reece. All she could summon as the manager led her from room to room was a nod and the occasional "mmm." Nothing—not the marble desk area, not the remote-controlled gas fireplace, not the enormous sunken tub, not the baby grand piano, not the cherry wood furniture nor the luxurious silk on the huge king-sized bed—mattered one iota to her.

She wasn't here to lounge, take baths, and enjoy frigging room service, after all, but to finish an investigation. Her computer from work was already in place. Several boxes of documents sat on the floor behind the desk—the Northrup documents and whatever the senators on the Legislative Audit Committee had turned over in response to her last open-records request. A fax machine was set up on a nearby end table together with a box of paper.

"We've handled high-security visitors before, Ms. McMillan, so please feel safe within our walls. No one will be able to get onto your floor, except the handful of staff with the security key to the elevator. Call room service for whatever you need, and one of us will bring it right up. No need to tip—the newspaper has taken care of everything. Don't hesitate to ask for me if you have any questions or concerns."

Kara managed a smile for the man, accepted his card. "Thank you, Mr.," she glanced down at the card, "Osterman."

The manager gave her a bright smile that didn't quite conceal the pity in his eyes as his gaze lingered on her bruised face. Then he turned and left her alone with Detective Irving.

The detective looked around at the suite and raised a bushy eyebrow. "Nicer digs than you'd find at a police safehouse, that's for damned sure. Better food, too, I'll bet. Now that you know where to find the bubble bath and caviar, let's go over the rules."

The rules were simple. No visitors. No outgoing calls unless she used the secured line. No revealing her location to anyone, not even her mother. No leaving her suite.

"Got it."

"It's bound to get a bit lonely up here, what with your son and mother out of town. You might be tempted—"

He was about to mention Reece, she knew. "I'll be too busy to be lonely."

But as she thanked Detective Irving and locked the door

behind him, Kara felt more alone than ever. She walked over to the tinted window, stared down at the busy street far below, then at the white-tipped mountains in the distance, feeling just as cold and bleak inside.

"You were just doing your job," she said out loud to herself.

But did you have to be so cruel about it?

A part of her had wanted to tell Reece she knew he wasn't the one who was shielding Northrup, but she'd squelched that voice. Nor had she been able to tell him how deeply it touched her to know all he'd done as a state senator to protect her. All she'd allowed him to see was her anger.

It still surprised her. When he hadn't been at her bedside, he'd been shaking up the health department and harassing the state attorney's office in hopes of uncovering what she could not ethically tell him.

The life of a woman I care very deeply about was in danger.

His explanation was so simple, so clear. And she'd thrown it back in his face.

You had no business getting involved.

She pulled the digital recorder out of her pocket, rewound, and hit play.

"The time I spent making love with you actually meant something to me. I couldn't stand by and do nothing while some lunatic tried to murder you. Sorry if you don't like that, but it's who I am."

"I don't need you looking out for me."

Shut up, McMillan! She cringed, her own words scraping like barbed wire over skin.

"Goddamn it, Kara, quit pushing me away! Is sex the only thing you're willing to accept from me? If that's all you want, then I'm not interested."

"I-I understand."

"Do you?"

"It's probably best if we go our separate ways."

"Christ! That's not what I said! How can you be willing

*to end our relationship without fighting for it first? How can
you be so willing to let go when we both know that what we
have together is special? Is that what you really want?"*

"No."

She turned off the recorder. It hurt to hear his anger, to
hear her own fear. That's what she'd been feeling—not fury,
but bone-deep fear. Fear that he cared for her too much. Fear
that she cared for him even more. Fear that she'd end up
alone and in tears, feeling shattered.

Which pretty much described how she felt right now.

She'd told him the truth—she didn't want to end their relationship.

*How can you be so willing to let go when we both know
that what we have together is special?*

The hell of it was that right now she had no choice but to
let go. She had an investigation to complete—an investigation that had nearly taken her life and Connor's. Until this
was over, she had no business thinking about anything else.

Suddenly exhausted, her head aching, Kara turned away
from the window, found her way to the bedroom, crawled
into the enormous bed, and fell into a weary asleep.

LATER THAT afternoon, Reece strode from the Senate cham-
bers, briefcase in hand, in a shitty mood despite the fact that
his education bill had just passed. He offered a canned quote
to the reporters who stood in the hallway and then headed
toward his office. Miguel had agreed to meet him there in ten
minutes.

His stomach rumbled, and he opted for a quick detour to
the cafeteria downstairs. He'd spent the lunch recess at the
hospital arguing with Kara and hadn't yet eaten. Although
the cafeteria had closed hours ago, there were vending ma-
chines that dispensed dubious fare for those brave or desperate enough to eat it. He'd just dropped five quarters in the
machine for something labeled "turkey and swiss" when he
smelled her perfume.

"I heard about your reporter." Alexis leaned against the vending machine, the white tips of her French manicure a sharp contrast to her skin-hugging black silk dress. "I'm sorry she was hurt."

He took the sandwich, moved over to the soda machine, dropped in three quarters, and punched Pepsi. "She wasn't just hurt, Alexis. She was almost murdered."

"You really care about her, don't you?"

Yeah, he did. But he wasn't going to discuss Kara with anyone right now, particularly not Alexis. He popped open his soda can and took a swallow. "Was there something you wanted?"

She smiled and took a step in his direction. "I think it's kind of funny that a senator who won't have sex with a lobbyist for ethical reasons sees no moral dilemma in fucking a journalist. Then again, good publicity is *so hard* to come by."

The fist of suppressed rage Reece had been carrying in his belly all afternoon came perilously close to striking. He forced himself to take another swallow. "Only you would measure every intimate relationship in terms of profit. But that's what whores do, isn't it?"

Her perfect face flushed an ugly shade of red. "Fuck you!"

"No, I don't think so." He turned and walked away.

Miguel was waiting for him by the time he reached his office, white cowboy hat tucked politely under his arm, his bolo tie clipped with a silver bear claw studded with turquoise. "You looking to get food poisoning?"

Reece juggled briefcase, food, soda can, and keys and unlocked his office door. "Missed lunch."

Miguel followed him inside, sat, and dropped his cowboy hat onto his lap. "You've missed a lot of things lately. How's Ms. McMillan doing?"

"They discharged her today. The cops took her to a safehouse." Reece put his briefcase down, sat at his desk, and opened the plastic wrap covering his sandwich.

"A safehouse? Like a women's shelter?"

"No, a police safehouse. A secret location." Reece stared at the concoction of bread, grayish meat, and orange cheese. "Until they know who is behind this, they're keeping her under police protection."

"Are you going to be able to visit her?"

"No. Only the cops know where she is." After today she probably wouldn't want to see him again anyway. He'd gotten angry, and he'd pushed her. But damn it, she'd pushed him, too. Did she really hold it against him that he cared for her enough to try to find out who was trying to kill her? Were her feelings for him so casual that his concern for her life felt intrusive?

"What about her son? I suppose he's with her."

"He's gone out of town for a while." Reece took a bite and chewed. "Ever heard of Northrup Mining, Inc.?"

"You mean the company Ms. McMillan named in her open-records request to all of us? No."

"Yeah, me neither. She seems to think someone on the Legislative Audit Committee is covering up for them, forcing the state health department to back off."

Miguel frowned. "That's a serious accusation. Do you think she's onto something?"

"Someone thinks she is. Someone's so sure she's near the truth that he's willing to kill her to stop her."

"I don't know, *amigo*. Seems like a long shot to me. But if anyone on the committee is dirty, my money's on Devlin."

"Mine, too. I've requested a list of his campaign contributions from the secretary of state's office."

"You're not getting involved with this yourself, are you?" Miguel looked genuinely alarmed, his brown eyes wide. "That won't look so good—you checking up on him. He won't like that."

"We're charged with holding government agencies accountable, Miguel. It's my job to get involved in this." Reece set his tasteless sandwich aside, lifted his briefcase onto his desk, and opened it. "I picked up a file on Northrup from the health department today. The file's been cleaned out. But I'm going to spend tonight playing a game of follow the money—find out who the company's key shareholders are, that sort of thing."

"Jesus, Reece!"

Reece looked up to see Miguel staring into his briefcase, a horrified expression on his face. He'd seen the Sphinx. "Relax. I've got a concealed-carry permit."

"Just what are you planning on doing with that?"

Reece pulled out the file folder containing the health department documents and shut the briefcase. "Hopefully nothing. I've been carrying it since Kara was attacked just in case."

But Miguel was shaking his head. "You're getting way too caught up in this, my friend. You need to get out of town for a few days, clear your head. Do you want whoever's after her to come after you?"

Reece bared his teeth. "You better believe I do! You didn't see what he did to her. Christ, Miguel! He's lucky the cops killed him first—two clean shots through the chest. I'd have shot him in the balls first."

"I can't believe this is you I'm hearing. What has she done to you?"

"She hasn't done anything. Self-defense is perfectly legal. It's not like I'm going to hunt the bastards down and kill them like a desperado. Besides, the worst possible strategic move these jerks could make would be to go after a senator."

"Oh, I don't know. If they're *loco* enough to try to kill a journalist, what's a state senator?"

"What I hope to be is a major pain in their ass. Now do you want to see these documents or not? I figure you and I can put our heads together and figure out who's behind this."

Miguel looked at his watch. "Not tonight. It's Hilaria's mother's birthday. Don't want to piss off my mother-in-law. But let me know if you find anything. Call my cell."

Reece took another swig of his soda and turned toward his computer, his mind already plotting out an Internet search. "Enjoy yourself. Tell Hilaria hi for me."

He heard his office door close, typed "Northrup Mining Inc." and "shareholders" into the search engine, and then hit return.

BY THE time room service brought her dinner of chicken soup—she didn't have the stomach for much else—Kara had organized all the Northrup folders by date and type of document. They lay in neat rows across the elegant cherry dining table and the top of the closed baby grand piano. The folders from the senators on the Legislative Audit Committee sat in eight tidy piles.

She sipped her soup, caught the latest on CNN, and surveyed her handiwork. She would start with the senators' files. If she could find out who was covering for Northrup, she'd have the keystone of her story. Of course, she still had interviews to do—Owens at the health department, Northrup officials, the governor, each of the eight senators, an expert on cement-kiln dust. It would be helpful if she could find an expert to comment on the content of the videos. For all she knew piles of paint-stripping, lung-shredding CKD were an industry standard. She would e-mail Tom and ask him to find someone.

She finished her dinner and put the tray outside her door in the empty hallway. The emptiness and utter quiet were unnerving. Quickly, she closed and locked her door, shutting out the silence.

Back in the living room, CNN droned on reassuringly. The gas fire danced over fake logs and cast an artificial cheery glow. Outside the window, the lights of Denver glinted like diamonds.

And now there was no more avoiding it. She could either start with Reece's file, which was by far the thickest, or she could set him aside and go through them based on probability of guilt—the odds being determined solely by her completely biased impression of each individual. If she went through Reece's first, she could prove that he had no connection to

Northrup and lift that weight from her mind. But if she truly believed him innocent, then why should she waste precious hours turning up nothing?

Oh, hell! Just make a decision, McMillan!

She grabbed Drew Devlin's file, a notepad, and a sharp pencil and then sank into the armchair closest to the fire.

REECE STARED at his computer screen, shock boiling into outrage. He'd had more difficulty tracking down Northrup's shareholders than he'd imagined. Still, he'd kept up the search, wading through self-congratulatory press releases about worker safety, quarterly earnings, and plant upgrades, until he'd found something.

TexaMent set to buy Northrup in $2.7-billion deal.

It was a headline from an old cement-industry newsletter published several years ago and cached online. And there on the front page beneath the headline was Mike Stanfield, shaking hands with another man in a suit. Behind him stood Prentice, sporting Armani and more hair.

Reece read through the article and pushed back from his computer. So TexaMent owned Northrup. Goddamn! How could he have missed something so damned important, so basic?

He grabbed his TexaMent folder and searched through pages but found not a single mention of Northrup Mining, Inc. He'd done some research on TexaMent before agreeing to carry the tire-burning bill, checking their environmental record and OSHA file, and never once had he heard of Northrup. He'd known TexaMent had a plant in Adams County, but he'd had no idea the facility went by a different name.

He shook his head and laughed bitterly. How stupid he must have seemed to Owens at the health department when he'd called up asking about TexaMent's record. Owens had been able to lie and tell the truth at the same time. No enforcement actions on record for TexaMent. None on record for Northrup either, if he were to believe the file Owens had given him.

My God, they'd played him for a fool! They'd sought him out with a proposal that had legitimate environmental uses, won his support knowing that the other members of his party would sign on if he, with his reputation, sponsored it. Then they'd brought Devlin out of hiding, thereby assuring themselves unquestioned bipartisan support. Was Devlin working for them? And what did Kara have on Northrup that made her such a threat to them? Was Stanfield aware of the threats on her life? Was he behind the attack, or was someone else at the Northrup facility to blame?

The thought that he'd shared a few meals with Stanfield sickened him and turned the rage in his stomach into a white-hot fury. He wouldn't stop until he knew the truth, and he would do it all above-board, publicly, sharing whatever he uncovered with Kara and the other media.

Kara. She was investigating Northrup, probably still unaware of its ties to TexaMent. She needed to know, and she needed to hear it from him. Otherwise, when she connected the two companies she would believe that he'd lied to her. After all, he was carrying a bill for TexaMent.

But that was about to change. He'd pull the bill tomorrow morning and launch an official probe into both companies.

Reece flicked through his Rolodex, picked up his phone, and dialed Stanfield's number.

HE STARED down at the lights of the city, tossed back the last of his scotch, and winced as it hit the ulcer in his stomach like a piercing arrow.

So the reporter had not only survived, but now she'd gone into hiding. Well, hired help wasn't always what you hoped it would be. He should have handled it himself from the beginning. Perhaps then things would never have come this far.

Now Sheridan had become a problem, too. Certainly, the senator wasn't the first man to think with his cock, and he wouldn't be the last. But his involvement with the reporter posed a serious threat. The situation needed to be managed.

It was time to try something different. They couldn't very well kill a senator outright, especially not after the failed attack on the woman he was screwing. That would bring the entire state bureaucracy into the fray and draw even more attention to the McMillan girl. But there were other ways to get Sheridan out of the picture.

As for the reporter, there was no point in wasting time trying to find her. He would make her come to him. And when she did, he would make sure to answer all of her questions—she deserved that much for all her hard and fruitless work.

Then she would die.

He wasn't a murderer. He was a risk manager. He'd built his fortune by staying one step ahead of everyone else, by using circumstances to his best advantage, by doing things other people were too afraid or too lacking in vision to do. Laws and rules were for men too weak to reshape the world after their own desires. He was neither weak nor afraid.

Boldness was a lesson he'd learned from his father, though not in the usual way. He'd always struggled to please his father, a moderately successful oilman, but he had somehow seemed to fall short of the mark. His father hadn't approved of his ideas for running the company and had gotten in his way whenever he tried to strike out on a project of his own. The solution to the problem came one day during a private lunch meeting when his father, who'd been in the middle of another tirade about the danger of taking shortcuts, had started to choke on a bite of steak.

His first impulse had been to call for help. But then, as he'd watched his father flail and turn purple, he'd realized that this was the break he'd been waiting for. And so he'd put down the phone and watched as his father had choked slowly to death.

After that, everything had been easy. He'd replaced the board of directors, hired managers who shared his hardnosed vision, and moved the company to a level of profitability his father had never imagined. Where he'd once cowered before his father, trying desperately to please him, men now cowered before him and raced each other to win his favor.

No one was going to take that from him now. Not some bitch of a reporter who liked to stick her nose into other people's business—and certainly not some self-righteous state senator.

He pulled his cell phone out of his pocket. He had several calls to make.

CHAPTER 23

KARA WASN'T quite healed yet. That was the only explanation for why she'd slept until ten—that and the fact she'd awoken in the middle of the night, heart pounding, body wet with sweat, sure she was fighting for her life. It had taken a moment to remember her attacker was dead, to remember where she was and that she was safe. It had taken much longer to fall back asleep again. She'd only succeeded after she'd curled up against one of the king-sized pillows and pretended Reece was beside her.

She crawled out of bed, mildly disgusted with herself for being so weak-minded, shed her pajamas, and walked naked into the enormous bathroom with its walk-in shower and sunken tub. She turned the water in the shower on hot, stepped in, and let the scorching spray wash her nightmares away. By the time she emerged from the bathroom twenty minutes later, she was awake and ready to work.

She called room service; ordered the huevos rancheros, some orange juice, and tea; and then slipped into a pair of jeans and her ivory silk blouse. She sat down to read over her notes from the night before. She'd read through Devlin's file and that of four other committee members and found nothing pertaining to Northrup—no memos to the health department, no bills, no requests for favors. She had, however, found an interesting note in Devlin's file.

What about this? Does the stupid bitch really think I'd give her anything incriminating?

Those words had been scrawled on a yellow sticky note that had somehow become stuck to the back of an innocuous e-mail to the health department about the annual Senate holiday party. Kara would bet anything that Devlin's intern had written it and that it referred to some document the intern felt Devlin might not want her to see. She was equally certain that its presence in this folder was sheer, delightful accident. She had saved the sticky note, tucked it carefully into her pile of papers, and made a note to interview his intern as well. If she found nothing, she might be able to use this in a lawsuit against Devlin to prove that he had broken state law by withholding requested documents.

The next file belonged to Miguel de la Peña. A moderate and a family man, he was closely allied with Reece. Kara knew the two of them were friends outside the Capitol as well. Not that any of that meant anything, of course. She opened the folder and had just glanced through the documents when room service knocked at the door.

"I hope you're feeling comfortable here." Mr. Osterman carried her tray toward the dining table.

"It's covered with documents. Sorry. You can just put it here on the coffee table." Quickly she moved her notes aside, the smell of bacon making her mouth water. "And, yes, I'm very comfortable. Thank you."

"Is there anything else I can get you?"

"No, thanks." She waited until he'd gone to dive into her breakfast. She couldn't remember the last time she'd been this hungry.

She reached for the remote and switched on the television and then surfed for the news. Being in the hospital and shut up in the hotel left her feeling cut off from the world. For all she knew, space aliens were parked over Washington, D.C., and peace had broken out in the Middle East.

Nell Parker's heavily made-up face and brassy blond hair popped onto the plasma screen television in such sharp detail that Kara almost winced. At thirty-five, the popular anchorwoman had already had her first lift.

"—was found dead this morning in the Capitol Hill neighborhood. She had been shot twice through the head. Police say there was no indication that she had been sexually assaulted, but until autopsy results are available later this week they can't be certain.

"While police said they could not discuss possible motives for the murder, a source close to the investigation told News 12 that the senator had reportedly been intimate with the deceased but that the two had become estranged.

"Again, police are currently conducting a search at the home of State Senator Reece Sheridan, who is believed to be the primary suspect in the shooting death of Alexis Ryan, a Denver lobbyist. Sheridan has reportedly agreed to submit voluntarily to questioning by police and is expected to accompany them within the hour from his office at the state Capitol to the justice center. We'll have more on this breaking story as it unfolds."

Kara stared at the television screen, her breakfast forgotten, blood pounding in her ears.

No! This wasn't possible! There's no way Reece could have murdered anyone! The police must have made some kind of terrible mistake.

She grabbed the remote and flew through the channels. Dog food. Mr. Clean. Minivan. Tampons. Oprah.

"—is expected to accompany the police to the Denver Justice Center for questioning at any moment in the alleged murder of his former lover, Alexis Ryan. We're here on the west steps of the Capitol, where only moments ago several officers from the Denver Police Department entered the building."

Hands trembling, Kara turned down the volume, grabbed for the phone, and dialed Tessa's cell number. One ring. Two. "Answer it, Tess!"

"Kara? Bless your heart! Aren't you supposed to be sequestered in a nunnery or something?"

"He didn't do it, Tess. He couldn't have done it."

Tessa was quiet for a moment. "It looks bad, Kara. They found a nine-millimeter handgun in his briefcase this morning, and they found a bloody tarp in the Dumpster behind his condo. They've got a search warrant for his home and his vehicle and have taken his Jeep into custody for forensic testing. He says he was at home alone and asleep last night, so he has no viable alibi. He admits that he had a fling with her a couple years ago and that the two of them haven't gotten along since she tried to trade sex for votes. But he swears he didn't kill her."

Then it dawned on Kara. "The TV stations don't have any of this. Did he give you an interview?"

"Yeah. An exclusive."

Kara closed her eyes and fought the lump that was trying to form in her throat. She knew this was Reece's way of reaching out to her, his way of asking her to trust him. He'd granted her paper an exclusive at a time when he needed every bit of good ink he could get. *What an idiot!* "How'd he look?"

"He looked pretty good, considering—got a cute bow tie on with suspenders. Classy."

"No, I mean how did he *seem* to you?"

"He's pretty shaken up, but he looks good, truly, Kara. He said he was certain the evidence would prove his innocence."

"God, I hope so, because he *is* innocent." She knew it just as she knew the sky was blue and the sun would come up in the morning. "Who's his attorney?"

"He has declined counsel."

"What?" Kara was on her feet now, pacing. "The cops will shred him to ribbons!"

"He says he has nothing to hide and therefore doesn't need an attorney." Tessa said something to someone else, and Kara heard Joaquin's voice in the background. "They're coming out now. I've got to go."

Kara hung up and turned up the volume on the TV.

" —walking down the west steps of the Capitol now."

Kara's heart gave a sick thud, and pain sliced through her stomach. Two officers flanked Reece as he walked gracefully down the steps and toward the squad car, jacket tossed over his shoulder. His head was high, but Kara could see the grim set of his jaw, the tension that brewed just beneath his skin.

The crowd of reporters pressed in on him with cameras and microphones and threw questions in his face, some of them rude.

"Is it true you've agreed to submit to a lie-detector test, Senator?"

"How do you respond to reports the murder weapon was found in your possession?"

"Will you confirm that you and Alexis Ryan were lovers?"

"Where does Kara McMillan fit into the picture?"

Reece stopped short and looked toward the television cameras. "I wish to express my condolences to Ms. Ryan's family. I have every confidence the Denver Police Department will discover who took her life and that justice will be served. The police will have my full cooperation throughout their investigation."

Kara saw the anger and humiliation in his eyes. She knew what this was costing him, felt his pain as if it were her own. He'd become a senator to be a better teacher, to prove to his students that one person could make a difference, to show the world that it was possible to hold political office without bending to the corruption that so often went with it. And now he was on display before the world as a murder suspect.

The police pushed through the crowd, opened the door of the squad car, and with a hand on Reece's head, guided him into the backseat. Then the door slammed shut, and he disappeared from view. The siren chirped twice in warning, parting the crowd, and the squad car drew slowly away from the curb.

Kara was halfway to the door, her purse in hand, when she remembered. She wasn't going anywhere.

* * *

PICTURES OF Alexis, her skull blown open, her eyes staring at nothing, lay on the table before Reece. Rage was a slow burn in his gut. No matter how much he had despised her, she hadn't deserved what had happened to her. No one deserved this. He hoped whoever had done this to her would soon be sitting where he was sitting.

"Let's get this straight. You argued with the deceased yesterday afternoon. Then you went back to your office, where you worked until approximately twenty-three-thirty."

"That's correct." Reece stared into the skinny cop's gray eyes. They'd been questioning him in this miserable little room for two hours nonstop. The skinny one, whose name was Charlie, was playing good cop, while the fat one, whose name was Stan, was clearly playing bad cop. They had grilled him on every aspect of his relationship with Alexis, on every step he'd taken yesterday evening. And yet it didn't seem to satisfy them.

Stan leaned across the table and spoke in a low and menacing voice. "And while you were in your office, the things she said really ate at you and pissed you off. You decided to track her down and have it out, didn't you? You grabbed your gun, tracked her down, and blew her brains out. Then you wrapped her in the tarp and dumped her in the park."

"No, I didn't. As I've already told you, I think someone is trying to frame me. I didn't give Alexis another thought after I turned my back on her. I went up to my office and did several hours of research on the Internet, which the browser on my computer ought to be able to confirm. I left the office at eleven-thirty, drove directly home, watched CNN for a while, and then went to sleep. I didn't see Alexis after our argument at all."

"That's a lie, Senator!" Stan's face grew red. "We got a bloody tarp pulled out of a trash bin behind your condo. We got an eyewitness who swears he saw a man fitting your description dump a woman's body in the park and drive away at oh-one-hundred. The numbers he saw on the license plate are a match for yours, Senator. You were there! You killed her!"

Reece kept his voice calm, well aware that the interview was being watched from the other side of the one-way mirror. "No, sir, I didn't, but someone clearly wants you to think I did. I slept alone in my condo until six this morning, when I got up, went to the gym, showered, and then came into the Capitol."

In truth he'd lain awake half the night, thinking not of Alexis and his petty argument with her, but of Kara, who was somewhere out there. Surely by now she'd seen the news and knew he was a suspect. Would she believe him guilty? Would she want to put off their relationship until he was cleared? Had she found the TexaMent connection and decided he was nothing but a liar?

Worse than the potential damage to his political career, worse than the knowledge that someone wanted to destroy him, was his fear that he'd lost any chance he'd had at building a life with her.

He loved her.

He wasn't sure when he'd realized it. Perhaps when, afraid and in pain, she'd admitted that she needed him. Perhaps the first time she'd come for him, lost herself against his hand. Perhaps that first night when she'd had too much to drink and had given him a hard-on just by asking ridiculous questions.

A part of him still struggled to grasp what was happening. He'd just gotten to his desk at the Capitol when two police officers had showed up at his office and begun to question him. He hadn't known Alexis was dead until they'd told him. The news had stunned Reece, but no more so than the realization that he was a suspect. He'd answered all their questions, and when they'd asked to search his Jeep and his office, he had been happy to comply. Then they'd found the Sphinx.

They didn't seem to care that he had a concealed-carry

permit. In a blink, they'd gotten a warrant to search his home and had continued to badger him for details regarding his whereabouts last night and his relationship with Alexis. Within an hour, a forensics team claimed to have found a blood-soaked canvas tarp in the trash bin behind his house and he'd become not only a suspect, but their prime suspect.

It was like a nightmare, only Reece couldn't seem to wake up.

Charlie gave Reece a sympathetic nod of the head. "I understand, Senator. Really I do. You're in a new relationship now with the reporter. You've been under a lot of strain with her being attacked and almost killed. Up comes Alexis Ryan. She insults your new girlfriend, and it all crashes in on you. You pop. It happens every day. Admit that you killed her in an uncontrollable rage, and you're looking at murder two. With your record—"

Reece leaned forward, disgusted. "I didn't kill her! I didn't so much as touch her! Someone is trying to frame me here! Do you really think I'd be so stupid as to murder someone and keep evidence of the crime in my briefcase?"

Stan glared at him. "When the forensics come in on this you're going to be arrested and then you're going to fry!"

Reece rolled his eyes. "Actually, the current means of execution in Colorado is lethal injection."

"You're a real smart ass, aren't you buddy?"

The door opened, and Chief Irving stepped in. "Charlie, Stan, take five."

The two cops stood, shared a questioning look, and then strode out of the room.

Irving shut the door behind them, pushed back a chair, and sat. "Hell of a day you're having, Senator."

Reece leaned back in his chair and ran a hand over his face. "Yeah."

"I'm going to tell you something that might surprise you."

"What could that be?"

"I believe you. I don't think you had a damned thing to do with Ms. Ryan's murder."

Reece met Irving's gaze and saw that he wasn't joking. "Why is that, Chief?"

"For one thing, forensics turned up no trace of blood in your Jeep. Nada. It seems unlikely to me that you could transport her body in a blood-soaked tarp and not get a single drop of blood in your vehicle. That casts some doubt on our anonymous tipster. If he saw your Jeep dumping the body, there should be blood. If there's no blood, I don't see how it could be your Jeep, and our tipster could be lying."

That was the best news Reece had heard in hours. "I didn't kill her."

"I know it." Irving nodded. "For another thing, the lab says there was no powder residue on your skin, and your piece hasn't been fired since the last time you cleaned it."

The suffocating knot of dread that had been building in Reece's chest began to loosen. "The last time I fired it was about six months ago."

"But more than that, Senator, I don't think you'd be stupid enough to commit a homicide, drive the body to a highly public location, throw a tarp with the victim's blood on it into your own damned trash can, and then keep the weapon on you. You might be a politician, but you're not an idiot."

Despite his situation, Reece grinned. "That's the nicest thing anyone's said to me all day."

"It all goes together too well. An anonymous tip leads us to the body, gives us your license plate number and the make and model of your vehicle. The victim has a sexual history with you, a history that includes public confrontations. The bloody tarp is found behind your building. A weapon is found in your possession. Hell, this case is wrapped up so pretty you might as well put a bow on it. I've been a cop for thirty years, and my gut tells me something's off."

"That's what I've been saying all morning."

"Of course, we're still waiting for the autopsy results and ballistic tests. If the slugs that come out of her brain match your weapon, you're going to be in a hell of a lot of trouble.

In the meantime, you might be able to cut through some of the bullshit by agreeing to a polygraph."

"Fine. I said I'd cooperate, and I meant it. The sooner your officers quit wasting time with me the sooner they'll find the real murderer."

Irving nodded. "If you don't mind, I've got a question for you myself."

"Ask it."

"Who's out to get you, Senator?"

CHAPTER 24

KARA TRIED to focus on the papers in her hands but found it almost impossible to keep her gaze off the television. At least once an hour, the local stations ran the footage of Reece being escorted down the steps and into the squad car, together with an update from outside the Denver Justice Center. There was nothing new to report, but it was clear that behind the scenes the research drones were digging.

The noon broadcast painted Reece as a good man who'd possibly gone wrong and included the photograph of him shouting into Galen's face. By one, he was a man with a dark side whose dislike for the victim and unpredictable temper were common knowledge at the Capitol. This time, the photo of him shouting at Galen was contrasted with photographs of Alexis Ryan as an innocent schoolgirl and a beautiful, successful woman. By two, they'd gotten an interview with the victim's weeping parents, whose grief was juxtaposed with Reece's fury.

Kara sat on the carpeted floor surrounded by documents, her stomach tied in knots of helpless rage. She knew lynch-mob reporting when she saw it. There wasn't one shred of forensic evidence to tie Reece to the lobbyist's death, yet he'd already been tried and convicted in the media. The man they described was not the man she knew, but she couldn't very well speak out publicly on his behalf, not when she, too, was investigating him.

My God, had she actually been thinking of calling one of the news stations and complaining about their coverage? Yes, she had. The thought pushed her to her feet, and she began to pace the room.

What exactly would she have said? *He can't have murdered anyone because he was kind and gentle with my son? He's innocent because no man who makes love like he does could ever kill a woman? He didn't kill anyone because I'm in love with him?*

The realization drove the air from her lungs. She sank into an armchair and buried her face in her hands. *So much for objectivity, McMillan.*

Perhaps she should turn this story over to someone else. Perhaps her mind was so clouded with emotion that she was unable to do her job. After all, Reece, through his tire-burning bill, was the only member of the Legislative Audit Committee she'd been able to tie to Northrup, but she still refused to believe he was involved with any of this.

Would she have felt the same way if she didn't know him personally?

No. She would have looked at the evidence objectively, and she would have assumed she'd found the guilty party.

And she would have been wrong.

It was a strange realization that left Kara feeling unsettled. She'd made a career out of piecing facts together. She'd followed logic, followed the evidence, and it had never led her astray. And now she was ready to toss both facts and logic out the window for some kind of—what? Emotional insight?

What a damned mess this is.

She leaned back in the chair, took as deep a breath as her healing ribs would allow, and fought to clear her mind. Her investigation was incomplete. Like a puzzle with too many pieces missing, the picture created by the information she'd acquired so far was deceptive. She didn't know what the missing pieces were, but she needed to find them.

Her next thought had her sitting upright, pulse racing.

What if whoever was after her had killed Alexis Ryan? What if whoever wanted her dead was trying to hurt Reece now that she was beyond their reach? After all, media coverage of the attack had linked the two of them. Whoever was trying to kill her surely knew she and Reece were at least friends. Or what if Reece had uncovered something during his own investigation that they didn't want him to know?

She stood and went back to pacing. What did they stand to gain by framing him with murder? Why not simply kill him? Why keep him around?

She stopped and almost laughed. They needed his vote. That had to be it. He was sponsoring a bill beneficial to Northrup, and they needed that bill to pass. Framing him for murder would tie him up and shred his credibility, at least until he was cleared. But it wouldn't prevent him from voting.

Movement on the television screen caught her eye. She turned up the volume.

"—has just stepped out of the building, and we're told that he's going to make a statement."

Cameras focused on Chief Irving, who faced the media gauntlet looking like a man who'd already had his fill of bullshit for the day. He stepped up to the dozens of microphones that were thrust in his face, waited for quiet, and then read from a written statement. "Today, police questioned State Senator Reece Sheridan extensively based on the circumstantial evidence against him in the homicide of lobbyist Alexis Ryan. Sheridan, who submitted voluntarily to questioning without benefit of counsel, cooperated fully with investigators, undergoing a polygraph test, which he passed, and submitting a blood sample for DNA testing. The police department is not seeking an arrest warrant against the senator at this time. Pending the outcome of forensic testing, Senator Sheridan remains a person of interest in this case."

Then Irving turned away from the crowd, ignoring the explosion of shouted questions, and disappeared back into the justice center.

Kara smiled despite her nerves. The impromptu press conference had served its purpose—to disseminate information and to distract the media throng so Reece could leave unobserved. They'd probably gotten him out in an unmarked squad car via the underground parking garage. She'd been fooled that way once—but only once.

Suddenly Kara needed to speak with Reece so badly it hurt. The last time they'd talked, she'd been angry with him. She'd made him think she didn't care enough about their relationship to fight for it. Well, he was wrong. She cared plenty. More than that, she believed in him. If nothing else, she wanted him to know that.

She crossed the room, picked up the secured phone line, and dialed his cell.

REECE THANKED the officer who'd driven him back to the Capitol and then shut the passenger door. He strode up the east steps, grateful that the ravening media horde was currently being distracted by Chief Irving's press conference over at the justice center. He needed to get to his desk. He had work to do.

He opened the heavy doors and walked into the rotunda. Every head turned his way, and the cacophony of voices faded to a stony silence. People he thought he knew well—colleagues, friends, and staff—stared at him with blatant suspicion and contempt. Carol from Senate Finance. Alan, the sergeant-at-arms. Even Brooke, his own intern.

Walking with deliberate slowness, he made his way through the unnatural hush to the rose-colored marble stairs and took them one at a time, fighting to keep the anger off his face. Whispers. Muttered curses. The heat of a hundred people staring into his back.

The hallway outside his office was no better. People stopped talking and glared. He unlocked his office door, closed it behind him, leaned back against it, and slowly released the breath he'd been holding. Chief Irving had warned him it would be tough, but Reece hadn't expected to feel so . . . *defeated.*

"You'll find out who your real friends are, that's for damned sure," the chief had said.

How could anyone who knew him believe him capable of cold-blooded murder? Sharp disappointment twined with a sense of betrayal, rose like bile at the back of his throat. For two years, he'd played this game. He'd tried to serve as an example, tried to show his students and the public that a person could make more of a difference by following the rules than by bending and breaking them. And where had it gotten him?

Today he'd been led like a criminal down the steps of the Capitol with the world watching. People he'd trusted now believed he was a murderer. Kara was likely lost to him forever. And Alexis was dead. As much as he'd disliked her, Reece grieved for her. They'd been lovers once, after all, and her last moments had been lived in terror and brutality. The image of her, sprawled lifeless on the grass, flashed into his mind.

He forced it down, forced himself to focus. He hadn't come here to win a popularity contest or to sort out his thoughts. He had important work to do.

The message light on his phone blinked red. Melanie had probably left him just as many messages here as she had on his cell phone. He'd called her back before leaving the justice center. She'd been frantic and had burst into tears when she'd heard his voice. She'd offered to house him, feed him, get him drunk on his favorite scotch, and beat the shit out of any reporter who came near her house. But what had touched him most was her absolute faith in him. She hadn't once asked him if he was innocent or guilty.

He'd told her he had things to handle at the Capitol but that he'd get back to her later about his plans for the night. As he'd hung up, he'd felt for the first time since his father's death that he had real family.

He sat at his desk, waded through his messages—most of

them from Melanie, the rest from reporters—and then turned to his computer. The first thing he needed to do was make certain that his tire-burning bill was on tomorrow's Senate agenda. He was going to kill his own bill, and he was going to kill it in the most public way he could—on the Senate floor.

Then he needed to get in touch with Kara somehow to tell her about Northrup's relationship with TexaMent.

He called up the bill status database and discovered that someone had already placed the bill on tomorrow's agenda. In fact, someone had placed it on today's agenda, but it had been postponed when a dispute over Western Slope water rights ate up most of the day's session.

And then it clicked. Stanfield had wanted him out of the way so the tire-burning bill, which had already passed second reading, could be passed before Reece had a chance to kill it. The bastard had been so cool on the phone last night.

"I guess we each have our jobs to do, Senator," he'd said, almost as if Reece's announcement that he was killing the tire-burning bill hadn't fazed him at all.

"Yes, we do. And part of mine is making certain Kara McMillan is safe. I don't know who is trying to kill her, but I'm warning you to stay away from her. Leave her alone, Stanfield!"

"Get a hold of yourself, Senator. You're beginning to sound like a lunatic."

Reece was willing to bet that as soon as he'd hung up the phone, Stanfield had gotten busy arranging to frame him for murder. He couldn't prove it, of course. He'd shared what he knew for certain with Chief Irving, who'd watched him through emotionless blue eyes that said he'd heard it all before—false protestations of innocence, lame excuses for guilt, the screams of the abused, the bereaved, the dying.

He'd written down a few names—TexaMent, Northrup, Mike Stanfield. "And this is the same company Ms. McMillan is investigating?"

"Yeah."

Reece had to give Stanfield credit. With one terrible act, he'd destroyed Reece's credibility, at least until he was cleared. He'd isolated Reece, humiliated him, kept him out of the Capitol for a day. And he'd disarmed him—he wouldn't get his pistol back until he'd been cleared. But Stanfield wasn't as clever as he thought he was. Someone had to have acted to get the bill placed on today's agenda, and that information would be part of the record somewhere. Whichever senator had changed the agenda surely had ties to Northrup and was the person Kara was trying to expose.

Reece read through the minutes for the day's session and sneered at the computer screen. "Devlin." The jerk could never say no to people with money.

In his trouser pocket, his cell phone vibrated. He withdrew it, saw that the caller's number was blocked, and hesitated. A reporter? "Reece Sheridan."

"I'm so sorry!"

"Christ, Kara, it's good to hear your voice!" And it was.

"This shouldn't be happening to you."

"I want you to know that I didn't—"

"Don't you even say it! If you think for one minute that I have even the slightest doubt about you, then I'm going to kick your very fine ass."

He closed his eyes, leaned back in his chair, felt relief rush through him. He hadn't realized until that moment how essential it was to him that she believe him. "Thanks."

"The news coverage has been terrible. If I were in charge, there'd be some reporters going back to j-school for a refresher course on 'innocent until proven guilty.' "

At the moment, he couldn't care less what reporters were saying. Kara believed in him, and that was enough. He knew he was grinning like an idiot. "Are you safe?"

"Safe as a gold bar at Fort Knox."

"Good, because they're relentless."

"I know. They did this, didn't they? The same people who tried to kill me killed her to hurt you."

"I think so." He needed to tell her. "I called the CEO of

TexaMent last night to let him know I was pulling my support for the tire-burning bill."

"The bill Northrup wants passed?"

"TexaMent is Northrup, Kara. They own Northrup. They bought it almost ten years ago."

"When did you find—?"

"Last night. I wanted to tell you, but it was late and I wasn't sure how to reach you. I was about to call Chief Irving and ask him to relay the information."

"Where are you?"

"At the Capitol."

"My God, you're brave!"

Someone knocked on his door, and Miguel popped his head inside. "Reece, I . . . oh. I'll wait outside, *amigo.*"

The day was getting better. Among his colleagues, Miguel, at least, hadn't deserted him. He nodded to Miguel, who saw the phone, smiled, and ducked out to wait outside his office door.

"How's the investigation going on your end?" Reece didn't want to hang up. He didn't want to say good-bye. He needed her.

"Not great. There are still too many pieces of the puzzle missing. But with this new information, I might be able to shake something loose. So far the only senator I've been able to find with ties to Northrup is you."

"I have a few thoughts about that." His gaze fixed on Devlin's name on his computer screen. He pulled a flash drive out of his desk drawer, attached it to his USB port, and hit copy.

Her next words took him by surprise. "I need to see you. Please, Reece, I have to see you."

"There's no way, Kara. You know that. I won't do anything that puts you in danger. I'm not exactly low profile these days. If I drive up in front of wherever they've got you hidden, someone is likely to film it and put it on the six o'clock news. Hell, the TV crews are probably staked out on my front lawn."

"Then don't go home. Wait until after dark, and take a cab from the Capitol." Then she told him where she was and rattled off instructions on how to get to her.

He tried not to listen. "Kara, we both know this is a bad idea."

"Bring whatever documents you have—disks, files, whatever you can grab. With my understanding of Northrup and your knowledge of how things work at the Capitol, we ought to be able to piece this together faster."

"What about your rule that you and I not discuss our jobs?"

For a moment she said nothing. "It's our lives we're talking about now, Reece. Please come."

What if they followed him? What if he led them to her? He couldn't take that risk. "I'll be there in two hours."

Chief Irving was going to have his hide.

KARA GLANCED at her watch. He ought to have been here ten minutes ago.

She stood in the doorway to her room, where she'd be able to hear him knock on the stairwell door at the end of the hallway. It was locked from the inside, but she'd already tested it and knew she could open it. There were no security cameras in the stairwells—she'd scouted for them—so all he had to do was climb thirty flights of stairs. Then she would let him in, and no one would be the wiser. Even if the bastards had followed him, they couldn't get to her. She wasn't going to open the stairwell door for anyone else.

She was about to call him again, when she heard it—the rap of knuckles against metal. She hurried to the end of the hallway, glanced through the skinny rectangular window, felt her pulse trip when she saw his face, and opened the door.

"Nice workout." Beads of sweat clung to his forehead, but he wasn't particularly out of breath. His jacket was slung over his shoulder, and he still wore the clothes he'd been wearing on television—starched white shirt, red suspenders, cute little bow tie. Classy. He bent down and kissed her forehead. "Let's get you back inside."

He tested the stairwell door to make certain it shut behind him, then wrapped an arm around her shoulder and walked with her into the suite.

"So what do you think?" Kara locked the door behind him and watched the expression on his face as he took in their surroundings.

"Not bad for a hidey-hole." He grinned, but she could see the lines of strain on his face, the shadows in his eyes. He tossed his jacket over a chair, pulled her gently into his arms, and buried his face in her hair. "God, it's good to see you."

For a moment they just stood there, just held one another. He was warm from his climb up the stairs, his scent and the strength of his body both familiar and reassuring. But for the first time since she'd met him, Kara felt the vulnerability beneath that strength. Somehow, his anguish seeped into her. Her heart gave a painful lurch, and hot tears came from nowhere to blur her vision.

She wanted to tell him, wanted him to know how much he meant to her, but she couldn't bring herself to say the words. Instead, she stood on her toes, brushed her lips over the day's growth of stubble on his cheek, and left a trail of kisses down his jaw to his throat.

He took her chin between his thumbs, searched her face, his brow furrowed. "Are those tears for me?"

She answered him in the only way she could, by taking his mouth with hers. His lips were soft, warm, pliant, and at first he let her set the pace. But when she slipped her tongue into his mouth, he ended the kiss and pulled back.

"I don't want to hurt you." His palm pressed gently against her healing ribs.

She pressed a finger to his lips and fought past her tears to find her voice. "Shut up."

CHAPTER 25

WHEN SHE kissed him again, Reece took what she offered, accepted the soft stroke of her tongue, the press of her soft body against his, the fisting of her hands in his hair. He tasted the salt of her tears, felt her shiver, and wondered at this intensity of emotion that seemed to be coursing through her.

Her fingers left his hair, found the ends of his bow tie, tugged, and then moved to unbutton his shirt. And still she took the kiss deeper, her mouth mating with his with an urgency and tenderness that unleashed an ache in his chest.

She was giving. For the first time since he'd known her, she was giving of herself, not just her body, but from her core. The realization broke over him like the crest of a wave, robbed him of breath, left him feeling stunned, shaken, naked.

He forced himself to stand passive as she pulled his suspenders over his shoulders and removed first his shirt, then his undershirt. Heat speared into his groin as her hands and lips explored his chest. And then she was on her knees before him, tugging on his zipper, stroking the length of him, taking him into her mouth.

Her lips were hot against his engorged flesh as she stroked him, her mouth and hand working in tandem. And her tongue—Holy Jesus God, what was she doing? Air hissed from between his clenched teeth. He buried his fingers in the silk of her hair, matched her rhythm, and let the force of her hunger carry him to the smoldering brink.

"Stop!" He fought for control and looked down into her confused eyes. "Not like this."

He lifted her to her feet and unbuttoned her blouse, taking time to run the silky cloth over her bared breasts. Then he peeled away her jeans and panties and lifted her sweet body into his arms. "Where's the bed?"

She pointed, then wrapped her arms around his neck and buried her face against him. God, it felt good—that intimate little gesture of trust, of need, of surrender. He carried her down a short hallway, into the darkened bedroom, and laid her down in the middle of the enormous bed.

She was the most beautiful thing he'd ever seen. Her lips were swollen, her cheeks streaked with tears. Her hair lay in a tangled mass over her breasts, one wine-colored nipple peeking through, begging to be licked. Yellow bruises stained her skin, a reminder to Reece of how close he'd come to losing her. He stretched himself out beside her and captured her mouth for another kiss.

Knowing hands sought out the most sensitive places, the surest ways to please. Skin slid over soft skin. Bodies twisted and rolled.

Burning for her, Reece could wait no longer. He settled himself between her thighs. "Don't close your eyes, Kara. Look at me!"

Kara did as he demanded and immediately lost herself in the tangle of emotions she saw there—lust, protectiveness, tenderness. And love. Yes, love.

Their moans mingled as he nudged his way inch by inch inside her and began to thrust in slow, silky strokes, his gaze never leaving hers. He felt so good, so absolutely right, and the tears she'd gotten under control only minutes ago trickled down her temples.

"Ah, Kara, sweetheart." He ducked down, kissed the wetness, and looked at her through eyes that seemed to understand.

The first orgasm took her by surprise, rolling through her like a tidal wave set on slow motion. Her gasp became a low, shuddering moan and then a cry as the pleasure overtook her, swelled, and grew even stronger. She dug her nails into the sweat-slick skin of his back and tried to ride it out. Still he kept the pace slow, his thrusts extending her climax until it became another.

"Reece, oh, God!" She panted his name, wrapped her legs around him, and pulled him closer, deeper.

She heard his breath catch, felt his muscles tense, felt his control slip. In the span of a heartbeat he was driving into her with a rhythm that had her hurtling toward yet another peak. But this time, he soared with her over that sweet edge into a void that held nothing but shattering bliss, nothing but skin and breath and entwined limbs. Nothing but the two of them.

"BE SURE it's room service before you open the door." Reece watched Kara slip into her white silk bathrobe, the warm glow of lovemaking on her face, the scent of sex clinging to her skin like expensive perfume. "And try not to look like a woman who's just—"

She put a hand over his mouth and smiled. "Shhh! You're not supposed to be here, remember?" Then she left him in the dark.

He heard the door open and then a man's voice mumbling. He'd have felt better if he'd been the one answering the door. He'd have felt better still if he had his pistol. Despite the precautions he'd taken to make certain he wasn't being followed, it was stupid of him to have come here. And yet, after what they'd shared, he couldn't truly regret his decision. He'd had plenty of great sex in his life, but never had he experienced anything like making love with Kara. Each time, it felt as if he'd died inside her, only to be reborn fresh and new and clean.

"You can just set it down here," Kara told the man. "Wow. Did I really order all that? I guess I'm really hungry tonight. Thanks."

Reece couldn't help but smile at the nervous tone in her voice. She was a pathetic liar.

A few moments later, the door closed, and Kara reappeared and spoke with an exaggerated English accent. "Dinner is served."

Reece slipped back into his boxers and followed her out to the main room, where three trays of food sat on the coffee table. As they shared a bottle of Chardonnay and feasted on clams on the half shell, fried calamari, shrimp, and a selection of antipasti, she gave him an overview of her investigation, starting with the whistleblower and ending with the documents she'd requested from members of the Legislative Audit Committee.

As he listened, he found himself fascinated by the way her mind worked—her sharp intelligence, her thoroughness, her ability to digest vast amounts of information and hold on to the details. He watched her shifting facial expression and saw there the passion she felt for her work, her thirst for justice, her determination to shine a light on the hidden wrongs of the world.

By the time she'd finished, the wine and the food were gone, and she had showed him what she believed were key documents, including the letter from someone on the audit committee ordering the state inspector to back off Northrup. Reece held the letter in his hand and stared at the blacked-out signature, anger and disgust rolling in his gut. Did the dark marker hide the name of a murderer?

She sat on the couch across from him and pointed to the document in his hands. "The biggest hole in my story is the identity of the person who signed that letter. Owens at the health department knows who it is, and I'll bet the governor knows, too. But neither of them is going to tell me."

"Probably not." *But if I apply the right pressure, they might tell me.* "Can you run your story without knowing who signed it?"

"I could run the story and simply quote the letter, but if I do that, whoever signed it will scurry for cover like a cockroach. He or she will do everything possible to cover any tracks and make my job harder."

"So where do we start?"

She stood, walked over to the piano, and picked up a stack of file folders. "Whoever signed that memo has some connection to Northrup, so we start with the Legislative Audit Committee. I've combed through these files, and so far the only person I've found with any tie to the company is you."

She dropped the folders onto the coffee table.

"But you were looking for Northrup, not TexaMent." Reece grabbed the folder on top and then got down to work.

An hour later, Kara was frustrated and fed up. She'd read through three files, complete with campaign finance records, and found nothing, not a single mention of TexaMent or Northrup. She placed the document she held back into its folder and found herself watching Reece.

He sat on the other sofa, frowning with concentration, the end of a pen between his obscenely delicious lips. Her gaze traveled from his feet, which rested on the coffee table— could feet truly be sexy?—up his long, muscular legs, over his navy silk boxers with their appealing bulge to his bare torso. What must it be like to live in that body, to have all that delicious muscle and velvety man-skin within reach all day every day? If Kara had his body, she'd be too busy touching herself to make it out of bed in the morning.

His voice startled her. "If you keep looking at me like that we're not going to get anything done tonight. And that would be a shame because I think I've found what we're looking for."

That had her on her feet. "Show me."

He sat up and spread documents from Drew Devlin's file across the table. "He's been getting hefty contributions from TexaMent for years. Look."

Kara read down the page and saw the entries on the campaign-finance reports that Reece had starred. "Who's Mike Stanfield?"

"It says here he's a businessman, but it doesn't identify the business. I just happen to know he's the CEO of TexaMent."

"That's it. It's Devlin." She felt her pulse pick up, felt that rush of adrenaline she always got when a story was finally coming together.

"It certainly seems so. Look at this." Reece circled Stanfield's reported address—a rural address with an Adams County zip code—then pointed to fifteen additional entries on last year's report that had the exact same street address but different names. "Either Stanfield runs a boarding house for wayward donors, or he's breaking the law."

She leapt to her feet, dashed into the dining room, grabbed the folder that held the original inspection report, and flipped through its pages. And there it was. She let out a whoop of triumph and almost danced back to the couch. "That's not Stanfield's house. It's Northrup."

Breathless, she tossed the report into Reece's lap and watched his face as he read through the first page. He stood, dropped the report on the table, and pulled her into his arms. "Ms. McMillan, I believe your story is in the bag."

"Well, not quite yet. I still have to interview several people, including Devlin and this Stanfield guy. I doubt either of them is going to be particularly inclined to confess on the record. Crooks never do."

"Just one of many reasons why bad guys suck."

"I can't believe I missed that." Her euphoria dropped a few notches. "I'd read through the campaign-finance reports line by line, and I missed it."

He kissed her hair. "Don't be so hard on yourself. They went out of their way to hide what they were doing. I only caught it because I know the players. You've done one hell of a job with this investigation, Kara."

But her mind was already on the next step. "I need to call Tom."

"I'M GUESSING a good forty or fifty inches, perhaps twenty to thirty for the main story and a couple sidebars."

While Kara spoke with her editor, Reece listened from inside the bedroom and made his own plans. He couldn't prove anything, but he was certain Stanfield was behind both the attack on Kara and Alexis's murder. The bastard certainly had money and arrogance enough to hire thugs to do that sort of dirty work. Based on his management of Northrup, he also didn't seem to give a damn whether he was breaking the law or whether his company was hurting people or the environment.

But Stanfield's winning streak was about to come to an end. Unless he got Reece locked behind bars or put a bullet through his skull in the next twelve hours, Reece was going to walk onto the Senate floor and kill his own bill. Then he planned to do a little interviewing of his own—first Devlin, then Owens, then Stanfield.

He was so lost in thought he didn't realize Kara was off the phone until she came into the bedroom. "How'd it go?"

"Fine, I think. Except that I get a terrible feeling my editor wants to have sex with my mother. He kept prying for information." She plopped down on the bed beside him, a look of revulsion on her face. "Tell me that's illegal."

He fought back a smile. "Strictly speaking, no."

"My mom and my editor. Oh, God!"

"Your mom can handle him. Lily is a smart woman—much like her daughter."

She glared at him. "She and I have next to nothing in common. She's into all that New Age stuff and—"

"She's incredibly intelligent. She cares about other people." He sat up, slipped her bathrobe off her shoulder, punctuated his words with kisses down the soft skin of her back. "She's sexy. She's brave. She's strong. And she loves her only child with every bit of her body and soul."

He pulled Kara's bathrobe aside, bared her luscious body, and then turned her so she leaned against him, her back to his chest. He cupped her breasts, teased their taut peaks with his thumbs, and watched them grow tighter still.

"What do you think you're doing, Senator?" Her eyes were closed, and he could feel her pulse quicken.

"Right now I'm getting you hot and bothered. In a minute, I'm going to go fill up that gigantic sunken bathtub. Then I'm going to climb into the water with you and make you scream."

"Politicians and their promises." Her words were breathy whispers.

"Sweetheart, this is one promise I'm going to keep."

KARA BACKED away from the sliding glass door, heart slamming in her chest. She saw the gun, saw the flash of light when it fired. Then she was running.

Connor sat on the floor in the hallway playing with plastic dinosaurs.

"Hide, Connor! Under your bed!"

She called for him, screamed for him, but he didn't seem to hear her.

Another gunshot. Behind her glass shattered.

"Connor, run!"

But Connor didn't budge.

Then the man's hands were on her, choking her. She fought him, fought to breathe, fought to live.

"Kara! It's okay! Wake up, sweetheart. It's just a dream."

Shaking, feeling sick, her heart hammering in her chest, Kara found herself sitting up in bed, drenched with cold sweat and clinging to Reece, who held her close, stroked her hair, whispered reassurances in her ear. Gradually, her trembling subsided, leaving only nausea and the lingering taste of horror. It had seemed so real. Why did it always seem so real?

"Do you want room service to bring you some tea?"

"No. Just don't let go of me." She buried her face in the warm strength of his chest.

"I won't."

REECE ROSE before dawn and shared a small pot of tea with Kara. She'd seemed to sleep soundly once she'd fallen asleep again, but there were shadows in her eyes, and he knew the nightmare lingered with her. He told her of his suspicions about Stanfield and warned her to be careful. Then they showered together, and he amused her by using her razor and girl-scented shaving cream on his face.

"You smell like baby powder," she said, sniffing him and laughing. "How pretty."

Afterward, he reluctantly kissed her good-bye and left the way he'd come, testing the stairwell door behind him. He wanted to get out onto the street and into a cab before anyone recognized him. As his face had been all over the television yesterday and was surely plastered on the front of every newspaper this morning, that wasn't going to be easy.

He made it almost all the way to the Capitol before the cabbie recognized him. The man stared at him in the rearview mirror. "Hey, you're that guy who killed that woman, right?"

"I'm that guy, but I didn't kill anyone."

"Whatever you say, buddy. Who knows? Maybe she deserved it. My ex-wife, if I whacked her, she'd deserve it."

Reece found himself feeling sorry for the man's ex-wife as he was forced to endure a recitation of the cab driver's marital woes. He was grateful when the gleaming gold dome of the Capitol came into view. He handed over the cab fare and walked straight up to his office, ignoring the stares, the whispers, and the small cadre of reporters that chased him up the stairs. He'd used Kara's fax machine to make copies of the key documents implicating Devlin and wanted to do a bit more research before confronting him. Perhaps Devlin had sponsored other bills on behalf of TexaMent.

He opened the file of documents he'd copied and glanced through them while he waited for his computer to boot. He had an hour before he needed to be on the Senate floor. And then Stanfield would get just a small piece of what he had coming to him.

CHAPTER 26

"TELL MR. OWENS I'll call back every fifteen minutes until I hear from him. Thanks." Kara hung up the phone. "Damn it!"

She'd gotten Devlin's voicemail—not surprising, as the Senate was in session this morning. The governor was supposedly out of the office and couldn't be reached until this afternoon. Owens was still in a meeting—a meeting that would probably last until her deadline had passed. Typical bureaucrat.

If she hadn't been locked up in this hotel, she would have gone to the governor's office and the health department and then camped out at the Capitol to wait for Devlin. She was a lot tougher to evade in person. But stuck at the top of a skyscraper, she could do little more than harass whoever answered the phone. The frustration made her want to scream.

That's not how her day had started. She'd awoken feeling warm and contented, Reece's arms around her, his lips pressing kisses against her temple. They'd shared the shower and a cup of tea. Then he'd grown serious and told her he believed Mike Stanfield was somehow behind not only the threats and the attack on her life but also the lobbyist's murder. He'd warned her to be careful, then he'd given her one last lingering kiss and headed off to the Capitol to kill his bill.

And that warm contentment had too quickly been replaced by worries—for Reece, for herself, for Connor, whom she missed horribly. She wanted Reece to have his name cleared. She wanted her life back. She wanted her son and mother to come home. She wanted to be able to figure out where her relationship with Reece was going without violence, nightmares, and threats hanging over both of their heads.

God, she loved him. She hadn't told him yet, as if not speaking the words would somehow keep her feelings from becoming too real. She hadn't meant for things to turn out like this. She'd never intended to lose herself over a man again. She'd always imagined that if and when she fell in love again, she would be very grown-up about it—no crazy pounding of the heart, no screaming sex in a sunken tub at midnight, nothing to interfere with her career or complicate her already complicated life.

She'd been wrong. Reece had brought all those things with him—pounding hearts, screaming sex, and a world of complications. But he'd also respected her, stood up for her, and gone out of his way to be thoughtful to both her and Connor. She'd never experienced that kind of easy connection with a man before. With Galen, she'd always felt there was something else she had to do to win his approval—be more sophisticated around his friends, who were so much older and more established than she; be better in bed; make fewer emotional demands. Her relationship with Tom, though it wasn't sexual, wasn't much different, as she'd struggled constantly to prove herself to him.

But with Reece, all she had to do was *be*. He'd accepted her as she was from the night they'd met. Getting lost in him felt an awful lot like . . . finding herself.

She got up from her desk, crossed the room to make herself another cup of tea, and pushed thoughts of him from her mind. She needed to get focused and put these interviews behind her so she could pound out this story. She'd already spoken to a cement-industry expert, who had viewed copies of the videotapes Tom had overnighted to him. The man had sputtered with outrage at the images he'd seen—piles of cement-kiln dust, pools of leaked oil, machinery held together with rags and duct tape.

"So what you saw in the videos is not within industry standards?" she'd asked him.

"Are you kidding me? If I were still doing worker-safety inspections, I'd shut that place down. I can't imagine what the workers are breathing every day. Ten years from now their lungs are gonna be nothing but scar tissue."

"Is there any chance whatsoever that the individual who made these tapes might have staged the conditions you viewed?"

"How could anyone do that? There's dust piled up on the ceiling beams. No way could anyone have set that up. What you're seeing is the result of negligence on the part of management. They're not putting the necessary time and money into maintaining their equipment, and it's causing dust and oil leaks. My guess is they've either cut back on their cleaning crew or that the cleaning crew flat out can't keep up with it."

"Why would management fail to maintain the equipment? Wouldn't that hurt the company in the long run?"

"Who cares what's gonna happen in ten or twenty years when you can turn a profit this year? Besides, the rock beds Northrup is mining are expected to play out in the next ten years. Why spend millions on upkeep for a plant you're gonna be shutting down?"

That information had taken her by surprise, and another piece of the puzzle had fallen into place. It was one thing for a company to let its equipment fall apart if that company planned on staying in business. Neglect would eventually impact the company's bottom line. It was a different situation entirely for a facility only years away from closing its doors forever. Like someone pushing to get that last five thousand miles out of an old car, the bigwigs at TexaMent would save millions if they could just hold the plant together with duct tape until it was time to shut down operations.

The lust for profit. It was the motivation behind all of this. From dumping solvents into the drainage ditch to squelching the results of state inspections to failing to maintain equipment, it all came together in millions at the bank. Even the tire-burning bill had its foundation in the desire for profit, as the company would be getting paid to burn tires rather than paying to burn coal.

Kara dipped her tea bag one last time, drained it with her spoon, and set it on the tray. She raised the cup to her lips and took a careful sip. The flavor of peppermint splashed over her tongue. Mulling over the facts, she strolled back to her desk, sat, and sipped.

How did Mike Stanfield feel about money? She needed to find out. She'd gotten a list of questions ready for him this morning just after Reece had left, but she'd been putting off calling him.

Chicken.

She tried to ignore her irritating inner voice and pretended for a moment that she hadn't heard it. But the voice was right. For the first time in her career, she was afraid to interview someone. The realization left her feeling stunned and disgusted. Had she really let them get to her? Had they intimidated her so thoroughly that she was afraid to make a phone call?

As if to redeem herself, she grabbed her notepad, reached for the phone, and dialed Northrup's number. In a matter of seconds, she found herself speaking with his executive assistant. She clicked the record button.

"He's not available at the moment, but he was expecting your call. He instructed me to tell you he'd be available this afternoon."

Kara hid her surprise. "What time do you expect him back? I'll call back then."

"He's marked himself out until four. Would you like me to take a message?"

"Just tell him Kara McMillan from the *Denver Independent* will be in touch this afternoon." She hung up the phone, chills pricking down her spine. The bastard was playing mind games with her. He'd left that message with his assistant for one reason—to intimidate her. He wanted her to know she wasn't going to catch him off-guard. He wanted her to believe he was one step ahead of her. Well, Mike Stanfield could go to hell.

She reached for a stack of documents, ready to begin working on the first sidebar—a timeline detailing findings in the state's inspection reports. Agitated, she succeeded in knocking the documents onto the carpet, where they scattered out of order.

"Great, McMillan. Perfect." She got down on her knees and tried to sort through them.

It was then her gaze fell across one sheet of paper, and she saw it. Forgetting everything else, she picked up the document—a citation against a shift manager for improper storage of solvents—and stared at the name. "Oh! Oh, God!"

She leapt up, picked up the phone, and called her source at the Colorado Bureau of Investigation. "Hi, it's Kara. I need a background check ASAP. The name is Juan de la Peña."

"SENATOR SHERIDAN, you have the floor."

Reece could see the gloating satisfaction in Devlin's eyes. He waited until the Senate chamber fell silent, gave Devlin his most genial smile, and then leaned into the mic. "Mr. President, I would like to make a motion that Senate Bill 46, regarding the burning of waste tires as fuel, be postponed indefinitely."

Devlin looked surprised, and for a moment he said nothing. "I find your motion to be out of order."

Go ahead, Devlin. Dig your grave deeper. "Point of order, Mr. President, the bill *is* on the schedule. It *is* my bill. And I *do* have the floor. How can the motion be out of order?"

The silence in the chamber seemed to deepen, and Reece knew the other senators were straining for the subtext, trying to figure out what was really happening in front of them.

Devlin stared at him for a moment, seeming to be at a

loss. Clearly, he'd expected Reece to try to pass the bill today. Perhaps he thought being framed for murder would bring Reece to heel. Fat chance.

"The bill has already passed first and second reading. Trying to P.I. it now is—"

Reece interrupted, almost enjoying himself. "Entirely in keeping within the Senate rules."

"I call a ten-minute recess for a reading of the rules." Devlin slid out from behind the president's podium, probably headed for a private phone from which to call Stanfield, when Reece intercepted him.

He spoke so only Devlin could hear him. "I think it's time you and I had a little chat about TexaMent."

Devlin looked at him through gray eyes that held contempt. Or was it fear? He motioned to a side conference room. "Make it quick."

As soon as Devlin shut the door behind him, Reece spoke. "How long have you been in Mike Stanfield's pocket?"

"What the hell are you talking about?"

"Oh, come off it, Devlin. I know Stanfield has been slipping you big bucks using his employees' names as cover. I've combed through your campaign-finance reports for the past few years and found dozens of contributions that all came from the same address—TexaMent's Northrup plant. What do you think an investigation would reveal? Did all those employees truly make contributions, or did the money come from TexaMent and Stanfield? How much is he paying you to be his lapdog? Whatever it is, it's sure as hell over the legal max."

Someone knocked on the door, and Miguel popped his head in, a worried look on his face. "Reece—"

"Not now, Miguel!"

Looking surprised and more than a little angry, Miguel shut the door.

Devlin glared up at Reece and puffed out his chest. "You can't prove anything."

"I think I can." Reece held up the stack of documents he'd photocopied. "I've got campaign-finance reports dating back to your first House campaign, and they all show the same thing—thousands in donations from one address, Northrup."

Devlin did a good imitation of surprise. "That's not my fault. You can't hold me responsible for his mistakes."

"Sure, I can, and so can the Secretary of State. I've also got a copy of the letter you wrote to the state health department demanding that they back off their enforcement action at Northrup." Reece shuffled through the papers and held the letter out so that Devlin could see it. Then he bluffed. "The signature is blacked out, of course, but Owens was more than happy to tell us who'd written it when he realized what was at stake."

Devlin's gaze dropped to the paper, and his nostrils flared. "I might have made a few phone calls, but I didn't write that. Owens is full of crap."

"Save it for the ethics hearing, Devlin. Northrup was faking its emissions reports, lying about its equipment, dumping toxins in the water, coating the farmland downwind with caustic dust, and making people sick. They were breaking federal and state environmental laws, and by forcing the health department to back off, you were aiding and abetting them."

"I didn't force them to do anything!" Devlin's face flushed an angry red.

Reece ignored him. "So how does it work? Stanfield pays the big bucks, and you watch his back?"

Devlin took a step in Reece's direction. "Do you think I'm the only politician who takes care of the people who fund his campaigns? That's how the game is played, Sheridan!"

"Speaking of games, you had it all worked out, didn't you? You waited in the shadows while Stanfield got me to sponsor the tire-burning bill to ensure the environmental vote and then you signed on."

Devlin sneered at him. "That was my idea. I found it rather funny, really. It seemed like a great way to win over the tree-huggers and piss you off at the same time."

Reece watched Devlin brag and decided to play to his ego. "I have to give you credit. It worked—for a while. But then Kara McMillan got those whistleblower tapes and everything went to hell, didn't it?"

"Some people don't know when to quit."

"You can say that again. Stanfield tried to get her to back off with threats, and when that didn't work, he tried to have her killed. Then when I figured out what was going on and tried to withdraw the bill, he had Alexis murdered and framed me."

Devlin watched him warily. "I don't know anything about that."

"I think you do." Reece held out several pages he'd printed out this morning. "I also happen to have your phone records, including those from two days ago. I know that shortly after I called Stanfield to tell him I was killing the bill, he called you at home. Two hours later Alexis was murdered."

Devlin's body jerked as if he'd been hit. "You can't access those records!"

"I already have. I suspect that when I bring this information to Chief Irving he might have a few questions for you."

"You're crazy! I didn't kill Alexis! I liked her!" He started to sweat. "Stanfield wanted the tire-burning bill put on the next day's agenda, that's all."

"I passed the polygraph, Devlin. Will you?"

He was shaking now. "All I've ever done is watch out for TexaMent's interests here at the Capitol—carry a bill now and then, watch over the health department. I've never conspired to kill anyone!"

"I'll leave that to the cops to sort out. In the meantime, there's the little matter of the tire-burning bill. You know damned good and well my motion isn't out of order. You called this recess to delay the vote. But we're going to go back out there, and you're going to approve my motion and call for a vote. Got it?"

"Are you blackmailing me?"

"No. If I were blackmailing you, I'd threaten to make everything I know public unless you cooperate. But I'm turning all this over to the police and calling for an independent audit no matter what you do."

"So what's to stop me from denying your motion just to spite you?"

"You don't have a leg to stand on, and every senator in that room knows it. Deny my motion, and you'll just look worse in the end. Besides, I have every word of this conversation on tape." Reece ignored the shocked look on Devlin's face, turned his back on him, and walked to the door.

"You can't do that! It's illegal!"

"If you paid more attention to the laws of the state you pretend to serve, you'd know that covertly recording a conversation is legal in Colorado, provided the person doing the recording is a party to the conversation. Ask legislative legal." Reece pushed open the door and found Miguel pacing in the hallway outside the door. He looked pale, sweat beading on his forehead.

Miguel stomped over to him. "Have you gone *loco?* We have to talk."

"It will have to wait, Miguel. I believe Devlin is about to call for a vote."

KARA READ through the lengthy background check the Colorado Bureau of Investigation had faxed over for her. Juan de la Peña might be the brother of a state senator, but he was also absolute scum. He had a juvie record stretching back almost to the day he was conceived—mostly petty drug charges, theft, vandalism, that sort of thing. He'd served a couple terms in prison, once in Cañon City for assault and once in Leavenworth for assault and possession with intent to sell. And now he was working at Northrup as a shift manager, where he'd been cited for improperly storing toxic chemicals.

It was interesting information. More interesting was the fact that Senator de la Peña hadn't seen fit to include among the materials Kara had requested the fact that his younger brother worked for Northrup. Reece was his close friend. Did Reece know?

Kara picked up the phone and dialed Tom's desk. "Hi, it's McMillan. I've got—"

"Have you heard from your mother today? How's she doing?"

"What? No, I haven't spoken with her yet today."

"Well, when you do, tell her I said hello."

Kara bit back a groan. Her editor had the hots for her mother. It was enough to make her ill. "Actually, I've called with some interesting information relevant to my investigation. Senator de la Peña's brother works as a shift manager at Northrup, but somehow the good senator didn't see fit to account for this fact in my open-records request."

"That is interesting. What do you know about the brother?"

"I know he's spent almost as much time in prison as out of it, mostly drugs. He served a five-year sentence in Cañon City in the nineties and spent most of this decade so far in Leavenworth."

"Leavenworth? Hold on. Let me get Novak in here." He bellowed for Tessa. "I'm going to put you on speakerphone. Tell Novak what you just told me."

Kara recapped the details. "He was released from Leavenworth in July 2004, and somehow he managed to land a job as a shift manager at Northrup. I don't know if he has any prior experience in—"

Tessa interrupted. "When did you say he entered Leavenworth?"

"It says here February 2000."

"That places him in Leavenworth at the same time as John David Weaver. Hellfire and damnation, Kara, you found the missing link."

CHAPTER 27

JOHN DAVID Weaver. *The man who'd tried to kill her.*

Kara was glad she was already sitting down. "You've been investigating him."

"Of course!" Tom sounded indignant. "Someone tries to take out one of my reporters, I'm damned well going to find out everything I can about him!"

It was perhaps the most caring thing she'd ever heard Tom say. Except, of course, that it was all about him. *His re-porter?*

"I've been following every lead I have, trying to kick this dead man's ass for you," Tessa said. "I've been hoping to tie him to Northrup or TexaMent, but so far all I've been able to prove conclusively is that he was a lifelong loser. He's been in and out of prison since he was fifteen. Seems he liked to hurt women."

When I'm done with you, you'll do anything I tell you to do. Or maybe I should let you die with me inside you.

His voice, steeped in hatred, filled her mind.

Kara squeezed her eyes shut and blocked out his words. "Yeah. I've got no trouble believing that. Is there any way Sophie can use her prison contacts to find out whether he and Juan de la Peña knew each other? Anything we can do to prove the connection will help."

"I'll have her get on it." Tom bellowed for her. "Alton! Get in here!"

"So what's this mean for your investigation?" Tessa asked.

"I'm not sure. We've already got a paper trail tying Devlin to TexaMent. Maybe it's just coincidence that Senator de la Peña has a brother working there. And even if his brother is caught up in this, it's possible that the senator is clean."

Tom made a sound of disgust. "He needs to explain why he failed to disclose his family ties to Northrup when he responded to your open-records request. I refuse to believe it was just an oversight on his part. Time for you to give him a call and play indignant reporter. In the meantime, I'm going to have Novak here see if we can persuade Irving to give us a crack at his case file in exchange for this bit of information you've unearthed. Someone had to be paying your buddy Weaver, and the cops are the only ones who are going to be able to access his accounts."

Her *buddy?* Tom had the sensitivity of a rock.

Kara let it roll off her. "The Senate's in session today, so there's not much chance that I'll catch de la Peña until late this afternoon, but I'll call now and leave a message."

In the background, Tom was telling Sophie to look into any in-prison ties between Weaver and Juan de la Peña.

Tessa spoke, the tone of her voice changing from professional to personal. "How are you doing, Kara?"

"Better."

"We all miss you. You need to come back before Holly drives Sophie and me nuts. She called me last night at almost midnight to ask—"

Tom's voice interrupted. "We'll fire you an e-mail if we find anything new. Otherwise, we'll have an I-team meeting by speakerphone tomorrow morning at nine. I want this story in the bag in forty-eight hours."

"Got it. And Tessa—thanks."

"My pleasure. We're a team, remember?"

Kara hung up and dialed Reece's cell phone. Something told her she needed to warn him.

* * *

As HIS fellow senators filed past him for their lunch recess, Reece packed his briefcase, a feeling of grim satisfaction in his gut. The bill was dead, consigned to eternal legislative limbo. Although there was no way to prevent someone from carrying a similar bill next year, at least he'd proved to Stanfield and to himself that he was not for sale, no matter what the price.

He shut his briefcase, reached into his trouser pocket for his cell phone, hoping Kara had left him a message, but his cell phone wasn't there. He grabbed his coat off the back of his Senate seat and reached into its pockets, but his cell wasn't there either. He'd used it to check messages this morning on his way into the Capitol, so he knew he hadn't left it in Kara's hotel room. Deciding it must be upstairs on his desk, he picked up his briefcase, draped his coat over his arm, and strode up the steps of the Senate chamber toward the door.

He needed to grab a quick bite to eat, but first he wanted to call Chief Irving and send Kara an e-mail to tell them both what he'd learned from Devlin. The bastard had all but admitted to working for Stanfield and to forcing the health department to back off its enforcement action at TexaMent. And although he'd denied having anything to do with the memo, the attack on Kara, or Alexis's death, he'd admitted that he'd gotten Stanfield's call the night of the murder.

Reece was so deep in thought that the crush of reporters waiting for him in the hallway outside the Senate chamber took him by surprise. The moment he opened the door, they rushed in on him, firing questions like bullets, cameras clicking, their flashes flaring like strobes. Unable to hear through the chaos, he held one hand up for quiet. Then, as he would do in a classroom of noisy teenagers, he spoke so quietly that everyone fell silent to hear him. "I can't answer your questions if you shout all at once. One at a time, please."

"Is it true you and Ms. Ryan had a sexual relationship?"

"Yes." Out of respect for her family, he refrained from pointing out that there was hardly a lawmaker at the Capitol who hadn't.

"What do you feel this scandal has done to your chances for re-election?"

"Ultimately, there is no scandal, because I had nothing to do with Ms. Ryan's murder. Right now the only thing that concerns me is seeing her killer brought to justice. I haven't given a single thought to being re-elected."

"Do you feel that passing the polygraph test ought to vindicate you in the court of public opinion?"

"Although we're all innocent until proven guilty, I realize people sometimes rush to judgment based on media reports. I suspect that those who've already judged me and assumed that I'm guilty won't be satisfied until I'm fully cleared."

Down the hall behind the media throng, Miguel paced back and forth, looking agitated. Reece hadn't yet had time to talk with him, as he'd gone straight from his confrontation with Devlin back to the Senate floor.

"Is it possible that the murder of Alexis Ryan was in some way connected with the failed attempt on reporter Kara McMillan's life?"

Reece hesitated. "That's a question best answered by the police. Thanks for your interest, and now if you'll excuse me, I've got to get some work done before session reconvenes."

He pasted what he hoped was a friendly smile on his face, ignored the burst of additional questions, and made his way through the crowded hallway toward Miguel, who glared at him.

"It's about damned time! What do I have to do—make an appointment?"

It wasn't like Miguel to be hostile or sarcastic. Reece studied his friend's face. "What's going on?"

"We need to talk, and it can't wait."

Reece glanced over his shoulder. "Well, we can't do it

here unless you want every word we say to be in tomorrow's paper."

"Let's go up to the observation gallery. It's usually pretty private up there, and I need air."

They stopped by Reece's office so he could drop off his briefcase—a quick glance revealed no cell phone on his desk, either—and then took the marble stairs past the presidential portraits on the third floor of the rotunda to the uppermost level just beneath the dome. A jumble of voices echoed up from the busy ground floor of the rotunda, more than one hundred feet below. French doors opened onto a narrow balcony that wrapped itself around the building, offering spectacular views in all directions.

Reece automatically gravitated toward the west and its view of the distant snowcapped mountains. He opened the door and stepped into the late February sunshine, Miguel following after him. Two hundred feet below them, people walked their dogs in the park, stood in groups talking, or hurried to their cars.

Reece heard Miguel's breathing behind him and felt an odd prickling down his spine. He turned to find Miguel standing there, a strange expression on his face. "What's going on? Has something happened with Hilaria or one of the kids?"

Miguel flinched, stepped back, and looked away. "It's my brother."

"Luis?" The last Reece had heard, Luis, who'd been a bit on the wild side in his younger years, was newly married and awaiting the birth of his first child.

"No. Juan." Miguel couldn't seem to look him in the eye, and Reece realized his friend felt ashamed.

"I'm sorry." From what Reece remembered, Juan was the fourth of Miguel's six brothers and had spent most of his life in and out of prison. Miguel rarely mentioned him. "Is he in some kind of trouble?"

Miguel looked down at the ground below and nodded, sweat beading on his upper lip and forehead, his breathing rapid.

Reece had never seen him like this before. He reached over and placed a reassuring hand on Miguel's shoulder. "Whatever it is, Miguel—"

"Stop it!" Miguel pushed his hand away and stepped back from him.

It took Reece a moment to realize Miguel was pointing a pistol at him and a few seconds more for the adrenaline to kick in. "What the hell?"

The gun shook in Miguel's unsteady hands. "I told you not to get involved! I warned you to stay out of it! Why didn't you listen?"

Reeling between disbelief and soul-deep shock, Reece looked up from the barrel of the H&K nine-millimeter semi-auto to the look of hellish anguish in his friend's brown eyes. He wondered if this was the gun that had killed Alexis and fought back the rage that surged from his gut. If he wanted to live through this, he needed to keep his mind clear. "Tell me what's going on, Miguel."

"Juan works for Northrup. He's a shift manager. I helped him get the job when he got out of prison. I thought it would help him straighten out his life."

"And it didn't."

"At first it seemed to. Then he got busted by his supervisor for dealing on-site. Mike Stanfield would have turned him over to the cops, except that he was my brother."

"So they didn't report him." Reece itched to turn on the digital recorder in his pocket but didn't dare move.

Miguel shook his head. "No. Stanfield even offered to get him treatment. Then when the health department came down on them, Stanfield told me I owed them a favor. I made a few phone calls, wrote a memo, got Owens to drop it. I didn't like it, but it seemed only fair, especially because Juan was one of the workers they cited."

Miguel had written the memo? This had to be a joke. It was anything but a joke. "But then Kara started digging, didn't she?"

"I didn't know anything about her connection to this until

she stormed in and took the health department records. I told Stanfield there was nothing I could do about it."

"Did you try to have her killed?"

"No! God, no! I had nothing to do with that!" But the look on Miguel's face told Reece exactly who did.

"Juan set it up, didn't he?"

Miguel swallowed, a convulsive jerk of his throat, then nodded. "The man the cops killed was a friend of his from Leavenworth."

"And Alexis?"

"Believe me, I'd have stopped him if I'd have known. When I heard she'd been killed and you were the prime suspect, I knew. Dear God, Reece, he killed her and then he used information about you that Stanfield had gotten from me to set you up."

The memory of Miguel staring at his gun flashed through Reece's mind. "You told Stanfield that Alexis and I had been lovers, and you told him I was carrying a gun."

Miguel nodded, lifted his chin, but sweat was running down his face. "Juan is my brother, Reece. I have to get him out of this."

"And getting him out of this includes killing me?" And then he understood. "You were going to push me off, weren't you?"

"Y-you turned around too fast. I couldn't." Miguel took a step toward him, gun trembling in his hands. "So now you're going to jump."

Reece laughed, a harsh sound. "I see. My death will look like a suicide. Everyone will think I nixed myself because of Alexis's murder, and what I know will die with me. Is this your idea, friend?"

Miguel flinched at the word *friend*, his face an image of torture. "No!"

"Well, that's some comfort. I suppose it's Stanfield's idea then?"

"He wanted me to push you, but I can't. I can't!"

"Too bad, Miguel, because I won't jump, and I won't let

you push me off. If you want me dead, you're going to have to shoot me. You're going to have to pull that trigger." Reece took a step forward.

Miguel stared up at him with astonishment. Then his jaw tightened, and for a moment Reece expected to find himself lying on his back in a pool of his own blood taking one last, rattling breath. A nine-millimeter round at close range would make a mess of his anatomy.

But then Miguel's aim wavered. "I can't!"

It was the break Reece had been watching for. In one move, he jammed his palm hard against the barrel of the pistol so the slide couldn't move to fire and clicked the release for the magazine, which fell to the granite floor of the balcony with a heavy clatter.

The gun had been fully loaded.

Miguel dropped it and gaped at him through eyes that held first shock, then deepest torment. He sagged against Reece, his entire body trembling. "*¡Madre de Dios, perdóneme!* Forgive me!"

Fury and pity warred inside Reece. He lowered Miguel into a sitting position, reached automatically for his cell phone, and remembered he'd misplaced it.

Damn it! If he left Miguel alone, lord knows what he would do. At this point, Reece wouldn't put it past him to jump himself. And there was the gun. There was probably still one round in the chamber, so Reece didn't dare leave it with Miguel. Nor did he dare touch it further, or he'd risk ruining the prints. Already under suspicion, he couldn't afford for anyone to draw the wrong conclusions about what had just happened here.

"I'm going to call for help, Miguel, but I need your cell phone."

"They're going to kill me! Or maybe he'll go after Hilaria and the kids!" Miguel seemed lost in his own misery. "Oh, Christ!"

Reece took the phone from his friend's pocket, dialed the security desk downstairs, and gave the sergeant-at-arms a quick rundown. He needed to call Chief Irving, but that could wait until Miguel was indoors again and the gun had been taken into custody.

"It's over, Miguel. It's going to be all right. You couldn't kill me because you're not a murderer. You were trying to protect your brother, and you got in too deep. But everything's going to be okay."

But Miguel shook his head. "No. No, it's not. Your cell phone—I took it. I gave it to my brother to give to Stanfield."

"You took my cell phone? But why would—?" Then it hit Reece like a fist.

If Stanfield had his cell phone, he'd have access to Kara.

He grabbed Miguel and shook him. "What are they going to do, Miguel? Goddamn it, tell me!"

KARA JABBED at the veggies in her salad, her frustration at a peak. She'd left two messages for Reece but hadn't yet reached him. She still hadn't gotten a hold of the governor, either. Worst of all, Owens's response to her demand for an interview had been to resign. He'd announced his resignation in a press release Tom had forwarded to her via e-mail.

"Guess he saw the writing on the wall," Tom had written.

Kara had known from the moment she'd read the press release how the state would play it. Owens had resigned and would take the fall for the governor. The governor would promise an investigation into allegations that Owens had caved to political pressures and gone easy on corporate polluters. But the investigation would, in fact, be a taxpayer-funded whitewash. In the end, the state's report would conclude that regulations were unclear, records were vague, Owens was understaffed, media reports were inaccurate, memories were unreliable, and nothing illegal had occurred. Then Owens, having been more or less cleared, would resurface in some other government post a few years from now, maybe even run for governor himself.

This was not how it was supposed to work. The innocent were supposed to go free. The guilty were supposed to be held accountable. And above all, the public was supposed to have unhindered access to the truth.

Galen would have made fun of her for her idealism. But not Reece. Not only did he seem to respect her for it, but he was even more idealistic than she was. She supposed it was one of the things that drew her to him. How many politicians ran for office because their students wanted them to?

She jabbed a slice of cucumber. How would Owens react if she showed up at his front door? He'd probably call the cops and accuse her of stalking or trespassing or some damned thing. Still, it was tempting. She could leave the hotel using the stairs, just as Reece had done, and she could prop the stairwell door open so she could get back inside. No one need know she'd gone out.

Even as she worked out the details in her mind, she rejected the plan. She'd promised Chief Irving she'd stay put. She couldn't lie to him.

She glanced at her watch, pushed her half-eaten salad aside, and reached for the phone. Surely the Senate had recessed for lunch by now. She dialed Reece's number, hoping this time to catch him this time and not his voicemail.

"Hello?" The man's voice was unfamiliar.

"I'm sorry. I must have dialed the wrong—"

"Ms. McMillan?"

"Yes."

"This is Mike Stanfield. I've been waiting for your call."

CHAPTER 28

FOR A moment Kara was speechless with confusion. What number had she dialed? She glanced at the LCD display on her phone, felt a rush of dread. Her finger flew to the record button. "What are you doing with Reece's cell'?"

His voice was cold, full of anger—like hate on ice. "You're a smart girl. Figure it out."

The realization hit her with the force of a body blow, drove the air from her lungs. *They'd taken him! Dear God, they had him!*

If she hadn't already been sitting, she would have sunk to the floor. She fought to regain her breath, to steady her voice, to clear the panicked chaos from her mind. "S-so you're a kidnapper now in addition to being a murderer?"

"I'm a businessman. And you, Ms. McMillan, are standing between my company and millions of dollars."

Panic sparked into fury. "Isn't that just a damned shame?"

"For the two of you it is. My men are waiting in the stairwell for you to come and open the door. If you don't, pretty boy senator here dies."

Then in the background she heard him. "Leave her alone, Stanfield!"

Reece! Anguish like pain sliced through her belly. They truly had him!

But at least he is still alive.

Stanfield's voice growled in her ear. "And don't think of trying to hang up on me and calling the police. If any of my men so much as smell a cop, I'll make certain your lover regrets the day he met you. Of course, he probably already does."

She barely recognized the menacing voice that came from her throat. "Don't you dare touch him!"

"I'm giving you thirty seconds to open that door. Twenty-nine . . ."

"You won't get away with this!"

"I suggest you put down the phone and open the door, or you'll find out just what I can get away with. Twenty-four, twenty-three."

Kara dropped the phone, her mind racing, her stomach twisting with fear. She couldn't secretly dial 911 because Stanfield was on the line. She didn't have time to send an e-mail. Besides, he would hear her typing. And if she didn't open the door for his men within the next twenty seconds, Reece would suffer, perhaps die. She couldn't let them hurt him.

Mentally ticking off the seconds, she ran to the door of her suite, threw it open, and dashed down the hallway. Three men in white work coveralls stood on the other side. One of them she recognized by his resemblance to his brother— Juan de la Peña. She could tell from the look on his face that he considered her a dead woman.

He held up his gloved hands, fingers splayed, then folded his thumb, counting. *Nine. Eight. Seven.*

Her mouth went dry. Would they shoot her on the spot?

Five. Four. Three.

What if they killed Reece anyway?

Two.

Heart slamming against her chest, Kara opened the door.

REECE PUSHED Miguel's car up to ninety and flew up the left lane of I-25 toward the exit that would take him to the Northrup plant.

What if he was already too late?

He'd called Chief Irving the moment Miguel had finished outlining what he knew of Stanfield's plan and related what Miguel had told him. Irving had ordered him to stay at the Capitol and sent two units to see if Kara was still where she was supposed to be and to protect her if she was, promising to call him on Miguel's cell phone with the news.

But Reece wasn't about to wait around to find out what his gut already knew. Stanfield had her, and if he wasn't stopped, he was going to kill her.

Because the cops still had his Jeep for forensic testing, he'd taken Miguel's keys and burned rubber out of the parking lot. Now he wished he'd taken Miguel's gun, too, though he doubted the sergeant-at-arms would have let him go charging out of the building with a loaded weapon. He could only hope there was a tire iron in the back. Otherwise he'd be facing Stanfield and his crew of hired thugs empty-handed.

This was his fault. It couldn't be a coincidence that this was happening the day after he'd been with her. Somehow, he'd given her location away. Goddamn it! If anything happened to her, he'd have the rest of his life to regret it and to hate himself.

Miguel's cell phone rang. "Sheridan."

"She's gone." It was Chief Irving.

"Goddamn it!" Reece pushed the gas pedal to the floor and kicked the speed back up to ninety, the car's max.

"There's no sign of struggle anywhere, no blood, nothing. Everything related to her investigation has disappeared with her—her files, her computer, even the phone."

"It was equipped to record. Stanfield must have suspected that."

"I don't want to know how you know that, because if I find out you compromised her safety in any way, you're going to find my boot up your senatorial ass."

And Reece knew he deserved it. "Understood."

"The last time she made a call was about thirty minutes ago when she dialed your cell number."

Thirty minutes ago.

Reece had been on the highway for about fifteen minutes, which meant they were about fifteen minutes ahead of him. More than enough time to pull a trigger. "Son of a bitch!"

He spotted the exit just ahead. He threw on the right turn signal, crossed lanes, took the exit doing sixty, then slammed on the brakes and cranked the car, tires shrieking, onto the two-lane county road.

"Please tell me you stayed at the Capitol like I told you to. Those weren't your tires squealing, were they?"

"Technically, no. I requisitioned the car from Miguel."

"Damn it, Sheridan! When this is over I'm going to haul your ass in for interfering with police operations, violating a goddamned lawful order, and pissing me off!"

"I don't think the latter is a crime, but as long as Kara is alive and safe you can do whatever the hell you want with me afterward. Who has jurisdiction out here?"

"The Adams County Sheriff's Department, and, yes, they've already dispatched several units, including the S.W.A.T. team. They'll get there before you do."

Ahead in the distance loomed white industrial silos as tall as skyscrapers.

"I wouldn't bet on that."

Kara sat on the floor of the van, her hands bound and her mouth covered with duct tape, her hope waning. She could see the security checkpoint through the windshield and knew they had arrived at Northrup. It seemed a lifetime ago that she and Holly had tricked their way through this same gate.

Juan de la Peña's fingers bit into her shoulder. In his other hand, he held a gun. He leaned down and whispered, "Are you afraid of what's going to happen in the next ten minutes?"

And in that instant, she recognized his voice. He was the one. He'd called her late at night, tried to frighten her, just as he was trying to frighten her now. She wouldn't give him the satisfaction, no matter how badly her stomach pitched and rolled. She glared at him.

He gave her a shove and muttered something in Spanish.

God, she was an idiot. There was nothing to stop Stanfield from killing Reece the moment his men had her. Her life was the only bargaining chip she'd had with Stanfield, and she'd already given it away. What would he have done if she'd hung up on him and called the police? Would he have killed Reece outright, knowing that she had all the information the police would need to convict him of murder one? Or would he have released Reece, hopped on his Cessna, and flown for the border?

She would never know. She'd been so terrified that Reece would die because of her that she'd given away the game. But that wasn't her only regret.

Why hadn't she called Florida this morning to talk with Connor? The thought of him—the innocence in his big, brown eyes; the smell of baby shampoo in his silky hair; the sound of his laughter—made her heart ache until she thought her chest would split. He was only four. Would he remember her? Would he remember how she'd drawn pictures for him with shaving cream, made him spaghetti, and read to him for hours? Would he remember how much she loved him?

A lump formed in her throat, and tears pricked behind her eyes.

And her mother. She'd take good care of Connor, even if she did get his chakras realigned. But Kara's death would crush her. Reece had been right. Her mother might be a bit eccentric, but Kara knew her mother loved her. She hoped someone would be there for her.

And Reece. Oh, God, Reece! If she got even one moment in the same room with him, she was going to tell him she loved him. She didn't care who was watching or listening. She wanted him to know. She wanted at least to give him that much. Perhaps it wouldn't matter to him now, but she would tell him just the same.

God, let him still be alive!

She'd never given much thought to what it meant to die, had never spent much time wondering if anything came after this life . . . And, damn it, she wasn't going to waste precious time doing that now! Here she was still alive and breathing, and she had all but resigned herself to being Stanfield's next murder victim.

Pull yourself together, McMillan!

She would feel her way through the next few minutes, try to find out where Reece was, and make certain he was safe. And then she would do everything she could to keep them both alive. And if she died, at least she would have justice. Every document in the van had been copied, and Tom and Tessa knew enough to wrap this story in the next twenty-four hours if need be.

And then there was the whistleblower.

Stanfield couldn't kill them all.

The van pulled inside what seemed to be an empty warehouse and lurched to halt. The doors were jerked open, and rough hands forced her across the floor of the van and outside onto her feet. She expected Juan to put his gun to her head and pull the trigger at any moment, fought back a wave of terror.

Instead, he pulled out a cell phone. "We're here." He nodded a few times, then hung up and turned to the other men. "The boss wants you to take this stuff to the kiln and throw it all in. I'm taking her to see him. We'll see you there in about five minutes."

Juan took her arm and pulled her roughly across the warehouse toward a door. The door led to a tiled hallway lit with fluorescent lights that led them past what looked like laboratories or testing facilities of some kind. At the end of the corridor was what seemed to be ordinary office space. It was the middle of the afternoon on a Friday. Maybe someone there would see her, realize she was being held prisoner, and call the police.

"Forget it, bitch." Juan seemed to read her mind. "We've

pulled most of the staff into a safety meeting. This plant is almost totally automated anyway, and everyone who's not in the meeting is loyal to Stanfield. No one is going to help you."

He shoved her through an open door on her right into what seemed to be a conference room with a long table and several chairs.

She recognized the man immediately. She'd seen him once before—in Owens's office at the health department dressed impeccably in his expensive suit, each silver hair on his head perfectly in place. He hadn't said a word then, but had stared at her through the coldest eyes she'd ever seen.

"If those are public documents you've got, you're not leaving until they've been catalogued and photocopied," she'd said to him then, as he'd tried to leave with several folders in his hand.

The look on his face had been pure loathing, just as it was now.

Behind him stood Galen, wearing a three-thousand-dollar suit and looking uncomfortable. The stab of betrayal she felt any time she thought of him lanced through her with renewed pain. It was one thing to leave her pregnant and alone. But how could he participate in this? She forced herself to ignore him and focused her gaze on Stanfield.

"I see from your expression that you recognize me, Ms. McMillan. But the circumstances are a bit different this time, aren't they?" Stanfield motioned to Juan, who forced her to sit in a chair and ripped the duct tape off her mouth.

It stung, made her eyes water. She gave herself a moment to steady her breathing, then looked straight into Stanfield's arctic eyes. "Where's Reece?"

He sat and adjusted his tailored trousers. "You've been pursuing me for a solid month, and that's the first thing you ask me? I'm disappointed. I expected something more challenging from a journalist of your reputation."

"It's the only question that matters to me right now."

"Too bad. You're going to have to wait for the answer."

Then a slow smile spread across Stanfield's face. "But not for long."

Galen stepped forward, stammered. "I-I had nothing to do with this, Kara. I had no idea—"

Four years of anger and hurt exploded. "Shut the hell up, Galen! It's a little late for you to be developing a conscience, isn't it?"

"I'd forgotten that you two know each other." Then Stanfield turned to Galen, the velvet of his voice not entirely concealing the threat held within his words. "I didn't invite you here this afternoon. You came on your own. You are bound both ethically and legally to maintain your client's secrets. Let me know the moment that starts to become a problem for you."

Galen blanched and took a step backward. "You know I would never betray a client."

But Stanfield had already dismissed him and turned back to face Kara. "I have a few questions for you—questions you need to answer if you want to see your sanctimonious senator alive again. Where is Henry Marsh?"

The question took her by surprise, though it shouldn't have. Stanfield wouldn't be able to put this behind him until everyone involved had been silenced. "Who's Henry Marsh?"

She wasn't prepared for the blow, a sharp jab to her battered ribs that forced the breath from her lungs. Dizzy with pain, she might have sunk onto the floor had her hair not been held fast in Juan's closed fist.

Juan's voice was a hiss in her ear. "Were those the ribs Johnny-boy broke? Sorry. I won't hit you there again. I'll make my own mark somewhere else."

She saw Galen take a step in her direction, then stop himself. *Coward.*

"Answer the question, Ms. McMillan, and we can avoid any further unpleasantness."

She pretended to fight for breath and whimpered at the pain—not entirely an act. She needed to stall, to hold on to the information for as long as she could. One thing was absolutely clear to her: the moment Stanfield had everything he wanted from her, she was dead.

"Mr. Marsh left Colorado weeks ago." She labored over her breathing. "He didn't give me his new address. I didn't want to know it."

Behind her, Juan moved, but Stanfield motioned for him to wait. "How did you get in touch with him?"

"I called his cell."

"Give me that number."

"I don't have it memorized," she lied. "It's programmed into my cell phone."

Stanfield looked irritated now. "Then give me your cell phone."

"You'll have to get it from the Denver Police Department. That's where it is."

The next blow landed on her cheek. It startled her, but it didn't hurt as much.

"Why would they take your cell phone?"

"Because Chief Irving didn't trust me not to use it while I was in hiding. They were afraid it might be tapped."

Stanfield laughed. "It takes a lot of money to buy that kind of technology, Ms. McMillan. You're hardly worth that."

"This is all about money, isn't it?"

He looked at her as if she were crazy. "Everything is about money, because money is power. Do you know what money buys?"

"Besides convicts and corrupt politicians, you mean?"

He gave her a cold smile. "Money buys everything, Ms. McMillan. Everything and everyone. It cost me a measly ten grand to hire someone to take your life. True, the money was wasted in the end."

"How much did you pay to have Alexis Ryan murdered?"

"Juan handled that for free—makeup work for a sloppy job done by a friend." Stanfield's gaze moved to the man behind her and then back. "It cost me less than that to find out where the cops had hidden you. Hackers come cheap these days. And of course, once we knew your boyfriend had gotten past security—one of my men saw him enter and not come back out until morning—we knew we could, too. It was just a matter of figuring out how."

Kara grasped for questions, tried to keep him talking. "Why go to all this trouble?"

"Your investigation would have dragged my name through the mud and cost this company millions. In fact, your interference already has cost us millions. We were going to cut seven million from expenses by burning tires, and now we're going to have to wait until next year."

"Pardon me if I don't give a damn."

"Of course. But I have two more questions for you. Who else knows about this investigation, and what kind of files do you have on your computer at the newspaper?"

Kara's mind darted for a way not to answer the first part of his question. Anyone she named would become a target. "The computer in the van *is* my computer from the newspaper. As for the rest of your question, I'll answer it when I know that Reece is alive and safe."

Please, let him be alive!

"You want to see the senator? Fine." Stanfield stood. "Juan, let's take Ms. McMillan to the senator. Come along, Prentice."

Galen looked like he'd rather do anything than go with them, but fell silently in behind Stanfield.

Juan laughed, jerked her up out of the chair, and forced her out of the conference room and back down the hallway. "Stupid bitch."

She glanced up at him. "You know, Juan, I read through your criminal record. You turned out to be a real loser, didn't you?"

That earned her another jab to the ribs, but it was worth it.

This time they took a different exit that led them down stairs and through a poorly lit corridor that seemed to go on forever. Cement kiln dust lay thick on the floor. As they walked, a roar like the grinding of heavy machinery grew louder until it almost hurt Kara's ears.

They exited through another door and climbed two flights of stairs that led them outside into the late afternoon sunshine, where the noise was a deep rumble beneath their feet. Before them, a tower of crossing steel beams and cyclone-shaped bins rose several stories high. From its center stretched a long rotating cylinder that must have been several hundred feet in length and almost wide enough to drive a small car through. At the base of the tower was a structure made of heavy steel. Two men stood near it dressed in yellow, hooded suits, their faces covered by shields. Fire suits.

Kara looked around, hoping and praying to see Reece, but he wasn't there. Dread crept down her spine, beneath her skin, into her heart.

Please be alive!

"This is the preheater tower." Stanfield pointed. "Everything that enters the kiln passes through here first and is heated to almost two thousand degrees Fahrenheit. This door is our only access, apart from the pipes that pump in raw, ground rock, but they're too small to pass a human body."

A human body.

It took a moment for her to understand what he was trying to tell her, for the horrid truth to sink in. Blood rushed from her head, made her knees weak. Her heart thrashed painfully inside her chest. She shook her head, her breath coming in shuddering gasps. "No! No! You didn't!"

A sneer spread across Stanfield's face that said, indeed, he had.

Behind her, Juan laughed.

Reece was *inside* the kiln.

He was dead.

He'd been incinerated.

And she was about to join him.

CHAPTER 29

HOT TEARS sprang to Kara's eyes and ran unnoticed down her cheeks, as she stared at the closed kiln door. A thousand thoughts ran through her mind in the span of a second. Had he suffered? Had he felt alone and afraid at the end? Did he know how much he meant to her?

Oh, God, Reece!

She met Stanfield's frosty gaze, her voice unsteady. "You son of a bitch! You think killing people makes you powerful? How pathetic and afraid you must be on the inside!"

Stanfield's smile became rigid. He motioned the two men in the fire suits toward the steel door and then took several steps backward. "We'll see who's afraid."

Juan jerked her back and put distance between them and the door. The men worked together to move the heavy bolts and slowly pulled the steel door open.

The blast of heat took her breath away. The white-orange blaze was painfully bright even in the daylight, and the roar was like that of a freight train. Red, glowing bricks lined the interior, even the door. She turned her face away and shut her eyes against the glare. "Killing me constitutes a major violation of the First Amendment!"

"To quote you, 'Pardon me if I don't give a damn.' Your computer and files have already gone into the fire," Stanfield shouted over the blaze. "You're next. Oh, don't worry. It won't hurt—at least not for long. I doubt you'll even have time to scream."

Her mouth went dry. Her legs began to tremble, her heart to flail in her breast. She didn't want to die. Not now. Not here. Not like this. "Y-you won't get away with this!"

Behind Stanfield, Galen vomited down the front of his suit and onto his expensive leather shoes.

Stanfield didn't spare him a glance. "I rather think I will. You see, Ms. McMillan, the kiln is hot enough to melt rock almost instantaneously. Imagine what it can do to flesh and bone. The water inside your body will instantly evaporate, and the compounds that make up the rest of you will chemically bond with the melted rock. In a few moments, there will be nothing left of you, not so much as the smallest bit of DNA. Without a body, your disappearance will remain a mystery."

He spoke as if he were discussing a science experiment, his words conjuring an unbearable image in her mind of Reece enduring what he described. Through a haze of jagged terror, she saw Reece in the flames, all that he was, all that he might have become, vanishing in a moment of unbearable agony. She squeezed her eyes shut against the image and tried to blot it from her mind.

And she realized Stanfield was right. The last call she'd made had been to Reece's cell phone. Stanfield hadn't been at the hotel, so there was no chance anyone would have spotted him there. The phone had been destroyed, so there was no recording. Apart from her call to Stanfield's secretary, there was no record of contact between the two of them. Chief Irving would search, but he would find nothing strong enough to charge anyone with murder.

Over the horrified pounding of her own heart, she heard laughter. They were laughing. Everyone was laughing, except for Galen.

Then something strange happened. The fog of grief and horror lifted, and her mind cleared, raw emotion fusing into a glassy calm she'd never felt before. She knew what she had to do. She could see it in her mind, each step. It was so simple. She could do it. She could survive.

The men in the fire suits were moving toward her.

Stanfield was still talking. "They can take the heat, but you can't. You'll begin to burn long before they throw you in. It's up to you whether you go in quickly or one excruciating step at a time. Tell me who else knows the details of your investigation, and I'll make certain you don't suffer."

Kara began listing made-up names in a whimpering voice, allowed herself to sink, as if legless with fear, toward the ground. When Juan bent down to adjust his grip and jerk her to her feet, she exploded upward, catching him full in the face with the top of her head.

He fell to the ground, seemingly unconscious, and Kara ran.

Life seemed to go into slow motion as she fled away from the tower, away from Stanfield, back toward the main gate. If she could only get outside the gate, back to the highway, she could flag someone down and escape.

Behind her, Stanfield shouted. "Close the kiln doors! Get her!"

She looked over her shoulder to see the men in the fire suits rip off their hoods and throw them to the ground. They were running after her, but she had taken them by surprise and had a head start. She ran, her legs pumping, her feet barely seeming to touch the ground.

A crack of a gunshot. The bite of fire in her shoulder.

And she realized her mistake. She was running in a straight line.

She threw herself to the side, rolled behind a front loader, and then was on her feet and running again through the first open doorway she saw. The inside was a vast cavern filled with pipes, catwalks, conveyor belts, and machinery. And dust—everywhere piles of dust.

The clarity she'd felt began to recede, and in its place was doubt. She wove her way through the machinery, trying to put as much steel as she could between herself and that gun. On she ran, darting past pumps, leaping over pipelines, ducking beneath conveyor belts, through a door, and into a room where a giant drum as big as a house rotated to a deafening racket. She covered her ears, slid behind some kind of waist-high circuit box, coughing from the dust and trying to catch her breath.

If only she knew her way around the plant like they did. If only she knew where she was. They were the hunters, and she was the prey—but only they knew the lay of the land.

Her gaze traveled around the room, searched for a safe path out, and then she saw.

Footprints.

Her own footprints.

The dust was so thick on the floors that it was like running across the surface of the moon or through fresh snow. Her footprints would lead them straight to her.

Unable to hear over the din, she darted out of her hiding place and made for the steel mesh stairs up to the catwalk. At the end of the catwalk was a door. Up and up and up she climbed, only vaguely aware of the burn in her thighs, the ache in her lungs.

Out of the corner of her eye, she saw a flash of yellow. The men in the fire suits had come through the door. They were below her now. They pointed. They'd seen her.

Faster and faster she ran. Along the catwalk. Toward the door.

Toward freedom. Toward life.

A bullet hit the safety rail beside her. She screamed and kept running.

Heavy footfalls rocked the catwalk beneath her feet. They were behind her. They were gaining on her.

She reached the door, grabbed the knob, and jerked.

It was locked. With a desperate sob, she kicked it, yanked at the knob again. And then, miraculously, it opened.

She threw the door wide open and found herself looking into Stanfield's angry face.

"No!"

She knew one moment of blinding terror, and her knees all but buckled. Then something struck the back of her head and exploded into pain. As she fell into darkness, her last thought was of Reece and Connor and pleasant smells drifting from the kitchen.

Your pretty mommy is awake. Show her how you set the table.

REECE HEARD voices and ducked behind a stack of steel barrels. Four men emerged from the building across from him. Two were dressed in protective yellow suits of some kind—fire suits, perhaps. The other two were dressed for a business meeting—Stanfield and Prentice.

The two in fire suits seemed to be carrying something heavy. Reece shifted position to get a better look, felt his heart explode.

Kara! Her name was an anguished shout inside his mind. Grief. Regret. Rage.

A torrent of violent emotions washed through him, drove him to his knees.

He was too late. He was too late. He was too late.

He battled back the molten fury that would have sent him flying toward them with nothing but his fists and forced himself to watch and wait.

They carried her past a front loader and around the side of a building toward . . .

The kiln. He'd studied cement kilns before agreeing to sponsor the tire-burning bill. He recognized the structure.

So that was how Stanfield planned to dispose of her body. No body, no murder.

But Reece wasn't going to let him get away with it. If nothing else, he would see that Kara got justice.

He followed them carefully, quietly. They stopped at the base of what had to be a preheater tower, dropped Kara roughly onto the ground between them, and reached for their hoods, which for some reason lay on the dusty asphalt as if they'd been carelessly tossed aside. Miguel's brother sat nearby, clutching what was clearly a broken jaw. Prentice stood, pale as a ghost and shaking, having apparently blown chunks down the front of his expensive suit.

Stanfield was shouting. "Hurry the hell up! I want this over with now! God, Prentice, you stink!"

Reece waited until both men in fire suits were facing away from him to make his move. By the time they knew he was there, he already had his arm locked tightly around Stanfield's throat. "Drop the gun and get away from her! Now! Or your boss is a dead man!"

The gun fell to the asphalt not far from Kara's head. The men stepped away.

"Now lie down on your stomachs, hands locked behind your heads! Do it! If you even try to get up, I'll break his neck!"

Stanfield's body jerked as he struggled for breath. His hands clawed at Reece's arm. But old and sedentary, he was no match for Reece's strength.

Reece squeezed harder, aching to send the bastard to hell. "Surprised to see me alive, old man? You're in for a lot of unhappy surprises today. The sheriff's on his way here, and when he gets here he's going to arrest you for murder."

"I-I had nothing to do with this!" Prentice began to babble. "I came here to talk over some property mergers, and I—"

"Shut your goddamned mouth, Prentice! She's the mother of your child! Does that mean nothing to you? You should have given your life for hers!"

Prentice stared at him. "M-my life? But she's not—"

"I said shut up!" Reece loosened his grip on Stanfield's throat and allowed the bastard to take a breath. Over Stanfield's coughing, he heard a moan, a soft, feminine sound.

Kara. She shifted, whimpered, and turned her head toward him. Her eyes were closed, but she was *alive!*

The warm rush of relief he felt was followed by a sharp blow to his stomach.

Stanfield elbowed him hard and stumbled out of his grasp toward the gun, toward Kara.

Kara heard what sounded like fighting—shuffling feet, grunts, fists striking flesh. It sounded distant, far away, as if perhaps it were a dream.

Then something hard pressed into her temple.

"Don't do it, Stanfield. The cops are here. The S.W.A.T. team is almost in position. If you kill her, they'll have you red-handed."

It was Reece's voice. *Reece!* But how could it be Reece's voice? He was dead, wasn't he? *Oh, God, Reece!*

With the flood of grief came awareness—the throbbing of her head, the cold press of asphalt against her back, the tingling burn of the cement kiln dust beneath her palms.

She opened her eyes and saw Reece being held by the two men in fire suits, Stanfield crouching over her, holding a gun to her head.

Reece was alive! But how?

She didn't need to know that now. What she needed to do was keep them both alive.

Stanfield wasn't looking at her; he seemed to be scanning the surroundings.

Carefully, Kara gathered a handful of cement kiln dust in her left hand and held it, ignoring her burning skin.

"I don't see anyone," Stanfield growled.

She waited until he looked down, then threw the dust in his eyes.

He screamed, pitched away from her, and covered his face with his forearm, the gun still in his hand.

Then all hell broke loose.

"Freeze! Police! Everyone on the ground!"

Shouts. Gunshots. A cry of pain. The crunch of dozens of booted feet.

And Reece was there, on top of her, shielding her with his body, his sweet weight pressed against her.

And then just voices. Cop voices. Chief Irving swearing.

It was over. It was finally over.

She looked up into Reece's eyes and saw the worry, the lingering shadows of fear. Relief and joy swelled like the sun inside her. Her eyes blurred with tears. "You're alive! I thought . . . They told me—"

"Everything's going to be okay."

And then she remembered. There was something she had to tell him. "I love you, Reece Sheridan."

He grinned. "I kinda figured."

THE NEXT several hours passed in a blur of cops and doctors as Kara and Reece were examined, treated, and questioned. Kara felt ashamed when she learned that Reece had been at the Capitol facing down Senator de la Peña when Stanfield had called her. It had been a recording she'd heard, part of Reece's last conversation with Stanfield the night before Alexis was killed. He'd never been anywhere near Reece.

"My God! I feel so stupid! I almost got both of us killed."

Chief Irving put a reassuring hand on her shoulder. "Don't be so hard on yourself. Men like Stanfield spend their lives manipulating people. You did one hell of a job out there. You used your brain, fought back, and stayed alive. That's what matters."

But Kara wasn't ready to let herself off the hook that easily. "I risked everything for nothing! If I had only hung up on him and called 911—"

Chief Irving interrupted her. "Quit second-guessing yourself. Stanfield is a clever man. He frightened you, pressured you, gave you no time to think. But he miscalculated in two important ways. He underestimated your strength and will to live, and he underestimated Senator de la Peña's conscience. You're not an easy victim, and the senator isn't a cold-blooded killer."

Reece had a black eye, which seemed to please him, as well as a few scrapes. She had a minor concussion, a shallow wound where a bullet had nicked her shoulder, as well as chemical burns here and there from lying in the caustic dust.

Only the burn on her left palm hurt enough to bother her.

But that didn't stop the doctor from trying to keep her in the hospital overnight.

"Just for observation," the doctor said.

Kara hopped off the emergency room gurney and glared at him. "Like hell! I have an article to write! There will be lots of people in the newsroom who can observe me. If I keel over, they'll know."

Reece shook his head. "Kara, I really think—"

"I know you're only trying to watch over me, but I almost *died* for this story. The moment the police reports are final the other newspapers will be all over it. If I don't get it in to-morrow's paper, I'll be playing catch-up on my own investi-gation!"

Reece looked at her doubtfully for a moment and then his gaze slid down her body. He smiled. "Fine. But tell me, little Miss Hospital Gown, what are you going to wear? Your clothes are saturated with CKD."

In the end, Kara prevailed. With Chief Irving to escort him, Reece retrieved some clothes from the hotel suite at the Loews and brought them back to her in the ER. Then, frown-ing the whole way, he drove her to the paper.

He glared at her as he pulled into the parking garage. "I'm staying with you, you know."

It felt so good to be with him. She smiled. "I kinda fig-ured."

She walked inside with him, the two of them hand-in-hand. The newsroom was in a state of chaos. IT had set up a new computer at her desk. The health department files sat in neat rows on a table they'd set up nearby.

"There she is—my hero!" Joaquin grinned, then nodded to Reece. "Nice shiner, Senator."

"Kara!" Holly ran down the hall toward her, threw her arms around her, and hugged her. "Thank God you're safe!"

Kara was astonished to see tears in Holly's eyes and felt her own eyes tingle. "I'm fine."

"When I heard from Tess that you'd disappeared, I—"

But Kara never got to hear what Holly was going to say, because Tessa and Sophie and Matthew crowded in, each of them claiming a hug from her and a handshake from Reece—except for Tessa, who kissed Reece full on the lips.

"I've been wanting to do that for a while now," she said. "Thanks for keeping her safe."

"Well done, McMillan! Welcome back!" Tom stepped out of his office, coffee in hand. "Welcome to the newsroom, Senator."

A little knot of worry Kara hadn't even realized she was carrying inside her melted away. She'd half expected Tom to toss Reece out of the building.

"If you're all done fawning over McMillan, let's get this meeting underway," Tom bellowed. "I want an edit plan in thirty minutes. Senator, you'll have to excuse us. Maybe you can grab a cup of sludge in the cafeteria."

"Sounds good to me."

But Kara didn't want to let go. She gave his hand one last squeeze.

He grinned, ducked down, and brushed his lips over hers. "I'll see you soon."

The staff filed into the conference room—including Holly.

Tom glared at her. "Bradshaw, what are you doing here?"

Holly lifted her chin. "I know you think I'm only good for interviewing celebrities about their love lives and latest trips through rehab, but Kara is my best friend, and they tried to kill her, and I'm going to help with her story, and if you don't like that, you'll have to pick me up and throw me out this door!"

For a moment Tom looked utterly surprised. Then he glowered. "Fine. Sit down and shut up!"

Holly sat, looking quite pleased with herself.

And Kara'd thought she'd seen everything.

REECE SAT in the newsroom near Kara's desk and watched as the news team pulled out the stops to get her investigation to press on time to make the morning paper. He'd never been in a newsroom before and found it to be nothing like the constant hustle and bustle he'd expected to find. Instead, it was more manic, with periods of intense quiet and concentration, during which the only sound to be heard was the clicking of a half dozen keyboards, occasionally interrupted by rushed discussion, dark humor, and profanity.

"Hey, Matthew, grab me some coffee while you're up."

"What am I, Tess—your bitch?"

"Yep, says so on your forehead."

Most entertaining to him was the way they seemed to speak in code. He'd had no idea that journalism was so specialized, and he realized that a well-managed news team had more than a few things in common with a well-trained police unit, including its own jargon.

"What's your slug?"

"We're putting a hammer on the main bar. What do you want for the drop?"

"We're going to start it above the fold, jump it to five, and spread the rest over two columns."

"Kara, what do you want for that cutline?"

"Production wants a head for the second sidebar." To which the reply was, "They're always begging for head down there. Don't they get any at home?"

Reece left Kara's side only twice—once when Tessa interviewed him about his being cleared of Alexis's murder and once when Sophie interviewed him for her story about events at the cement plant today.

"What do you have to say to those who believed you guilty?" Tessa asked.

Reece bit back the words he might otherwise have said and tried to see it from the public's point of view. "People wanted justice for Ms. Ryan and, understandably, misdirected their anger toward me. I'm ready to move forward with the legislative session, and I hope I have the public's support."

Sophie's interview was much tougher. "You saw them carrying Kara out of the building across from you, is that correct?"

For a moment, Reece found himself back in that horrid, desolate moment. "Yes. I saw her, and I thought she was dead. I thought I was too late, that I was no longer fighting to save her life, but to keep her body from being disposed of like trash. I never want to feel that way again."

Tears welled up in Sophie's eyes. "Thank God you were there! They would have burned her alive!"

Reece nodded, smiled, and wiped the tears from her cheeks. "Is that part of your interview?"

Sophie laughed. "No. That part is off the record."

As the evening wore on, Reece noticed the way everyone seemed to be watching over Kara. They got her cups of tea without being asked, ran to fetch files for her, and cast covert glances her way. And he realized that they had come close to losing her, too.

But as the evening wore on toward midnight, Kara began to fade. He knew it was only strength of will that had carried her this far.

She lifted her left hand from the keyboard, shook it, and winced.

Reece took her hand, loosened the bandage. "Let me put more of that prescription cream on it."

She didn't argue with him—proof, he supposed, that it must really hurt.

"How are you holding up?" He asked as if he couldn't see the exhaustion on her face.

"Okay. Just a little more to go."

She finished at a little past one, her face pale. "I'd read through it again, Tom, but I just can't. I—"

"Go on, and get some sleep, McMillan. We'll take it from here."

Reece guided her back to his Jeep, helped her climb inside, and buckled her seat belt.

"Where are we going?" she asked, half asleep beside him.

"Back to the hotel. The suite is booked through the end of the week. Seems a damned shame to waste it."

* * *

SATURDAY MORNING dawned bright and blue, one of those Colorado mornings where the sky seems impossibly wide and bright. In the streets of Denver and throughout the metro area papers made their way into racks and onto front porches and kitchen tables.

"Greed," read the headline at the top of the *Independent*. "Investigation of cement plant reveals environmental crimes, government corruption, murder."

People walked down the sidewalks reading of the reporter who'd nearly been killed in her search for the truth and of the senator who'd been blamed, betrayed, and redeemed.

Moira and Ed Farnsworth read it over their morning coffee, called Dottie and Carl Perkins over, and spent most of the morning together discussing it. Moira set her china cup down daintily in its saucer. "Well, I think we should sue the bastards."

Miguel de la Peña read the story from inside his cell at the Denver County Jail and wept. He'd be going home today. Well, not really home. Because he'd turned state's witness, he, Hilaria, and the kids were going to be placed in protective custody until the case was resolved. He only hoped his family and Reece would one day forgive him.

Juan de la Peña read it shackled to his hospital bed, bleary from the anesthesia they'd given him when they wired his jaw back together. He got through the first paragraph before throwing it across the room. He forgot about his jaw, tried to shout, and ended up whimpering like a baby.

Galen Prentice, having made bond late last night, read it in his lawyer's office and swore he'd never known that any of this was going on. He slammed the paper on his lawyer's desk. "I'm the victim here! Why doesn't anyone understand that?"

Drew Devlin hadn't read it yet when the police knocked on his front door and asked if he'd be willing to come down to the station to answer a few questions. He got the chance to read it at his leisure while waiting in booking for his lawyer. "It's lies. It's all bullshit," he told the toothless drunk sitting next to him.

Mike Stanfield was unable to read it. Although doctors had successfully removed the S.W.A.T. team bullet from his liver, cement kiln dust had burned his corneas so severely that he wouldn't be reading much of anything for a while if ever again.

But thirty floors up, Kara and Reece slept in one another's arms, oblivious.

CHAPTER 30

KARA WAS lost in the most erotic dream. Reece was cupping her breasts, his thumbs drawing circles around her aching nipples, his lips on her throat. Then he entered her from behind as she lay on her side, his cock moving thick and hard inside her, his fingers busy between her thighs.

She awoke to the sound of her own cry just as the climax washed through her, hot and sweet.

He leaned down and kissed the corner of her mouth. "Good morning."

He was still inside her. And he was still hard.

She smiled. "Good morning."

A half hour later, she lay with her head against his chest, her body still pulsing with pleasure. She ran her hand over the muscles of his chest and toyed with a flat brown nipple.

"Don't tell me you're still feeling frisky after that." His voice, still rough with sleep, rumbled in his chest.

"Maybe."

He shifted, brought her closer, and stroked her hair. "Sorry, sweetheart. Unlike you, I have to reload."

"Actually, that's probably a good thing, because I'm sore. Every muscle in my body aches."

He slid gently out from beneath her, sat up, and looked down at her through eyes dark with worry. "Stay here."

She couldn't even think about getting up. Her legs ached. Her ribs ached. Her head ached. Her shoulder throbbed where the bullet had grazed her. Her skin stung in the places where the cement kiln dust had touched her. She was a wreck.

He strode across the room, gloriously naked. "Would you like some tea?"

"Yeah, thanks."

In a moment he returned with a cup of steaming tea and a bottle. "Drink. Then lie down however you're most comfortable."

She sat up slowly, wincing, took the tea, and stared at the bottle in his hands. It held an amber-colored liquid. "What's that?"

"Massage oil. I found it in the bathroom." He grinned, sat beside her. "I figure the gold-medal winner in the Run from the Bad Guys Olympics deserves some TLC."

She laughed despite herself, sipped her tea, and then lay down on her back.

His hands worked over her slowly, gently, massaging the almond-scented oil into her skin. Her muscles began gradually to loosen, the pain to lessen, and she found herself telling him in detail what had happened at the plant.

How she'd tried to stall Stanfield with questions. How she'd demanded to know whether Reece was still alive. How her heart had nearly broken through her chest when she'd believed that he was dead. How, as they'd been about to throw her into the blaze, a strange clarity had come over her. How she'd escaped from Juan and run. How she'd tried to hide. How her last thoughts before she'd been hit on the head had been of him and Connor.

He listened, his hands soothing her, forcing her to relax when she grew tense, easing the memory of fear and rage away.

Tears slipped from the corners of her eyes. "The worst of it was wondering how much you'd suffered and knowing I'd never have the chance to tell you I love you."

"It's over. Stanfield can't hurt you or anyone you care about again." He bent over her, kissed her, and wiped away her tears. Then he stood and scooped her into his arms.

"Wh-where—?"

"After a massage, it's time for a hot soak. My soccer coach used to do this for us."

She laughed. "Hopefully not exactly like this!"

"Well, most of the time he made love to us *after* the massage and soak."

Her laughter was the most beautiful sound in the world to Reece. He filled the sunken tub with steaming water, helped her climb in, and then waited until room service had brought their breakfast—champagne, omelets, and fresh fruit—to join her.

As they fed each other and sipped champagne in the soothing heat, he told her how enraged, desperate, and helpless he'd felt driving down the highway, counting every second, fearing he was already too late.

"And when I saw you, watched them drop you on the ground as if you were garbage—good God, Kara! I could have killed every one of them with my bare hands and enjoyed it!"

She lifted herself and kissed him. "It's over. Except . . ."

"Except what?"

"What about Miguel?"

A white-hot shard of pain sliced through his gut, and his words came out harsh and angry. "What about him?"

"I can't imagine how much it hurt to realize he'd betrayed you. He was your best friend, Reece, and he tried to kill you."

"I don't think he was ever truly a threat to me, but he gave Stanfield everything he needed to hurt you." He remembered Miguel's sobbing as he poured out his story to the sergeant-at-arms, felt the seeds of pity, and ignored them. The anger was still too strong. "I've always admired him for being such a devoted family man. It's strange to think his devotion nearly brought him down."

"I hope someday you'll be able to forgive him."

"Forgive, probably. Trust? I doubt it." He picked up the champagne and refilled their glasses. "I don't want to talk about him. I want to talk about how much I love you."

A smile spread over her beautiful face, and she seemed to glow. "You finally said it!"

"I've said it before."

She shook her head, still smiling. "No, you haven't."

"Yes, I have."

"No, you haven't."

"Okay, fine. Maybe I haven't. But I do. I love you, Kara McMillan."

"Good." Her gaze traveled down his body, and her pupils dilated. She bit her lip.

He felt himself grow hard. "What are you thinking?"

Her hands slid up his water-slick chest. "I'm thinking how if I had your body, I would never leave the house. I would stay in bed all day every day because I wouldn't be able to stop playing with myself. Truly, I don't know how you do it."

He set his champagne aside, leaned against the back of the tub, and stretched his arms out along its edge. "Well, sweetheart, don't let the fact that you're not *in* this body stop you. Go for it. Feel free to consider me your own personal playground."

By the time they were out of the tub and dressed it was almost two in the afternoon. The red message light on their phone blinked furiously. Kara brushed her wet hair and watched while Reece listened to the messages and took down the details on a pad of paper.

When he was finished he turned to her. "There are five messages from Tom offering you a raise and two from your mother saying she's heard the news and wants to know you're safe. And let's see: CNN, Fox News, CNN again, Larry King, the *New York Times,* the *Columbia Journalism Rev*—"

"You're kidding me!" She grabbed the list from him, read through it. "Jeez. And this story wasn't even that well written. I was so rushed—"

He snorted. "Oh, give me a break!"

"And what's this? Someone calling to find out if you want to run for *Congress*?" She felt her humor evaporate and looked up at him. "I guess we both have some choices to make, don't we?"

"You say that like it's a bad thing."

Maybe it was.

Kara called Henry Marsh first and gave him the full story. "If you hadn't stepped forward, Mike Stanfield would have gotten away with it. You truly are a hero, Mr. Marsh."

"Hell, I didn't do anything. I sure am sorry for what you went through. If I had known what would happen, I'm not sure I'd do it again."

"Will you be moving back to Colorado now?"

"I don't know. I'm kind of liking Tennessee, truth be told. We might try things here for a while. I got a good job at the hardware store, and my wife is happy. Don't know what could be better than that."

Kara wished him well and then returned her long list of messages. She gave what seemed like a dozen interviews and set up half a dozen more, the whole time asking herself one question: what did she want?

She thought she knew. No. She *knew* she knew. But could she just ask for it? Could it be that easy?

For so many years now she'd had so few choices. She'd worked hard at her job, paid the bills, and made ends meet. She'd worked hard at being a good mother, too, and tried her best to give Connor the life he deserved. When it came to meeting her own needs, satisfying her own desires, she'd never had the time, the money, or space to worry about such things. Could she afford to do so now?

"Love you, too, Mom. Can't wait to see you. Bye-bye." She hung up the phone and turned to see Reece reading through her article, his face grim.

He looked up from the page. "How's Connor?"

"He loves the beach. Now he's fascinated by pirate ships.

I guess my aunt has been telling him pirate stories. They'll be coming into DIA tomorrow at 12:57 on United."

"We'll take your car. I don't think the Jeep will fit all four of us plus luggage, and we'll need Connor's car seat." He spoke the words as if there were no question that both of them would be going to get her son and mother, as if he were a part of her life, a part of her family.

It was now or never.

Kara took a deep breath and plunged in. "Reece, I know what I want to do, and I'm just going to come out and tell you. We've never had 'the talk'—you know, the relationship talk?"

He set the paper aside, "Someone always avoided it."

"Well, yes, but, whatever." She gestured impatiently. "It comes down to this: I don't want to be with a man who's going to say he loves me one minute and gets sick of me the next. I don't want to be with a man who will be sweet to Connor and then abandon him. I'd rather be alone than go through that."

He stood. "I—"

She pressed her fingers to his lips and ignored her fears. "Shh! Let me finish. I don't want to give up my career. And I don't want Connor to be an only child. I want a husband, Reece, a mate for life. I want a man who really loves me, who will stick by me no matter what, even when he gets bored with me and thinks I'm old and ugly. I want babies— at least one more, probably two. And I want to work as a freelance journalist so I can stay home with them. I want a father for Connor, someone who will adopt him, become his legal parent."

"Anything else?"

"I want a puppy. For Connor." It felt good, once she got it all out. "Even though I love you, Reece, and can't imagine a single day without you, I'd rather end it right now if you don't want me in the same way, if you're not comfortable with my—"

"Demands?" Reece offered gravely.

"Yes."

He nodded, met her gaze, and suddenly she couldn't breathe. She'd laid it on the line this time. Everything that mattered to her was on the line.

"In that case, I guess there's only one thing I can say."

Her pulse tripping, she waited.

He tucked a finger beneath her chin and tilted her face toward his. "Kara McMillan, will you marry me?"

EPILOGUE

Eighteen months later

Kara glanced at the clock. It was four-fifteen. She needed to start supper soon, but she could probably squeeze out a few more paragraphs first. Her book deadline was still six weeks away, but given how little writing time she got with a new baby, she wanted to take full advantage of every moment of peace and quiet.

She'd been offered the book contract while she and Reece were in Costa Rica on their honeymoon. Penguin had offered her an ungodly sum to write a nonfiction account of the TexaMent investigation and its aftermath, and she'd gone almost overnight from being a newly unemployed journalist trying to build a freelance career to being an author with more than a year's salary in the bank.

She'd never written a book before and, at first, it had seemed like an overwhelming task. But she'd gotten to work on it and discovered that writing a book wasn't all that different from writing a news article—a book was just a lot longer. The hardest part had been the emotional toll of reliving it all again.

After she'd written the chapter in which John Weaver tried to rape and kill her, she'd begun having nightmares again. Those nightmares had gotten so bad at one point that she'd become afraid to go to sleep, sure that in her dreams she'd be running and running and running, only to find herself staring into Stanfield's face and the unbearable heat of the kiln. Reece, afraid that the dreams were exacting too high a cost on her and their unborn baby, had asked her to put it aside for a time. She hadn't, and despite his frustration with her, in the end he'd seemed to understand.

But the nightmares had passed. She was almost finished writing about the trial and other events that had followed. As a result of his brother's heartbreaking and tearful testimony, Juan de la Peña had been sentenced to life without the possibility of parole. He'd been killed a few months later in a prison fight.

For testifying against Stanfield and his own brother, Miguel had received a suspended sentence. His dignity and self-respect recovered, but his Senate seat lost, he'd thrown himself into building a support program for family members of convicted felons. Sophie had written an article about it that had garnered attention from across the nation. And in a gesture that had brought a lump to Kara's throat, Reece had sponsored a bill that allowed Coloradans to donate a portion of their income tax refunds to the organization.

Galen had avoided a trial by pleading guilty to a watered-down conspiracy charge. In return, he'd gotten a year's probation, a sentence that had outraged Reece. Galen had also been disbarred and was now unemployed and living with his seventy-year-old mother.

Devlin had claimed to the end that he'd never known anything about murder plots or threatening phone calls or fraudulent campaign donations, and the jury had believed him.

Stanfield, despite a legal team that included five glitzy criminal attorneys, had been convicted of first-degree murder, two counts of conspiracy to commit murder, two counts of attempted murder, several accounts of assault, and numerous environmental crimes, for which he'd been sentenced to a total of one-hundred-twenty-five years in prison. Then he'd had to face a long civil trial for mismanagement at the hands of TexaMent's shareholders. Kara found it somehow fitting that he was now using all the money he'd made trying in vain to appeal his way out of prison.

TexaMent had faced a trial of its own. Its executives had claimed not to know what was happening at their Northrup plant, which the feds had shut down within days of Kara's article being published. The company had settled out of court with its neighbors and been slapped with a few million in fines—which they were now trying to collect from Stanfield.

Kara had debated adding a couple chapters to describe what she jokingly referred to as the "Harrowing of the Senate," but that was really Reece's story to tell, not hers. He'd chaired the ethics committee hearings that had taken more than a year to complete and spent countless nights going over testimony and reading through records and transcripts. In the end, the governor had resigned in disgrace and more than a few lawmakers had found themselves paying restitution for expenses improperly charged to the taxpayers. Few of them were even bothering to run for re-election. Devlin was one of the stubborn ones—but polls showed him losing in a landslide.

The whole ordeal had put Reece in the spotlight, loved as a hero by some, loathed by others. His re-election campaign was going well, and he was expected to win with about 80 percent of the vote in his district. If members of his party had their way, he'd be running for Congress in two years. But they didn't know her husband the way she did. Though he never complained, she knew he wanted nothing more than to return to teaching.

"If we teach kids ethics and we teach them how their government is supposed to function, this sort of thing will be less likely to happen," he'd said more than once.

Her idealist. God, how she loved him! Not a day went by where she wasn't grateful for those three margaritas and Holly's inept meddling.

Whatever he decided to do, Kara would support him, just as he'd supported her in her career decisions.

Over the nursery monitor came a whimper that, Kara knew, would quickly develop into a lusty cry. She hit save, closed her document file, and left her desk to get Caitlyn from her crib.

"Hey, sweetie. Is someone hungry and wet? Come here, precious one."

Kara quickly changed her baby daughter, who contented herself for a short time by sucking on her little fist. With Kara's dark hair and Reece's blue eyes, she seemed a perfect blend of the two of them.

She was almost eight weeks old and had been born at home in the bed where she'd been conceived. It had been Kara's idea to have a homebirth with her family around her. She loved the old Victorian house she and Reece had bought and restored and hadn't been able to stand the thought of going through labor in a hospital again. It was one of the best decisions she'd ever made.

Her labor had been so much easier and faster this time, with the pain overwhelming her only toward the very end. But then her mother and Reece had been there to help her through it, together with the midwife and Reece's sister Melanie, who'd become a good friend. Holly, Tessa, and Sophie, whose job it had been to entertain Connor during Kara's active labor, returned at the last minute, just in time to watch the actual birth.

Reece, whose love had sustained her through the last excruciating hour, had been the one to catch Caitlyn. With the guidance of the midwife, he'd eased their daughter from Kara's body. Then he'd looked up at Kara through eyes filled with tears, a look of amazement on his face. "It's a girl!"

Kara would never forget that moment for as long as she lived—even if in the next instant she overheard Holly tell Tessa and Sophie, "If I ever have a baby, I'm going to have a Brazilian wax first. Keep it pretty, you know?"

"Honey, when you've got an eight-pound object coming out of your cooter, the last thing you're going to care about is how it looks," had been Tessa's reply.

Kara smiled at the memory, picked her daughter up off the changing table, and tried to soothe her fussing. "Hold on just a minute, sweet pea. I know you're hungry."

She followed the sound of a child's laughter out to the backyard, where Connor was still trying to teach Jake—the black lab pup Reece had brought home from the pound one afternoon—to pull his red wagon like a sled dog. She sat in the porch swing, nursed her baby, and watched her big boy play in the late afternoon August sunshine.

He was five now, almost six, and he'd be starting kindergarten in a few weeks. Reece had already taught him how to read at first-grade level and do basic addition, and Kara cherished the bond that had formed between them.

"Watch, Mommy! Watch what Jakey can do!" Connor had attached Jake's leash to the handle of the wagon, and when he walked forward, the pup—now more of a dog, really—did, indeed, pull the wagon.

"That's great, Connor. He likes to play with you."

But the moment Connor hopped in the wagon, hoping for a ride, Jake hopped in the wagon, too.

She laughed with her son, looked at the new baby at her breast, and wondered that her life should be so sweet, so rich, so . . . happy. She allowed herself to relish the moment, the scent of her rose garden, the warmth of the breeze, the tiny baby sounds Caitlyn made as she nursed.

When Caitlyn was full, Kara carried her back inside and placed her in her infant seat on the kitchen table, then popped some chicken in the microwave to defrost.

The garage door opened.

Reece was home early.

He walked through the door, a smile on his handsome face, briefcase in hand, suit jacket slung over his shoulder. The sight of him never failed to make her heart beat faster. He walked over to her, kissed her, and then went to kiss the baby. "How was your day?"

"Quiet. Connor spent most of the afternoon outside. Caitlyn just woke up from a good two-hour nap."

"Get lots of writing done?" He tossed his jacket over the back of a chair, set his briefcase down, and opened it.

"Some. How were things at the Capitol?"

"Had a little run-in with Devlin. He wants to sponsor a bill to forbid anyone from taping a conversation without the knowledge and expressed consent of everyone being taped."

Kara laughed. "I bet he does."

"It won't pass." When Reece looked up at her again, there was an amused glint in his eyes. "I saw your mother enjoying a romantic lunch with Tom."

Tom had been wooing her mother since the day they'd met in the hospital. Kara had been proud of how her mother had constantly turned him down, upbraided him for his bad manners, and generally told him to shove off. She refused to believe her mother could have given in. "What makes you think it was romantic?"

"Perhaps the fact that they had their tongues in one another's mouths?"

"Oh, I think I'm going to be sick!"

Reece chuckled. "One other thing came up today."

"What? Now they want you to run for governor?"

"Nothing like that. Just this." He turned to his briefcase, pulled out a white envelope, and handed it to her, his gaze soft.

Kara stared at it for a moment, realized what it was, and looked up at Reece in amazement.

"Go ahead. Open it."

Pulse racing, she ripped open the envelope, pulled out a thick document, unfolded it, and read. "Oh, my God! It's done! It's really done!".

He pulled her against him, kissed her forehead, and they held each other for a moment. "Prentice's parental rights are forever terminated. He's out of your life for good, sweetheart. Should we tell Connor?"

"Oh, yes!" Kara hurried to the back door, her heart dancing. "Connor, come inside! We have something special to tell you."

Connor bounded indoors, followed by a panting, wagging Jake.

Reece sat at the table, lifted Connor onto his lap, and took the precious document from Kara.

Almost unable to contain her emotions, Kara pressed her hands to her face and watched.

"Do you know what this is?" Reece asked.

Connor shook his head.

"It's our final adoption papers. These papers say that by law I am your real father now—and you're my son." At those last words, Reece's voice broke.

Connor's face split into a wide grin, and he threw his arms around Reece's neck. "I have a daddy! I have a real daddy!"

Kara watched through eyes blurred by tears as Reece hugged his son—their son—and saw on her husband's face how much Connor's love and affection meant to him. Then Reece's gaze met hers and he mouthed the words, "I love you."

And in that moment, which would stay with Kara for the rest of her life, the world was perfect.

Turn the page for a special preview of
Pamela Clare's next novel

HARD EVIDENCE

Coming soon from Berkley Sensation!

TESSA TURNED into the underground parking garage, but had to drive down two levels before she found a spot. Her parking karma sucked.

She turned off the ignition, grabbed her briefcase, glanced at her watch.

Damn!

Why was she perpetually twenty minutes late? Did Christiane Amanpour or Barbara Walters or Jane Pauley have this problem? Somehow she didn't think so.

They don't have Tom Trent for a boss either, Novak.

She hopped out of the car, locked it, and hurried to the nearest stairwell, rehearsing the questions she planned to ask Chief Irving as she ran up the steps, the staccato click of her heels reverberating off the concrete walls.

Why, if Denver were a major crossroads for sex trafficking, was there no police task force assigned to combat the crime? How many reports of trafficking had they received over the past five years and how many had they investigated? Most important, who in the department had had access to that police report, who had altered it, and why?

¡Por favor, Señor, ayúdeme! ¡Me van a matar!

Please, sir! Help me! They'll kill me!

The girl's terrified screams echoed in Tessa's mind, made her stomach knot.

Gun shots. Shattered glass.

So much blood.

Whoever had doctored that report thought he was being clever. He was probably strutting around upstairs in his uniform feeling impressed with himself and thinking he had it all under control. But he apparently hadn't realized one of the witnesses was a journalist. And he had no idea how far that journalist would go to see justice served.

Well, he'd find out soon enough.

Lost in her thoughts, Tessa ran headlong into a wall of chest and found herself staring up into a pair of hard blue eyes.

Julian.

Startled, she jerked back from him, almost lost her balance.

Strong arms grabbed her, steadied her, held her fast. "We just keep running into each other, don't we, Tessa?"

He was dressed as he'd been the first night she'd seen him—dark hair tied back in a ponytail, black leather jacket, jeans.

Somehow just the sight of him was enough to make her mouth water and her brain go blank. But standing close to him like this made it hard to breathe. "Wh-what are you doing here?"

Clever, Novak! He's some kind of cop. What do you think he's doing here?

"I'm the 'shady criminal type,' remember? Criminal types belong at the police station." He bit his lower lip, frowned, gazed at her through narrowed eyes. "But if I didn't know better, I'd say you're following me."

She tried not to remember what it felt like to be kissed by those lips or nipped by those teeth. "Why on earth would I want to follow you? It's not as if you're going to get all chatty and tell me who you really are or what angle you're working on the Ramirez shooting."

"Not likely." Then his mouth turned up in a slow, sexy smile that made her insides melt. "Maybe you're hoping I'll kiss you again."

Heat rushed into her cheeks, and she gaped at him. "You're delusional, Darcangelo!"

He grinned a self-satisfied, smug grin that told her he knew exactly what that kiss had done to her. "Am I?"

She forced her expression to go ice cold and pulled herself out of his grasp. "I hate to wound your male pride, but I haven't given you or that little peck on the lips a single thought."

Head high and shoulders back, she stepped around him.

Julian was tempted to laugh. She might pretend to have sleet for blood, but he'd never known a woman to melt down quite like she had over a single kiss. But why argue with her about it when he could prove it?

In one move, he had her up against the wall, her delicious ass pressing against his thighs, her wrists shackled by his hands, her arms stretched out on either side of her head.

"Wh-what the—?"

"Shut up." He ducked down, brushed his lips down the curve of her cheek, ran the tip of his tongue over the whorl of her ear. She smelled good enough to eat, her perfume subtle and sexy and so female. Hungry for her, he sucked her earlobe into his mouth, pearl and all.

He heard her quick intake of breath, felt her body tense.

"You . . . are sooo . . . arrogant!"

"I said shut up." He released her right wrist, cupped her chin, turned her head to the side.

Then he kissed her deep and hard.

And she melted.

Her body seemed to go liquid, every soft, feminine inch of her backside pressing against him. The contact sent a bolt of lust blazing through his gut, made him painfully hard, his erection straining to be someplace better than his jeans.

In a heartbeat, the kiss turned rough. Teeth scraped skin, bit, nipped. Tongues invaded, clashed, plundered. He felt her hips move, her ass rubbing against him, betraying her need. Then her head fell back against his chest, and she whimpered.

The sound was like gasoline on the fire already raging in Julian's veins. He groaned, felt his control slip. He hadn't meant for it to be like this. He'd kissed her to wipe that conceited look off her face, to prove to her that she wanted him—not to get caught up in wanting her.

But he wanted her. Right now. Right here.

Trailing little bites down the silky skin of her throat, he let go of her left wrist, wrapped his arm beneath her breasts to steady her. Then with his other hand, he reached around, slid his hand up her thigh and under her skirt to cup her through her panties.

They were silk. And they were already damp.

Tessa was lost. She was lost in his scent, in the hard feel of him behind her, in the heat of his lips on her skin. If there were some reason she shouldn't be doing this, she couldn't remember what it was.

Then she felt the pressure of his hand against her, and her knees went weak. Rather than knocking his hand away and demanding that he stop, she found herself pushing against the pressure, parting her legs for him. "Oh, Julian!"

Liquid heat spread through her belly, began to build. And when he flicked his thumb over the hard bead of her nipple, she moaned, the sound reverberating up and down the stairwell.

A door opened.

Footsteps.

He growled deep in his throat, cupped her hard, ground his erection against her. Then he whispered. "If you try to tell me next time I see you that you haven't been thinking about fucking me, I'm going to call you a liar."

With that, he released her and was gone.

Shaking, her body on fire, Tessa struggled to compose herself. She straightened her skirt, picked her briefcase up off the floor where it had fallen, and smoothed her hair. How had she let this happen?

A police officer passed her on his way down the stairs, gave her a nod.

And then she remembered.

Chief Irving!

She glanced at her watch—*damn damn damn!*—and ran the rest of the way up the stairs.

PAMELA CLARE began her writing career as an investigative reporter and columnist, working her way up the newsroom ladder to become the first woman editor of two different newspapers. Along the way, she and her team won numerous state and national journalism awards, including the 2000 National Journalism Award for Public Service. A single mother with two teenage sons, she lives in Colorado at the foot of the Rocky Mountains. Visit her website at www.pamelaclare.com.

BERKLEY SENSATION
COMING IN SEPTEMBER 2005

Too Wilde to Tame
by Janelle Denison

New in the *USA Today* bestsellingWilde series. "No one does hot and sexy better" (Carly Phillips) than Janelle Denison.

0-425-20528-2

The Angel and the Warrior
by Karen Kay

"Karen Kay's passion for Native American love shines through" (*Publishers Weekly*) in this sexy new novel.

0-425-20529-0

Someone to Believe In
by Kathryn Shay

Kathryn Shay steamed up your nights with her firefighter romances. Now she's back with a story of love on opposite sides of the political fence.

0-425-20530-4

Touch Me
by Lucy Monroe

A debut historical from "a fresh new voice in romance" (Debbie Macomber).

0-425-20531-2

Personal Assets
by Emma Holly

From *USA Today* bestselling author Emma Holly, "one of the best writers of erotic fiction" (Susan Johnson).

0-425-19931-2